PRAISE FOR *THE YOU I SEE*

"**Freeman perfectly captures the uncertainty and intensity of a friendship on the verge of queer romance,** and the contradictorily cosmopolitan and conservative Houston is a perfectly rendered setting...**the author consistently returns to the simpler, sweeter, and more classic beats of love triumphing over all.**"

- Kirkus Reviews

. . .

"***The You I See*'s powerful ability to refute stereotypes on all sides makes for an especially authentic, realistic story of growth. It is highly recommended as a key acquisition for young adult libraries; especially those looking for non-traditional explorations of the subject for LGBTQ collections and discussion groups.**"

- D. Donovan, Senior Reviewer, *Midwest Book Review*

. . .

"**An honest, yet sensitive, character-driven, and uplifting story of two gay teenagers growing up and beginning to identify and express their own sexual identities... A positive and uplifting story that definitely needs to be told. The story is light-hearted and encouraging, and readers will easily find themselves rooting for the success of Brandon and Alex's relationship...** Perhaps if the world was exposed to more stories such as this one, it would become more familiar, and there would be less rejection and hatred."

- Lynette Latzko, *Feathered Quill*

. . .

"**A continuously hopeful story of friendship, young love, and the celebration of sexuality.** *The You I See* may be funny, but it hits on a number of emotional moments. It is immensely uplifting in this way. This would be a great choice for readers confused about their sexuality or those who find it difficult to accept it."

- 5/5 stars; Manik Chaturmutha, *Independent Book Review*

. . .

"An eloquent tale about two young men who face the odds to stay true to themselves. ***The You I See* is a quiet but essential novel with a profound and fascinating look at the issues of identity, and Danny Freeman explores it with a degree of intelligence and compassion.** This is a great read for its deep understanding of the human connections we make and how these form us to become the best person that we can be."

- 5/5 stars; Vincent Dublado, *Readers' Favorite*

THE YOU I SEE

DANNY FREEMAN

atmosphere press

In memory of Thérèse Gagnon, my little Big Sur flower, who believed in my writing more strongly than I did and told me the only sin I might ever commit would be to stop writing.

"The world is violent and mercurial – it will have its way with you. We are saved only by love – love for each other and the love that we pour into the art we feel compelled to share: being a parent; being a writer; being a painter; being a friend. We live in a perpetually burning building, and what we must save from it, all the time, is love."

– Tennessee Williams

CHAPTER 1

My Grandmother Allen once told me that life was like the lottery. "You can go far on talent, hard work, and persistence, but I've lived long enough to know that chance and blind luck play an oversized part in everyone's life, Alex.

"I met your granddad through sheer coincidence. We were both stranded at the train station in Chicago in January 1939, in the middle of a blizzard. I was trying to get back here to Houston, and he was trying to get to Austin. He bumped into me in the station's crowded café and spilled some of his lukewarm coffee down the front of my coat. A spark of electricity crackled between us as he pulled out his handkerchief and handed it to me. And the rest is history! It was all pure chance!" Her eyes sparkled with the joyful memories.

"So, keep your eyes open, sweetie," she counseled me. "You never know when your whole life might change in an instant. Life hands out all kinds of surprises, and the best of them come when we least expect them. They can knock us over like a two-ton truck – unexpected, unsolicited, yet undeniably the very thing we never knew we'd been looking for all along."

I finally knew what she meant the first time I saw Brandon Marshall. It was a one-in-a-million chance that we even met.

The odds were astronomically low that two such opposite personalities from drastically different families could have ever found a way past our disastrous first encounter. Yet, meet we did; survive our first encounter we did... and the rest? It was like hitting one jackpot after another.

Brandon and I stood across from another in a sandwich assembly line. The boys to my left and his right were in charge of the bread. The boys to my right and his left were responsible for the jelly. Brandon and I had one simple mission: spread a good deal of thick, store-brand peanut butter on impossibly thin slices of cheap white bread. Within minutes, my hands were covered in peanut butter. I was a neat-freak kind of boy as a general rule. But on that Sunday morning in an overly loud church kitchen, I wouldn't have noticed if someone emptied a bucket of the stickiest maple syrup on my head. All I could think about was the stunning guy who stood across from me.

"So," Brandon said, "first thing to know: it's not always like this... this kind of *I Love Lucy* chocolate-factory-show-meets-Sunday-School chaos. We do actually have class every Sunday, but the high schoolers are taking food to the homeless later today. We're too young to go feed the homeless, so we do this instead. Something about catching TB. Ever heard of that?"

He looked across at me but plowed ahead before I could answer. This was his primary style of talking, I was soon to learn: a mile-a-minute, rapid-fire, how-could-he-go-so-long-without-a-breath freewheeling monolog. He expected me to listen, but I never got any sense he actually wanted me to respond. "They only do it once a quarter. You came on a bad day for your first time here. Or maybe a good day if you actually like making 150 peanut butter sandwiches." He chuckled and winked at me.

Brandon was a good eight inches taller than me, and his shoulders seemed twice as wide as mine. He had incredibly fair brown hair that flopped around each time he shook his head. No matter how it landed, it settled in just the right way. He had the bluest eyes I had ever seen, and his clothes set them off perfectly: a pink-and-blue striped polo shirt and blue jeans. I swear, he looked like he just stepped out of a magazine.

All three of his collar buttons were undone, and my eyes were drawn to something I had never seen on a boy my age: a pronounced dip down the middle of his chest between two discernible plateaus of newly developing pec muscles. He laughed more than anyone I knew, and he seemed to find his own jokes the funniest. He had a smile that lit up that hot, noisy church kitchen. I was captivated by his beauty and delighted by his unstoppable flow of words.

"Next thing to know: there are four Michaels connected to the youth group. It's very confusing at first. There's Michael Walker the youth minister. You know him. He brought you in here. He's got a wife named Susie. She's around somewhere. Everyone calls him just plain Michael. Then there's Michael Waller. He's the junior high Sunday school teacher. I mean, seriously? Walker and Waller? It's like they planned to go to church here together and help lead the youth group just to confuse us with their almost-the-same last names. I don't know where he is, but you'll meet him soon. Everyone calls him Wally." He snickered to himself.

"He started teaching class three years ago. They said he was just supposed to teach one month to give someone else a break, but he's never left. Half of us think he stays because he likes us. Half of us think he stays because nobody else is crazy enough to teacher junior high. I definitely think it's option two. Who actually likes to teach junior high kids? They said the other guy who used to teach us had to go see a shrink."

Brandon snickered again. I sensed him looking at me. I paused mid-swipe across a crumbling slice of white bread and looked up. He flashed me an all-knowing, we're-in-on-that-joke kind of smile. I felt paralyzed by his radiant grin.

Brandon looked down and forged ahead. "Anyway. Back to the Michaels. Next Michael is Michael Thompson. He's Joel's dad. He comes on trips and helps Michael keep everyone under control. Everyone calls him Mike. So, that's the first three: Michael, Wally, and Mike. Then there's Michael Abbot. He's an eighth grader. Over there." He flourished his sticky knife and pointed. "That tall boy over there stuffing bags with chips. Try to keep them all straight. Okay?" He looked up at me. I nodded. He smiled, looked back down, and pressed on.

"Third thing: avoid Joshua at all costs. He's the seventh grader down there folding up the tops of the lunch sacks. I mean, there's a reason he is doing that job. We always give him the lame jobs because he screws up the important ones. It would take him ten hours to do your job, and it would take that long for me to tell you all about him. Just trust me. Avoid him."

I looked up. Brandon gave me a wink. I looked side-to-side. Did the other boys hear that? It didn't seem the sort of thing you'd say at church about someone else at your church. I didn't know much about Christianity at that point in my life, but I knew enough to know that loving your neighbor was pretty much Jesus' main teaching. The boys all around us were caught up in their own loud chatter, oblivious to Brandon's comments about Joshua. Over it all floated the rising and falling bursts of laughter from the junior high girls in the corner. It didn't seem anyone but me was listening to a thing Brandon said.

He must have seen me eyeing the group of girls in the corner. Their heads seemed conspiratorially close together. They occasionally glanced up at certain boys before falling into ear-piercing shrieks. "And just avoid them, too. All the girls here are the lamest. Most of them are scratchers. Know what I mean?" He looked at me knowingly again. "Trust me, Alex. Steer clear."

He lapsed into a brief silence to take the lid off a new jar of peanut butter, and I looked back down to focus on my task.

Brandon shouted angrily, "Hey, hey, hey! You little moron!" I looked up, thinking he was speaking to me. I realized he wasn't, and relief swept over me. The boy on his left, the jelly boy, was showing some dance move to the boy next to him. In the midst of wild, flying arm movements, his jelly-coated knife scraped against Brandon's forearm. Brandon glared down at the offending boy. He was a foot taller than jelly boy, who cowered under Brandon's withering scowl.

"This is a new shirt, Jason! I just got it for my birthday. Then Mr. I-Wanna-Be Michael-Jackson here smears me with jelly!" Jason muttered an apology.

Brandon furrowed his brows. "Yeah, you should be sorry, Jason. Watch what you're doing from now on." Brandon looked back at me smugly and gave me a wink. He grabbed a paper towel from the countertop and wiped his forearm. He muttered to himself softly, "Goddamn jelly's everywhere now." He lifted his pink sleeve and wiped the lower half of his upper arm. I stood and stared, my knife suspended mid-sweep. I had never seen a guy my age with such rounded biceps.

Brandon looked up and saw me staring at his arm. He winked again. He tightened his right bicep, and the mounded tissues contracted into a hard tennis ball. I couldn't look away.

"These babies don't come easy. I do chin-ups, push-ups, and crunches five days a week. Joel wrote down a routine for me. And I have a few small baby-weights. They're old hand-me-downs from my brothers. I think I love working out more than anything else in life." He paused and considered something silently. "Well, there's something I love more, but it's not something I tell everyone about."

I nodded mutely. He let his sleeve drop back in place. We both looked down to our task again. Brandon asked, "Do you play any sports?"

"Not really. I'm hopeless with balls." Brandon snickered. I

felt a red blush coming up my neck, so I hurried on. "But I love to run. My dad's a runner, and he's taken me with him since I was really young. We run together four or five mornings a week before school and work."

"Oh, yeah. Where do you run? At a gym on a treadmill?"

"No, as long as it's not raining, we run in Hermann Park on weekdays because it's close to our apartment. Then we run in Memorial Park on Saturday mornings."

Brandon looked stunned. "Oh, my God! That's so cool! My dad would never take me running with him. Not that he runs. But if he did, he wouldn't take me. He thinks I talk too much. He always says, 'Least said soonest mended.' But wow! Just wow! You go running with your dad. How far?"

I felt on solid ground for the first time in twenty minutes. "Usually seven to ten miles. It kind of depends on how much time we have and how we feel."

His jaw dropped, and his peanut butter knife froze in mid-air. "Holy cow! Ten miles? My brother couldn't even run ten miles. And he's, like, 17."

A man stuck his head in the kitchen and shouted. "Wrap it up everyone. You've got less than ten minutes to finish, and that includes cleaning up. I'll be right back. Come on! Hop to it!"

Brandon lowered his voice and said, "Speaking of dads. Here's the fourth thing you have to know right away: my dad is the preacher here. You'll hear him later. I usually tune him out because I hear all the same things at home all the time. You can't imagine what it's like living with a preacher. Every conversation is about God and includes some Bible story. And just so you know, we are nothing alike. So, don't think I am a mini-preacher waiting to catch you in your sins and tell you how bad you are. I promise I don't report back to him on anything. Some of the kids used to think I gave Dad a full report on the drive home. Like I would really do that! All your secrets are safe with me." He flashed me that brilliant smile.

"And my mom is an English professor. What do your parents do?"

"My dad works at MD Anderson. He's a researcher, and my mom is also a professor."

"Oh, cool! Where does she teach? Maybe they work together, and we are destined to become best friends."

"She works at Rice. She's a math professor."

"Oh, my God! My mom just teaches at HCC, you know, the junior college. It's the place where professors go if they're not quite good enough for Rice or UT or a place like that." He snickered to himself. "Or at least that's what my brother told me. You'll meet him later. His name is Will. He's in 11th grade. He's a total nerd. I mean, he's super smart. I can't believe he'll be gone the year I start high school. I'm gonna need all the help I can get. Are you smart? Maybe you can help me with my homework."

He paused and eyed me suspiciously for a few seconds. It was the longest silence since he began. He said, "You know, I have a feeling you're really smart. Something about you screams 'I'm smart.' But you're not nerdy at all." He paused again and seemed to wonder if that was possible: could I be smart and not nerdy?

He resumed the interrogation. "Do you have any brothers or sisters?"

"No, I'm an only child."

"Wow! I always wanted to be an only child. I can't imagine having the whole house to myself and being able to do whatever I want! I've got two even older brothers, too. I mean, not including Will. You won't meet the other two for a long time. I hardly ever see them myself." He left this mystery unexplained and suddenly switched gears. "So, what's your favorite TV show?"

"Um... I don't really watch TV. My dad says you get nowhere fast by watching too much TV and anywhere you want by hardly watching at all. We watch PBS a couple of nights a week. I like NOVA, the science show."

I seemed to have inadvertently pressed Brandon's mute button. He stood frozen, knife suspended mid-swipe yet again. His mouth was slightly open for a good five seconds before he asked, "You don't watch TV? Man, where do you come from? No TV? You really mean it?"

My neck and cheeks burned with embarrassment. "Well, I, uh…" I stammered. "I mean we watch some shows. Just not a lot. I've seen *The Love Boat* a few times at my grandparents' house!"

Brandon hooted with glee. "*The Love Boat*? Lovey-dovey *Love Boat*? You call that watching TV? God, Alex, you are something else." I felt like a tourist without a map in a non-English speaking country.

He carried on, unaware of my misery. "Don't tell me! They also watch *Fantasy Island*, right? 'De plane, boss, de plane!'" He roared with laughter. "Really, Alex! You gotta come over to my house! You gotta see some real TV shows!"

He sensed my discomfort and changed tactics. "So, do you know any good jokes?"

I thought to myself: 'God, what is this bottomless pit opening up in front of me?' I messed up every joke I ever attempted to tell! When I heard them at school, I usually had no idea why they were funny. I stuttered, "Ummm, n-n-o. I can't think of any."

He abandoned his peanut butter duty and stared at me. The plight of the homeless paled in comparison to my plight as a helplessly uncool, from-another-planet, nerdy junior high boy. "Well, I'll tell you one I heard from my brother. He likes country music, for some crazy reason. How can you be that smart and like country music?" He snickered. "So, anyway, it's a country music joke."

He paused, looking at me through narrowed eyes. "You don't watch PBS and listen to country music, do you?" I shook my head vigorously in the negative. "Good. I was about to give up on you. There's just some things I can't accept in a friend. You could like PBS or country music but not both. I'd draw a line there." He chuckled. "Anyway, this is the joke. What did one of Dolly Parton's tits say to the other one when she was doing the back stroke in a river near her home?"

My neck and cheeks lit up again! Guys at school said 'tits' all the time. My parents never said I couldn't curse; they just said I couldn't use crude or vulgar language. I didn't know for sure, but I had a sense that 'tits' was both vulgar and crude. Why else would the boys at school say it so far from the teachers and the girls? Why else did they shoot each other sly looks and chuckle to themselves when they said it?

We both froze again: me from sheer panic and Brandon from utter confusion. When he regained his wits, he asked, "You do know who Dolly Parton is, right?"

I knew I was doomed either way. If I said no, I was hopelessly lame in the eyes of this coolest of guys. If I said yes, I wouldn't understand the joke without him explaining it to me. Then he'd know I really didn't know who she was. Then I would be a double loser because I lied *and* because I didn't know whoever Dolly Parton was.

Once again, he seemed to sense my distress. "Okay. Never mind! It's not really that funny." He hesitated for a second. "You're not kidding me, are you, Alex? You really don't know who she is? You know, *Nine to Five*?" He made a strange gesture with both of his hands, circling them around in front of his chest. "You know?"

Some kind of realization broke upon him. He eyes widened. He gasped for air as he asked, "Do you even know what tits are? I mean, come on. I know you watch PBS and probably read books for fun, but you know what tits are. Right?"

Of course, I knew, but I couldn't answer! My tongue felt glued to the top of my mouth, held fast by gallons of peanut butter.

He looked deflated and defeated. Had anyone ever stymied him like this before? He was a non-stop-talking, laugh-a-minute wonder boy, and I was his undoing. I was a brick wall he couldn't plow through. He had never met a PBS-watching, no-clue-who-Dolly-Parton-is, afraid-of-the-word-tits kind of boy before.

I looked around me in a rising panic. All the activity and noise in the kitchen had died down. The jelly boys next to us looked frozen in time, eyes fixed firmly on me. In the middle of my own frantic confusion, I hadn't realized ours were the last voices in the kitchen. My humiliation was complete. I had failed whatever test they hand out to the new Sunday School boys. I realized in one second of clarity that I was done for. I was the loser kid who couldn't even make a friend at church, the one place where kids are supposed to be nice to one another and everyone felt like they belonged.

Eons passed. I heard the slow crunch of tectonic plates far below my feet. I saw myself as an old man, sitting alone on a park bench without a friend in the world. My future was a bleak lonely haze. Whatever chance I thought I had to become Brandon's friend was over, nipped in the bud, like an azalea that bloomed a few days before spring's last frost.

Nobody in the whole room said a word, not even the impossibly loud group of girls in the far corner. Every eye rested on me. It was all over. I knew I could never come back.

Tears welled up in my eyes. I set down my knife without looking up. I turned away from the table and bolted from the kitchen. I stumbled outside into the warm, humid morning air and sat at a wooden picnic table under the shade of a giant oak tree. I laid my head on my arms and wept.

A few moments later, the table wobbled and the wooden seat across from me creaked. I looked up, and a pair of impossibly blue eyes stared straight into mine. "I'm sorry, Alex. I'm the world's biggest jerk! I know I am. My mom always tells me I'm like a dog with a bone. Like, I get going on something, and I won't let go! I didn't mean to embarrass you. I'm a total asshole! I'm the worst friend you could ever have! Call me what you like. I deserve it! You can hit me as hard as you want. Or kick me in the balls! Go on! I deserve it." Brandon's smile was a mix of playful mischief and honest sentiment.

I was stunned. I couldn't believe he had come to apologize. He must have thought I was the world's biggest baby sitting at that table crying on my own. What kind of kid runs out of Sunday School in a flood of tears after some gentle teasing? I was dazed and helplessly out of my depths.

He reached across the table, arm outstretched, hand extended. "Are we still friends? Will you forgive me? Can we start over?" No one had ever said such words to me before. I melted in an instant, my all-consuming shame replaced in a flash by a toe-tapping happiness which was unexpected and exhilarating.

I reached out and took his hand. We shook fiercely. His mega-watt smile returned in earnest. I couldn't help but grin.

"Yeah," I said, "we're still friends. It's okay. I know you didn't mean to get me upset. I'm just a dork about things like TV shows and jokes. I must seem strange to you."

He ran around to my side of the table and threw his arm around my shoulder. "Come on, man! You're not a dork, and you are *not* strange. Seriously, you're the coolest guy I've ever met. You're so different. I mean, why be like everyone else, right?" He pulled me tightly to him, and we started to walk back toward the church kitchen. "We've got fifty more sandwiches to make in ten seconds. Joshua took your place, and I gotta get you back in there. I mean, you gotta save me from Joshua!"

Just as we were about to go into the kitchen a tall guy came walking our way from across the parking lot.

He called out, "Hey, hey, Brandino. Did y'all finish the sandwiches? Ben and I are coming to load up the boxes –

except I have no idea where Ben is! He can be a dick when he wants to. He's good at leaving all the work to me."

Brandon's eyes darted to mine with a questioning look. Did he wonder if I knew what the word dick meant? I did know that. I knew what dick meant.

The mountain of a guy turned to me. "Hey man! What's up? Are you Brandon's friend? What's your name?"

I stared up in wonder. He was in an orange Astro's t-shirt and blue jeans. He filled the t-shirt in an eye-catching way. His rock-hard arms strained at the thin sleeves. I noticed his rounded shoulders and how his thick, veined neck stretched out the collar's fabric. I was awestruck and mute.

Brandon slung his arm over my shoulder again. "Joel, this is Alex Kennedy. Alex, this is Joel Thompson. He's my brother's friend. He practically lives at our house. I told you my brother was a super nerd. Well, Joel likes him anyway, but I think Joel just hangs around to get answers for all the tests. And of course, he hangs around our house because I am there. I am way cooler than Will, and Joel knows it." He snickered.

Joel reached out and punched Brandon on the shoulder. Brandon swayed against me. Brandon looked up at Joel, and said, "Easy, man. I've still got a bruise on my chest from that football you launched at me last week in the pool. I swear, you almost knocked me out."

Brandon used his free hand to pull his shirt down slightly. "See! Look at that bruise." I looked with pleasure. There was a nasty purple bruise spread across the left side of his chest.

Joel sighed and said, "Come on! You've told everyone a million times about that bruise. It was an accident. And it's not as if you haven't left your fair share of bruises, cuts, and scratches on me."

Joel winked at me. "You gotta watch this one. If he invites you over to swim and says he wants to wrestle you in the pool, just watch out. He kicks. He scratches. He bites like a girl. He even squeals like a girl!"

"I do not," Brandon cried out. He let his arm drop from my shoulder and started gesturing wildly with both arms. "That was an accident! Your arm was right in my way when I was gasping for air. You basically made me bite you. I didn't have any choice. I was about to drown!"

Joel winked again. "Okay, Alex. I warned you! Don't believe his sad stories, explanations, and teary apologies after the fact. Brandon always goes for the jugular. Knives out, fists out, and direct kicks to your crotch when you least expect it."

Brandon squealed in the unguarded way seventh graders do when their honor is on the line. "I do not kick people in the balls! That was an accident, too! You are so huge. I've got to kick any way I can and hope to land a blow! You're the one who stuck your crotch right in front of me."

Joel doubled over in laughter. He straightened up when his laughing died down a bit and said, "I'm telling you this guy is too much. Don't say I didn't warn you."

Joel stuck his hand in the air just above my head, palm out, ready for a high five. "Well, Alex, welcome to our church. If you've met Brandon and survived, then you've made it through the worst we have to offer. Everyone else is WAY nicer and more normal than he is."

I jumped up to slap his palm and somehow managed to finally say, "Nice to meet you, too. Brandon's not too bad. He's pretty funny to me."

Joel grabbed Brandon and locked his head between his forearm and upper arm. He said, "And you, Brandino, be nice to this guy. I can tell we want to keep him around. You chase off all the new kids who come here." Brandon was squirming to get loose, and Joel tightened his arm even more. Joel's rock-hard bicep had a trance-inducing effect on me. He finally let go and gave Brandon a huge push, almost knocking him over.

"Ow," shouted Brandon. "Child abuser! This is child abuse! I'm telling my father! You'll be sorry, Gregory Joel Thompson!"

Joel walked off to meet another guy by the back of the church van who was struggling with a box full of sack lunches.

Brandon threw his arm over my shoulder again. No friend had ever done this before, and he'd done it three times in ten minutes. "That, over there, is Ben. He's Joel's best friend. My brother is like Joel's second best friend. We call Ben and Joel the gods of the youth group. When we go to camp in the summer, Ben and Joel throw the junior high boys around in the pool like they're toys. And when they go to the showers, I swear to you, half the younger guys go down at the same time just to have a look."

I blushed again, imagining those two guys throwing me in the pool and coming naked out of the camp showers. I felt my penis harden. I panicked, fearing that Brandon would notice.

Brandon let his arm fall from my shoulder. "Wow! What a morning! You are so cool! I can't believe you're coming here now." He stopped, grasped me by both shoulders, and turned my body to face him straight on. "Are you coming here from now on? You've got to come back!" He threw his head back and shouted, "You gotta save me from Joshua!"

Ben and Joel looked over at us and laughed.

I shuffled my feet a bit. I knew the story behind my parents' decision to visit the church, and I didn't imagine they would be eager to come back. At that point, however, I couldn't imagine not coming back to Bissonet Avenue Church of Christ. I had never met anyone like Brandon, and I couldn't imagine never seeing him again.

"I don't know. We just came this one time because we got invited by some people who go here. I don't think my parents are very serious about it. We're not really a churchy family. They'll talk to me about it later. They'll want to know if I want to come back."

Brandon grinned from ear to ear. "Well, tell them yes, yes, yes, and a thousand times yes. Tell them you met the coolest guy in the youth group, and he says you have to come back."

He paused and smiled. "I mean me. I'm the coolest guy! Not Joel!"

He patted me on the back and said, "I knew when you walked in that we'd be friends. I just had this feeling…"

Had I realized that, too, when I walked in? Did I think I'd eventually become friends with the most beautiful guy in the room? Looking back, the thought never crossed my mind, but as my parents and I drove away from church later that morning, I realized I couldn't imagine my life without Brandon.

CHAPTER 2

OCTOBER 1987

I saw Brandon each of the Sundays following the 'Dolly Disaster', as I came to call it in my memory. He always stood waiting for me under the oak tree close to the wing of the church building where the junior high class met. He'd start talking to me from a distance before I could even hear him clearly. He always came to sit with me and my parents in the auditorium during the worship service. My parents' original plan for a 'one-and-done' church visit crumbled in the face of my budding friendship with Brandon.

Every other month, on the first Sunday evening, the entire youth group gathered for a devotional. Brandon's family was hosting the devotional in October, and Brandon just assumed I'd be coming.

As we walked from Sunday School class to the auditorium on the last Sunday in September, he said, "You gotta come next week. Ever since you've been coming to church, Joshua has been leaving me alone. You're like my lucky charm or my... um. What's that word for something that wards off evil?"

"A talisman?"

"Yes! That's it! God, you're so smart. What's it like to be so smart?"

"I don't know. I don't really think about it."

"Well, that just shows how smart you are. I mean, I am only average when it comes to brainpower. So when I really get something, I feel totally smart. But when you're smart all the time, it must just feel like everything is so simple. Like for you, 2+2=4 is as simple as $E=mc^2$." He snickered. "I bet you're amazed I know about $E=mc^2$, aren't you?"

I tried to hide a smile. He poked me in the ribs.

"Well, I don't read science books for fun or watch NOVA like you do. Will likes to make me feel stupid, and he told me the other day I was so dumb I'd never understand $E=mc^2$. I asked my mom what it was all about. She told me not to worry about it until high school, but I bet you already know all about it."

"I get the basic concept, but it's complicated. Energy and mass are the same thing, more or less. The mass of something is the measurement of the amount of energy it contains. You know, the mass times the speed of light squared?"

Brandon's eyes glazed over. He blinked a few times and shook his head. "Yeah, that's what I was thinking. I mean, like, who doesn't know that?" He chuckled and patted me on the back. "Well, anyway, Mr. You're-My-Get-Away-From-Me-Joshua-Talisman, you don't have any choice! You! My house! Devotional! Be there! Or I'll come hunt you down."

. . .

As soon as the final 'Amen' rang out at the end of the evening service the following week, the youth group made a mad dash for the doors at the back of the auditorium. I lost track of Brandon in the crush of bodies. I was dazzled by the quick change from indoor lighting to bright sun, and I just followed the crowd, hoping I'd eventually run into Brandon again.

I began to panic when I couldn't see him anywhere. I realized I would have to take a chance on an open seat in one of the church vans. I saw Michael Walker, the youth minister, standing by a blue van, calling the last four or five kids his way. Just as I resigned myself to join the small herd of misfits who had missed their chance to ride in the cool kids' van, I heard Brandon's voice call out.

"Alex! Alex! Over here." I turned in several directions and finally saw an arm waving from a nearby car. My heart leaped and tumbled.

He called out again, "Alex, over here. We have room for you. I'm riding back with my mom. Come on!"

I ran over and asked, "Are you sure you have room?" What a lame question! His mom and a young girl were in the front, and he was alone in the back.

He shot me a crooked smirk. "Well, I think I can squeeze you in back here. I'm not that fat, you know."

I hopped in. Brandon patted me on the back as I fastened my seatbelt. "I thought you were right behind me. Then I turned around, and you were gone. Then I about had a heart attack as I saw you headed toward the church van. Joshua had just gotten in, and there's no way I was gonna let you get on that van. He's not edging into our friendship." He snickered and winked at me.

Mrs. Marshall spoke up quietly but with a firm edge to her voice. "Brandon, that's enough. There's plenty of Alex to go around. And you know what I've said about your attitude toward Joshua. Fix it, young man."

Brandon looked down sheepishly and said, "Yes, ma'am. I know." He looked at me and grinned a little. "Sorry. Just ignore me when I say things like that."

I nodded to acknowledge the apology, and I felt a keen sense of elation: 'our friendship'! He said 'our friendship'!

As we pulled away from the church, Mrs. Marshall spoke up from the front seat again. "Alex, I've met your parents and spoken to them on their previous visits. I am so glad you're coming to Bissonet. Where do y'all live? I've never thought to ask your parents."

"We live off Fannin, north of Hermann Park. A few blocks over from the Museum of Fine Arts. You can throw a rock from our lobby and almost hit the Mecom Fountain"

Mrs. Marshall looked at me through the rearview mirror. "Oh, yes. In one of those apartment buildings? Which one? I recall seeing a few newer ones, plus some older ones, right?"

"We live in the old one that's closest to the park. It used to be a warehouse where they stored cotton before it went to the port. They remodeled the building and turned it into apartments. We have the whole top floor for our apartment."

Brandon asked, "You mean you don't have a backyard? No pool in the back? We have a pool in our backyard. I can't imagine not having a yard and a pool."

I shrugged. "Well, I guess I've never missed what I've never had. Dad says it's better to live by the park with all that space than to have our own yard that we have to spend tons of time taking care of. When he's outside, he likes to enjoy being outside and not have yard work to do."

Mrs. Marshall said, "You know, it's not a bad idea. My boys have always been my yard crew, but I still spend so much time weeding and taking care of the flower beds. Being so close to the park must be nice. It's like having a gigantic backyard without the hard work." She paused and smiled at me in the mirror. "We live up ahead – just south of the Village. I suppose we are about half-way between the church building and your apartment. If you ever want to come over, you'll be close by. Where do you go to school?"

"St. Martin's."

"Oh, the Episcopal school on Main?"

"Yes, ma'am."

"Well, that's wonderful. You must be very accomplished if you got in there. My second oldest son Matthew had two friends who went there. They were two of the most intelligent and well-spoken teenagers I've ever known. I have a feeling you are like them in many respects."

Brandon patted me on the shoulder and said, "Yeah, for sure! I bet your IQ is, like, off the charts... probably double mine!"

"It's not that big of a deal. It's not the most important thing about me."

There was twinkle in his eye as he asked, "What is the most important thing about you?"

"My parents always tell me the most important thing about me is the way I treat other people. What does it matter if I am smart but also a jerk?"

He flashed me his mega-watt grin. "Well, I can tell you this: you're the nicest guy I know by a long shot. I mean, the guys at my school fall into two categories: smart assholes and dumb assholes!" He snickered.

"Brandon Marshall! Watch your mouth, young man. You've just complimented Alex on his character, then you go and say something like that!"

"Sorry, Mom. It just slipped out, but you know it's true. I'm just callin' it like I see it. I mean, you said so yourself... not those words, but you're always telling me to avoid the wild boys at my school. They're all wild! Just some are smart and some are dumb!"

I glanced up at the rearview mirror and saw a definite upward slant at the corners of Mrs. Marshall's eyes. I imagined Brandon was one of those kids who was hard to punish: how could you reprimand or even spank a kid that had you suppressing an all-out belly laugh when you were trying to scold him?

There was a lightness to her tone when she said, "Well, that may be true, but your language is the issue I'm most concerned about. I can't have you cursing like a sailor. You should be setting a good example for Alex and for Carrie." A hard edge quickly stole into her voice. "Seriously, Brandon, if you don't keep a reign on that tongue of yours, the wrong word will slip out in front of your father one day... and you know how that will end for you. You're on thin ice as it is after your stunt at school last week."

We all lapsed into silence. I wondered what Brandon's stunt may have been. Carrie whispered something to Mrs. Marshall. Brandon asked her a question about the math class they shared at school. She seemed not to hear him or to ignore him on purpose.

He looked at me slyly and whispered out of the corner of his mouth. "Awkward! We went together for three days at camp last summer! Then I dumped her. Now she hates my guts."

We turned right at Kirby and headed south, passing Rice Village and its jumble of eclectic shops and trendy restaurants. A few blocks later, we turned east and drove about half-way down the tree-lined street. Mrs. Marshall turned into a narrow driveway and pulled into the garage. We all climbed out.

She leaned close to me and gave me a soft kiss on the cheek. "Welcome to our home, Alex. You are very welcome here!"

She caught Brandon by the arm as he rounded the back of the car. They walked over to the far side of the driveway. Brandon looked straight at me for a few seconds as his mother spoke to him. Then he looked down and shook his head over and over. I couldn't hear Mrs. Marshall's words, but her voice carried just enough so I could make out its serious yet gentle tone. She finally patted him on the shoulder, and they turned towards me in unison.

"Now go on, sweetie. You better keep Alex by your side," she said with a dry chuckle. "Joshua will be here any minute."

Brandon lunged at me, grabbed my arm, and tugged me with him. "You're coming with me! If Carrie comes near me, I need someone to witness. She scratches. I still have the scars from camp. And we gotta get our Joshua radar up and working. Prepare yourself for evasive maneuvers if he heads our way!" I let him lead me, feeling slightly dazed that the coolest guy in the junior high youth group continued to claim me as his own.

The teen horde soon descended, and a crush of young, sweaty bodies filled the backyard. There must have fifty or more. Apparently, we were going to eat and have the devotional outside. Brandon said his mom told Michael Walker there were just too many people to sit comfortably inside for the devotional.

He whispered to me, "It's really because Joshua White threw up last summer when we had the July joint devo here. Three kids spilled their drinks on the new carpet in the den. And some kids left plates with pizza crusts under my dad's chair in the study. After that, Mom said, 'Never again. You all can stay outside and sweat to death next time.'" He paused and said indignantly, "She said this to me! As if it was all my fault that these church kids are slobs."

I couldn't help noticing Brandon's pool, complete with slide and diving board. "Wow! What a cool pool. I'd swim all summer long if I had my own pool."

"You'll have to come over next summer when it's pool time again. The water's still quite warm, but we have this rule in my family about not swimming past the end of September. I'll ask my mom later if you can come swim next summer!" The following summer seemed like an eternity away. I wondered if he would forget his invitation by then.

The devotional started with a lot of songs I had never heard before. It seemed like every eye was on me as I sat there in silence. Brandon and I shared a cushion he grabbed from a bench on the deck, our backs against a low brick wall near the garden gate. He leaned close while someone was praying and whispered, "Don't worry. You'll learn all the words soon. We sing the same songs over and over. I bet God is so tired of these same songs all the time." He chuckled at himself. One of the nearby adult chaperones let out a quiet but harsh, "Shhh,

Brandon. Be respectful."

He gave my ribs a quick jab with his elbow. I opened my eyes. He winked twice and whispered, "Better not hang out with me. I'll get you in trouble... me and my mouth!" An even louder chorus of shushing erupted from the nearby adults.

Michael's lesson was about sexual purity. It wasn't a topic I had ever really thought about before. He said it was wrong for the kids in the youth group to do anything more than hold hands with their boyfriends or girlfriends, especially if the other person wasn't a Christian. Anything else, he said, was sinful and dirty and we could expect a harsh punishment of some kind from God.

I shuddered as he plowed ahead. "Let me be clear, guys: no touching anything but hands; no kissing; no sitting so close that your legs and shoulders are pressed together; no draping your arms around each other; and no sex of any kind, ever, until you are married. If someone tries to pressure you to do any of these things, you can be sure they are being tempted by Satan. And so are you. You have to resist Satan with all you have, even if it means losing your girlfriend or boyfriend. No girlfriend or boyfriend is worth eternity in hell, and you can be sure God will hold you accountable, even if you've been baptized. You don't get a free pass to do what you want after you've been baptized."

He went on like that for another five minutes, quoting verses from the Bible which said it was better to cut off your hand that caused you to sin than to spend eternity in the fiery pit of hell.

I'll never forget his final words. "I wish I didn't have to talk about this, guys, but you have to know that all this talk here in Houston about accepting gay people and protecting gay people from being fired from their jobs, and all these lies about how homosexuality is not a choice, well, it's just that: it's all lies. God hates homosexuality even more than he hates all the other sexual sins. God made it clear in the Bible: homosexuality is wrong; it's perverted; it's an abomination; and all those gay people out there who are intent on shoving their lifestyle down our throats are destined for hell. It's just that simple. They will burn for eternity, and there's no point in trying to water it down to make Mayor Whitmire happy. She can talk all she wants about equal rights for gays, but she's an agent of Satan at work in City Hall."

There were snickers and stifled laughs all across the backyard. I looked around, and, I swear, every teenage eye was turned on me. I bet you could have seen the red glow of my cheeks from outer space.

After the final prayer, Brandon disappeared without a word. I got in line between some high school girls. I wondered what I should do. Did a lowly seventh grader introduce himself to high school girls? Should I slink away and let them merge together, amoeba-like, into a single mass of frizzy hair and feathered bangs? I looked behind me and saw all the junior high boys at the very back of the line. I felt lost without Brandon by my side. I wanted to run out the side gate and sprint the two miles back to my apartment. I wanted to forget about the Church of Christ and never look back.

I felt a tap on my right shoulder. I turned that way only to feel a tap on my left shoulder. I turned that way and caught a glimpse of Brandon darting back to my right. He pulled my arm and dragged me with him. "Come on! I got us a spot inside. Just act cool."

As we walked away, the girls in front and behind of me dropped into low whispers, then soared into high-pitched laughter, with sideways glances at Brandon and me.

We went around the side of his house and through the front door. He led me to the kitchen where a swarm of moms bustled about. No one seemed to notice us. He motioned me to keep following him. Up on the bar between the kitchen and breakfast room lay a buffet of pizza. We filled our plates, grabbed a can of Dr. Pepper each, and went back to the foyer.

Brandon sat down, patted the floor beside him, and said, "Come on. Sit here." I sat beside him, and he turned slightly toward me. The tile floor felt cool and inviting. We could see all the other kids through the back windows of the living room from our vantage point. I was relieved to be out of the noise and chaos.

"I thought this was better than being outside with that motley crew. Plus, I want to avoid the mosquitoes. For some reason, mosquitoes love to bite me." He lifted up his yellow shirtsleeve. There were several small red marks above his left elbow. I couldn't help but notice the dense heft of his arm again. I was in awe of Brandon's arms.

He fingered the bite marks. "I got these Friday night when I was mowing the grass. Those damn mosquitoes seem to swarm me the second I step outside. I've got these on my arms, plus tons on my back and some on my legs. Stupid little mother suckers!" He chuckled to himself. "I'm surprised I didn't get any bites just now during the singing and stuff."

He took a few bites of pizza. I realized I had been frozen, pizza and drink totally forgotten after the sight of his shapely arm. I realized, too, that he was staring straight at me.

"Are you okay, Alex?"

"Sorry. Yeah. I was just thinking about something else."

"Oh, I didn't know I was boring you. Let me go see if Joshua wants to join you! I'm sure he can keep you in stitches!"

I must have looked alarmed. He threw his head back in laughter, trying not to let any food fall from his mouth. "I'm kidding! I'm kidding! Gosh, you are so serious. I'm just joking. I guess you don't really know about Joshua, do you?" I shook my head. "Joshua and his family moved here the summer between fourth and fifth grade. His birthday is right before mine, even though I am older."

I must have looked puzzled.

"Oh, I forgot! You don't know my secret. Even though I'm in the same grade as you, I'm a year older. I'm already thirteen. When I was toddler, I had a really bad speech problem. The only people who could understand me were my parents and brothers. So, I started going to a speech doctor when I was four. I don't remember all this, you know? I just know what they tell me." He paused to take a breath. "Strange, when you think about it. I only know what my family tells me about being little. I guess it could all be a lie."

I had never considered this before, either. I took my parents at face value when they told me stories about what I was like as a baby and toddler. There were always so many things they knew about me that I never knew about myself. I wondered when the balance would shift: when was the day I'd I finally know more about myself than they did?

"Anyway, my parents decided they didn't want me to go to kindergarten because I would have to be in speech class at school. They didn't want the other kids to tease me, and they didn't want me to miss time in class. I'm not sure what they thought I'd be missing. Like, how to color inside the lines, maybe?"

He chuckled at himself, and I laughed, too. I was mesmerized. My house was so quiet all the time, and I spent so much time alone. I had never known a boy my age – or near my age – who talked as much as Brandon did.

"Anyway! Sorry, I get all distracted! So, I had this bad speech problem, and I had what you call a late birthday. I wasn't going to turn five until August 22. If I went to kindergarten after that birthday all the other kids would be months and months older. Like, some of them with birthdays in September would be turning six just a few weeks after school started, and I would only be a few weeks into being five. Mom said when you're five a little age difference can be a big thing. Especially when nobody can understand you."

I started to wonder if Brandon's steady stream of talking was his way of making up for years of muddled speech as a little kid. I listened carefully but couldn't hear any kind of speech problem. He sounded just like any other guy.

"So, they decided to keep me out of school that year. I kept going to the speech doctor. I don't mean they cut my tongue or something! God, that would be awful if they cut on your tongue because you mumbled. Seems like it would make it worse. Don't you think?"

I nodded in agreement.

"And then I started kindergarten the next year; like the same time you would have. So, I'm in seventh grade but already thirteen. Anyway, so back to Joshua... I went to Joshua's birthday party just a few weeks before mine. My mom was trying to be nice to the newcomers, I think. His family had just moved here. He was turning ten, and it was a total baby's party. I mean a BABY party." He snorted and winked at me. "So, then I had to invite him to my party. Did I already say? My birthday is August 22. When's yours?"

"August 15."

"Wow! Just wow! So close..." He eyed me suspiciously again. Some unseen wheels turned in his mind. He fell silent and kept staring at me.

After twenty or so seconds, Brandon snapped out of his trance and went on, "Anyway! Then it got worse. Joshua was in my fifth grade class at school, and he followed me everywhere, every day. He sat by me at lunch every day. He stood by me in the water line every day after recess. He waited for me outside the bathroom EVERY DAY! I couldn't even pee in peace!" He shuddered at the memory. "And... and... he invited me to spend the night at his house EVERY Friday for the whole semester! Finally, my mom made me go over to his house during Christmas break. She said it would be rude if I turned him down any longer. Do you wanna know what happened?"

I nodded, knowing resistance was futile.

"First of all, he farts all the time. His room was like walking into a gas factory! Then he made me play with Legos for hours! I thought I was gonna fall asleep with Lego bricks in my hands. It was that boring!"

I gulped and wondered what he would think of my Lego collection.

"Then it just got ten times worse. It was time for bed. I slipped on my sleeping shorts. He looked horrified and asked where my pajamas were. My pa-ja-mas? I stopped sleeping in pajamas when I was, like, four. But Joshua pulled his pee-jays out of the closet. They were Santa Claus pajamas! I kid you not, Alex. And he had Santa Claus slippers to match! And then he takes all that stuff, leaves the room, changes in the bathroom down the hall, and comes back looking like the Big Man himself."

I shook my head and laughed. "So, did he have a surprise pair for you, too?"

Brandon gasped. "Oh, God, I never even thought about that. No, it got worse. He only has a little boy bed. I had to sleep on the floor. Did I mention he farts? Did I mention he has four dogs? Did I mention the carpet smelt like farts and dog piss? All I got was a quilt to lay on, a pillow, and a quilt to cover with. It was like sleeping in a dog toilet."

I laughed so hard some Dr. Pepper came out of my nose, and happy tears blurred my vision. Brandon seemed pleased that I had appreciated his performance. He basked in the glow of my admiration, like a Hollywood star stepping out on the red carpet at the Oscars.

"So, yeah, just avoid Joshua. He's nice enough, but if you're just a little bit nice to him, he will never, ever leave you alone again! You don't have to be mean, but just avoid him. It's the only way to save yourself from that carpet."

"I'll keep that in mind."

He clapped me on the shoulder. "Oh, one more thing. Don't be friends with Eric Williams. He's best church friends with Joshua. They do everything together. It's like a deal: you get one, you get the other. Like, you get fries, you get ketchup. Eric's alright, but it's not worth the risk of getting invited over by Joshua. I swear, I can still smell that odor."

I said, "I have a friend at school named Eric. He's pretty nice. Who are your best friends at school?"

Brandon sighed, "I don't really have any best friends at school. I mean, I know everyone in my grade, but I just don't have one or two close friends. Even here at church, I just kind of hang out with everyone. What about you? Are you best friends with this Eric?"

"Well, I've got three best friends at school: Eric, Kevin, and Abdul. I don't really see them much outside of school, but we spend a lot of time at school together. We always invite each other to our birthday parties, but that's about it. Maybe a movie or two in the summer."

"What about cousins? Do you have a lot of cousins to make up for being an only child?"

"No. I just have one cousin, but she lives in Seattle with her mom. I'm the only child in my whole family here in Houston."

"Wow! I can't imagine that. I have twenty-three cousins!"

"What? How on earth is that possible?"

"Well, Dad has two older brothers and a younger sister. And Mom has one older sister, one younger brother, and three younger sisters. All of them have kids. So, you know, my family is like rabbits. Someone's breeding every time you turn around. They all live in Nashville or near it. My Dayton cousins are the worst. They're honest-to-God hillbillies. I think they drank moonshine in their baby bottles. It explains a lot." He snickered and gave me a conspiratorial wink.

I went silent, pondering what it would be like at Christmas with three brothers plus twenty-three cousins. I didn't even have the imagination for it. Brandon stared at me for a long time again. I wasn't sure what he wanted. Was I supposed to talk more about my family? Was I supposed to ask him a question?

I cleared my throat. He came back to awareness with a

jerk. He asked me, "So what did you think about your first devo?"

"Um... well, I felt a bit awkward not knowing the songs. And, uh, that lesson was kind of intense. I've never heard that kind of religious language before. I remember my granddad watching a TV preacher one time, but he was only watching to make fun of it. The preacher was talking about hell and telling people to send him money and ask Jesus into their hearts in order to get saved. It was weird."

I paused for a few seconds, wondering how much I ought to say. "All the stuff about going to hell because you kiss a girl... I mean, it's a bit much. And my parents really like the mayor. She wants everyone to feel welcome and at home here. She says people who are gay should have the same rights as everyone else, and my parents agree. My dad does some volunteer work at one of the AIDS clinics, and his lab at the hospital is investigating ways to treat people who have both cancer and AIDS."

"Really? Wow! I mean, my dad is just like Michael. He hates gay people so much. Except he doesn't call them gay. He calls them queers and fags and Sodomites. He thinks AIDS is God's punishment on them. He hates the mayor even more. He calls her the 'Whore of Babylon-on-the-Bayou.' He says women have no business leading at church or in the government. They should stay home and take care of their families."

"But your mom works!"

"Well, she doesn't do everything he says. Sometimes, I don't think she really loves him."

"I don't think your dad's gonna like my mom very much. She's the chairwoman for the local chapter of NOW, and she was an advisor for Whitmire's campaign in '85."

"What's NOW?"

"The National Organization of Women. It's a feminist organization dedicated to women's full equality."

"Oh, God! My dad hates the feminists nearly as much as

he hates the gays. You gotta tell your parents to keep all that quiet. Dad would never let me be friends with you if he found out all that stuff."

"Your dad sure does hate a lot of people."

"Tell me about it! It's his favorite hobby – talking about all the people he hates. Don't get him started on the Democrats or scientists or atheists!"

He said it with a playful tone, but I thought I saw some deeper emotion play out across his face.

"What about all of them out there?" I gestured to the swarm of teens we could see through the windows in the living room. "What do they all think?"

"They all think what their parents and Michael tell them to think. My brother Will throws around those words all the time: faggot, queer, lesbian. He calls the mayor a dyke Jew."

"What does that mean?"

"Dyke?"

I nodded.

"It's, like, the female word for faggot. Like, a lesbian, but a hateful way to say it."

"She's not a lesbian! She's married to a man. He can't call her that!"

I hesitated a second before asking, "And what do you think?"

"About what?"

"About gay people."

He went silent. The mood between us seemed tense. He let out a sigh and looked up at the ceiling. "I don't know. How do I know what to believe when my dad says one thing and your parents say the opposite?"

"Well, what does your own heart tell you?"

He turned his face to me, and his piercing blue eyes bore straight into mine. "My own heart?"

"Yeah, deep down. My parents always ask me what my heart feels about something."

"What does that mean?"

I paused and tried to remember a time when I wasn't sure what my heart was telling me and how my parents told me to listen to it more carefully.

"Well, when you think about gay people, do you feel like you want to call them names – like faggot and dyke – and tell them how bad they are, or do you want to treat them just like ordinary people? Do you think they deserve your understanding or your hatred? What does your heart tell you?"

"Dad says we can't trust our hearts. He says the inclination of our hearts is always to evil. He says that if I follow my heart, I can be sure I'm sinning. I have to follow the Bible, not my heart."

I couldn't think of a thing to say. I knew Michael and Will's kind of hateful talk swirled around parts of Houston, but I had never met people who said those things. It made me a little hesitant and unsure about Brandon. I also didn't know what to make of his dad's advice to ignore the still, small voice of the heart. I'd never heard anything like that in my whole life. What kind of religion told people not to trust their best instincts?

I suddenly realized I knew very little about Brandon. Was he like his dad and Will but just hid it well? Did he think the same thing about gay people and the mayor? Was there a hateful side to him I hadn't seen? My heart told me no, but another part of me felt wary. A sour taste filled my mouth, and I feared that some unseen fault line was about to shatter my new friendship with Brandon.

He gave me a wry smile, switched topics on a dime, and said, "So, the big question, my friend, is who do you like? Because I have it from a very trusted source that Rachel Bishop wants to go out with you."

"Who's that?"

"She's the one out there by the grill." He pointed toward the big window opposite us in the living room. "The one with the long brown hair in the pink shirt. She told Laura, Laura told her brother Josh, and Josh told me. Not Joshua White. There's two Joshuas technically. But Laura's brother's name is just Josh. Anyway, he told me that she likes you. Rachel not Laura! She wants to go out with you. She said she thinks you're totally cute. What do you think?"

I hesitated. "I don't know her at all. What's she like?"

"Well, she's a scratcher, too. Most of those girls are scratchers. Seriously! I went to the nurse twice at camp last summer because of scratches! And those were just the times I was bleeding."

I wondered what went on at this camp. I had visions of horseback riding, swimming, campfires, and making crafts. Isn't that what kids did at church camp? All the talk of scratching girls and furtive romance scared me a bit.

I said, "Um, I... well, I'm not sure. I don't even know her. Let me think."

Brandon leaned over and tapped me on the forehead. "Wise move, man! That high IQ must be true! I was gonna tell you to say no to Rachel, unless you really liked her. I was gonna warn you, but I would let you make your own mistake if you wanted. That's what kind of friend I am. I should tell you several other girls think you're totally cute. They all talk about you in the bathroom according to Laura. You know they go to the bathroom in big groups? Well, it seems one of the groups is the 'we think the new boy Alex is hot' group. But the 'Brandon is even hotter' group is bigger. Mine's bigger than yours."

Brandon chuckled at himself. He was like nobody I had ever met before. I never knew what to expect out of his mouth. It both excited and frightened me.

"Will told me who to avoid when I came to the youth group. So, I thought I would pass on the same info to you. Stay away from the scratchers. I'll make a list later so it's clear."

"Where's your brother? I haven't seen him tonight. And

where are the others?"

"Will's working tonight. My two oldest brothers don't live here anymore. Matthew's a junior at UT. He's 20. Jacob is married and lives up on the north side of town. I think he's 27 or 28. He was so old when I was growing up, it was like he wasn't even my brother. He and my dad fell out over something, and I haven't seen him since I was four. I was what you call an unexpected blessing. Just when Mom and Dad thought they had it all done – surprise! They saved the best for last!" He flashed me a winning smile and held his arms straight up in the air.

There was a sudden commotion outside. Several teenagers huddled by the pool, pointing and laughing.

Brandon jumped up. "Oh, shit! There's people in the pool. I'll hear about this all week, and I wasn't even there!" I ran after him.

We stumbled out the back door as kids streamed out the gate and down the driveway. The powerful lights on the side of the house lit up the whole poolside scene. As the crowd parted, I saw Ben and Joel by the side of the pool, half smirking and half trying to look sorry. They were drenched and shirtless.

Brandon grabbed my arm and pulled me along behind him. We walked up a bit closer. Mr. Marshall and Joel's dad were gesturing wildly in front of Joel and Ben. I stood transfixed.

Everyone in the youth group talked about Ben and Joel all the time. Brandon called them the gods of the youth group, and I couldn't help but agree. They were the two biggest high school guys I had ever seen. Even when they had shirts on, you could see their rounded biceps. As they stood by the pool, wet and shirtless, I finally got to see their broad shoulders, full chests, and rocky six-packs. My penis swelled up. I stole a quick glance at Brandon, worried he might notice what happened to my crotch, but he wasn't looking at me. His eyes were fixed on Ben and Joel.

He turned to me and said, "Wow! Just wow! I think they get bigger every few months. When they'd come to the pool at camp last summer, I swear every guy watched them take off their shirts and dive in. I mean, they don't even look like teenagers. I want to take my shirt off in three or four years and look like that. What do you think, Alex?" He poked me in the ribs.

I muttered quietly, "Yeah, they're big. Like football players I've seen on TV."

"I know! Joel is the QB at his high school. Ben is captain of the wrestling team at his high school. They meet up at some local gym a few afternoons a week." He looked at me and threw his arm around my shoulder. "Let's make a pact. That'll be me and you one day. Muscles all over and gods of the youth group." He tossed back his head and shouted in the air, "Watch out, world! Alex and me are next!"

Mr. Marshall turned on his heel with fury. Brandon gasped and seemed to draw near to me for protection. Mr. Marshall took several strides toward us. "Brandon Geoffrey Marshall! Tell me you are not the fool I hear screaming in my backyard." Spittle flew from his lips. "You have a guest, a new friend from church, right next to you. You should be setting an example. You are not an animal in the zoo. Get inside and help your mother clean up after your friends." His voice boomed even more loudly. "Now – before I ground you until Halloween!"

I rocked back on my heels as Mr. Marshall advanced toward me. In a calmer voice he said, "Alex, you are welcome any time. Please forgive my son for not being his best on your first visit." He shook my hand and turned away.

Brandon and I slumped back to the house. His mom called out to us as we entered.

"Just a second, honey." We both turned to look at her. She laughed and said, "I mean, you, Alex. You're a honey here, too. I called your mother just after we arrived. I told her you had come with us and that she and your dad shouldn't drive to the church to collect you. She said one of them would be here by 8:30. Stand out front and look for them. They may miss the house number since it's dark now."

I nodded and said, "Thanks. Can I help you clean up?"

She shook her head and said, "No! You're our guest! It's been a pleasure to have you here. Brandon asked if you could come swim next summer. You are very welcome. As a matter of fact, you'll be in trouble if you don't come back before then."

Mrs. Marshall leaned close to me and gave me another kiss on the cheek. Then she turned to Brandon and stroked his cheek. "Now, my real honey, go wait with Alex. See him off safely, please. Then get straight upstairs to the shower. And lights out at 9:00. Not a second later. Don't give your dad any more reasons to shout."

Brandon and I wandered out to the porch. All the streetlights had come on. The church vans and high schoolers' cars were long gone. I was glad for the peace after the raucous backyard and Mr. Marshall's explosion.

I looked at Brandon and asked, "Are you okay?"

He was staring down at his feet. "I guess. It's the story of my life. I can't do anything right. He praises Will for everything he does, but he bites my head off for the smallest things. It's just..." His voice broke off as Dad pulled up.

I patted his shoulder. "I'm sorry if I was in the way and made it worse. Are you gonna be okay?"

He looked at me with his characteristic wry grin. "Sure. I'm gonna be okay. You're not in the way. In fact, you made it easier somehow. Call me this week. I want you to come over soon."

I grinned from ear to ear. "Cool! Have fun at school."

"Of course! It's a laugh a minute."

I ran down the sidewalk, my feet barely touching the pavement, and hopped inside for the quick ride home.

CHAPTER 3

Every fall, the church youth group went on a retreat the weekend before Thanksgiving. When I first heard about it, I wasn't sure I wanted to go. Brandon called me a few days after Halloween and said I didn't have an option. He teased me, "Bring your permission forms on Sunday or you'll be in big trouble. If you don't, I'll suggest to Joshua that you really want to go to his house for a sleepover. It'll be a night to remember. Lemme tell ya!"

I brought my forms the next Sunday. Brandon stood a few feet away with his dashing grin and two thumbs raised high as I gave my paperwork and registration check to Michael Walker.

The fleet of church vans and family cars descended on Camp North Pines by 8:00 on a cool Friday evening. The camp was only forty miles north of downtown Houston, but it seemed a world away from the bumper-to-bumper commuter traffic we crawled through to get there.

As soon as we unloaded our belongings, Brandon grabbed me by the arm and tugged with urgency. "Come on, come on! We gotta get to the cabin before Joshua. I heard him telling Eric White that he was going to save a bunk for you." A look of grim determination settled on his face. He muttered, "You sleep next to Joshua? Over my dead body!"

Brandon led me down a poorly lit path to the cabin designated for the junior high boys. Joel's dad, one of the weekend chaperones, was already inside. He seemed to be guarding several bunks near the door. He smiled at us when we came in and said, "The adults are over here on this side. Far from the bathroom, for obvious reasons!"

Other boys were already rolling out sleeping bags on their bunks and arguing about who was going to snore the loudest. In the far right corner of the cabin, between the bathroom door and a window, two beds stood side by side. Brandon dropped his bags at his feet, dashed across the cabin, and hurled himself onto one of the mattresses. He shouted mid-air, "Claimed! Brandon and Alex claim these! Back off everyone! Back off!"

I looked around. There hadn't actually been a mad stampede to those beds. Brandon's 1880s-land-rush theatrics seemed a little unnecessary. But that was Brandon in his purest form: all-in all the time and way-over-the-top-eager about everything!

Joel came in a few seconds later loaded down with his suitcase, pillow, and sleeping bag. I was surprised that he seemed to be coming in to stay. I figured he would be in the cabin with the high school guys. He put his stuff on one of the bunks his dad had been reserving and muttered under his breath – something about being stuck in the nursery with the babies.

He sauntered over as Brandon and I organized our belongings. He sat on the foot of the bed I claimed, the one closet to the bathroom. He gave us each a high five and looked over at the squabbling mass of boys on the other side of the cabin. "How do you put up with those morons? You two are the only normal junior high guys. You are so lucky to have each other this weekend."

Brandon chuckled and said, "Well, why do you think we claimed these beds? We might get a few bad whiffs from the bathroom, especially after Joshua and Eric use it, but at least we're over here by ourselves. We'll leave the crazy ones for your side." He looked up from his suitcase. "Hey! Why are you in here, anyway, Joel? Why aren't you with the high school guys?"

"Well, in case you forgot, Ben and I fell in your pool at the joint devo. We got totally chewed out by your dad, my dad, and Michael. The only way Ben and I could come on the retreat was to agree to stay in separate cabins and not hang out together this weekend. So, we have to pretend we don't know each other. It's fucking stupid." Joel looked over his shoulder to see if his dad heard him. His dad didn't seem to hear him, and Joel carried on, "So, I think I'll let you two hang out with me, if you want." Brandon giggled and winked at me. "Otherwise I'll go crazy putting up with those boys over there. I won't be responsible for what I do to them, I swear."

Joel stood and stretched his arms. His long-sleeve t-shirt lifted up, and I could see his hard, contoured abs. I was close enough to reach out and touch them. I'd have given anything to run my hands across those ridges.

"So, I'll see you at the campfire. Save me a seat. Later, dudes." He walked off.

Brandon punched my shoulder. "What a weekend! Your first retreat! Plus, we've got beds together far from Joshua. Plus, Jackie is not here this year." Who was Jackie? "Plus, we get to hang out with Joel. Plus, it's actually cold enough for a campfire this year. It was so hot last year. We were all in shorts and t-shirts. It ruined the effect of a November campfire. It's gonna be an awesome weekend.

"Come on! We gotta go get a good seat for the campfire. I sat right in the path of the smoke last year and coughed all weekend. When I got home, Dad actually accused me of smoking cigarettes on the retreat." He snorted. "As if! God, they are so nasty. I'd never smoke in a million years. Come on!" I followed him out of the cabin, leaving my belongings half in place and half scattered about.

The campfire was indeed awesome. The night was turning colder quickly, and the fire seemed to draw everyone to it. We roasted marshmallows and made 'Smores. There was a long round of crazy camp songs. I didn't know a single one, but nobody seemed to notice. It was a bit chaotic, and Brandon's euphoria rubbed off on me. I'd never thrown myself so fully into something so silly before.

Once everyone was exhausted, Michael started the serious songs. I recognized a few more this time, and I joined in on some of the repetitive choruses. Joel sat right between Brandon and me. You would never have known it by looking at him, but he had a beautiful voice. It was loud and strong while also being clear and soothing. He sang low and high notes with ease. I loved listening to his voice, and I soon forgot I didn't know many of the words.

Michael's lesson was short and, thankfully, not about sexual purity. When he finished speaking, some of the older teenagers started the youth group theme song, *Love is the Way*. We all stood and wrapped our arms around those next to us.

Joel's dense left arm rested on my shoulder and neck. Brandon wrapped his right arm around my waist. I kept trying to focus on the words of that last song, but I couldn't ignore the strength and warmth I felt from my two new friends on either side of me. I never knew I could feel so safe and happy between two such friends.

Joel pulled me in closer at the end of the song and said, "I'm really glad you came, Alex. You're a good friend for Brandon. He needs someone like you who can calm him down. Try to keep him outta trouble, okay?"

I looked up and said, "Sure, Joel. I'll try. He's a good friend to me. He's the best friend I've ever had."

Later that night as all the other boys drifted off to sleep, Brandon and I whispered back and forth for a while. He had pushed his bunk right next to mine because he felt a draft from the window.

He leaned in close to my head. "Rachel still wants to go out with you. Just like half the other girls here. Why don't you give it a chance tomorrow? Ask her! And this place is a great place for kissing. Plenty of places to go off and not be seen. I can be the lookout for you two."

I shook my head. "I don't know. I didn't really come here to kiss Rachel. I don't want to go out with any of the girls yet. Give me some time, okay?"

He sighed and rolled on his back. "I try so hard and see all the thanks I get." I looked over at him, worried he was really mad. He gave me the irresistible wry smile I had come to love over the previous few months. He winked at me and said, "Good night, *mi amigo*. Get some beauty sleep. You need all the help you can get." He closed his eyes and kept chuckling for a few seconds.

. . .

I opened my eyes to find Joel towering over me, with only a towel wrapped around his waist. Steamy light streamed out from the bathroom, and Joel glistened with that fresh-from-the-shower look. It was still dark in the cabin. No one else seemed to be awake.

Joel looked down at me and winked. I could hear a playfulness in his voice as he said, "Mornin', Alex! What are you doing up and dressed already? Got a date I don't know about?"

He pulled the towel off and began drying his back and shoulders. His penis dangled right in front of me. Where was I to look when the god of the youth group was stark naked, only a foot away? I looked up at the ceiling, even though I could tell he was looking into my eyes.

"I was cold and awake already. Then I heard the shower. So, I thought I'd put on my clothes and wait for Brandon to get up. I didn't know it was you in the shower."

Joel whispered, "I don't think he's getting up any time soon. I don't even see his head."

I looked over at Brandon's bed, thankful to have something else to look at. Sure enough: Brandon was completely huddled inside his sleeping bag. I don't think he had moved all night.

Joel continued to stand close as he dried off. He seemed to be taking a long time. I still didn't know what to do with my eyes, so I went back to staring into the darkness above me.

"You can look at me, you know. All the guys at camp watch me when I'm not looking. I am used to it. They even do it in the locker room at school. All the freshman keep staring at us older guys, and then they turn away as soon as they think someone's seen them watching us." He laughed and bent over to dry his legs.

I once read a book in school about bronze statuary in ancient Greece. My eyes lingered over the impossibly sculpted male bodies that filled every page. Joel looked as if he had just stepped out of that book, as if the stirrings I felt in my loins in fifth grade magically brought one of those statues to life. I wanted to reach out and touch Joel's body so badly. I was dizzy with desire.

He shook his head over me and snickered. "I hear you haven't been baptized yet. They call this christening in other churches, but my dad calls it 'dry cleaning.' This will be good enough until we get you all the way under water." He shook his head again and water from his still-damp hair sprinkled over me. "In the name of the Father…" He shook his head again. "In the name of the Son…" He shook his head again. "In the name of the Holy Spirit…" He shook his head a final time, smiling down at me. "There you go. That'll keep you out of hell for now."

He draped his towel around his neck and held out his arms. "Come on. Let's go over to the dining hall and get something warm to drink."

I grabbed his hands and let him pull me up. I slipped my coat on, looked back at the lump of Brandon inside his sleeping bag, and crossed the room to wait by the door.

Joel put on his pants and shoes. He lifted his arms to apply some deodorant. Then he held his arms up and flexed them both for me. I was awestruck. He gave me a huge smile, and said, "It's nice to see someone who likes my guns. They take a lot of hard work, you know." He slipped on a t-shirt, pulled a sweater over his neck and torso, and grabbed his coat.

He grinned and whispered, "Come on. I know where they keep the hot cocoa."

We wandered up a tree-lined path to the dining hall. A small glass thermometer hung on a nail by the main doors. Joel leaned in to see it. "Wow! It's 28°. That's the coldest it's ever been on any retreat here. That hot cocoa is gonna be awesome."

We stepped into the welcoming warmth of the dining hall. The kitchen and serving line were to our right. There were rows of tables in front of us and off to the left. Past the tables was a large open space with chairs arranged in a circle. On the far side of the circle was a fireplace, already lit, and two wooden rocking chairs.

Joel motioned to the fire. "Someone's got the fire going! Sweet! Go on down there. Go warm up. I know the ladies who work in the kitchen. They're here every year. I'll go sweet talk them into letting me make us some cocoa."

He joined me in a few minutes, holding a brown plastic tray with two mugs of hot cocoa and two Styrofoam plates with a sausage biscuit on each. He handed me a mug. "Watch out. It's really hot. And look what else I got for us!" He handed me one of the plates. "I'm tellin' you, it's all about who you know. If you're in with me, Alexo, you're in for the good stuff."

I smiled and thanked him for the cocoa and biscuit. I was hungrier than I realized and glad, too, for the warm cocoa.

He looked over at me between two bites and said, "Alexo! I like that." He paused and repeated it slowly so it sounded like 'Uh-lexo'.

"Do you already have a nickname?"

"No. It's just Alexander or Alex. Most people call me plain Alex."

"Then Alexo it is. You don't mind?"

"No. It's good. I like it."

Joel munched on his biscuit, took a swig of the cocoa, and said, "I feel like I know so much about you, but I don't know you... if that makes any sense."

I was confused but nodded anyway. We had only spoken a few times at church after that first Sunday. How did he know anything about me?

"I mean, Brandon talks about you non-stop whenever I'm over at their house. I spent the night with Will two weekends ago. Brandon gave me your life story or at least as much as he knows. I know all about your running. I know you're an only child. I know you go to St. Martin's. I know you're, like, the smartest, nicest kid there. I know your parents are mega smart. I know you don't watch TV. I know you read books most seniors can't get through."

I shook my head. "He told you all that?"

"And more! Seriously, he thinks the sun shines outta your ass. Or you hung the moon and the stars. Or whatever metaphor you wanna choose. If it paints you in a positive light, he says it and then amps it up a bit more. He doesn't make friends easily, but you've won him over somehow."

He reached over and ruffled my hair as I blushed.

"What's your secret, Alexo? I know a few girls in the youth group who'd love to know the way to Brandon's heart. I mean, they've been trying to figure him out for years. Then you come along, and in two months he's following you everywhere.

Some of those girls are mad at you. The others all think you're totally hot. Don't pretend you haven't seen. Their heads all swivel in unison when you walk by. They sense something different in you." He winked. "Cute and kind. Quiet and smart. Chicks dig that, lemme tell ya."

I blushed again. Joel cackled and said, "God, you're easy to embarrass! That makes it too easy for me! And, I should add, all the high school boys think you are impossibly cool. They're all asking me, 'Who is that cool new kid in the junior high group?'"

I choked on my hot chocolate.

Joel finished the rest of the biscuit and slurped his cocoa. He dusted off his hands and put his palms behind his head, leaning back slightly in the rocking chair. "Seriously, man. You sound ten times smarter than any of the high school guys when you start talking. Not that you talk too much. In fact, you need to talk more." He paused and rocked forward, patting me on the knee. "You are a man of mystery… our youth group enigma. Tell me something I probably don't know about you. Surely, you've kept a few secrets from Brandino."

I gulped. "What do you want to know?"

He scooted closer to the fire and reached over to pull my chair closer, too. "It's drafty in here. Get closer. We've got, like, thirty minutes before anyone else comes in. Nobody gets up early the first morning. It's just you and me for now."

I hesitated. As much as I liked Joel, I wasn't sure to what extent he was serious and to what extent he may have been teasing me. Sometimes his grin was kind, and sometimes some other intention seemed to lurk behind it.

"Um, I really like classical music." I paused and waited for him to laugh or say something sarcastic. He didn't say a thing. His eyes were all kindness and friendship, as if he was genuinely interested in me.

I said with a little more confidence, "Do you remember how you mentioned I was an enigma?" He nodded. "Well, one of my favorite compositions is by the British composer Elgar. He wrote a collection of pieces called *Enigma Variations*. The best one is called *Nimrod*. When I listen to it, it makes me think about the sunrise. The beginning is soft, with just some gentle strings, and you can imagine all living things stirring to life just before sunrise. Then it builds to this loud moment as horns and other instruments join in. All this emotion swirls around you, and you can imagine the sun just coming over the horizon. Then there is a moment where the whole song crescendos to its peak. You feel it in your heart. It's like everything in the world was holding its breath and then exhaled in one giant rush as the sun peaked over the distant hills."

Joel stared at me intently for a few seconds before saying, "Wow! Where do you come from? And where is all this deep stuff coming from? None of the high school guys would have a fucking clue about what you just said." He slapped his hand over his mouth and said sheepishly, "God, I'm so sorry, Alexo! I have a bad habit of cursing! I'm a horrible example. If I do it again, you can take a free hit on me anywhere you want. Deal?"

I grinned and said, "Deal!"

He urged me on, "Well, keep going, keep going. Time is ticking."

"I hate sports of all kinds. Except running and swimming. I was always horrible at all the games we played in PE in the lower school. If I could just run, I was happy. But when I had to throw, dribble, or catch a ball, I was falling all over the place. By fourth grade, the PE coach just let me go run by myself when it was time for any sport with balls. Have you ever seen *Chariots of Fire*?"

He furrowed his brow and said, "No, but I know it's about running."

"Yeah, it's about this man in Scotland who is the best runner in the country, and he's preparing to go to the Olympics. At one point, he's scheduled to run in a race on a Sunday.

But he won't run on Sunday because he's a very pious. He says it's wrong for him to run on a Sunday. He says a line like this: 'When I run, I can feel his pleasure.' He means he feels God's pleasure. I'm not sure what he means by that, but I think I feel it, too. Like when I run, and nobody else is around, I can feel something I can't describe. It's like a kind of peace and happiness I never feel any other time. Maybe that's what God's pleasure feels like."

Just as I finished, the main doors at the far end of the dining hall opened swiftly, and a swarm of loud girls came rushing in. They saw us and several came running our way.

Joel looked startled. "Oh, shit... oh, sorry! Come on, man. Come on! Follow me!" He jumped up from the rocking chair. I darted after him. We ran down the opposite side of the dining hall from the small cluster of girls heading toward us. He threw open the back door just as I reached him.

He cried out, "Run, Alexo. Run like your life depends on it!"

We sprinted around the back of the dining hall and out across the large clearing. I easily outpaced him. I saw his startled look as I passed by him.

"Holy shit," he exclaimed. I looked back and saw him doubled over, sucking in great gasps of air. I slowed to a jog and turned around. I trotted back to his side.

"Did you get winded?" I asked.

He collapsed to the ground, simultaneously laughing and trying to catch his breath. "Holy hell, you're fast! Sorry I keep cursing around you. My dad would kill me if he heard me cursing in front of a junior high kid, especially one who hadn't been baptized."

After a few seconds, he stopped laughing so uncontrollably. His breathing returned to normal. He looked up at me and said, "Yes, I did get winded. I can never run on a full stomach. Plus, you turned on your rockets, and I tried to keep up. I think I pulled a muscle. You're like lightning! I didn't know you ran like that!"

He shook his head and smiled at me. "I'm telling you, those girls were after you. You're a marked man."

I looked up the path and saw lights on in the cabin. Some of the boys were milling around on the porch. I said to Joel, "We'd better get back. Brandon will wonder where I am."

We headed back to the cabin. Joel made the most of his injuries, moaning dramatically as he leaned against me. I could hardly stand, but I loved the feel of his body's weight pressing in close to me. We stumbled into the cabin, laughing, and every eye turned our way as we entered.

I saw Brandon immediately. He was sitting on his bunk, looking small and alone. He looked back and forth between me and Joel. His expression darkened, and he cried out, "Where have you been? Why didn't you wake me up if you were going out? I would've come with you!"

I shrugged and sat down on his bunk. "Your head was totally inside your sleeping bag when I woke up. You didn't even move when I got up and changed clothes. I thought you needed the sleep, so I left you alone. Then Joel came out of the shower, and he said we should go get some cocoa. I didn't want to wake you up. We just sat by the fire and talked until the junior high girls came in. You didn't miss much, really."

He didn't reply. He stood up, sighed, put on his coat, and left the cabin without looking back.

. . .

The morning passed by in a whirlwind of activities: breakfast, chores, silly songs, devotional songs, prayer time, and a long lesson by Michael. Brandon studiously avoided me all morning. I tried to speak to him during the silly songs, and he bolted away from me like a stray electrical spark. When we sat down for the lesson, he made a dramatic point of sitting on the opposite side of the circle from me. Every person in the room sensed there was something drastically wrong between Brandon and me. At one point in the lesson, I looked to my left and saw Joel staring at me from a few chairs down. He shrugged at me and mouthed the words, 'What's up?' Tears flooded my eyes, and I quickly looked away.

After the lesson, the girls stayed inside the dining hall to play games, and the boys went outside for a game of football. Michael said everyone had to play. He kept saying the game was just for fun and nobody needed to take it seriously. He threatened the loss of afternoon free time for anyone who got angry, started shouting, or began playing too roughly.

Michael designated Ben and Joel as team captains. I ended up on Joel's team after a blind lottery. Brandon was on Ben's team. He glared at me from across the fifty-yard line on the first play. He had never looked at me so coldly, and I couldn't imagine any way to repair whatever chasm had opened up between us. I knew he was angry at me for hanging out with Joel while he still slept, but I couldn't see why he was so upset. I wanted to be with him more than anybody else, even more than Joel. Didn't he get that?

I attempted to look eager for the first few plays, but I soon employed some stealthy diversionary tactics and stayed close to the sidelines on each play. I figured the best thing to do was keep my head down and try to look interested, feigning an exaggerated sense of engagement. I ended up running back and forth along the sidelines, no matter if my side was offense or defense. I'm sure Michael noticed, but I guess he went easy on me since I was still new. Perhaps he also sensed the tension between Brandon and me and decided to let it all slide in an effort to make things easier on me.

Joel noticed my tactics, too, and left me to myself. Whenever our side had the ball, he aimed his missile-like passes to the opposite side of the field from me, even when a good receiver was open near me. I was thankful for his kindness and sensitivity.

Brandon was way too intense. No matter what the play was, he was right in the middle of the action. At one point, I heard Joel quietly ask him to calm down a bit. He took Brandon aside and said, "It's all supposed to be fun, man. You look like you wanna take off someone's head! Take it down a few notches!"

The next few plays only made Brandon angrier. He was as tall and broad as the biggest freshmen and sophomores. He didn't seem to have any control, knocking down the junior high boys without a backwards glance.

Finally, Michael's voice boomed out across the field, "Alright, Brandon Marshall. You're out! Get out of the game! You know what I said. Joel tried to tell you to take it easy. It's called flag football for a reason. I won't let you hurt anyone! Get over here and sit!" He pointed to the ground beside him, like he was calling a dog to heel.

An awkward hush fell over the field as everyone stared at Brandon. He blushed a deep red. He looked so small and fragile from where I stood. Several of the high school guys snickered as Brandon walked over to Michael.

Play continued. After several starts and stops, I made my way to the side of the field where Brandon sat alone. I tried to approach him as nonchalantly as I could, hoping I could get his attention and at least offer a smile or wink.

Michael turned to me and stared me down. He shouted at me: "Leave him alone, Alex. You can't make this better for him. He's gotta grow up sometime. He might as well start now. Just back off."

. . .

Later at lunch, Brandon came in once everyone else was eating. Michael came in right behind him. He bent a little to whisper in Brandon's ear. Michael pointed to the serving line and then motioned to the end of a table on the far side of the room, far away from where I was sitting. Brandon got his lunch and went to sit by himself. He sat with his back to the rest of the room. He didn't seem to be eating, just staring out the window.

I looked back to the chaperone's table. Michael was sitting down and didn't seem to notice me. I summoned all my courage. I stood up and walked over to Brandon, with my eye on the chaperone table the whole time. Michael's loud shout across the football field still rang in my ears. I didn't want him shouting at me, but I had to make some kind of amends to Brandon.

I sat down opposite Brandon. He didn't even look at me. I wondered if I was making things worse. I glanced at the next table over and saw Joel looking straight at me. He gave me a subdued smile and a wink.

Brandon's eyes were red. He looked down at his food and wouldn't meet my eyes. He cheeks were rosy and mottled. I noticed a small amount of moisture at the top of his lip. He had been crying and crying hard. I didn't know what to say. I thought back to the night of the October devotional when Mr. Marshall yelled at Brandon. Brandon had the same distant, sad look, and I realized there was a whole part of Brandon I didn't understand.

I asked, "Are you okay?"

He looked up at me. Tears pooled at the bottom of his eyes. I didn't know what I ought to say. I felt useless. And I was scared. Could one wrong move on my part be the end of our friendship? I felt as though I was on an icy pond. One wrong move and a thousand cracks might split open beneath my feet.

He didn't reply at first. He stared into my eyes for several seconds, then looked away. I sighed and started to rise.

He reached out and grabbed my wrist. "No, don't go. I mean... please don't go. I didn't mean to ignore you all morning. I just didn't know what to do. I was angry and sad, and I didn't know what to do."

I didn't know how to respond. I just said what seemed easiest. "It's okay, Brandon. I didn't think you were ignoring me." I knew for a fact he was ignoring me, and it pierced me like a long, sharp dagger all morning long. If I hadn't been distracted by my own running, I would have sat on the sidelines and sobbed through the whole football game. "I just thought you were tired or maybe cold."

His eyes held a look I didn't understand. He said softly, "Is that what you thought? That I was cold? Maybe I was. I don't know. I just know I'm sorry now. I didn't mean to ignore you. I don't mean to act like a jerk. I just do. I get so tired of myself sometimes. I don't know how to stop." He buried his face in palms and shook his head back and forth. He looked up again. "God, I'm a mess. I don't know what to do. I'm the shittiest friend on the planet."

I smiled at him. "Why don't you eat? That hamburger is so cold now it has icicles on it."

He gave me a subdued smile in return. He took a few small bites, and I told him about Rachel and Joshua.

"They boxed me in at the serving counter earlier, and I couldn't find a good way to get away from them. Then Joshua saved me a seat. He cried out to me in front of everyone and waved to me wildly as I turned away from the serving line. How could I pretend not to see him? Rachel followed close behind. I was trapped. I spent the whole lunch listening to her talk about who liked who, and Joshua was rambling on about a new dinosaur tape he got. He asked me about seventeen times if I wanted to have a sleepover and watch the dinosaur tape with his family!"

Brandon smiled in earnest as I finished. He seemed to flip some switch, and the old Brandon I knew became animated again. He chuckled and said, "Man, what a way to spend your first lunch on your first fall retreat. I think you should definitely do the sleepover with Joshua. I bet he has dinosaur pj's. And dinosaur slippers. Maybe he'll let you wear them."

He snickered at the thought.

I felt on firm ground again. He kept going and said, "I'll come up with a plan for tonight so we can avoid them. They don't get you for two meals in a row. I have no problem being rude to either of them. We'll sit at the end of the table and ask Joel and Ben to sit next to us. Then we'll be walled off." He raised his hand for a high five. I slapped his palm. He threw back his head, shaking with laughter.

I looked over at Joel. He gave me a thumbs-up.

After lunch clean-up, Michael came over to us and asked Brandon to follow him for a minute. They stepped over to a far corner of the dining hall. I couldn't hear what Michael said, but Brandon's body language reassured me he wasn't getting another tongue-lashing. In fact, his eyes lit up, and he smiled from ear to ear. Michael extended his hand, and Brandon shook it fiercely.

Brandon ran back to me, tossed his arm around my shoulder, and exclaimed, "Michael changed his mind about making me sit out of this afternoon's free time. We can hang out together all afternoon. You are so lucky. If I wasn't in the picture, you'd be Joshua's primary target. It would all be over for you, you sorry-ass loser-man."

Brandon and I spent a glorious afternoon together. The sun was strong and bright, even for late November. He took me on several of the trails that went off in various directions through the thick pine forests that surrounded the camp. He was a laugh-a-minute, non-stop talking machine. We ran into Joel just as we came back to the main clearing. He asked us if we wanted to go down to the small lake and see if any of the boats were available. We agreed and followed him to the lake.

Luckily for us, one of the large row boats sat idly in the calm water. Joel winked at us and said, "Climb in boys. I'll row you around while you keep making up."

Brandon clambered to the front of the boat, and I sat in the back. We both faced the middle, staring at each other around Joel's sturdy presence in the middle of the boat.

After a few minutes of aimless chatter, Brandon said, "Well, there was no making up for Alex to do. It was all my fault. I just got so mad that you two went off without me. I know it's stupid, but I just felt left out. I already apologized to Alex. And I want to apologize to you, too. You two are the coolest guys I know. You're the last people I'd ever want to hurt. Being here with you two makes this the best retreat ever. I don't wanna go home and back to school."

Joel slowed his rowing. We drifted in the middle of the lake, well away from a small canoe with several girls on the far shore. He said, "Thanks, Brandon. That's really mature of you to say. You were a bit of a jerk this morning. Actually, you were a colossal dickhead. I don't think you know what a special friend you have in Alexo. He'd have every right to tell you to shove off after the way you treated him this morning. I think he should knock your head off if you ever do that again. Or I'll do it for him if he wants."

"I know! I feel so lucky he forgave me."

I spoke up. "Don't worry about it. You're pretty easy to forgive. I don't think I could stay mad at you for very long. And I'd never knock your head off. Friends can make allowances for each other." I don't know where the words or the courage came from, but I went on. "You're the best friend I've ever had. I don't ever want to do anything that would make you think anything different, but I also hope you'll talk to me if you ever feel that way again. I'd rather talk to you than have you ignore me and be mad."

Brandon nodded and looked down. "I'll try! I promise I'll try. Just knock me around if I act like a jerk. Sometimes that's the only way to get through to me."

We all fell silent for a minute. Joel resumed his rowing and said, "Seriously, you two are about the best friends I've ever seen! And you've only known each other, like, three months. You better hang onto each other. Good friends don't come along very often. If you keep it up, you'll be absolutely inseparable by the time summer rolls around."

Brandon winked at me from the other end of the boat, and I swear my heart took flight. For the first time since we got in the boat, I didn't even really notice Joel's beautiful arms as they pulled at the oars. I stared at Brandon's handsome face in the fading afternoon sunlight and never wanted to look away again.

. . .

Brandon's plan worked at dinner. We sat at the end of a table and arranged for Joel and Ben to sit next to us. We were walled off from the onslaught of Joshua and Rachel. Michael decided to lift Joel and Ben's punishment, and they had the chance to spend the last evening actually being friends again. Brandon was in rare form. He seemed transformed from the sulky guy who glared at me across that mid-field line before lunch.

Despite my happiness to have him back, I had an unsettled feeling at dinner as I watched him laugh and trade barbs with Joel and Ben. I wondered to myself: 'When's the next time he might turn on a dime like he had this morning? When's the next time he would upend my world with his silence and distance? Would our entire friendship feel like walking a tightrope?'

After we helped with kitchen duty, the four of us made our way to the campfire for the final devotional. Brandon slung his arm over my shoulder. He leaned on me heavily, with stumbling steps, pretending that someone had spiked his punch at dinner, hiccupping and slurring his speech with exaggeration. His weight against me made me feel safe and warm again. I didn't want that long walk to the campfire to ever end.

After Michael's lesson, we all stood to sing *Love is the Way* again, everyone with their arms around each other's shoulders. The weeping from the junior high girls on the far side of the circle reached a fever pitch. I felt Joel's body shaking next to me. I looked up to see if he was crying, too.

He had a wide grin on his face. Looking down at me, he whispered, "They all cry on cue at every campfire. It's like a law of nature!" I chuckled, and he pulled me in closer.

As the song ended, all the guys quickly dropped their arms from around their friends' shoulders and shuffled off. I saw Ben slip away from the other side of Joel, but Joel and Brandon didn't move away from me. The three of us stood there, staring into the intense fire, some unspoken, unshakable bond holding us immovably in place.

CHAPTER 4

Two weeks before Christmas break, Brandon called me on Thursday evening. We had settled into a rhythm where we spoke on the phone every Thursday once we finished our homework. I always let him call me because he took longer to finish. I never got in a 'hello'; Brandon just started talking as soon as he heard me pick up my receiver.

"So, my friend, have I got a deal for you." I could hear him grinning over the line. "My parents said you can come over to our house and spend the night on New Year's Eve. Did you hear that? Oh, yes, baby! Our first sleepover on New Year's Eve! Go! Now! Now! Go find your parents and ask. I'm not waiting one second longer. I'm gonna wait here until you come back."

I laid the phone on the kitchen counter and skipped down to my parents' bedroom. I figured they would say yes. Brandon invited me to spend the night the weekend after the fall retreat, but both his parents got sick that weekend. We had to cancel at the last minute. Ever since then, all our plans to coordinate a night that was good for both families fell apart.

My parents didn't hesitate. Dad said, "Sounds like a grand plan, my man. Tell him we'll talk to his parents on Sunday and make plans for dropping you off and picking you up." Mom grinned and winked at me.

I beamed from ear to ear. "Thanks! I gotta go back. He's waiting on the phone."

Brandon exploded with excitement. I literally had to hold the receiver away from my ear. "It's gonna be the best New Year's ever! Whoop, whoop! Oh, yes, New Year's Eve with Alex at my house!" I could imagine the victory dance happening on the other end, and I admit I did a little joyful jig myself when we hung up a few minutes later.

. . .

Dad accused me of opening the car door before he shifted into park as we pulled into Brandon's driveway around 6:00 on New Year's Eve. He gave me a kiss on the forehead and ran his hand through my hair. "Have a great time. I can't believe we won't see you until next year! We'll miss you so much!" He snickered at his joke and waved to me as I walked up the brick path to the Marshalls' front door.

Brandon flung open the door and pulled me in before I could even ring the bell. A tsunami of words flowed out of him as he led me up the stairs to the second floor. "Alex, oh friend of mine. I was about to give up on you. Where have you been? What have you been doing? Fixing that amazing hair of yours?" Snicker, snicker. "I thought you'd never get here. I've been staring at the clock in the den for ten hours. I think I've gone cross-eyed."

"You told me to be here by 6:00. It's, like, 6:00 on the dot!"

"Alex, Alex, Alex... I said be here *by* 6:00, Mr. 180-IQ. That means you can come any time before. I mean, I was ready for you by lunch. Actually, I was ready for you weeks ago. Why's it taken you so long to get your ass over here?" He snickered and poked me in the ribs. "Don't take me so literally. Just show up any time you want. Lemme give you a tour of the whole second story first. Then I'll show you the best bedroom on the planet! Be thankful, my friend, that Joshua did not get you to come over to his house. He's got the lamest, babiest room in the world. Mine's like bachelor pad to the max, man. To the max!"

We stood on the landing, Brandon's arm draped around my shoulder. He pointed to the left. "Down there is a linen closet. It's got extra blankets and pillows. That kind of stuff. Towels. Some old clothes. Get whatever you need. Across from that is the bathroom. It's got a huge walk-in shower. It's the best."

We turned right. "This first room on the left is my old room. It's very small. When we moved here, I had to take the smallest room. Definitely a baby room." He didn't even open the door. "And over here, we have Will's room. He's hardly ever here. I swear, I think he sleeps more at other people's houses than ours. Next, here on the left is Matthew's old room. He's the one at UT, remember?" He opened the door and pointed to the far window and a desk beneath it. "That's where I do my homework. I have to do my homework in here because my dad says I get too distracted in my own room. And that phone on the desk is the one I use to call you. Just so you can imagine where I am when I call."

We reached the end of the corridor, a set of double doors in front of us. As he swung the doors open he said, "And this was my other older brother's old room. When we first moved in here, this was Jacob's room. Then Matthew stayed in here when Jacob left for college. Mom and Dad said Will could move in here when Matthew left for UT, but he said he didn't want to mess with moving. So, they asked me, and I said yes! This was a craft room for the old couple who lived here before us. That's why it's got these wood floors, to make cleaning up easier, and why it's so big."

It was the biggest kid's bedroom I had ever seen. It stretched the whole length of the end of the house. It was, perhaps, fifty feet long and thirty feet wide. Brandon took me on a slow tour.

Over to the right, as we stepped in, was Brandon's bed. "Here's the bed, obviously. We'll crash here later. Are you okay sleeping in the same bed?"

I nodded and smiled. It was a queen bed and looked enormous compared to my small single bed at home. Its headboard and footboard did not match. On either side of the bed stood two small nightstands. These did not match either. There were tall, wide windows above each nightstand. Up above the bed was a large picture of a pod of dolphins leaping at different angles out of a clear blue sea.

He must have been following my eyes. He said, "I love dolphins. My dream is to swim with them one day."

Straight across from the door was a large window. In front of it sat a small, simple table with slender silver legs and a smooth, clean surface. "That's my sketching table. That window gets the best light all year round, though not as much around the summer solstice."

I was about to ask for more information when my eyes drifted to the left, and I saw a small rack of weights. Brandon pulled me over to the weights.

"These are my weights, as you can tell. My dad only lets me use weights that are less than fifteen pounds right now. My two oldest brothers had a big set of weights. Will never uses them, so they're basically all mine now. Dad says I can slowly work my way up to the bigger weights next year. I'm hoping I can add the seventeen-point-five and twenty pounders by Spring Break. You'll have to come over again and celebrate when I do! I'll get you working out soon and help you get rid of those stick arms you have." He winked and grinned at me.

He picked up two dumbbells, raising and lowering them alternately, squeezing tightly when each weight neared his shoulder. He had on an old t-shirt with extra short sleeves. His beautiful biceps swelled and peaked with each contraction. I couldn't help but feel weak in the knees.

Brandon put the weights back and gave me a quick double bicep pose. My penis hardened in response. He nodded to the wall and said, "And this is Gary. Can you imagine looking like that?"

Brandon had tacked a large poster above the rack of weights. On the poster stood a man in a very shallow pool, with water only up to his ankles. Far in the out-of-focus background were palm trees and many-colored flowering plants. Nearer in the background, though still out of focus, a sparkling shower of water fell from an unseen source. He was the biggest man I had ever seen. I didn't know there were so many muscles on the human body. Every one of them stood out in stark relief. My penis hardened again as I looked at the mountain of a man smiling back at me in his impossibly tight swimming trunks.

I shook my head and looked at Brandon. "No, I don't think so. I can't imagine looking like that. I think it's a little over the top."

Brandon threw his arm around my shoulder. "Well, I don't think I wanna be *that* big. Joel said you have to take tons of steroids to get that big. He knows a guy at his gym who takes them. Joel said they work, but they're not really good for you in the long run. You look good for about five years, and then you look like you're sixty when you hit thirty-five. I just wanna be normal big, if that makes any sense. I wanna be buff but not too buff!" He sighed and shook his head, nodding to Gary. "I'd be happy being about half that size in ten years."

He pulled at my arm. "Come on, stop drooling. We'll come work out with Gary later."

Next came a large metal-frame contraption that looked suspiciously like a medieval torture device. "And this is my deluxe captain's chair," Brandon explained. "Sometimes they just come with this bottom half, but mine has this frame around the top and those handles for doing pull-ups and leg raises. I only got it because Matthew paid for it with his own money a few years ago." He patted me on the back. "Don't look so worried. I'll break you in gently."

Farther along the wall sat a long chest of drawers with various books, framed photos, and an old piggy bank sitting on top. There was an old family photo; Brandon looked to be about three or four. I finally got to see his mysterious 'older older' brothers, as he liked to call them. They were both as handsome as Brandon. I saw a startling resemblance between Brandon and Jacob, whereas Matthew and Will looked more alike. Beside the chest of drawers stood a tall floor lamp in the corner. A huge picture window took up most of the space on the adjacent wall. It overlooked the yard below, the covered wooden deck, and the pool I remembered from the first devotional in October.

To my amazement, all around the window, on each side and below, Brandon had pinned dozens and dozens of sketches to the wall. They were a mixture of pencil and ink, mostly grouped by theme.

On the right side, nearest to us, was a cluster of familiar Houston landmarks: Sam Houston astride his horse in Hermann Park, finger pointed toward the site of the battle of San Jacinto; the soaring Transco Tower and its famous curved fountain in the foreground; the picturesque, European-style Mecom Fountain not far from my apartment; a series of archways on a building at Rice University; the bold geometric bulk of Pennzoil Place; the neoclassical south front of the Museum of Fine Arts; a detailed close-up of the elegant top of the Epperson Building; the main venues in the downtown theater district: Jones Hall, the Alley Theater, and the Wortham Center; the old Rice Hotel, where Kennedy spent his last night before his ill-fated trip to Dallas; the austere elegance of the Rothko Chapel; the whimsical tent-like entrance to the gold-domed chapel at the University of St.

Thomas; and so many more.

Underneath was a grouping of African animals, amazingly lifelike, ready to jump off the page. Next to them came a grouping of cars and other vehicles. Then came a cluster of various trees in full leaf. We passed slowly, from right to left, in front of each collection. Brandon had never been so quiet before. He was breathing gently but quickly beside me. I could tell he was looking at me closely.

I stopped and threw my arm around my friend's shoulder. "Wait... Brandon? Are these yours? You did all these? Really?" He grinned and seemed pleased. I wondered if he expected some other reaction from me. Did he think I would see his drawings and find some reason to criticize them?

I took a step back and said, "Wow! I had no idea you could draw like this. Why have you kept this a secret all along? I wish I knew a long time ago that you had this talent. So much talent! My best friend is a secret Van Gogh. Oh, my God!"

He gave me a sly smile and slipped his arm around my shoulder, too. "Well, a guy's gotta have a few secrets, right? I mean, I'm sure there's lots I still don't know about you, Mr. I-like-Elgar-Mozart-and-Chopin." He said 'Choppin' just to annoy me. He had discovered my love of classical music at church one Sunday a few weeks before Christmas. He got in a dig every chance he could.

"You have a gift! I've never, ever seen anybody our age who can draw like this. I don't even know any adults who can draw like this. These are like the sketches that Da Vinci did. This is unbelievable talent! You could do an exhibit at the Museum of Fine Arts... like, New York, not just Houston!" I shook my head, aghast.

He gave me an over-exaggerated bow. "Finally, someone who gets that I am a genius. Not a genius like my brothers. But a genius in my own way." I heard the familiar humor in his voice, but I heard, too, the slight note of sadness I would come to know more and more in the years ahead. Perhaps he hoped

I was finally a friend who understood him, who could appreciate him for who he was and not for all that he lacked compared to his brothers.

On the left side of the window was a cascade of various sketches: his brothers and parents, older people I assumed were his grandparents, dogs and cats, fish, dolphins, and assorted birds. They varied in quality. Some were remarkably life-like. Others seemed hastily drawn, with sloppy lines and distorted proportions. Yet each one had a kind of life and passion about it. There was something in those sketches that went beyond a pen, a hand, and a piece of paper. There was a force and energy in each one. It couldn't have all been done by skill alone; there was a hidden source of inspiration in my friend. I suddenly saw him in a completely new light.

Brandon stood very still beside me. I almost forgot he was there. I was utterly captivated by his art, his creativity, and whatever it was he put of himself in those magnificent drawings. I suddenly realized I only knew a very small part of my new friend. Up until that moment, I often thought I knew all about him because of his non-stop talking. I assumed everything there was to know about him came out in words. As I stood admiring his art work, I realized some hidden, secret part of him expressed itself without a single word. Perhaps the truest part of Brandon came shining through those sketches of trees, buildings, and dolphins and those intricately realized portraits of his loved ones.

We moved on silently. On the adjacent wall was a small, low table with a new-looking color TV on top. Next to the TV a battered end table held a radio-cassette player combo. On the wood floor beneath the table, an old orange crate held a jumbled collection of cassette tapes. I could see a few artists' names on the ones near the top – Michael Jackson, Madonna, The Police, Whitney Houston, Huey Lewis and the News, Chicago, and Amy Grant.

In the middle of the room, a long couch covered in an old

Sesame Street sheet sat facing the TV. At the end of the couch closest to Brandon's bed stood a well-worn weight bench. He nodded toward it and said, "And, this, of course, is my weight bench, right here by the weights. You should realize now: resistance is futile. You'll be spending a lotta time on this baby, here." He snickered and poked my ribs. "You've got some serious catching up to do."

We completed the circuit of the room. He smiled and threw his arm around my shoulder again. "So *mi* room is *tu* room, okay, *mi amigo*? Whatever you want to do, whenever you want to do it, just do it! Don't ask. Don't worry. Pretend like we're brothers and this is your room. Actually, if you were my brother, I'd kick your ass if you came in here." He chuckled to himself. "No, seriously, consider yourself part of the furniture!"

I was stunned. I never wanted to leave. The friend of my dreams had the room of my dreams.

. . .

Thirty minutes later, we headed back downstairs for dinner with Brandon's parents and Will. Matthew was home from UT on Christmas break, but he was spending the night with some old high school friends over in West University Place. Nobody said anything about Jacob and his wife, so I assumed they wouldn't be coming. I had wondered if I might finally meet Brandon's elusive oldest two brothers, but I quickly realized it might be a very long time until I ever saw them.

We offered to help with last-minute preparations in the kitchen. Mrs. Marshall said she had everything under control. Mr. Marshall was outside grilling hamburgers, and Brandon said it was best to leave him alone when grilling. I wondered what was sacrosanct about grilling but decided not to ask. I had developed a slight fear of Mr. Marshall, and I was happy to stay out of his way as much as I could.

Brandon and I settled on the couch in the living room. I sat at one end and expected him to sit at the other. Instead, he sat right next to me, his left knee pressed against my right knee, his shoulder impossibly close. I wondered what Michael Walker might think.

"You'll probably think it's strange, but we have July 4th food on New Year's Eve. Hamburgers, homemade French fries, and baked beans. I don't know why we do it. It's just some family tradition. Then we usually play some games and eat dessert a little later. Mom made her famous 'Better than Sex' chocolate cake." He snickered. "Dad hates the name, but Mom insists on calling it that. And there's ice cream. Then we'll watch Dick Clark's *Rockin' New Year's Eve*. It used to be more fun when all my brothers were around."

He paused and considered something before speaking again. "Although, I guess it's actually been a really long time since we were all together on New Year's Eve. Not since Jacob was in high school, I think. And I was just a toddler then. I barely remember him living here. Most of my memories are with Matthew and Will. I bet you think that's weird, huh? To have a brother so old I can barely remember him living at home?"

"Not weird; just different. Sometimes I wish I had a brother. But I think I'd want to be the oldest. It'd be more fun to be the older one. I bet it's hard to be the youngest."

Brandon sighed. "You have no idea. Being the youngest son of a preacher is shitty. My life is a lonely, painful sojourn, my friend." He leaned into my shoulder and smiled. "But you make it a billion times better by being here! You just need to move in with me upstairs." My heart skipped a beat or two at the thought.

As we sat around the table for a few minutes after dinner, Will asked if my family watched Dick Clark on New Year's Eve. I heard a slight snicker from Brandon.

"No. We usually have dinner together and play a few

games. My parents let me have a sip of champagne around 11:00, and then I go to bed."

Brandon looked shocked. "You mean you've never actually been awake for the stroke of midnight? Ever? And you've never seen Dick" – snicker, snicker – "Clark?"

I saw a line tighten in his father's jaw.

"Um, no. We usually watch an opera or a musical from Broadway on *Great Performances* on PBS."

Will asked, "You really mean you don't know who Dick Clark is, not just that you've never seen his New Year's show?"

Brandon snickered somewhat more loudly. I saw Mr. Marshall's knuckles whiten as he absent-mindedly held his knife.

"Um, no, not really. We don't watch Dick Clark. Who is he?"

Brandon couldn't resist. "Really? You've never heard of Dick Clark?"

I shook my head. Brandon's snickering inched up another notch. A noticeable shift took place in the emotional atmosphere. There was a hidden dynamic at play, and some part of me sensed it was going to surface soon.

Brandon laughed and said, "You know? Good ol' Dick. Good ol' Uncle Dick. Dickety-dick-dick Dick Clark."

Mr. Marshall's fist came slamming down on the table. Several glasses overturned. Cutlery clattered. Everyone jumped in their chair. My heartbeat took off like a rocket, and a sickening feeling welled up in my stomach. Mrs. Marshall turned white as a sheet. Will scraped his chair back slowly. Brandon, who had been leaning his chair back on two legs, looked terrified. His chair dropped back to all four legs with a thud.

"Brandon Geoffrey Marshall! Why must you embarrass us in front of your friend," his father roared. "Why must you embarrass *yourself* in front of your friend? Why must you act as though you had been raised by monkeys? Why must you take such infantile delight in a commonplace name? Why must you make every word a dirty joke? And why do you treat your friend with such contempt simply because his parents have decided that he need not watch hours of mindless television or listen to dirty rock music? What has this young man done that is so wrong that you would mock him in your own house and treat him with such disdain?"

I hesitantly lifted my eyes to meet Brandon's. He didn't look up. A deep crimson blush covered his neck and cheeks. He sat immobilized, except for his chin, which trembled with the effort of concealing what surely would have been a wailing cry if he lost control. Tears pooled in his eyes.

His mother laid a restraining hand on Mr. Marshall's clenched fist. "Robert, not now. Please, not tonight." Her voice shook with emotion, and her eyes, too, brimmed with tears. I glanced over at Will and saw a look of intense anger in his eyes. For his brother? For his father? For me, because I caused all this?

Mr. Marshall inhaled sharply. He looked squarely into my eyes. "Alex, for the second time in as many of your visits here, I must apologize for my son's behavior. I must also apologize for my behavior. It is unacceptable for me to speak like this in front of you. Perhaps you and Brandon should go up to his room. We all need to cool down. I'll be up in a few minutes."

I swallowed loudly and let go of my tightly held breath. Such scenes never happened at my home. My dad never raised his voice to me. The only time I can remember him yelling at me was a time I almost stepped out in front of a car when we were crossing McGregor on a morning run. He hadn't been angry then; he'd been scared for my life. I wondered what it must be like to hear such words, not just shouted across the table, but shouted at me? Part of my heart shriveled up as I pondered what that would feel like.

Brandon gained control of his voice. He stood up and looked at his father. He said softly, "Yes, sir. I'm sorry, Dad."

He looked across to me. "Alex, I'm sorry. I didn't mean to be rude to you." His eyes darted toward his father and back at me. "I didn't mean to make fun of you. You're my best friend. You really are." His voice broke. I nodded and smiled as best I could.

Mrs. Marshall stood up and put her arm around Brandon's shoulders. "You two go on up, sweetie. Maybe we can skip the first game. How about dessert in an hour or so? We'll let our food get settled. How does that sound?" Brandon nodded and leaned into his mother's shoulder. She squeezed him more tightly and kissed his fair brown hair.

I followed Brandon slowly up the stairs. He walked right in front of me, yet he seemed a million miles away. There was a distance between us I could neither fathom nor cross. I wanted to make things better for Brandon; I just didn't know how.

He slumped down on the bench at the foot of his bed. I sat beside him. He muttered beneath his breath, "I hate that asshole! He's a fucking dick!"

We sat for some minutes in silence. He didn't move. I was lost at sea until a sudden inspiration struck. I looked over at Brandon. His eyes were closed. I poked him gently in the ribs. "Hey, Brandon?"

He opened the eye closest to me. "Yeah?"

I put on my most serious face to keep myself from laughing. "I didn't want to tell you this earlier, but Joshua actually invited me over to his house first... I mean before you invited me here. I told him I'd come by and watch Dick Clark with him if you got too boring. So, I think I'll head on over. Okay? I'll see you around. Okay?"

Brandon's other eye popped open, and a flicker of a smile played on his lips. He tackled me with force, tugging me off the bench and down to the floor. He wrestled me onto my back, pinning my arms at my sides. He was just inches away from my face. His smile returned. His eyes sparkled.

He shook with laughter and said, "Oh yeah? Oh yeah? Well, listen, my little stick-arm friend – if you walk out that door, it's over. Do you hear me? You can't go sneaking around behind my back and then expect me to take you back. So, make a choice! You stay here or you go to fart-smelling, dog-piss Joshua's room forever." He leaned in closer and said through gritted teeth in mock anger, "I mean forever. It's either me or fart-smelling hell on earth."

He collapsed on top of me, his body pressed fully up against mine. His left thigh pressed hard into my groin. My dick began to swell with pleasure, and I hoped against hope that Brandon wouldn't notice. I silently prayed, 'Please, God, not now! Please, not now!'

Brandon shook with laughter and rolled off me. He grabbed my hand as he rolled onto his back. He looked over at me, still holding my hand, and said, "Seriously, Alex, you're just gonna have to move in here with me. I've got to have someone on my side in this house. Do you see what it's like? He does that all the time. And just at me. He's never yelled at Will in his whole life. Never!" He let go of my hand and sat up. "I'm the only one he treats that way. It's like he hates me! Me! I'm his own son. I promise you, if I ever have kids, I am never gonna scream at them like that."

I sighed and nodded in agreement. I was about to speak when we heard a slight knock at the door. Mr. Marshall came in, clearing his throat.

"Please stand, Brandon. We need to speak."

I got up, too, and started for the door. Mr. Marshall reached out a hand and touched my elbow. "No, Alex. Please stay. You must hear this, too."

I wanted to run from the room. I thought about it seriously for several seconds, yet I also felt impossibly compelled to stay near my friend, no matter what.

Brandon stood facing his father. Mr. Marshall was only a few inches taller, but in that stand-off Brandon seemed somehow stooped and shrunken. Mr. Marshall stared straight at Brandon and asked Brandon to look him back in the eyes. Brandon turned his head slightly upward.

"Please recite to me the verse you know from Psalm 34."

Brandon cleared his throat and said, "The face of the Lord is against evildoers, to cut off the remembrance of them from the land."

Something within me recoiled at the scene playing out in front of me. I felt physically sick again, like I did at the dinner table when Mr. Marshall erupted in fury.

"And now the verse from Romans. You know which one."

Brandon shifted his weight from foot to foot. His eyes darted my way. Mr. Marshall sighed, and said, "It's no use looking to your friend. This is about you and your soul. He is here to listen so that he might learn and inwardly digest this lesson."

Brandon cleared his throat again and softly recited, "There is no one who is righteous, not even one; there is no one who has understanding, there is no one who seeks God. All have turned aside, together they have become worthless."

Mr. Marshall held up his hand to stop the flow of words. My stomach clenched with disgust, and I felt small beads of sweat form on my brow. This was a kind of parenting I knew nothing about. Fear and confusion coursed through my every vein.

"You know the Lord looks down on wrongdoing, Brandon. He simply will not tolerate your sinfulness and rebellion. You have been baptized, and, by God's grace, rescued from the punishment that awaits so many. But your friend here has not been baptized yet. You have a duty to him to lead a godly life free from stain and blemish, yet you seem to do just the opposite at every turn. How will he know the beauty of the Lord's way if you refuse to live it out in front of him? How will he make a decision to turn from his own sin and trust the Lord if you live in such a way as to mock the righteousness of God?

You may think it's harmless fun to laugh at the word 'dick,' but your frivolity masks a deeper rebellious streak in you. You cannot fool God."

Tears welled up in my eyes. I wanted to scream and shout at that bully of a man. I wanted to throw him from the room and kick him down the stairs. I wanted to take my friend in my arms and make him laugh until he forgot all about the evening's horrible events.

Mr. Marshall pulled Brandon close to him. He rested his chin on Brandon's head and whispered into his hair, "You may think I don't love you, but I do. My love for you compels me to say these things to you for your own benefit, to spare you the suffering your own sins will bring upon you. How could I say I loved you and not say the very thing you most need to hear? What kind of father lets his own son walk freely into the fires of hell?"

I saw Brandon's shoulders gently shake as Mr. Marshall pulled back. Soft tears ran down Brandon's face, but I didn't sense they were tears of healing or relief.

Mr. Marshall turned to face me. "You must realize that the Christian life is a constant battle against sin. Brandon will not always set you the best example. When he does, you should follow. When he doesn't, you should forgive him. You are very welcome in our home, but you must take us as you find us." He turned and walked quietly from the room.

Brandon slumped onto the bench at the end of his bed again. I was about to speak when the door opened again. Mr. Marshall looked directly at me.

"Alex, let's have a little talk in my study. Perhaps Brandon could use some time alone to pray and consider where he stands with the Lord if you come with me."

Down in Mr. Marshall's study, I stood awkwardly in front of his desk. He had seated himself in the swivel chair behind it. Mr. Marshall took his glasses off, wiped a handkerchief across his brow, and sighed heavily. He looked directly into my eyes. I felt naked and exposed in his harsh gaze. I looked for a sign of softness around his eyes or some glimmer of gentleness around his mouth. I saw nothing but stony self-righteousness.

Without blinking or looking away he said, "You are a kind boy and a good friend to my son. He is a mystery to me. I know at school that he is well-liked. His teachers tell me he is the most popular boy in his grade. I understand this. He is a hand-some boy, if I may say so. He's always had a winning smile. And since he is a year older than the other boys, he stands a head above them. He is stronger and more physically capable than they are. When you are twelve, a boy who is thirteen can seem impossibly older, especially one with Brandon's build."

He paused and put his glasses back on. He lowered his gaze, looking at one of several picture frames on the desk. I couldn't see who was in the frame from my side of the desk. I finally saw a softening of his eyes. Was Brandon in that frame? I hoped with all my heart that he was, that the faint glimpse of tenderness was for Brandon's sake.

"Yet Brandon does not have any close friends like you. I think he teases the other boys too much. They like him yet fear him. He senses this and doubles-down on his teasing and sarcasm, much as he did with you this evening. He is like a shark. He smells blood in the water and cannot pull back."

He paused again and looked back at me.

"You must realize this for your own sake, Alex. You are a good friend to Brandon, but you may be hurt by him at some point. Probably more than once. And, of course, I have a duty of care to my own son, too. I cannot let you hurt him."

I gulped and wondered what I could ever do to hurt Brandon.

"His soul is in my care. It's my duty to see that he goes to heaven one day. If he has friends in his life who are not on that same journey with him, then I must be sure they do not lure him away from his eternal goal. I must protect him from himself and from anyone who does not share that goal." His gaze into my eyes intensified. "I mean anyone, Alex. Even you. At some point, you must make a choice to become a Christian or remain in your willful disobedience. There is a price to pay no matter what you choose. Just be sure you know what those costs are. Do you understand me?"

I was aghast. I did understand. For the first time in my twelve years on the planet I understood that a grown man, a man sitting just three feet away from me, was threatening me. After the first waves of dread and fear swept over me, another wave of emotion came on fiercely. I was unexplainably angry. I knew I would protect Brandon and my friendship with him regardless of the cost. I knew what Mr. Marshall wanted from me, and I knew he would never back down.

I held his gaze and replied, hoping my voice would hold, "Yes, sir. I understand."

. . .

In the first hour of the new year, Brandon and I wearily climbed the stairs to his bedroom.

Mrs. Marshall had called up to us around 9:00. We went downstairs for a game of Scrabble, followed by dessert and the end of Dick Clark's *Rockin' New Year's Eve.* We were a subdued party by that time. Will had decided to go over to Joel's house around 9:30; only Brandon, his parents, and I watched as the famous ball in New York City dropped to welcome in 1988. Not even Dick Clark and his blindingly white teeth could lift the somber mood of the Marshall family. After the ball descended and the on-screen confetti settled, I wondered what all the fuss had been about. I felt oddly homesick and longed for the easy familiarity of my life with my parents. The current of emotions in Brandon's family left me feeling adrift and confused.

I lay beside Brandon in his bed in the silent house. The

room was warm and stuffy, so we decided not to pull up the sheet or comforter. We never moved after that. He was soon fast asleep, breathing calmly, just a few inches to my left. I wondered if he was dreaming and what he might be dreaming about. I hoped it was something happy, something that might restore him to his old self by morning.

He had been distracted and quiet since his father left the room earlier in the evening. When I returned to his room after the talk with Mr. Marshall, we listened to a few songs on some of his tapes. Then I looked back over the sketches on his wall while he sat silently and sketched something new at his table. He wouldn't show me what he sketched. He demonstrated how to do a few exercises with his weights, but his heart wasn't in it. I didn't know how to reach him. Even my cleverly delivered string of Joshua-jokes failed to pierce his lonely, distant world.

I sighed and turned on my left side. I stared at Brandon in the soft light coming from the single lamp in the far corner. I let my gaze drift over his handsome face and down his shapely torso. I wanted to reach out and place my palm on his chest, to feel its gentle rise and fall. I wanted to comfort him and offer back some of the joy he had brought to me. I had never felt so protective of anyone in my life. It was a new and unsettling sensation, making me feel both wise beyond my years and way in over my head all at the same time.

. . .

Dad picked me up from the Marshalls' just after 9:00 that first morning of 1988. Brandon woke me about 8:20 to tell me that breakfast was waiting. Mr. Marshall was in his study with the doors closed. Brandon, Mrs. Marshall, and I had a quiet breakfast of eggs, bacon, and biscuits. I had a sense Brandon was feeling better, though we spoke very little in the dash to eat and gather up my belongings.

Relief swept over me when Dad and I stepped off the elevator and made our way into our apartment. There in that eighth-floor loft I felt safe. I understood the emotional dynamics. I had no fear of unexpected eruptions of shouting and anger. I had no fear of unsaid words and frosty silences. I was, in a word, at home.

When Mom came down the hall to greet me, I burst into tears. She and Dad were both very quiet as they hugged me tightly and let me sob myself dry. I loved my parents for many reasons, first among them was their ability to be near me without asking a ton of questions or prying into my thoughts and feelings. I knew they were always present, always ready to listen, but I never felt pressure to speak in haste.

Later that morning, after I gave my parents a partial retelling of the previous night's events, I sat in my favorite chair by the west-facing window in my room, looking out at the north end of the Rice campus and, farther off, the Transco Tower looming over Uptown. I held a sketch in my hand. I had discovered it just a few minutes earlier at the bottom of my bag, beneath the clothes Brandon had gathered up for me while I brushed my teeth after breakfast.

It was a sketch of Brandon and me. We stood side by side, his left arm around my shoulder, my right arm around his waist. It was us but not us. I recognized our faces but not our bodies. He had drawn our bodies with added muscle; not as much as Gary, not by a long shot. But he drew us as he imagined we might be in five or six years. The sketch was slightly comical, our current faces drawn on top of well-built, older bodies. Across the top of the paper he had written in chunky block letters:

FROM B TO A:
BEST FRIENDS NOW AND ALWAYS.

In smaller lettering across the bottom he had written:

ALEX AND BRANDON'S 1988 NEW YEAR'S RESOLUTIONS!!

(1) Save each other from Joshua no matter what! Just say NO! Make Nancy proud!

(2) Beg our parents for as many sleepovers as possible!

(3) Keep on working out together! Stick arms, be gone!

I smiled and laid the drawing lightly in my lap. I breathed out a deep sigh and closed my eyes. I felt a new and unexpected stirring inside: an oddly-paired sense of satisfaction and longing, like I had discovered a magic kind of food that simultaneously filled me up and left me wanting even more.

CHAPTER 5

January and February passed quickly. My teachers seemed to think my fellow students and I had gone soft over the winter break, and they piled on the homework in a secretly orchestrated plan to chain us to our desks at home. I continued with chess club, violin practice, and orchestra, but I felt frayed around the edges by the end of each week.

At the back of my mind, like some sleeping dragon ready to wake in a split second, was the memory of Mr. Marshall's threat on New Year's Eve. I knew at some point he would push me harder. I knew it was only a matter of time until he launched the next offensive in his bizarre battle of wills. I felt out of my depths, like I was playing some game whose rules I scarcely understood.

Dad and I picked up the pace on our morning runs, especially grateful for the cool mornings before the summer heat returned to Houston. Brandon started coming with us most Saturday mornings. His dad dropped him off at the corner of Fannin and Cambridge, just behind Palmer Memorial Episcopal Church, where we were always waiting for him. At first, Brandon was not able to run as fast or as far as us, so we ran as much as Brandon could and walked the rest.

My dad was good at making it seem like he himself was winded and tired, when all along he had an eagle eye on Brandon so he could judge when to slow us all down. Brandon seemed not to notice. I got the sense he was just happy to be with us and relieved to be around a father who never blew up in unexpected rages.

As February drew to a close, Brandon and I made big plans for Spring Break. I was going to spend at least three nights at his house. Brandon wrote out an entire itinerary, planned to the hour, full of exclamation points and smiley or frowny faces. One Sunday in late February, he showed me a small sample of his schedule at church during his dad's sermon:

> 9:00 – 12:00 – go to Hermann Park: run, toss Frisbee, hang out; get ice cream?
> 12:00 – 1:00 – lunch at my house
> 1:00 – 2:00 – me sketch ☺ and you read ☹
> 2:00 – 3:00 – lift weights with Gary… resistance is futile, my little stick-arm friend
> 3:00 – 4:00 – swim, if it's warm enough
> 4:00 – 5:00 – watch TV

His schedule went on and on for pages. I had never seen him so organized. We continued our regular Thursday night phone calls, and at least half of every phone call consisted of schedule updates in the weeks leading up to Spring Break. Every Sunday morning at church, he presented me a hand-copied schedule with a new adjective added to the ever-growing title: "A and B's Amazing, Astounding, Freaking Awesome, Joshua-free, Impossibly Cool and Fun Spring Break Adventure."

As Spring Break drew closer, I found it increasingly hard to concentrate in classes, and I had absolutely no patience for my violin lessons. Brandon filled my mind, and thoughts of our upcoming days together became the substance of my never-realized childhood dreams.

Growing up as a practically friendless only-child meant I missed out on many typical childhood experiences. The more I thought about it, I realized Brandon had missed out on a lot of those experiences, too. His parents were nearly twenty years older than mine and couldn't have been as agile and athletic as my parents were when I was a free-roaming toddler. He may have grown up with three brothers, but the two oldest were never his childhood playmates.

In a sense, our friendship became a way for both of us to make up for some of those lost, lonely years. In our excitement to be together as much as possible, we intuitively knew we had to squeeze in as much childhood fun as we could before the weightier pains and pleasures of adolescence came our way.

Disaster struck the week before Spring Break. He called me frantically on that Monday evening. I had just come home from chess club. I hadn't even eaten.

His voice was strident and abnormally high-pitched. "It's my damn Dayton cousins! Mom and Dad decided they would surprise me with a secret visit from my cousins. Never in my entire life have my cousins from Dayton come here for Spring Break. We've never gone there. I only see them at Christmas." He was breathless, but he couldn't seem to stop. "Mom just told me this morning on the way to school. She dropped this bomb on me, kissed my cheek, shoved me out the car door, and waved wildly. It was like, 'Here, honey, let me ruin your life for you right before I shove you from the car. Have a great day!' Honestly, I had no idea this was coming. We're screwed, Alex."

I jumped in without thinking. "You mean you never told your parents you were planning for me to come over? You just assumed they'd say yes? You idiot!" I heard him gasp softly. I should have paused, but I was unable to stop. "When were you actually going to ask them? The day before I came over? God, you've ruined our whole break! All those schedules for nothing! All that planning for nothing! All our excitement for nothing! It's all over now. Thanks, Brandon. How could you be so stupid?"

I heard my own voice but didn't recognize it. I couldn't believe the words that came out of my mouth. I knew I had a sharp tongue at times. I sometimes spoke harshly to my friends at school if I was tired or upset, but I wanted to be better for Brandon's sake. After New Year's Eve, I promised myself I would never lose my temper or shout at Brandon. Nevertheless, I did both things without even thinking. I wasn't any better than his bully of a dad.

Brandon was silent in a way that brought about a painful tightening in my stomach. I knew he was fragile deep down inside. Had I gone too far?

"Brandon, are you there?"

"Yeah. I'm here. I'm really sorry. I just thought they'd say yes. We never do anything as a family on Spring Break. I spend the whole time at home year after year. I thought they'd be happy for you to be here and keep me occupied and out of trouble." He sighed. "And now I've got my five cousins coming. You have no idea what kids from Tennessee are like. They're like Joshua times five... even louder and crazier. God, it's gonna be awful."

"Well, I could still come over. Maybe we could still do a sleepover before they arrive. Or I could come while they're here, you know? I could be a distraction. Maybe they can sleep in the other rooms, and we can still hang out in your room."

"It's no use, buddy. I already brought up all those ideas. Dad said no. You and I can do something the Saturday afternoon before we go back to school, but that's it."

"Can I stay over that night, on that Saturday?"

"I wish you could, but Dad just said no, no, no and no." He paused for a second. "I wonder if he's mad at you? He made it sound like I shouldn't spend so much time with you. You'd make things a lot easier if you got baptized. He doesn't like me having friends who aren't baptized."

I gulped. My stomach had released a bit as we spoke, but it tightened again. I felt sick and hot. The pieces all fell into place: the surprise visit from the Dayton cousins; the small concession to a single afternoon together at the end of Spring Break; the comment about Mr. Marshall not wanting Brandon to be around un-baptized friends. Mr. Marshall had been deadly serious on New Year's Eve. He wanted me to know he was not playing around. Our torpedoed Spring Break plans were evidence of his ongoing strategizing against me. I thought to myself, 'Well, alright, Mr. Marshall. I can play your game. If getting baptized is the price I have to pay to be your son's friend, it's a price I can pay. I'll fly to Israel, and you can dunk me in the Jordan. Then leave me the hell alone!'

"Listen, Brandon. I was gonna tell you soon. I've been thinking about getting baptized. I was just waiting until I was totally sure. I'm sure now."

I could hear the smile in Brandon's voice. "Really? I thought you were gonna hold out forever! I thought you would be that one kid in the youth group who really didn't believe in God but hung around anyway. It was gonna be so cool. Like, I would know this secret about you that no one else did. My best friend would be the secret atheist, like a mole inside the CIA."

"Well, it's time I do it. Everyone expects it, and I've been thinking about it a lot. I just hadn't said anything to you because I needed to talk to my parents first."

"Oh, they said okay? When's it gonna happen? I didn't even know!"

"They're totally fine about it." I had to keep on lying. "I've been studying with Michael for weeks. I just asked him not to tell anyone, even you. I figured if I started studying with him and he told everyone, then it would be bad if I decided not to get baptized in the end. So, we've just kept it quiet."

"Well, that'll shut my dad up! He told me he didn't think you were ever gonna be baptized and that he didn't want you to be a bad influence on me. He said I was wild enough without a friend who wouldn't submit to Christ."

That colossal jerk of a man! What kind of father was he?

"It just shows you what a moron he is, Alex. You're the best influence I have, and you're not a Christian. Most of the kids at church are horrible influences, and they all got baptized years ago. Bunch of hypocritical assholes, is what they are."

"Yeah, well, I can't do anything about them. Neither can you. I can only do what I think is right. Being baptized is right for me. If it satisfies your dad at the same time, then it's like winning the lottery. It'll make God and your dad happy, and I get to go on being your best friend. It's a win-win for everyone."

"Hey, I gotta go. Mom's staring me down. She knows I didn't even start my homework yet. She's been distracting Dad so he wouldn't realize I'm on the phone with you. Let me know as soon as you decide what day you're gonna get baptized. If it's not a Sunday, I want to make sure I am there."

"Okay. It may be a few more weeks or even a month. I'll keep you posted. Talk to you later!"

. . .

I brought up the topic at dinner the next evening. It didn't go as I expected.

"I think I am ready to be baptized. Is that okay with you two?"

Dad looked up from his plate, his eyes wide with surprise. He held up his hand as he swallowed. He took a sip of wine. I looked across at Mom. Her eyes were fixed on Dad. I looked back to him. For the first time in a long time, I felt on uncertain ground with my parents.

Dad cleared his throat. "This has come suddenly. I didn't know you had been thinking about this. Tell me what you're thinking."

This was my dad's classic ploy. He never asked easy questions; he never left room for a simple 'yes' or 'no.' I spent my whole childhood explaining what I was thinking and feeling. It got tiresome, especially when I knew they knew I was trying to be less than straightforward.

I muttered, "I just think it's time. I know I believe in Jesus, and I want to get baptized."

His gaze pierced me more deeply. "We will support your decision, but it's really important you make the decision for yourself without any pressure from anyone else and without any fear."

I wondered: how could this man know me so well? I loved my dad so much, but I often felt exposed before him, like he could see inside me and understand me better than I could understand myself.

"I'm not afraid. Nobody is pressuring me. I just want to do it."

Mom said, "Honey, you really must be clear. You must be genuine. It can't be based on fear but on love."

Why did they keep repeating that word 'fear'? Had they been rehearsing in case I ever brought up the topic? Had they somehow intuited what I was thinking and decided they must prevent it at all costs?

"I'm not afraid. I want to do it so I can be a good Christian. I want to do it because it's the right thing to do. I thought it would make you happy. Why is that wrong?" I thought I could hold myself together, but my voice broke slightly on those last few words. I knew everything that was at stake for Brandon and me. I couldn't imagine my life without him.

Mom reached across the dining table and took my hand. I looked into her eyes. I saw the familiar gaze which always made me feel safe and warm, a look of unshakeable love. "It's not wrong. We do support you. We just don't want you to rush or make the decision for the wrong reason. Why don't you keep thinking about it, and we'll talk again this weekend?" I started to speak up, but she kept talking. "No, no. I am not trying to get you to change your mind. Just think about what we said and what we asked you. If you feel the same way this weekend, then we'll talk to Michael on Sunday and see what's next. Okay?"

I nodded in agreement. Dad spoke up, "Of course, we will support you. We love you and want you to follow your conscience."

Two weeks after Easter, Michael lifted me up out of the cold baptistry at the Bissonet Avenue Church of Christ. The first people I saw on the steps on the far end, just where they'd been when Michael lowered me into the water, were my parents. Dad looked quiet and somber. A slight smile crossed Mom's lips, but it never reached her eyes. Just behind them, grinning with delight, stood Brandon. He started whooping and clapping, and all the kids and teenagers behind him joined in.

Still wet from the waters of baptism, I figured I was in a win-win situation. If God was real, I had just made him happy. Even if God wasn't real, Brandon was very real, and I had paid the price required to maintain our friendship. Either way, my friendship with Brandon seemed on solid ground again.

. . .

ii.

My baptism worked its magic on Mr. Marshall. As April drew to a close and the heat of May began to build, Brandon and I became inseparable on the weekends. Dad and I continued to meet Brandon for an early run on Saturday mornings. Brandon would then spend the rest of the day with us, and his mom or Will would come pick us up around 4:00. We'd go back to his house for dinner and a sleepover. We begged for Friday night sleepovers, too, but both sets of parents said we needed a night at home to rest after a busy week at school.

A tragedy in the Marshall family held a silver lining for Brandon and me. Mr. Marshall's oldest cousin, Frank, died suddenly after a heart attack the first weekend in May. Brandon's parents made plans to fly to Nashville for the funeral. Will had already planned to be away that weekend with his academic decathlon team, and the Marshalls decided to let him keep those plans. Mrs. Marshall asked if Brandon could spend the weekend with us since they were leaving late Friday afternoon and wouldn't return until nearly midnight on Sunday.

I could barely concentrate at school the week leading up to his first sleepover at our apartment. When Friday afternoon finally rolled around, I was down in the lobby waiting for Brandon when the Marshalls pulled up a little after 4:00. As I made my way out of the front doors, Mrs. Marshall waved at me through the front passenger window. Mr. Marshall lifted a single finger from the steering wheel as a subdued greeting.

Brandon hopped out of the back, and I burst into laughter. He was dressed in his best church clothes: blue suit, crisp white dress shirt, blue and green argyle tie, and his shiniest shoes! He spun around and bowed toward me, a huge grin spread across his face. He grabbed his backpack and overnight bag from the back seat and came to stand by me on the sidewalk.

His mom rolled down her window and said, "Alex, I am so sorry! He insisted on coming in those clothes. You know what he's like! He's got it in his mind that he's spending the weekend at the Ritz or something." She laughed and shook her head. Brandon tossed his arm around my shoulder and pulled me close.

She continued, "Okay, you two. Have a good weekend. And Brandon..." Her smile dropped away. "Seriously. Best behavior, all the time! Please don't embarrass us! We'll see you Monday after school. And, Alex, please thank your parents again. You three are lifesavers. Your mom has our number in

Nashville if she needs us. Be good, be good, be good." She blew a kiss, and they drove away.

Brandon gave me a crooked grin and said, "As if I am ever anything but good. I am fucking good all the time!"

I burst out laughing again, grabbed his bag from his hand, and said, "Come on up. My parents can't wait to see you! They're so excited to have you here!"

When we came through the front door, my parents were waiting with a banner that read: 'Welcome to our home, Brandon!' We had made it the night before. I could tell Brandon was surprised and pleased. My parents passed the banner to me, and each of them gave him a big, welcoming hug.

Dad said, "We are so glad you're here! Think of this as your home away from home."

Brandon said softly, "Thanks. I will. Nobody's ever welcomed me into their home like this." Mom winked at me. Everything had gone just as we planned!

My parents flapped around Brandon for a few seconds, asking about his day at school. He basked in their attention and concern. Sometimes I loved my parents so much I could burst. They were the best ever!

Dad said, "And what's going on with this jacket and tie? Do you have plans later we don't know about? Do you have some big date?"

"No, I just figured you wore a tuxedo at home. I don't have one of those, so I came in the nicest clothes I have. I didn't want to be a rude guest!"

Dad assumed a serious expression and said, "Well, yes we do wear our suits to dinner on weeknights, but not on the weekends. We just wear a simple blazer on the weekends; no tie necessary."

Brandon chuckled but gave me an uncertain sideways glance, as if to verify that Dad really was joking. I winked at Brandon and shook my head. He looked relieved!

Mom said, "You need to watch out, Brandon. You'll have a trail of girls following after you next year and in high school. They like a handsome guy in a suit. And they like a boy with nice arms, too." Brandon blushed a deep scarlet. That was not something I saw very often! Nothing ever seemed to embarrass him. I, too, felt a little awkward as I pondered Mom's comment! When did she notice Brandon's arms? Then, again, he had the best-looking arms I had ever seen on any seventh grader. The more I thought about it, I couldn't think of any eighth, ninth, or tenth grader I knew whose biceps could compete with Brandon's.

We took his belongings to my room. He changed into some khaki shorts and a blue t-shirt. Then my parents led him on a tour of the apartment. Brandon acted as if he was in a palace in a foreign country. I had never seen him so subdued and polite. He seemed in awe, as if they were indulgent royalty, and he was a lowly member of the grateful public admitted out of kindness or *noblesse oblige*.

He particularly admired the views from every window. There were two large windows in my corner room. One looked south along Fannin Street. In the foreground were the Hermann Park reflecting pool, the Houston Zoo, and the Japanese Gardens. Just beyond the edge of the park the Spanish-revival architecture of Hermann Hospital marked the start of the immense Texas Medical Center, with its burgeoning skyline extending several miles to the south.

The adjacent window faced west. When we went back to my room after dinner, he stared out the second window at the view over the north end of Rice University, the leafy neighborhoods along Bissonet, and the booming uptown skyline clustered around Post Oak Boulevard and the Galleria. At the south end of the Galleria, the Transco Tower stood like a proud sentinel over the throbbing metropolis. Dusk deepened, and millions of lights slowly came to life in the moist, warm air.

He said, "I always knew you lived a different kind of life than I did. I just had no idea what to expect. Your apartment is like a museum. You have real art work on the walls and sculptures on tables. Everything is smooth and clean. There's no clutter anywhere. All the furniture in your room matches, like it came out of some Italian design studio." He chuckled. "I mean, you've seen my house. It's like a bombsite!"

"It's not a bombsite. It's just that your family likes different things than mine. You've got a lot more decorations on your walls and sitting around on tables. It's just different. And you've got the coolest teen room on the planet."

He seemed not to hear me. "It's like my family is *Sanford and Son* and your family is *Dynasty*. And your parents! They are so cool. I didn't even understand half of what they were talking about at dinner, but you did. You were, like, listening and following along. They talked to you like you were an adult, like you had a brain and your own ideas. I felt so embarrassed when they realized I had no idea about F. Scott Fitzgerald's books. I mean, I know the name, but all I know is he wrote some books. You read those kinds of books with them for fun in the evenings. No wonder you're the smartest kid at the smartest school in Houston." He paused and sighed. "It's just so different here, like another planet, and not just two miles away."

I wanted to jump in and reassure him, but he was in a kind of trance and the words poured out of him. "And your parents are so calm. Your dad actually laughs and tells stories! It's like he actually likes you. I mean, it's so obvious he likes you. He wants to be around you and wants to show you affection. I saw him hug you twice as we washed the dishes! Twice in one evening! The only time my dad hugs me is after he shouts and screams and feels bad about himself."

My parents went to bed early and left the living room to us. I only had a twin bed in my room, so we decided ahead of time that Brandon and I would sleep on the floor in the living room. We laid out two completely unzipped sleeping bags and covered those with a few more blankets to soften the density of the hard wood floors. Then we piled on more blankets to cover with, along with pillows from the couch and the guest bedrooms. It looked comfy enough for watching a movie and getting some sleep. Brandon told me ahead of time he'd bring a movie from Blockbuster. I always left the movie choices to him. It was easier in the end!

We got ourselves settled on the floor, side-by-side, with our heads propped up on a mound of pillows. Brandon had actually kept his shirt on. I knew he had done so out of courtesy, probably under strict orders from his mom. I was slightly disappointed. I never got tired of looking at my friend's shapely body as he pranced around shirtless at his house.

He told me a few jokes as we lay there together. He couldn't even finish one of them for laughing so much.

"Shhh," I said. "Not so loud! My parents don't mind some noise, but I don't want to wake them if they've already fallen asleep."

"Sorry, sorry, sorry... but, seriously, I can't imagine either of them coming out here in a rage even if we did wake them up. They're so nice and so calm. I could definitely live here with them. Let me know if you ever wanna trade families." He paused and gave me a sly grin. "Do you think they'd mind if I slipped out of my shirt?"

I grinned back and said, "No, I don't think so. You're like another son to them, and they see me without my shirt on all the time. One boy's body is just like another's."

He assumed a horrified expression. "Alexander Nathan Kennedy! You did not just say what I think you said! You did not just say that my body is just like yours, did you?" He was trying his hardest to maintain his horrified look. It wasn't working. I could hear the laughter seeping through the serious tone of his voice. "Have you looked in a mirror lately? I am like a Greek god compared to your Mickey Mouse body!" He burst out laughing, but caught himself quickly, putting his hand over his mouth.

I mustered up my meanest expression and said, "You're hardly a Greek god, and I'm not exactly Mickey Mouse. I can stand up for myself when attacked so maliciously, you know? It's not too late for me to call Joshua. I told him to be on standby just in case I got tired of you." I snorted at my own comeback.

Brandon spluttered, "Oh, yeah? Oh, yeah? Well, have a look at this and tell me you can even come close, Mr. I've-Got-Spaghetti-Noodles-For-Arms. Cast your eyes on this body, my little stick-arm friend!"

He started to pull off his shirt but stopped half way. I could see his tight, shapely abs slightly contracted from trying not to laugh so much. He gave me one of his wickedly sly smiles and said, "You know, I've never, ever seen you with your shirt off. Never once in all these months! You always change in the bathroom by yourself or when I am in the bathroom and you're in my room. You know me: I'll strip down right in front of you. But you are so secretive! What are you hiding from me? Come on! Show me what you got, Alex!"

I sat up but hesitated. I had two great fears in that moment: one – that my parents would come out and see Brandon and me comparing our bodies; two – that Brandon would find my body somewhat disappointing. The running I did with Dad kept me lean and trim all over, but I didn't have the same shape and size as Brandon. I imagined he weighed at least twenty more pounds than I did, and none of it was from extra fat! Our difference in shape and size was part of what attracted me to him. I wanted to be more like him, but I also enjoyed the fact that he was bigger, taller, and stronger than I was.

Brandon sensed my reluctance and started to chant softly: "Take it off! Take it off! Take it off!" God, he was something else!

I put my finger up to his mouth and said softly, "Okay,

okay. But if my parents come out, I will kill you. I mean, I will kill you with a capital K and dump your dead body on Joshua's doorstep." He snorted. "I will be so embarrassed if they see us."

"Well, you said they've seen it all before. But they haven't seen this beautiful body of mine! Come on. Stand up." He reached out and took my hands in his. We stood up together. "Come on. On the count of three, at the same time as me, slip off that ol' shirt of yours. One... two... three."

We slipped our shirts over our heads, and he let out a loud whistle. I put my finger up to his lips again. He whispered, "Okay, okay, okay! Geez! I'm quiet!"

He reached out and patted my flat stomach. "Oh, my God! Look at those abs!" He dropped his voice, somehow monitoring himself even in his excitement. "Seriously, man. I admit, they're not a rippling as mine, but you're a whole year younger, you know. And you don't do crunches and hanging leg raises like I do. But, damn, those are tight abs." He paused and eyed me suspiciously. "Or do you do crunches behind my back? Have you been keeping something from me? Are you trying to show me up? Do you have to make me look bad to make up for feeling bad about yourself?" He managed to stay quiet but was doubled over in laughter. He was practically in tears. He was the funniest guy he knew, no doubt about it.

I laughed and shook my head. "No, I promise! I think I just stay slim because I run so much."

"Well, my friend, it's working. Keep it up." He reached over and patted my stomach again. "Keep it up, and we'll start doing crunches and leg raises every time you come over. We'll have the best teen abs in Houston, my friend. Everybody will be drooling after us."

He collapsed down to the floor and pulled me with him. We wrestled back and forth a few seconds. I could tell he wasn't putting his full strength into our battle. He let me pin him down, and he looked up in mock surprise.

"There you go, Alex. How's that for friendship? I figure I better let you win every once in a while or else you'll develop some inferiority complex. You've got the brains, and I've got the brawn, but I know you are secretly, madly jealous of me. I know you want this body."

I slugged him hard on the shoulder. He let out a loud yelp. We both froze and looked toward my parents' door. I really didn't expect them to come rushing out, but I wanted Brandon totally to myself for the whole night. Thankfully, the door stayed shut.

I gave Brandon a thumbs-up and asked, "So, what movie did you bring?"

He hopped up and went to my room. He came back with the movie behind his back, just as I started to slip my shirt on. He ran up beside me and snatched the shirt from me. He tossed it over to the other side of the room.

"Oh, come on! Go free! Let it all hang out! Dazzle me with those abalicious abs!"

I couldn't believe the things he said sometimes. I also couldn't believe the way he made me feel, like I was on top of the world and never wanted to come down. I wanted our night to go on and on forever.

He held up the VHS case in front of me and announced, "I present to you, kind sir, for your viewing enjoyment, *The Princess Bride*." He bowed and held it out to me. "My friend Ryan at school saw it with his parents around Christmas. He said it's the best movie ever, even though it sounds like a little girl's movie. He said we'd laugh our asses off."

We got some drinks and snacks from the kitchen, set up the VCR, and settled on our palette in front of the TV. Within minutes we were caught in an enchanted spell. I even lost sense of Brandon's presence beside me, though his intermittent fits of laughter reminded me how real he was. I gave myself fully to that unexpectedly magical movie and let it seduce me into its fantastic tale of adventure, treachery, comedy, friendship, and love.

Half-way through the movie, our snacks long finished, Brandon shuffled a bit beside me. He leaned his head in close to me and let it rest up against my shoulder. As Prince Humperdink plotted to bring about Westley's death, Brandon sighed and whispered, "This is the best movie ever! Make it go on forever. Don't let it stop."

I whispered back, "As you wish."

. . .

Brandon continued to come on Saturday morning runs with Dad and me in the weeks that followed. When Brandon first joined us a few months previously, Dad and I changed our Saturday morning runs from Memorial Park to Hermann Park for the sake of convenience. Dad decided he wanted to switch back to the longer trails in Memorial Park since the weather was warm again, and we began picking up Brandon early each Saturday morning. Brandon told me he'd done some running on his own to work on his endurance and speed. I could tell a difference. He kept pace with us perfectly, and we never had to stop early for his sake. Dad noticed this and complimented Brandon. I swear I saw a tear in Brandon's eye, even as he grinned from ear to ear.

Much to Brandon's delight, Dad bought a small set of light weights which he kept in the trunk of the car. After our runs, Dad would read the paper and sip some coffee on a park bench, while Brandon and I exercised in the grass next to him. Without fail, we would wind up in a pile on top of each other, shrieking with laughter, arms twisted, legs flying.

I once caught Dad looking at us out of the corner of his eye. I took some pride in knowing how to read his usually muted expressions. But when I saw him watching Brandon and me that one morning, I couldn't decipher his emotions very clearly. It was an odd mixture of joy and pride, with a bit of uncertainty mixed in, too.

The three of us would go back to our apartment and shower. Then we four would go get lunch somewhere along Montrose or over in the Village. We once took Brandon to our favorite taco stand on Fulton across from Moody Park. He said they were the best tacos in the world. On the Saturday nights I stayed over at Brandon's house, Dad and Mom would drop us there after lunch. Then Brandon and I would spend the rest of the day and night together.

I went through a kind of cultural education with Brandon which would have seemed odd to any other kid in Houston. Even at my school full of kids from highly educated families, I was different. I never knew the music they spoke about, the TV shows they watched, or the movies they went to see. Those things were all foreign to me, just as my family's interests seemed to them to be relics of a long-lost civilization. None of my friends went to symphony concerts and Broadway musicals at Jones Hall, live drama at the Alley Theater, the summer Shakespeare festival in Hermann Park, or art lectures at the Museum of Fine Arts. In fact, Brandon looked at me like I was speaking Swahili the first time I mentioned the recent Horton Foote play I saw at the Alley with my parents.

The Marshalls had a mountain of VHS tapes, nearly all of them recordings of TV sitcoms: *M*A*S*H, Good Times, The Jeffersons, Alice, Cheers, Fantasy Island, Sanford and Son, The Golden Girls, The Cosby Show, Family Ties, The Carol Burnet Show, I Love Lucy,* and many others. Brandon introduced me to an episode or two of each show and let me choose which ones I wanted to watch some more. For some reason, I came to love *M*A*S*H, Alice, The Golden Girls,* and *Good Times.* Brandon got a kick out of this.

"I knew it! I knew it," he exclaimed. "I knew you would pick the shows I like the least!" He chuckled to himself and slapped me on the back one Saturday evening in late May. "How can we be so different and yet be best friends?"

"Oh, come on! You like *M*A*S*H*. You always laugh at Klinger and snicker every time someone says 'Hot Lips Houlihan.' And I know you like *Alice*, too. Your favorite saying – come on admit it – is 'Kiss my grits.' You are Flo at heart! And you're, like, Blanche in a guy's body! You are so Blanche. Don't tell me you don't like those shows!"

He tried to assume a pose of righteous indignation, but I could see he was fighting back a belly laugh. I knew I got him with that comment about Blanche! He stared me down and said, "I never said I didn't like them! I just said those are the lamest of the ones I do like. And whatever I think is lame, you like. And whatever you think is lame, I like. You are my personal lame-o-meter. If I need to know if something is lame or not, I ask you, dear sir. You always pick the lamest choice no matter what! Then I have my answer!"

I gave him my dirtiest look, and a real zinger came to my head. "So, you think I always pick the lamest options, huh? Well, let me just remind you that I picked you as my best friend! So, if I always pick the lamest things, what does that say about you, dumbass?" Some of his bad habits were slowly wearing off on me, but I only cursed at him when we were teasing each other.

He spluttered, "Well, well... Oh, yeah? Oh, yeah?" It didn't happen often, but I left him speechless.

We eyed each other suspiciously, each glaring as malevolently as we could. He usually outlasted me in glaring contests, but a small twinkle came into his eyes while I managed to keep my steeliest gaze firmly in place.

He leaned into me quickly, wrapped his arms around my waist, and we toppled over in a heap of limbs and laughter. Being a year older and several inches taller, he had the upper hand in our wrestling matches no matter how prepared I thought I was. He pinned me to the ground, his body hovering just above mine. We were both shirtless, another one of his habits I picked up without noticing. My eyes took in his dense shoulders and the bicep muscles that seemed to get bigger with every passing month.

His breath was warm on my forehead as he laughed and said, "Well, Mr. Even-Bigger-Dumbass, don't forget that Joshua is ready and waiting to be your best friend. All I have to do is call him up, tell him we broke up, and he'll be knocking at your door."

He let his body fall on me. I couldn't believe what it felt like to have his hard body pressed against me, skin on skin, his heartbeat pulsing against my chest. He shook with laughter. I wanted to laugh, too, but he had squashed all the air out of my lungs. He rolled off me and stretched out next to me. "So just remember that, you sorry-ass loser-man. Me or Joshua? Who'd you rather have?" He reached over and ruffled my hair.

I laughed but had to stifle what I really wanted to say: 'Oh, there's no doubt about it! No doubt at all! I'd have you, Brandon; I'd have you every time!'

. . .

iii.

We sat on two towels on the deck in the Marshalls' backyard on a warm Sunday morning near the end of May. The end of school loomed large in our consciousness. We had spent the previous few weeks planning our summer. Both sets of parents had promised that we could spend some time to-gether, but mine had seemed a little reserved when it came to particulars. I wondered what was going on, afraid they might end up changing their minds about the plans Brandon and I were making. Yet, I knew deep down they wouldn't let us make so many plans if they had no intention of letting us actually spend time together. That sounded more like Mr. Marshall than my parents, and Brandon kept assuring me his parents were onboard.

"Okay, Alex-man. I've added some things to our list. We definitely have to go bowling one day. How did we not think of that earlier?" I stifled a groan. My aunt Karen took me bowling the previous summer with some of her friends and their children. It was awful. I was all thumbs. Gutter ball after gutter ball! But I knew better than to rain on Brandon's parade. He was a freight train of optimism and joy. He kept going, "And we didn't add ice skating. Everyone goes ice skating at Christmas. But why not summer? It'd actually be better in the summer. Falling down will feel the best. All that ice to cool us off."

I said, "I've been skating at the Galleria in the summer before. My Aunt Karen took me two summers ago. Let's definitely go! Are you sure your parents are going to go along with all this? Like, how are we going to get to all these places? I keep telling you to ask them about that. My parents both work all day. Well, Mom works less in the summer, but there are a lot of days when she can't drive us around."

Brandon gave me his best smile. "O ye of little faith. I've got a plan! I've got people on board! It's all gonna be good. I promise! My parents are 100% okay with all my plans. I check with them, like, every other day." He rolled over on top of me, pinning my arms to the ground. "Trust me, my little stick-arm friend. Your best *amigo* has it all under control!"

The back door opened, and Mrs. Marshall stuck her head out. "Come inside, you two! It's already 7:45. Time for breakfast, and then you have to get a move on. I need to leave at 8:30. I've got to make a quick stop at the store to get some more coffee filters for the Sunday School class."

Brandon's dad always went to the church building very early on Sunday mornings, so breakfast was just Mrs. Marshall, Brandon, and me. I never had any idea where Will was on Sunday mornings. I don't think he spent many weekend nights at home. I asked Brandon about it once. He said, "Am I my brother's keeper? I have no idea where he goes, when he goes, or who he's with. What do I care? The more he's gone, the more we can do whatever we want upstairs."

We followed Mrs. Marshall into the breakfast room. She had prepared a big breakfast for us – cinnamon rolls, eggs, bacon, orange slices and milk. I noticed that Brandon had a huge smile on his face. He was up to something. I noticed Mrs. Marshall seemed happier than normal. They were both up to something.

She motioned to me. "Come on, Alex. Have a seat. Don't let it get cold. Brandon asked me to make a big breakfast to celebrate the almost-end-of-school."

After a few bites, Brandon looked at his mom and asked, "Have we waited long enough? Can I please, please tell him?"

She grinned. "I think so. Go ahead and tell him. I think you'll explode if I make you wait any longer." She looked at me and winked. "Getting Brandon to keep a secret is like asking Nixon to tell the truth! Impossible! He's been close to exploding for the last few days."

Brandon burst out, "Your parents and mine have been planning our summer behind our backs just as we have been planning our summer! They knew what we were doing, and they kept their plans from us just to tease us!" He shot his mom a look of fake disdain. She stuck out her tongue in return.

Brandon squealed and said, "And guess what, Alex, guess what?"

"I have no idea. What? Just tell me!"

He practically screamed, "You get to spend the whole summer here, or almost the whole summer! They got it all planned out! One of your parents will drop you off here Monday, Tuesday, and Wednesday mornings. We'll hang out all day. Then they'll come get you before dinner. Then you'll come back on Thursday morning and stay through Saturday morning. We'll still go run with your dad. And if we want, your parents said I can come over on Saturday nights to your house." He paused dramatically. "I mean, it's like we'll be brothers for the summer. Well, I already have three. But you don't. Now you'll have me!" He threw his arms in the air. "Me! And you! All summer!"

I was speechless. I spent part of each summer shuffling from family member to family member while my parents worked – a week with Aunt Karen and two weeks with both sets of grandparents. Then Mom would take off one week, and we'd spend that together. Then Dad would take off another week, and we'd spend that together. Then they would both take a week off together, and all three of us would go on vacation. I always felt a kind of indifference about summer, but I knew the summer that stretched out in front of me was going to be the best summer ever.

I smacked my forehead. "So that's why they've been acting so weird every time I bring up summer plans! They keep telling me, 'We'll figure it out later. We'll talk about it later, Alex.' Mom just said a few days ago, 'Yes, you can see Brandon, but we're not going to make firm plans right now.' They've been saying that for weeks."

Another realization dawned on me. I turned to Brandon. "And you've known? You've known all along? You giant turd bucket." I gasped and looked at Mrs. Marshall. She laughed and threw back her head. Then I knew where Brandon got that gesture. That was exactly how he did it, too.

He sputtered, "No, no, no! I didn't know for weeks! I mean, they told me a few days ago! It was your parents' idea to keep it from you as long as we could. They even wanted me to act all upset and say that I was gonna have to go Nashville and spend the summer with my grandparents. But I just couldn't do it! I mean, I wanted to be that cruel to you, but I didn't think I could pull it off."

"You really mean it? You really mean that plan you just told me is what we're gonna do? All those days together? All those sleepovers? Really?"

Mrs. Marshall shook with laughter. "It's really true. Between me, Mr. Marshall, and Will, we'll get you two to all the places you want to go. Oh, and Joel offered to help, too. He'll be another chauffeur. You two must be really loved to have all these people doing everything they can to give you a summer to remember." She paused for a few seconds and added wistfully, "And what a great friendship you two have. It's the sweetest thing I have ever seen. Now, go, go, go! You've got about thirty minutes!"

Brandon and I darted from the kitchen, half-stumbling and weighing each other down, as we tried to mount the stairs with our arms around each other's shoulders. We reached the top, and he said, "I'll go shower first. I'll be two minutes."

I went back to his room to gather up my clothes and the few things I brought with me. I could hear Brandon, at the other end of the house, singing some made-up tune in the shower, "It's gonna be the best summer ever with my best pal Alex. It's gonna be the best summer ever with my best friend ever. It's gonna be..."

CHAPTER 6

Summer – that magical word, those wistful two syllables! For the first time ever, I anticipated the start of summer with a feverish intensity that obliterated every other thought during the last week of seventh grade. Summer 1988 broke over me like a tsunami and opened me up to a world I had never known. There, just on the cusp of leaving my childhood years forever, I experienced a long-denied childhood joy: a lazy, hazy, seemingly endless summer with my best friend constantly by my side.

Brandon and I slipped into a familiar routine. He would sit up against one of the moss-draped oak trees in his front yard, waiting for the first sighting of my dad's car as we turned off Greenbriar each morning. He would jump up and wave. By the time we pulled into the Marshalls' driveway, he would be standing at the spot where our car always came to a rest, practically waiting to pull me from the car.

We'd already have on our running shorts, and off we'd go for a short jog around his neighborhood. We'd come back to his house, change into swimming trunks, and cannonball into the pool. Between serious bouts of dunking and wrestling, we'd swim lazily for a few minutes or float on a raft. By 9:00

we were both starving, and we'd head inside for cereal and long-cold scrambled eggs. Then we'd lounge outside in the shade of the covered deck as breakfast digested.

Our parents insisted we do some kind of activity to stimulate our minds and keep us mentally sharp over the long summer. I had recently discovered the mysteries of Agatha Christie, and I eagerly introduced Brandon to her world of locked rooms, isolated country mansions, red herrings, and ingenious, surprising solutions. I read *And Then There Were None* on my own the weekend after school ended. I decided it would be a great book to read aloud to Brandon in our late-morning laziness.

He was suspicious at first. "Don't read me something boring, Alex! I've seen those Charles Dickens books in your bedroom. Those books are bigger than the Bible. I don't want to hear a book as long as the Bible! And no long words I don't even know! I'm not a brainiac like you! I like short, simple stories."

I read aloud to him the back cover of my tattered paperback.

He said, "So, ten people come to the island, and someone picks them off one by one? Obviously, there's some crazy person on the island. Sounds boring."

I sighed. "Think about the title! There's only ten people on the island; they all die and then there are none. But who did it, and how, if they all die in the end? It's one of the greatest mysteries of all time. It's super short. I read it right through on Saturday. I promise: you'll love it!"

On the first Tuesday of our summer, we sat in one corner of the deck where the built-in benches met at a right angle. I was propped up with a pillow behind me, legs out in front of me. Brandon lay perpendicular to me, his head resting on a pillow nestled against my waist. He looked up at me from time to time, his eyes rolling back to make contact with mine.

He listened with surprising attention. He was hooked by

the time I read about the first victim, the handsome and arrogant Anthony Marston, poisoned by his own cocktail.

Brandon muttered, "Yeah, he deserves to go first. What a prick! He's more worried about his car than the kids he ran over. Serves him right! Who gets it next? I bet it's Lombard. All the jerks get killed first. Right?"

Brandon moaned in dismay with each new body. He never correctly predicted the next victim and often said he was certain he knew the identity of the killer, only to see that person meet their end just after his prediction.

I read on: exit Emily Brent. Brandon remarked caustically, "Well, that old bitch deserved it! Serves her right for turning out that poor girl!"

When Justice Wargrave turned up as victim number six, Brandon squealed with surprise. "Wait, wait, wait! I thought it was the judge! It makes sense for it to be him. That whole record at the beginning, you know?" He imitated a British accent. "'Prisoners at the bar. How do you plead?' I mean, that is just what you hear in court. But now the judge is dead. I bet it's Lombard. It has to be. If it's not Wargrave, it's gotta be Lombard."

We took a break for lunch and picked up the next day. I kept reading as the bodies piled up until there were only two remaining guests.

"I knew it, I knew it," he crowed as Vera Claythorn and Philip Lombard stood near the pounding surf on Indian Island. "I knew it was all down to Lombard. What did I tell you, Alex?" He hooted in the air. "I could write this myself. I knew it all along."

I tried my best to hide a smirk.

He went silent as I read about the shot that took down Lombard. Vera Claythorn, gun in hand, was the last person standing.

"What? What? You mean it was Vera all along? How in the world?" He was indignant. "No, no, no! You're like my mom when I was a kid! She'd change the story on me to see if I was really paying attention. You read that wrong. Lombard's got to shoot Vera! And who's gonna kill her? I thought they all died! What is this stuff you're reading to me?"

I chuckled and said, "You sound like the boy in *The Princess Bride*. You're, like, 'Hold it, hold it, Grandpa. You're reading it wrong. She didn't marry Prince Humperdink!'"

He gulped.

I said mockingly, "Shall I continue?"

He kept moaning as I read aloud the famous post-script and intricate explanation of the ten murdered corpses. "How did I miss that?" Moan and sigh. "That's not fair. I mean, how was I supposed to figure that out?"

He sat up when I closed the book. "You mean that's it? Wow! What a story! I had no idea there were books like that out there. I read some of those choose-your-own-ending mysteries in fifth grade, but they were lame compared to this! I think we have to read more of these. That Christie lady is clever as hell! And you've got the best reading voice ever. I could listen to you all day! God, I don't want this summer to ever end. I just want it like this forever. You. Me. The pool. A good book. Forever and ever."

. . .

Some days, in between a shared Agatha Christie book, I would continue reading another book on my own, and he would spend time sketching next to me. He was often quite secretive when sketching. It was the one bit of privacy he claimed for himself. I came to respect this and never asked to see what he was working on.

We'd eat lunch with Mrs. Marshall and then go upstairs to watch some TV. We made a deal and traded turns picking what we'd watch each day. Mrs. Marshall insisted we only watch an hour of TV per day. She knew how little TV my parents allowed me to watch, and I think she feared they might consider her an inferior mother if she let us wallow for hours in front of the screen.

After our allotted hour, we'd do a workout. Brandon was a task-master when it came to the weights. He didn't even give me any say in the matter. He just barked his orders, corrected whatever I had done wrong, and pushed me harder whenever I lagged or hesitated.

"Come on! Concentrate, Alex! Feel the muscle! Keep your form good!" I swear I could hear him in my sleep sometimes.

One of Brandon's great joys that summer was the introduction of heavier weights. Mr. Marshall said he didn't see any harm in adding the twenty pound weights as long as Brandon was careful and slow. Brandon attacked the new weights with a passion. He'd sometimes carry them around with him: downstairs, around the pool, and out under the trees. Some kids had favorite toy animals. Brandon had favorite dumb-bells.

On Mondays, Tuesdays, and Wednesdays, one of my parents would pick me up by 4:00. On Thursdays and Fridays, when I spent the night with Brandon, we'd linger around the pool until dinner. On some Friday nights we played Scrabble with Mr. and Mrs. Marshall. The games never went well for Brandon. He insisted that I only spell words with fewer than four syllables. If I laid out a word he had never heard before, he shot me sly, dirty looks when his parents weren't watching.

Even when I tried to hold back and go for easy words, I ran circles around Brandon. If I tried to help him by looking at his letters or making suggestions, he'd sulk and glare at me. The night I spelled 'ambidextrous' was particularly tense for a few minutes. Fortunately, Brandon's capacity to hold a grudge lasted about ten minutes!

In addition to our lazy free-time, Brandon and I had chores to do almost every day. Thursday was trash collection day in the Marshalls' neighborhood, so Brandon and I emptied all the trashcans in the house each Wednesday and rolled the big bin out to the curb as soon as I arrived on Thursday morning. We usually cleaned his bathroom, tidied his room, and vacuumed upstairs on Thursdays. The heavy-duty work was Friday morning. Long before we became friends, Brandon mowed, edged, and trimmed the front yard and back yard every Friday morning during the summer. He joked with me that first Friday: "Seriously, like, right after I stopped wearing diapers, Dad stuck me behind the lawn mower. I've been doing this since forever. I was mowing before I learned to read and write. I'm just like a workhorse as far as he's concerned."

After we helped clean up the lunch dishes on our second Friday together, Mrs. Marshall sat us down for a stern talking-to. "Now, boys, you've got to get serious about the yard work. When you do it on your own, Brandon, it takes you about two hours. It's taken the two of you together about four hours last Friday and today!

"I was watching you today. I looked out the window once, and you–" she patted me on the shoulder, "were tying his legs up with the extension cord, and he was hopping around like a demented bunny for some reason. Then I looked out the window a few minutes later, and you–" she thumped Brandon's chest, "had Alex inside a big trash bag up to his waist. Then you hoisted him on your shoulders and pretended you were about the throw him in the pool. A few minutes later he was sitting on your back, lotus-style, while you were trying to do some push-ups. Honestly, boys, every time I looked out the window, you were on the grass rolling around, arms and legs flying everywhere, laughing like hyenas! I mean, trust you two to turn yard work into a Steve Martin and Martin Short duo!"

She paused and a slight edge came into her voice. "Seriously, Brandon, think for one minute! If your dad showed up unannounced and saw you two playing instead of working... I mean, just imagine it, baby."

Brandon tensed up beside me.

She shook her head and continued, "It would make his explosion on New Year's Eve seem like a stroll through the park. And you left grass clippings on the front walkway last week. I had to talk him down from the ledge all weekend. You two are on a knife's edge, and you don't even know it. And it's only the second week of summer."

I spoke up. "I'm sorry, Mrs. Marshall. The grass clippings were my fault. I swept the front walkway while Brandon finished trimming around the trees. I guess I just missed some. I've never done yard work before. I'll be extra careful from now on. And I'll stop being silly. I promise!"

"It's sweet of you to apologize, but it's all Brandon's responsibility at the end of the day." She took his hands in hers. "I am so glad you have Alex here with you, sweetie, but it will all come crashing down around your head in two seconds if you keep on like this. Find some way to have fun, but do it correctly. Maybe you should stay inside, Alex, while he does the yard work. Or maybe just sit and watch on the deck. Maybe if you're out of the way, he'll focus and hurry and do it right so he can get back to you."

Brandon nodded and put his arm around my shoulders. "Yeah! You just put your feet up and bark orders at me. I mean, even though you don't have any siblings, you're a natural when it comes to bossing me around like I'm your baby brother. I close my eyes sometimes, and you sound just like Will." He winked at me and ruffled my hair.

"No, no, no! We'll do it together. I insist! I've got to do something to pull my weight around here." Brandon chuckled and gave me a sly look. I could tell he wanted to say something totally sarcastic or inappropriate, but his mother's presence caused him to hold his tongue.

Mrs. Marshall's expression softened, and she said, "Well, sort it out between yourselves, and come up with a plan for next week. And get back out there and check for grass clippings on the driveway. I think I saw some from the kitchen window. Also, there are some wavy lines on the grass out front near the street. Get the mower back out and go over that area again. Get the lines straight, Brandon. You know what your dad's like about straight lines in the grass."

She kissed us both on our cheeks and took Brandon's chin in her hand. "Consider this your stern warning, sweetie. Don't give your dad any ammunition to use against you. You know I say all this to save you from that." She reached out and stroked my arm. "And, Alex, he thinks you are mature and responsible. That's part of the reason he allows you two so much time together. If he starts to think you're a bad influence on Brandon, all bets are off. Even I won't be able to help."

I swear my stomach sank about ten feet. I nodded meekly. I understood what she meant better than she realized. Brandon teared up a bit and kissed his mom gently on the cheek. "I know. I love you for it. I'm sorry I'm not better, but I'm gonna do better from now on. Alex is making me a little better every day."

. . .

ii.

In early July, we spent a particularly hot day at the zoo. It was our second visit in three weeks. Brandon brought his sketch book on both trips, and we spent long stretches of time sitting on benches while he sketched various animals. He rarely let me look on as he sketched at home. There at the zoo, however, he let me watch his deft, magical fingers bring the animals to life on paper.

We always sat impossibly close together as he sketched, our legs pressed up against each other's. Invariably, I sat on his left side so his right hand was completely free. He wore tank-tops on every outing all summer long, except for ice skating, of course. When I sat close to him on a bench at the zoo, I could feel the alluring shape of his bare tricep through my own thin cotton shirt.

Just after finishing our brown bag lunch, we found an empty bench in front of the chimpanzee enclosure. He laid his pencil down after several moments and turned to me. He had a serious look on his face.

"What do you think? Did we really descend from chimpanzees or monkeys?"

"Well, not these particular chimpanzees," I replied lightly. He stuck his tongue out at me. I continued, "They're probably not much older than my parents according to that plaque. That's an odd thought, isn't it? They could have kids our age."

Brandon was unusually pensive. "My dad says that evolution is just a theory. It's like scientists don't really want to believe in God, so they make up a way to explain where humans came from that doesn't involve God. He said God made the world look really old, even though it isn't, just to test our faith. What do you think?"

"Well, Dad's a scientist. He believes in God, and he knows that evolution is real." I paused and tried to gather my words. "We studied about evolution in life science class last year. I asked my parents about it. Dad said evolution is not something you believe in. It's not like Santa Claus or the Tooth Fairy. You don't get to decide whether you believe it or not. He said it's like gravity. Nobody says, 'Well, I don't believe in gravity.' That would be stupid. Gravity and evolution are the same kind of concepts. They are real, even if we decide we don't like the idea. It's just you can see gravity at work any time, but it's harder to see evolution at work in the space of a few seconds."

I looked at Brandon hopefully. Had I helped?

"I don't know. My dad says we all came from Adam and Eve. He believes they were the first people. He said you can't be a Christian and not believe that."

I hesitated before speaking again. I felt like I was in a minefield. "Well, maybe you don't have to decide now. You could talk to my dad about it. He could explain to you how we know humans and chimpanzees came from a common ancestor. He can give you some examples and explain it better than I can. Plus, how can you believe Genesis is literally true? There are two different stories of creation in the first two chapters, and the details totally contradict each other."

"Well, you gotta promise me one thing, buddy. You cannot tell my dad that you believe in evolution. You can't even let it just accidentally slip out that you think evolution is true. He would flip the hell out! I mean it! It would be the end of our friendship. He wouldn't let you near me. Our whole summer would come to an end in three seconds. It would be worse than you not being baptized."

"Okay. I promise. It's our secret." I stuck out my hand. He took it, and we shook.

He became still and very quiet again. He was looking intently at the chimpanzees. He spoke softly at last. "Well, when you look at them, you have to admit they look kind of like us, and we kind of look like them. I notice when I am drawing them it's just like sketching a person. Well, not exactly the same, but close."

He stopped and turned to me. "Isn't that funny? I may not have noticed that if it wasn't for my sketching. My mom told me one time that my sketching was a way of seeing the world, like I could see the world through my two eyes and through my sketches." He paused, a gentle smile on his face. "I like that. I can see both ways, with my eyes and my sketches."

I smiled. "Yes, I bet you'd really notice the similarity if you were trying to sketch a chimp and then wanted to do a self-portrait."

His quiet, somber mood broke in an instant. He roared with laughter and tumbled onto the ground. The chimps looked up, surprised by the sudden noise on an otherwise calm summer afternoon. "That was a good one, smartass! That was your best ever, I think!"

He extended his hand to me. "Help me up!" I stood up, pulled with all my might, and he jumped to his feet. He slung his arm around me. "Well, I do know this. None of those chimps have a friend like you. I am so glad we evolved to what we are now because I would not be your friend if you looked like that chimp over there and went around sniffing other people's butts. I mean, I'd draw the line at that." He snorted all the way to the exit.

CHAPTER 7

The youth group went to the same camp every summer in the third week of July. Brandon had been the previous two summers. He never talked much about camp other than to say who went out with whom, who dumped whom, and who scratched whom. When I asked him if I should go, he threatened great harm would come to me if I didn't.

We sat together on the long ride to the Hill Country, where Camp Brazos Hills nestled amidst the rolling landscape between Austin and Llano. The rest of the church van was chaotic, but we somehow managed to stay in our own little cocoon, oblivious to the loud voices and strident laughing of the other junior high boys around us.

Not long before we arrived, Brandon turned to the dreaded subject. "Okay, you hottie! You're gonna have to make some decisions. Rachel is still after you. You do know that?" I nodded. "Well, Christy told me that Anna and Jennifer both want to go out with you at camp, too. I mean, there's gonna be pressure. You'll have to make a decision. And then you don't even know who's gonna be there from the other churches."

Brandon caught me off-guard! Back when we first became

friends, he talked about dating at camp on a regular basis. I was always uncomfortable and a little discouraged because I never wanted to be with anyone but Brandon. I didn't notice it as it happened, but I eventually realized he brought up the topic less often as our friendship deepened in the winter and spring. He made a casual reference to Carrie, his girlfriend at camp the previous summer, one day in June, but he was otherwise silent about the prospect of dating any girls at camp. I suppose my subconscious thought the matter was dead and buried.

I was dazed. Something about church camp drove all the sexually repressed church kids into a manic frenzy. Brandon told me a girl from a church in Waco actually kissed Joshua the previous summer. He said, "It makes me feel better for him, you know? We give him such a hard time. It's good to know he can get girlfriends if he wants. Or at least one girl. Of course, only a girl from Waco would be likely to kiss Joshua." He shuddered – whether at the thought of Joshua kissing any girl or a girl from Waco pushing herself on Joshua, I could only wonder.

We settled into our cabin in the late afternoon. Most of the boys in our cabin came from our church, but there were six boys from a church in Austin. Our cabin counselor, Jake, was a college student from Abilene. He seemed nice enough. It was his first time being a counselor at Camp Brazos Hills. Brandon cast a mischievous glace my way when Jake said this. I asked Brandon about it later.

He said, "Those are the best kind of counselors to have. They're like substitute teachers. You just tell them what happened last year and then do whatever you want."

The first two days rolled by in a blur of activities: early morning cold showers, rather dismal breakfasts, singing, lessons, group games, more singing, somewhat better lunches, kitchen clean-up duty, swimming, sports, canteen, free-time, dinners with bizarre combinations (spaghetti and corndogs;

taco salad and fried catfish), more singing, the campfire, and late night cabin devotionals. Brandon had been right. In between all these activities a flood of messages and notes got passed around. Couples united gleefully and parted bitterly with amazing speed, sometimes in the span of a meal or a round of singing. The couples who lasted more than a day or two garnered a fair amount of respect and awe.

Brandon plunged into the fray on Monday morning. He somehow arranged, through the help of several intermediaries, to go out with Cathy, a girl from a church on the north side of San Antonio. She seemed nice enough. She trailed along after us all day Monday. I felt a bit sorry for her. She was definitely the odd-person-out in our lopsided threesome.

After dinner on Monday, Brandon and I had a few minutes alone in the cabin. He had a plan. "Okay, my little stick-arm friend. Your good looks and charm have the girls lined up and panting after you. And your hair! I swear, I've actually heard girls talking about your hair!" He chuckled; I blushed. "Cathy has a friend from her church all lined up for you. You've probably seen her. She's the one with the curly brown hair." I sighed and rolled my eyes.

"Oh, come on! You just ask her out. Her name is Sarah. She'll say yes. Half the girls, no three quarters of the girls – that's more, right? – are lusting after you. I mean, you could have your pick of the girls. Just ask Sarah out. Then when we four are together, they'll have each other for company, and it'll be like old times for us." He spoke of 'old times' like it was years ago, not just the previous week.

I continued to be confused and upset by Brandon's dogged insistence about having a girlfriend. I had no interest in dating any girls at camp… or anywhere else. I was happy to be with Brandon every waking second, and I thought he felt the same way. For the previous ten months, he seemed to be happy to have me all to himself. He had rebuffed every guy in the youth group – not just Joshua – who tried to be part of our little twosome. I never wanted it any other way, either. Then he suddenly wanted to pair me off with some girl who, sweet as she was, I didn't even want to be around. I was utterly disheartened.

After a long round of haggling, I finally agreed. I kissed a girl at a school dance at the end of sixth grade, but that was a debacle and something I never wanted to repeat. Making a serious attempt to ask out a girl was virgin territory for me! Brandon assured me it was very simple. I took some convincing!

"Listen, Alex! You're making it so hard! You aren't asking her to marry you. You're not even asking her to be your friend! Sheeeesh! She's gonna say yes to you no matter what you say. Even if you mess it all up and say you hate puppies, she'll say yes. It's like the best win-win situation ever." In the end, he wore down all my defenses.

We walked back up the path from our cabin to the main clearing. Cathy had already prepared the scene. Sarah sat by herself on a bench near the dining hall. As we walked closer, Brandon gave me a push and said, "Go get her, tiger!"

The whole silly mess was over in seconds. Sarah seemed more excited than I expected. She took my hand and pulled me off the bench. I tried to wiggle my hand free, but she had a vice-like grip. Brandon and Cathy were waiting for us under a nearby tree. It was time for the evening activity in the east soccer field. The four of us began to make our way over. Brandon and Cathy walked slightly in front of Sarah and me.

Sarah seemed to forget I was there as she and Cathy launched into a steady stream of gossip about the other girls who hadn't yet scored their own guy. She dropped my hand in the midst of much gesturing. I breathed a sigh of relief.

I couldn't take my eyes off of Brandon in front of me. I realized for the first time in some months how much he seemed to have grown since we met the previous September. I was with him all the time, but I saw him differently in that instant. He had on one of his usual tank-tops, and I couldn't help but notice the rounded heft of his shoulders and the size of his rapidly growing triceps. I let my gaze drift down to his tight ass, and I admired his shapely calves. I felt myself go hard and wished the girls would just go away.

Brandon let Cathy's hand slip from his, and, as if on cue, the two girls caught up with one another. He slowed his pace a fraction, and I caught up with him. He threw his left arm over my shoulder and gave me the biggest grin possible.

He winked and whispered, "See, I told you! The girls are all sorted, and we've still got each other! Inigo and Fezzick come out on top again!" I wanted to laugh. I wanted to cry. I wanted to skip and shout. I wanted his arm around me like that all night. I wanted to hold my best friend's hand forever.

. . .

All the counselors and staff at Brazos Hills emphasized a particular rule over and over: no cliques and no exclusive friendships. Since the camp attracted kids from all over Texas, the counselors wanted every kid to have a circle of friends to which they belonged. The adults didn't mind all the romantic matches. I think they even looked on the constant break-ups as a sign that nobody got too serious in the course of six days.

To my surprise and delight, Brandon and I seemed to float above this rule against exclusive friendships. We stuck together all week: at every meal, every game, every swim time, every lesson, every devotional, and every campfire. Maybe the fact that we each had a girlfriend was a kind of invisible shield that protected us from the counselors' approbation. The only time we weren't hooked at the hips was during boys' group sports. Brandon threw himself into every game with complete abandon. He was the guy who caused all the outfielders to back up when he came to bat in softball and the guy who parted the sea of bodies as he ran to the goal line in flag football.

I held back from the rough-and-tumble sports. No one seemed to notice or care. I wondered if Brandon would drag me in kicking and screaming, but he was happy to have me watching and cheering him on from the sidelines. From time to time, he'd look over to where I sat and give me a big smile and wave. It was as though he was checking to make sure I was still there.

On Wednesday, during a remarkably violent game of flag football, I sat on some mini-bleachers under the shade of a solitary oak tree. Every other guy was playing. Two junior high girls sat at the opposite end of the bleachers, higher up in the full sun. The rest of the junior high girls were off in one of the covered pavilions playing volleyball or doing crafts. I wondered why those two girls were watching the boys, sitting in the hot sun by themselves. They never paid much attention to the game; every time I looked their way, they were looking at me.

Halfway through the game, Joel came up and sat beside me. He clapped me on the shoulders and gave me a hug. "Hey, hey, Alexo! What's up, man? Why aren't you out there in the middle of that?"

He winked at me and ruffled my hair. He had on a pair of blue shorts and a yellow tank-top which accentuated his sun-bleached short brown hair. It had been a long time since I had seen his bare arms. They were bigger than I remembered. I could hardly take my eyes off them. I glanced over and saw the two girls looking our way, eyes glued to Joel and me.

"So, I heard a rumor that you are going out with someone named Sarah. Am I right? Is she cute?"

I nodded shyly. He continued, "You sly ol' fox. You could have your pick of the girls. I tell you, all the high school girls here know who you are. They come up to me and say, 'Is that totally hot skinny kid from your church? Is he really going into eighth grade next year? Oh. My. God. He's so cute!'" He mimicked a slightly nasal, high-pitched voice, with a touch of valley girl thrown in.

"I can't believe they say that about me. It's Brandon they can't take their eyes off of."

"Oh, I don't know, man. Sure, they notice Brandon. But they notice you, too. You think when people are looking at you two that they're always checking out Brandon." He paused and pulled me in closer to his chest. "Not, so, Alexo. Not so. They've got their eyes on you more often than not! I mean, look no farther than these girls up behind us. They are so mooning over you. I even think some of the guys have their eyes on you. But, hey, you didn't hear that from me!"

I felt like I had fallen through Alice's looking glass every time a conversation took a turn to who liked who, especially when someone – usually Joel – mentioned that it wasn't just the girls who sometimes took notice of me.

He continued, looking out to the field, "There's ol' Brandon, speak of the devil. God, doesn't he know it's supposed to be flag football? It's just like the retreat all over again. You give him a ball, and he goes mad. I'm surprised the counselors let him get away with it."

I wasn't too surprised myself. I overheard Jake and some of the other counselors saying it was no bad thing to let the boys play rough at sports. It was a way they could toughen up each other, the counselors said. Over the course of my first few days at camp, I realized the college-age counselors had a kind of church-camp-meets-*Lord-of-the-Flies* mentality. I was glad I stayed out of it all.

Joel went on, "And you two are practically, like, conjoined twins these days! You know I am supposed to drive you around a few places after camp? How in the world do you two get so many people to re-arrange their schedules and drive you around?"

"I think it's my wit and charm and his brute strength."

Joel shook with laughter. "That is so true. You do have wit

and charm. Man, you will be dangerous with the ladies in high school! I'm just telling you now!"

He dropped his arm from around my shoulder and turned toward me more fully. He had a look on his face I didn't quite understand. He lowered his voice, perhaps to prevent the two girls from hearing him.

"There's probably something you don't understand about Brandon. Do you remember that morning at the retreat when he got so mad at you and blew up on the football field?"

"Of course."

"Has he ever done anything like that again?"

"No, just the once."

"Well, what you've got to understand about Brandon is that he thinks he is never good enough. I'm not making this up. My mom is a psychologist, and she was talking to me about this one time after Will spent the night with us. Will told us about some of the things Brandon had been doing back at the beginning of sixth grade – a whole year before you came along. He was getting in trouble at school all the time. He was picking fights. He was talking back to his teachers. And his parents... well, his dad, was giving him hell all the time. I think Brandon was so miserable. He used to swim with me and Will whenever I was staying over at their house. And Brandon would fly off in raging fits at the smallest incident. He'd just erupt. It was kind of scary at times. I joke about him kicking me in the balls, but, God, he would get out of control. He'd lash out at the smallest little thing."

He paused again and looked away toward the field. "And my mom said she thought he felt like he couldn't measure up to his brothers. Each of his brothers were, like, the perfect kids at school and at church. He thinks they're so much better than he is. And in this weird kind of way, his dad just made it worse because he pointed it out all the time. Will used to tell me about the times when Mr. Marshall would scream and shout at Brandon. Mom said it was this awful spiral where Brandon didn't feel he measured up to his brothers. So, he acted in a way to get another kind of attention. Then his dad punished him and told him to act more like his brothers. That just made Brandon act up all the more. It sounds like some crazy shit, doesn't it?"

Just then, Brandon looked over at me in between plays and gave me a big thumbs-up. I waved and returned the thumbs-up.

Joel continued, "And then you come along, and Brandon finds in you the kind of friend he needed at just the right time. I don't know what it is about you, but something about you is just what he needs. Brandon actually has a hard time making friends. You'd think he's the most popular boy at his school, but he's not. Everybody knows him, sure, but he's not got any close friends except you. You, however, could have your pick of friends. Everybody loves you! Just on the surface of things, it would seem like you two were an impossible combination. But somehow you two started being friends. I think he's scared to death that you'll find out what he's really like and that you'll stop being his friend."

Tears welled up in my eyes. I wiped them and said, "That doesn't make sense. He ought to know by now I'm not going to do that. He's the best friend I've ever had."

"My mom says most of us act the way we act without giving it much thought. We just kind of react to what goes on around us, and most of the time what we do doesn't make any sense. In fact, she says most of us go around shooting ourselves in the foot – doing the very thing we don't mean to do."

We sat in silence for a moment. Perhaps for the first time in my life I realized how little I could really know about other people, especially, and ironically, the people I loved the most. Even though I loved Brandon like a brother, there was part of him I didn't understand and might not ever understand. It filled me with sadness and loneliness, as if a crushing weight rested heavily against my heart.

Joel shook his head as if to clear his mind. "Wow! I didn't mean to get all heavy on you! Did I make you sad? I was just trying to help you understand Brandon a little better. I thought maybe it would help if he ever acted that way again. I mean, if he acted like he did at the retreat again. I just don't want you to get hurt and think you have done something wrong. Have I totally depressed you?"

"No, I'm okay." Really, I felt heartbroken and lost. "I think I get it. He's my best friend. Why would I ever push him away or stop being his friend? Why would I do the one thing that would hurt him the most? That would be cruel. He needs to know someone loves him and wants to be his friend, even when he acts like a jerk."

Joel sighed and put his arm around my shoulder again. "Man, Alex! You are wise beyond your years. I can't have these kinds of talks with any other guy I know. Not even Will. Every girl for a hundred miles is gonna want to be your boyfriend as you get older! Girls love a thoughtful guy, especially if he's cute and has soulful eyes. My mom said you have the most soulful eyes she's ever seen on someone so young. Poor Brandon is gonna get dumped when some pretty girl turns your head in another year or so. He won't know what hit him. He'll start spreading rumors about her just so he can get you back!"

The thought of picking a girl, no matter how beautiful, over Brandon made my stomach constrict. I shivered.

"Tell me you are not cold! It's like three hundred fucking degrees out here." He paused for second. "Hey, what are you two doing at free time today?"

"We're gonna go sketch and read. We usually go to one of those swings between the fire circle and the west pavilion."

"What do your girlfriends think about that?"

"Well, we don't tell them what we're gonna do. They go do their own thing. And we do ours."

We watched Brandon make a dash for the goal line and

spike the ball when he crossed it. He looked over at me again and struck a pose, showing off his biceps, round and tight like softballs.

Joel said, "He looks about four years older than you, but you act about five years older than him. You're calm, cool, and collected. And he's all over the place. My mom says he's like a giant Labrador. Actually, she says the same thing about me. She said Brandon seems more like a brother I would have than a brother Will would have." He paused. "I wish I had a friend like you when I was in junior high. You would have been a good friend to me, I bet. Just like you are his best friend. And it's funny that you are his best friend and the best kind of friend for him. Know what I mean? I mean, sometimes your best friend is the worst kinda friend you could have."

"He's the best friend I could have, too. I never imagined I'd have a friend like him."

"Really? You think that? I can imagine you without him a lot more than I can imagine him without you. Most people probably think he holds your friendship together, like the big sporty guy is being nice to the smart, shy kid. But I think it's really the other way around. The smart, shy guy holds it all together."

He chuckled and wiped his sweaty brow. "I've got a plan. They let us older high school guys have additional swim time if we do extra chores after lunch. I know for a fact that all the guys want to start a game of soccer today. I hate soccer, so it was just gonna be me doing the extra kitchen chores. I thought I'd just swim by myself for a while, but you two should come. If you two come help me in the kitchen, we can go swim together. I'll get my counselor to talk to your counselor. How about it?"

"That sounds great! It would be a relief to swim without two thousand guys in the pool all at once. I'll tell Brandon. Where should we meet you?"

"Just come to the back of the kitchen after lunch. It'll take, like, fifteen minutes and then we'll have a whole two hours to swim."

. . .

Brandon and I changed before lunch and slathered sunscreen all over one another. We caught up with Joel after lunch at the back door to the kitchen. The after-lunch kitchen duty mainly involved putting away dishes as they came out of the dishwasher. Once all the other helpers were out of the way, we emptied the trash, wiped down the counters, and set out stacks of plates for dinner near the serving line. It took us less than fifteen minutes.

I thought a suspicious counselor might stop us as we made our way down to the pool, but the campgrounds were mostly deserted. It was a blast furnace of a day. The thermometer on the back of the dining hall showed 102°, and the hottest few hours of the day were still ahead. It appeared everyone had decided to spend rest time in their cabins or other shady places. I thought it odd for some of the high school guys to trade extra swim time for a game of soccer on the hottest day of camp. Still, it gave us the pool to ourselves. I wasn't going to complain.

As we walked beneath the shade of the oak trees, Joel said, "Your counselor was totally cool about you coming. He said you were the two most mature boys in the cabin, and he felt safe letting you come with me. I told him I'm CPR certified, so it's all good. If one of you starts to drown, I can pull you out." He paused and smiled. "Well, if you go down, Alex, I'll dive straight in. But with you, Brandon, I might have to give it some thought. I'm still scarred from some of those kicks you delivered last summer."

Brandon let out a holler and jumped on Joel's back. He beat his fists on Joel's shoulders and cried, "When are you ever going to drop that? It was an accident." Joel hoisted him up farther, and they galloped down to the pool ahead of me. I wanted to run after them, but it was too hot. I never ran in the middle of the day, especially when it was so hot.

I walked through the gate a minute behind them. Brandon was already in the pool. Joel had just stripped off his clothes and was pulling on his trunks. I threw down my towel and pulled my shirt off over my head. Joel whooped and hollered, "All right. The Bissonet boys are in the pool." He ran over my way, turned his back to me, and said, "Come on! Your turn! Hop on!"

I jumped on his back, locking my legs around his trim waist and throwing my arms around his shoulders. I could feel every hard muscle in his torso, and his rock-like arms pressed close against me as he took a running jump into the pool. We hit the water with an almighty splash.

For the next ten minutes, it was a complete circus. Brandon dunked me. I dunked Brandon. Joel dunked us both with a kind of force that took my breath away. Arms and legs flew all over the place. There were shouts, groans, gasps, and shrieks of laughter. Brandon was hollering at his loudest, and Joel roared with laughter. It's a wonder no counselors came to see what was going on. Joel tossed me around with ease. I slammed up against Brandon over and over again. I got too much water up my nose and down my throat.

I broke free from Brandon's grip at one point and swam to the side. I hung on the pool's edge and took big, deep breaths. I was dizzy and disoriented by the lack of air, constant motion, and dazzling sunlight.

Joel and Brandon stared after me in surprise and concern. Joel swam over with two or three strong stokes, Brandon close on his heels.

Joel asked, "Are you okay, my man? Did you get choked? Did I hurt you? I am so sorry! I forgot and got too rough!"

I shook my head. "No, it's okay. I got too much water up

my nose and down my throat. I got winded, and I felt like I was gonna go under. I'm okay now, but I think I might sit out for a minute."

Brandon hopped out of the pool. He squatted down in front of me on the concrete and extended both arms. I grabbed his hands, lifted my feet to the pool's edge, and Brandon pulled me up. We sat down together, with our legs dangling in the water. He practically sat on top of me, our shoulders and legs pressed closely together. He leaned his weight against me and said, "Yeah, I'm sorry, too. I got way too rough. It's a good thing I wasn't kicking. I may have gone straight for your balls without noticing it. Then I'd get another year of misery from Joel."

Joel heaved himself up out of the water. He sat down on my other side.

In a mocking tone he said, "I know, Brandon! God, you were way too rough. I mean, Alexo and me were just trying to float and chill and relax, and you were, like, off your chain! A wild man!" He made a motion with his arm like he was cracking a whip. "I mean, like, down, Brandon, down! Back you, wild beast!"

My breath slowly returned to normal, but it was too hot to sit under the sun's fierce heat for long.

I looked at Brandon and said, "Let's get back in, but could we have a few minutes of calm swimming? I don't mind you being rough, but I need a little calm first."

Brandon jumped into the pool. Joel looked over at me. "Come on! Give me a push from behind, hard as you can! Take out your anger on me!"

"I'm not mad at you. Or Brandon. Honestly." Still, I stood up and I gave him a huge push about two seconds before he was ready. He went tumbling in.

We floated together in a small little pod for a few minutes. It was much calmer, and a sense of peace and happiness washed over me. Brandon must have felt the same way.

He looked at me and said, "This is just like being back home. Just you and me hanging out in the pool, not with fifty other kids around. Now it's just this big lug-head who's butting in."

Joel made a move to dunk Brandon. I cried out, "No! Please! Just leave it. Don't start again." He looked startled and settled back down.

After a few more minutes of floating and gentle swimming, we decided to get out. A row of wooden lounge chairs sat down at the far end of the pool enclosure. Huge oak trees on the other side of the fence threw shade over most of the chairs. We laid our towels out on the chairs, leaned ourselves back, and rested in the shade. I was on the left, Joel was in the middle, and Brandon was on the right. Nobody spoke for some minutes. I could hear faint, intermittent shouts from the soccer game. Otherwise, the afternoon was still, silent, and scorching. The blazing heat seemed to scrub all sound from the shimmering air.

Brandon finally broke the companionable silence, saying, "We're gonna have to break up tomorrow, Alex. I mean, break up with the girls. I don't wanna leave camp with these expectations that Cathy and I are still a couple. She'll want to write letters back and forth and call each other. It's way too much hassle. It's better to do it tomorrow. Then we'll have a day of freedom on Friday."

"I don't know. It seems kind of cruel. We just asked them out, and now we turn around and give them the ol' heave-ho? It seems mean. I wouldn't want someone to treat me that way."

I heard Joel chuckle. Brandon was undeterred. "Oh, come on, Alex. Did you think you were signing up to be best friends for life? It's not like you were proposing to her when you asked her out! Going out at camp is just what you do. It's not 'until death we do part.' Grow some balls and break it off. You can be such a sissy sometimes."

Joel spoke up, a hard edge in his voice. "Hey, hey, hey! Enough with that! You should be glad your friend isn't a dickhead like you. He's got a point. These girls have feelings. Being nice is not the same thing as being a sissy. In fact, it's the other way around. It takes courage to be nice if it ends up making you look weak to some people."

Brandon burst out, "I know they have feelings, and if they suddenly had stronger feelings for someone else, we'd be toast! It's not like I am going to be mean! I'm going to totally make her feel good. I'll say I've been an awful boyfriend. I'll admit I haven't paid her enough attention, and I that want her to be free to go back home and find someone better than me. I've spent time thinking it all out. I'm going to do everything I can to make her feel good."

I couldn't imagine such bald-faced lying. "I think that's worse! Just tell her the truth. Just tell her you want to break up before camp ends. She'll see through your other lies. You shouldn't have asked her out if you didn't really want to go with her."

"Oh, well! Look who's talking, Mr. I'm-Gonna-Spare-All-The-Girls'-Feelings! You didn't really want to go out with Sarah. You two hardly speak. She thinks you're super hot, but you hardly look at her! She's noticed! She thinks you don't like her. She feels bad about herself because you asked her out! And now you act like *you're* better and nicer than *me*. Don't tell me not to hurt people's feelings! Take a look in the mirror. You're pretty good at it yourself!"

I lashed out, "Brandon, you're a jerk, do you know that? You're the one who pushed me into asking her out! You're the one who kept going on and on! I did it for you, alright? And now I feel awful about it. And now you're making fun of the fact that I actually care about other people's feelings! Not everything in the world is about you and your feelings. You can be the most selfish person I know."

Brandon got up so hard and fast his chair scraped across

the concrete. I thought he was going to jump across Joel and take me down. The venom in his voice shocked me as he said, "Well, listen you little prick. Who said I care what you think? Just shut up, Alex. Just shut the fuck up!"

Joel roared out, "Brandon, shut your fucking mouth! Now!" He jumped up and stood inches from Brandon. Joel shoved him hard, and Brandon began to stumble back. Joel reached out a hand to steady him, but Brandon shouted back, "Fuck off yourself."

I was petrified. My stomach felt like I was on a plane that was plunging to the earth from 40,000 feet in the sky. I saw Joel raise his hand, ready to strike Brandon across the face. I jumped up, too, and cried out, "God dammit, you two! Stop! Stop! This is ridiculous!"

Joel lowered his hand. Brandon slumped down in his chair. He buried his head in his hands and shook with loud sobs. Joel stood towering above him, every muscle taut and straining. Joel shook his head, as if coming back to himself. He seemed to change in a second. Every tensed muscle suddenly relaxed. He sat down and put his arm around Brandon's shoulders. He whispered softly, "God, I am so sorry. I just lost my temper. I'm so sorry. I'm so sorry, Brandon. I would never, ever hit you out of anger."

Through muffled sobs Brandon said, "Yes, you would have! If Alex hadn't shouted, you would have hit me. And I would have deserved it! I'm such an asshole! How can I say that to my best friend?"

I went over to Brandon's chair and sat right up against him. I put my hand on his leg and said, "It's both our faults. We're tired. It's hot. It's been a long week for us. And, Joel, too. We all just snapped. It's okay. It's all gonna be okay. I don't think you meant any of that."

He looked up. His face was mottled and red. "It's not okay. I screamed and cussed at you. I didn't mean to. It just all came out before I could even control it. You're the last person in the world I would ever hit or curse at. But then I go and do it anyway! I don't know why!" His voice broke again. "God, I'm so sorry. I'm so sorry."

"You didn't really curse at me. You just said 'prick.' I mean, I can say it over and over. Prick. Prick. Prick. Prick. See? It's no big deal, you big prick." I heard a small change in the tone of Brandon's sobbing. I carried on. "I mean, if you had said, 'Alex, kiss my grits,' then I'd really be mad at you! But we're best friends. Best friends fight sometimes. It'd be weird if we always got along. I mean, I know I'm perfect and always easy to get along with, but I don't mind putting up with you. I can let you be a prick and still like you!"

He looked up at me and smiled. I leaned in and gave him a big hug around his head. I could feel him shaking with laughter instead of sobs. I looked at Joel and winked. He reached over and patted my back. He mouthed silently, "Nice one. Nice one."

Brandon broke free of my hug and laid his hand on my thigh. He looked me in the eyes, in some way that seemed new, and said, "Man, you are the best friend I could ever have. I really am sorry. You deserve a better friend than me."

Joel spoke up, "No. He doesn't deserve or want a better friend than you; he just wants you to be a better friend to him. There's a big difference."

Even as Joel spoke, Brandon held my gaze. I thought about my conversation earlier with Joel, about how Brandon felt like he never measured up to his brothers. A deep well of compassion for my friend bubbled up inside me. I knew I had a sacred duty to him. I could be the one person in his life he could trust no matter what. My parents once told me I couldn't really fix the hurting parts of Brandon, but I knew I could do my best to not make his pain any worse. Like a doctor, I could at least do no harm.

I said, "You know we'll shout at each other again at some point, but I'm still your best friend. I always will be, and if you don't like that it will be humiliations galore for you!" I slid into my best Vizzini impersonation, lisp and all. "I mean, I can't compete with you physically, and you're no match for my brains."

Brandon didn't miss a beat; our minds were totally in synch. He turned into Westley and asked, "You're that smart?"

"Let me put it this way. Have you ever heard of Plato, Aristotle, Socrates?

"Yes."

"Morons!"

Brandon grabbed me with both arms, threw his head back, and shouted, "God, I love this guy! I. Love. This. Guy." He paused and smirked at Joel. He threw his head back again and said, "And this hippopotamic landmass here is not too bad either."

. . .

Brandon and I gracefully broke up with both girls the following morning. We kept it simple, no drama and no lies. Neither girl seemed overly bothered. I guess Brandon was right about that. I had expected sobs and tears. Sarah said she was going to break up with me the next day anyway. She said she was just trying to be nice by waiting.

She glared at me scornfully, saying, "But I guess you didn't think about that. You didn't think about doing the nice thing for me." I felt awful and tried to apologize. She stormed off before I could even finish. I knew I deserved that kind of treatment, though I was happy to escape without a scratch. Somehow it felt fitting. I was worried she would be the one left feeling bad, but I was the one who turned away in shame.

Despite the hound-dog mood that settled over me for a few hours after the break-up, one good thing came out of the whole mess: Brandon and I spent every waking second of the last two days together.

During free time on Friday afternoon, Brandon and I sat together on a swing beneath the shade of a small cluster of oak trees. An unopened sketch book sat in his lap, and I tucked my barely-read copy of *A Murder is Announced* between my right hip and the edge of the swing.

He turned a little, looked me in the eyes, and said, "I want to apologize again for what happened on Wednesday. I was way outta line. To be honest, I wasn't mad at you because you were wrong. I was mad at you because you were right. You have such a kind heart, and you're always thinking about other people's feelings. I have gone out with, like, ten or so girls at camp and school, and I never really think twice when I dump them." He paused and shook his head. "I mean, even that phrase is awful! I sound like an asshole when I talk about dumping a girl. Like she's a piece of trash or something. I just never realized how mean it was. You helped me see that. You help me be a better person, Alex."

"I'll be honest. I was scared. You switch from your normal self to outta control in seconds. I don't like not knowing when you might blow up at me." I couldn't believe what I was saying, but something in me told me I had to. He had to understand how I felt. "It doesn't change how much I want us to be best friends, but it does make me wonder if I am safe. I just can't handle that. I can't handle your screaming and cursing. And if you ever hit me, my parents would end our friendship in an instant. And I'm not sure I'd want to be around you if you hit me. Why set myself up for more of that?"

"God, Alex, I'd kill myself if I ever hit you. I don't think I could. I mean, I wouldn't if I was thinking straight and could control myself."

"Well, that's the point. You seem to lose control and you stop thinking. You don't know what you might do in that situation. And I don't want to walk around on eggshells with you."

"What does that mean?"

"I don't want to be around you never knowing when I might say or do the wrong thing and you'll blow up at me! If you hit me as hard as you could, you could really hurt me."

He went silent and hung his head. I saw a group of girls on their way to the pool for girls' swim time. I was pretty sure Cathy and Sarah were somewhere in that mob. Several heads swung our way, and I heard faint laughter drift back to us from across the wide field.

I reached over and put my hand on top of Brandon's hand where it rested on his leg. He flipped his hand over and laced his fingers through mine from below.

"How can I make you trust me? How could I convince you I'd never, ever hit you?"

"By never hitting me! And keeping your temper under control. By telling me you are angry or upset long before you feel like losing control!"

"You make it sound easy!"

"Well, no, I think it's actually the opposite. But are you willing to put in the kind of work it will take? Joel's mom's a counselor. Maybe you could talk to her and see if she has ideas about it."

He went silent again. I heard some voices back behind us, and I pulled my hand away from Brandon's.

He let out a long sigh and said, "I would see a million counselors if that's what it would take to be your friend and convince you I am serious about never hurting you."

"Well, I don't think it would take that many! You're not that messed up." I nudged his knee with mine. He smiled and leaned heavily into me. "I mean, maybe 999,999, but I think a million is too much."

"I deserve that. Heap on the insults! I deserve them all!"

"No, you don't. You don't deserve a single one. And anybody but me who insults you is gonna have to deal with me as a consequence." I glared at him, using my right fist to pound my left palm, looking as menacing as I could.

"Oh, God, Alex, don't! You'd make the worst villain in the history of humanity. Nobody ever feels threatened by you! Well, at least not threatened by your anger. Maybe your good looks and speed when running! But not your bulging muscles." He chuckled and reached over to squeeze my left bicep. "I mean, that is not intimidating, Mr. Praying-Mantis-Arm-Man! Not even a little! Just stand back and behold."

He flexed his right bicep. I reached over to stroke the mound of hard muscle. It was the first time I had touched him so intimately since camp started. I couldn't believe how good and right it felt. It was a billion times better than holding hands with Sarah!

He grinned and said, "Okay, that's enough. I don't want you to get in trouble. You never know who's hiding behind some tree somewhere."

We sat in silence for a few minutes, happy again in each other's easy presence. I had one more thing on my mind and asked, "Was there something else going on inside you when you got so mad? Did I do something to upset you without realizing it?"

"Honestly, no. Well, I mean, I did have something else on my mind, but I don't think I could even put it into words."

"Is it about me?"

"Well..." he hesitated and ran the tip of his pinky up and down the side of my leg in a gentle caress. "I mean, yes and no. It's about you but also about me. I don't know how to say it." He sighed and stared off into the far distance. I had a sense it was the wrong time to push him. He'd tell me in his own time.

He turned his head and smiled at me. I said, "Well, you know you can tell me anything, anytime."

He put his arm around my shoulder. "I know. I feel impossibly close to you. One day I'll try to put it all into words. One day..."

. . .

ii.

We got back to Houston a little after 3:00 on Saturday. I showered and went straight to bed. I didn't wake up until Sunday at 10:00. Mom and Dad let me sleep instead of going to church. We had a late breakfast, went for a walk in the park, and I was in bed again by 7:00 on Sunday evening.

Brandon and I slipped back into our summer routine within days. We both sensed our Arcadian summer was fading away too quickly by that point. Even though we had a full five weeks left, the days seemed cruelly numbered as we heard the oncoming rush of that freight train called 'The First Day of School' rumble our way.

Joel was true to his word. He switched to late afternoon and evening shifts at his job, and he became our all-around-Houston chauffeur in those waning weeks of summer. I say he became our chauffeur; the truth is, he became our third *amigo*. Not only did he drive us around, he stayed with us and joined in whatever we were doing. He was a bit like an older best friend, an older brother, and an impossibly cool young father all rolled into one.

Joel invited us over to his house the last few Friday mornings of the summer for a training session. He and his older brothers had turned the third bay of their family's spacious garage into a small gym. Brandon was in hog heaven when we went over. He wanted to add on as much weight as possible, but Joel kept him focused and steady. A few times, Brandon tried to push Joel to let him lift heavier weights or do something Joel said he wasn't ready for. Brandon always skated right to the edge, but one harsh look from Joel shut him up every time. Joel and I shared a few secret winks and sly smiles on those occasions.

On our second-to-last Friday morning together, Brandon and I were sitting side by side on a bench opposite from Joel as he rested between sets on another bench. As we sat there in the hot, humid garage, I happened to glance down at Brandon's lap. He had on an old pair of shorts that were just a little too small for him. I couldn't help but notice the bulge at Brandon's crotch. Sitting there, staring at Joel, I realized Brandon was as hard as I was. It left me dazed and confused.

I asked myself, 'Why is Brandon hard? Is he aroused by Joel for the same reasons I am? And if so, what was all the dating at camp all about?' I knew what I wanted to believe, but I dared not hope for too much.

Mrs. Marshall had to take Brandon to the dentist for a check-up and cleaning just after lunch that day. They left me alone on the deck. It was an impossibly sultry day in late August. I was miserable, even in the shade. I had just started *The Murder of Roger Ackroyd* and couldn't wait to find out why it was such a shocker when it was published in 1926. I decided to go in and continue reading upstairs.

I changed out of my sweaty clothes, cooled off under the ceiling fan, put on a fresh set of clothes, and stretched out on Brandon's bed. I looked up between chapters and caught sight of a stack of sketchbooks on Brandon's drawing table. He normally kept the table clear. He said he couldn't concentrate with clutter around him. He had a stash of old sketchbooks stacked in his closet, but he never asked if I wanted to look through them.

I stared at that stack of sketchbooks and wondered why he had brought them out. Did he plan to show me something? I considered if I should have a glance through them or leave them alone. Curiosity got the better of me, though I felt slightly uncomfortable. I got up off the bed, walked over to the table, and examined the cover of the top sketchbook. Brandon had dated it: *January 1 – February 25, 1987.*

I looked at some of the other covers. All of them had dates of varying lengths; some spanning just a few weeks and others spanning many months. His sketching seemed to come in waves and troughs. The books were not in any kind of order. This irked me, so I took a minute to arrange them chronologically. The first book started in March 1985.

I began leafing through the sketchbooks. The beautiful sketches made me feel instantly connected to Brandon. His stunning style was as familiar to me as his voice, his cheeky grin, and his strong body. Somehow, his sketches made me feel physically close to him. Something of him was in them.

I marveled as I traced the development of his skill and precision. The older sketches had a kind of childishness about them. They were still quite skillful and better than anything I could sketch. Yet, even if the books had not been dated, I could have easily lined them up in chronological order just by noticing the command he gained over his skill and technique as the months and years flew by.

I finally reached the last sketchbook: *June 8 – August 5, 1987*. It was the one he had with him at camp. He must have filled up the last few pages in the days after camp. Even though we often sat side by side on our favorite swing when he sketched at camp, I knew better than to peek or ask to see. He kept them hidden until he was ready to share them. It dawned on me suddenly: he hadn't shown me a drawing in a long time. Maybe a month or more.

I was shocked when I opened the book and saw the first page. I couldn't take in what I saw. It was me. I was on that first page, sitting by the side of the pool, head slightly turned to the viewer, with a playful grin and bright, happy eyes. I hadn't posed for that. I suppose he just saw me there in his mind's eye. It was exquisitely done.

I flipped the page. I stared at myself again. This time, I was sitting in my usual place on the deck, a copy of *The Body in the Library* in my hands. Across on the opposite page, I stood on the diving board, arms held aloft in a double-bicep pose. He had sketched my arms very generously. It didn't take much to imagine the grin he had on his face as he did so. I flipped another page. I lay on his bed, my head propped up on a pillow, looking at the viewer. This was how we often lay on his bed when talking, bodies fully stretched out, our heads just inches apart on our pillows. As I continued to turn the pages, I saw myself in drawing after drawing. I saw myself as Brandon saw me.

I felt a surge of joy! My beautiful friend had filled a book with sketches of me. It sparked a kind of feeling in me I couldn't begin to describe. A sensation like flying or floating; an excitement that felt like falling in love, at least the kind of love that almost-eighth graders could experience... except that I had already fallen in love months before, from the moment I stood across from Brandon as he talked a mile-a-minute and wiped cheap grape jelly off his bare arm.

Then I reconsidered: perhaps this wasn't the feeling of *me* falling in love but the first glimmer of hope that *Brandon* had fallen in love with me. Was that the overriding emotion I felt? The first, unexpected, and impossibly wild hope that he might love me, too? And love me in the way I loved him?

I heard the rumble of the garage door below. I raced to set the sketchbooks back on the drawing table. Then I realized I had left them in a neat, chronological stack – the exact opposite of how I found them. I heard the back door open and slam shut. In a frenzied panic, I shuffled the books and left them in a haphazard stack, their spines at various angles. I think that's how I found them! I heard pounding steps rush up the stairs.

"Where are you, sorry-ass loser-man? I'm just going to pee," Brandon shouted from the landing. "I'm so ready to swim, and I'm gonna drown your skinny ass." I heard his laughter trail off down the hall.

. . .

Brandon spent the next night at our apartment, the last sleepover at my place for the summer. It had been an emotional day for me, and Brandon kept asking if I was okay. He was worried he had done something to make me mad or upset. 'Just the opposite,' I said to myself, 'just the opposite, Brandon.' Still, I was confused, and I must have seemed distant as I sorted through my thoughts and feelings from the day before.

Before Brandon and I started a movie, the four of us sat on the balcony, looking out over the vast metropolis as dusk settled and lights came on. Mom and Dad kissed us both goodnight, told us not to stay up too late, and took our ice cream bowls inside. Brandon and I sat in silence for several moments.

Brandon scooted his chair up close to me and draped his legs over my knees. "I know we still have a week to go, but I just gotta say it's been an amazing summer. I mean, the best summer of my life. I never thought summer could be so much fun. I just wanna go back to June and start all over again. I'd do it all again." He paused and looked sheepishly at me. "Except for the pool scene at camp. I don't wanna do that again. Never, ever."

"I know. I never thought I'd ever have a summer like this in my life. I think back to last summer, and it seems like a different me. I don't even know that little kid who spent the whole summer inside with his nose stuck in a book."

He chuckled. "I'm glad to know I have expanded your world so much. You did need to get out some more! No more going back to life before Brandon! You have to admit, as much as I drive you crazy, your life is better with me in it." He sighed and a serious expression came over his face. "I think your quiet mood today infected me a bit. I've been thinking all evening about school and how different it's going to be for us in ten days. We're gonna go from four or five sleepovers a week to maybe two or three a month! If we're lucky! If my dad doesn't go ape-shit crazy the first time I get a B or C on a test."

"Well, we just have to make next week the best week of the whole summer. I promise I'm okay. I'm just tired. I'll be my normal brilliant and funny self by Monday. I promise."

"Good! That's the only reason I put up with you: because you're brilliant and funny. I mean, if it came down to your arms, I would have dumped you a long time ago." He snickered and reached out to squeeze my arm. "You know I'm just kidding. You're the best person I know. Seriously, Alex, I wouldn't change a thing about you."

Our last week together was pure bliss, and summer came to an end just as it started: two inseparable friends; our constant, laugh-a-minute, back-and-forth bickering; long morning runs; matching our wits against Ms. Christie; lazy afternoons in the pool; quoting our way through *The Princess Bride* for the twentieth time; talking late into the night, only inches apart; waking to each other's impossibly close presence.

CHAPTER 8

FALL 1988

The dreaded weight of back-to-school normality fell upon me hard. My teachers sensed we had all gone soft over the long summer break. They smelled blood in the water and circled around us with giddy delight. Eighth grade seemed to bring a disproportionate increase in the amount of homework. I was overwhelmed at times the year before, but the new workload was a blizzard compared to seventh grade's light shower of gentle snow flurries. In desperation, I dropped out of chess club by the third week of school. I kept up with the violin and orchestra. My parents said I needed a creative outlet. If I had to drop something from my schedule, chess club was the obvious choice.

Brandon and I spoke on the phone every Thursday evening, and we saw each other at church most Sunday mornings. We managed a few sleepovers in September and October, but I missed him like an absent limb most days.

. . .

The Friday before Halloween we got a special treat from our parents: permission to go watch Joel's football team play their crosstown rival, followed by a rare two-night sleepover at

Brandon's. Brandon had been toeing the line at school and at home. He managed to pull off all As on his first two report cards. He was actually a really good student. He just had to work twice as hard as his brothers. He thought that meant he wasn't as smart as they were.

I kept telling him he was just as smart. "Brandon, you are smart. Honestly! It's just that your brain works in a different way. You get to the same place in the end, just by a different way." He never seemed entirely convinced that was a compliment.

Will and Brandon picked me up a little after 5:00. It was one of the first genuinely cool nights that fall. The air was crisp and clear. A recent cold front had pushed all the usual Houston humidity far out into the Gulf. It promised to be an amazing weekend, a much-needed reminder that life was more than schoolwork and violin practice.

We made our way west down traffic-choked Holcombe as the city lights came on in the quickly descending autumnal dusk. When we got to the stadium, Will laid down the rules.

"Okay, losers. Dad says I have to keep you two in sight all the time. That doesn't mean you have to hang around me the whole time. You just need to sit somewhere lower down in the bleachers from me. Don't go wandering off. This game is a big rivalry, and there will be people everywhere. I know you're not third graders, so don't act like it. Don't embarrass me!"

I looked over at the stands and saw they were mostly full. Will went on, "So don't go off by yourself. Stay together all the time. If you want to go somewhere together, look up and get my attention first. There's only two places you can go – bathroom and concession stand. They're right next to each other. Got it?"

We nodded. Will had a touch of Mr. Marshall about him which I found distinctly annoying. "And if you go off and don't come back in five minutes, I am coming after you." He thumped Brandon's chest. "And I'll be telling Dad later, too."

Will smirked at me and said, "One word from me, and you, my loser brother's friend, will be in your own sad little room the next two nights. And my moron brother will be crying into his pillow. Stay close! Don't wander off! Do whatever I say!" He glared at Brandon. "Got it, dickhead?"

Neither of us said anything. We knew he had us in his crosshairs. We fell behind him as he joined his friends, and we made our way up to the ticket gates.

Brandon leaned close to me and whispered, "He's like Inspector Gadget meets Hitler, with a little of the Six-Fingered Man thrown in for good measure." I snorted and tried to stifle a full-out laugh. Brandon lowered his voice even more and said, "I mean, I could actually kick his ass. I weigh more than he does even though he's four years older than me. He might be a few inches taller, but I could knock his teeth out. And he knows it."

"Well, don't! You can kick his ass sometime when our sleepover is not at stake. Then you can go for it!" I grinned up at Brandon. "In fact, I'll hold him down."

"Now that's a plan, my little attack dog." He tossed his arm around my shoulder and barked madly. Will looked back, scowling. Brandon shut up fast.

We found a place in the bleachers about five rows lower than Will and his friends. Brandon explained the plays in detail. I pretended to be interested and nodded along with regularity. He saw through my pretense.

"So, when they finally get someone across the line with the ball, the rest of the team comes, and everyone jacks off together."

I came to with a start. "What? My, God… no, they don't."

"Oh, so you were half-way listening."

"Sorry, Brandon. My eyes glaze over when you go on and on about sports. It's like I got born without the sports gene. I just hear the Charlie Brown teacher voice when you drone on about football or baseball."

"What do you mean you got no sports gene? You have the running gene for sure. And if I have to drag you kicking and screaming, you'll learn to love your weightlifting genes." He chuckled. "Joel keeps telling me I should play football next year. Just to give it a try. But I don't know. They don't always let you play in high school if you didn't in junior high. But Joel says the coach would put me on the freshman team in a heartbeat. What do you think? I value your advice more than anybody else I know."

I shrugged. "Well, do it if you want to. But would you really enjoy it? I mean, it seems like football is something guys only do if their dad makes them or if the guy himself really loves it. I don't think your dad cares either way, and I know for a fact you don't love it deep down. It's not like you go around thinking about football all the time."

"Oh, do you know that for a fact? Do you really know what I love? Do you know me that well, Alexander N. Kennedy?"

I sensed a shift in the atmosphere between us. I paused for a second, collecting my thoughts and gathering my courage, and finally said, "As a matter of fact, I do know what you love. I know you better than you think I do." Brandon's secret drawings of me reeled through my mind like a film on a screen at the Cineplex Odeon.

He smiled and said, "Well, well, well! What does that mean? How do you know what I love?" He threw his arm around my shoulder. I noticed several nearby teenagers look our way. I wasn't sure what they had heard or what they were thinking. It was so loud with the band blasting away, the crowd's constant cheering, and the booming voice on the PA system. Surely, they couldn't hear us, could they?

I pulled myself away from Brandon a bit and tried to calm my own racing pulse. He didn't seem to notice; instead, he leaned in closer to me.

I felt flustered with the sudden talk of love, knowing what I longed to say but could never imagine myself saying. I said,

"I just mean that football has never seemed that important to you. Yes, you are good at it. Yes, you could probably take down players two or three years older than you. But I don't think it's something you really care about. Not like sketching or running with me and Dad." I hesitated. "I know for a fact you like hanging out with me more than you like playing football or anything else. You might have to give up a lot of things you really love to do in order to do something you only halfway care about."

"God, you're right. I hadn't thought about it that way."

"Plus, I'm sure they start practicing weeks before school starts. We'd have to kiss a big chunk of next summer good-bye."

"Well, that settles it!" He threw back his head and hollered, "To hell with football! I just want you, Alex!"

Several heads turned our way again, but nobody said anything. Brandon had that effect on people. Most other teens our age, and even older ones, tended to back down a bit once they got a good look at Brandon.

A few minutes later Brandon suggested we get a drink. He ran up the bleachers to tell Will what we were doing. While he was gone, I asked some guys next to us if they would save our seats. They agreed, but their smiles didn't seem very genuine. I thought I detected a hint of malice in their eyes, but I didn't have time to over-analyze anything.

Brandon raced down the bleachers and hollered at me to follow as he passed. We made our way to the concession stand underneath the bleachers. Out of the corner of my eye, I noticed Will and two of his friends coming our way.

Brandon leaned in and whispered, "Will is keeping an eye on us but trying to be cool about it. He's gonna stay close but not actually acknowledge us. Should we ignore him or embarrass him?"

"Seriously? He's got the power to ruin our plans. Let's play nice, okay?"

"Good call, man! I knew I kept you around for a reason!" He put his arm around my shoulder as we stood in line and slowly inched our way up to the counter. Will and his friends were several places back in line. As we started to walk away with our drinks, he called out, "Hey, Brandon. Wait for me over there by the ramp. I need to tell you something."

We walked away, weaving through the rowdy crowd. I became aware too late of the two guys from the stands walking behind us. They were getting incredibly close.

I heard a word ring out.

"Faggots."

A sharp, crushing pain exploded in the center of my back. I lost control of my drink, and it went flying from my hand, as if in slow motion, drenching an older couple just in front of us. I stumbled forward, off balance and shocked, and I fell straight into the older woman. I tried to catch myself so I wouldn't crush her beneath me. I felt a searing pain in my palms as they grated across the pavement, and a deafening thud filled my ears as my head crashed down.

At the same time, I heard a torrent of words and sounds behind me. Angry words ricocheted around. "Why don't you homo faggots go somewhere else?" "I'm gonna rip your fucking mouth off." "Brandon, stop." "Go get security." "Brandon, enough!" "This boy is hurt." And along with these words, other sounds remain deeply lodged in my memory: The sound of bone on bone. Running feet. Grunting. Groaning. A shrill whistle piercing the air.

Then it all went black.

. . .

I regained consciousness in a fog of pain and confusion. My head hurt fiercely. At first, I couldn't focus my eyes. I only saw blurred shapes and watery colors. I blinked and blinked again. Slowly, my focus sharpened, but my eyes hurt with the effort.

I was in a small hut of some kind, lying on a tall table like the one in the school nurse's office. Brandon stood next to me on my right, his hand on my shoulder. Will stood on the other side of me. A lady with an official looking name tag stood next to Brandon.

"Alex, I'm Nurse Watson. Do you know where you are?"

"At Joel's football game."

"Alex, do you know the date?" I told her.

"Do you remember what happened before you lost consciousness?" I nodded hesitantly.

"Alex, how many fingers am I holding up?" I told her.

"Alex, follow my finger as I move it back and forth. Stop if you feel dizzy." I managed to track with her finger. I felt a little dizzy. My head and back throbbed with pain.

"Do you take any medications? Any blood thinners?" I shook my head.

Nurse Watson patted my arm and said, "I've called your parents and an ambulance. They'll both be here soon. How badly do you hurt?"

"My head really hurts. And my back." I paused and looked down at my bandaged hands, as if they didn't belong to me. "And my hands sting." I teared up.

She patted me on the chest. "Yes, you took a nasty fall. You hit your head on the concrete. I hear you were twisting as hard as you could to avoid knocking other people over. I think your heroics actually caused you to fall harder." She paused and smiled. "You poor, poor boy. You poor, brave boy. I don't think they'll keep you long at the hospital, but it's better to be safe than sorry when you've hit your head on concrete like that." She looked at her watch. "They really should be here soon. Rest your eyes, sweetie. Keep the light out of them. It will help with your headache."

I closed my eyes as she turned to Will and said, "I'm going to step out and see if the ambulance is here. One of our counselors wants to meet Alex's parents at the front gates.

Since you know what they look like, please go up there with her. Her name is Mrs. Barlow. She's right outside. Go with her to meet his parents, and then bring them back here. Okay?"

I opened my eyes a fraction to glance at Brandon as he stroked my arm and fidgeted beside me. His face was tense and strained. Nurse Watson smiled at him and said, "And you, Mr. Best-Friend-of-the-Year, you can stay here, but don't get Alex excited. No laughing. No getting up. Stay calm and quiet. Both of you."

Brandon gave her his most winning smile and said, "Will do! But he's tougher than he looks." He looked down at me and winked.

When the nurse and Will left, Brandon grinned at me. "I beat the shit out of that guy. His friend had to pull me off him. And Will had to pull me off *him*. I was just in a blind rage. I just wanted to hurt those assholes for hurting you."

I sighed and closed my eyes. "I don't know if that makes me feel better or worse. Did you really hurt the other guy? I don't think he did anything. Just that one guy kicked me, I think."

"Oh, God, what does it matter? He called you a faggot and kicked you to the ground! He deserved what he got! And more! I was so pissed when I realized what happened!"

Even with the paralyzing brain fog, I remembered one thing clearly: my attacker said "Faggots." Plural. But I wasn't up for an argument.

"I just saw red when you went flying forward! I spun on those guys before they even realized what happened." He was breathing heavily, and I could hear the anger in his voice. "Nobody picks on you without me doing something about it. My job is to keep you safe, got it?"

"Thanks, but I'm okay now. It's going to be okay." I lowered my voice. "I just need you to be quiet for a minute. The noise makes my head even worse."

"Oh, God! Okay! Sorry, buddy! I didn't think about the

noise." He squeezed my shoulder even harder and took my hand in his other hand.

A second later the door opened, and my parents came rushing in. They seemed relieved when they saw me. I wondered later if they had imagined me in a much worse state. No telling what Will had said to them on the walk from the main gates to the first aid shed.

Brandon filled them in on more details, and I closed my eyes. The lights were too bright. Brandon was too loud. The pain was too intense. It was all too much. I just wanted to go home and cry. And I never wanted to hear that hateful word again.

. . .

The ER doctor at St. Luke's sent us home a little after 2:00. She said I would be fine with plenty of sleep and complete bed rest all weekend. Brandon initially insisted on going to the hospital with us, but my parents sent him home with Will once I was in the ambulance. As much as I loved him, I was thankful he didn't come to the hospital.

After my parents kissed me goodnight and shut my bedroom door sometime around 2:45, I began to think about the night's events. Sadness descended like a dense fog, and not just because of the physical pain. The safe, seemingly impregnable cocoon I had lived in for so long broke open with that swift kick to my back. The guys who attacked me didn't know me. They simply saw something between Brandon and me they didn't like. They followed us. They targeted us and shouted "Faggots."

The word rang out over and over again in my aching head. Its lingering echoes birthed a sense of fear in me I had never known before. My stomach felt tight. My heart raced. The truth was out in the open. Someone had noticed. Two people had noticed; maybe more. Like some ancient genie asleep for many centuries, what I knew for so long but never completely understood burst into my awareness: I was gay. In most people's eyes, I was a faggot.

I woke with that word still ringing in my ears. My head hurt, but I also felt more clearheaded. I glanced up at the clock on the wall to my left. It was 8:45. I had lived to see Saturday morning. My eyes drifted down to the nightstand to the left of my bed. There was an old-fashioned school bell, the type with a long wooden handle, sitting on the nightstand. A small note rested in front of the bell, propped up at an angle. It read: "Alex, do not get out of bed on your own. Ring this bell when you wake up. Love, Dad and Mom." I sat up slightly, took the bell by the handle, and gave it a soft ring.

My parents must have had on their sonar ears. They were at the door within seconds. They came in quietly, without turning on the overhead light. Mom partially raised the blinds on the west facing window. Diffuse morning light illuminated their faces. They looked worried, relieved, happy, and sad all at once.

Dad pulled my desk chair close to the right side of the bed and sat down, laying his hand on my chest. Mom sat on my bed, wedged up close to my hips. She rested her hand on my leg.

Dad spoke first. "How are you feeling, Alex? Better?"

"Yeah, I think so. My head still hurts. And my hands. But I feel clearer. I felt like I was underwater last night. Everything felt muddled and muffled. It's all a blur now. It's like I remember it, but it seems like it was ten years ago." I yawned. "But I am still very tired."

Mom patted my leg. "Well, sweetie, you can keep sleeping as long as you like. Do you want something to eat or drink?"

I shook my head. I felt a little nauseous. "No, nothing sounds good."

Dad replied, "That's completely normal. It'll pass soon. I know you don't want anything to eat, but how about some water or some apple juice mixed with Sprite? I don't want you to get dehydrated."

"Maybe both. Then I can sip a little of each and see what tastes better."

Mom hopped up and left the room.

Dad looked into my eyes. "We love you so much, Alex. We want to keep you safe and sheltered forever, but we know you have to grow up. We want to talk to you about what happened and how you're feeling inside. But not now. It can wait until you're ready."

Mom reappeared with two glasses on a tray. She set the tray on the nightstand. "Can we help you up to go to the bathroom?"

"I think I'm okay. I just want to take a few sips and go back to sleep. Maybe just the water for now." Mom picked up one of the glasses and brought it up to my lips so I could suck through the straw. I nodded when I'd had enough.

Dad leaned in and kissed my forehead. "When you wake up later, ring the bell. You might get dizzy if you get up quickly, and I don't want you falling. Once you get up a few times without being dizzy, we'll know you're okay."

Mom kissed both my cheeks. She lingered close for a second and said, "My beautiful, precious boy. I'm so sorry they hurt you."

I teared up and began sobbing. My face, awash in tears, twisted in anguish as the delayed shock from the previous evening surfaced in full. My parents began to cry, too, but they didn't say anything. They simply let me cry myself to sleep, sitting close by on either side of my bed.

I woke again around 4:15. My parents spent the next couple of hours tending to me in their kind, quiet way. I was back in bed by 7:30 and soon fast asleep. As they left the room that evening, they told me we'd all stay in from church on Sunday. I was relieved. I wasn't sure I wanted to see Brandon. I wondered why. Was I angry at him? Did I feel ashamed? Was

I uncertain how he would respond to me? It felt like my best friend had become a complete stranger, as if some impossibly wide canyon had opened up between us overnight. Something seemed to have hardened inside me, and strange new emotions left me feeling uncertain and frightened.

I felt almost normal by Sunday morning. My appetite returned. I had a light breakfast of oatmeal and orange slices. Mom made chicken quesadillas and guacamole for lunch. My headache was gone by then. The scrapes on my palms were less red and inflamed, though Dad said I'd need to keep them bandaged for at least a week. It would make playing the violin and writing at school impossible. Dad and Mom both agreed I should stay home for at least two days. Dad had already made arrangements with the lab so he could stay home with me.

We had a light supper of apples, peanut butter, and yogurt. Afterwards, we sat together on the couch in the living room. Dad was at one end. I rested my head in his lap. Mom was halfway down the couch, and I draped my legs over her lap. Dad laid his hand tenderly on my head. Mom's arms rested above my knees.

She started the conversation. "Alex, are you up for a talk? Your dad and I want to talk to you about something."

I nodded.

"First, Brandon has called about a hundred times." She chuckled. "No, not really. He called a few times yesterday when you were sleeping. We told him we'd tell you he called. We asked him not to call back today. I made sure he knew we were not angry with him. We just wanted you to have plenty of peace and quiet today. And Joel called twice to check on you. He said he'd call you later this week. I think he wants to come by.

"We called Kevin just to let him know you'd be out of school a few days... so he wouldn't worry. We didn't tell him much – just that you'd had an accident but would make a full recovery. He said he'll call you soon, too. We'll call the school tomorrow morning and get your absences sorted for the next few days. Oh, and Abdul called about thirty minutes after we called Kevin. I guess Kevin passed the news on. Abdul's mother offered to bring some food over. We told her we thought we'd be okay, but it was sweet of them to offer. You've got a lot of good friends in your life."

"Thanks for being my secretaries. Sorry if you've been overwhelmed by all this."

Dad shook his head and said, "Nonsense! It's what parents do. We just wish none of this happened."

Mom cleared her throat a bit. "When we met Will at the stadium gates, he told us what happened. He told us that the boy who kicked you yelled out the word 'Faggots.' Do you remember this, sweetie?"

Tears pooled in my eyes, but I was determined not to cry. "Yeah, I remember. I think he yelled it at both of us but kicked me because I'm smaller. I guess I look like an easy target."

Dad looked down into my eyes. "You are not an easy target, Alex. None of this is your fault. You didn't do a damn thing to deserve this. Got it? This was not your fault. And it wasn't Brandon's fault." I wasn't so sure about that last part.

He continued, "Do you remember the couple you fell onto?" I nodded. "They were at the first aid shed when we arrived. The woman is an Algebra teacher at Joel's high school. She told us she knew both of the boys involved. It seems they get in trouble often and start fights for the smallest reasons. She wanted to make sure we knew you had nothing to do with starting what happened. We wouldn't have believed her if she said otherwise!"

He paused and looked over at Mom. She took up the thread of conversation. "Sweetie, we want to ask you some questions. We want you to be honest with us, but we also want to give you the freedom to not answer if you don't want to. Okay?"

A wave of anxiety swept over me. I had an idea where this was going. I knew I was impossibly safe with my parents, but

I also knew my world would never be same if I answered honestly the question I thought was coming my way. I never for a moment doubted my parents' love for me. I knew they would love me just the same whether I was gay or straight or confused. On another level, however, I knew there was no turning back if the words 'I'm gay' ever came out of my mouth.

She took a deep breath before asking, "Do you know what the word faggot means? Do you know it's a hateful way of speaking to someone who is gay?"

I nodded.

"Do you know why those boys might have said that to you?"

I nodded again.

"Do you think they were saying that to you alone or also to Brandon?"

I shrugged.

She paused, and there was a slight tremor in her voice. "Alex, do you think you're gay?"

The apartment seemed unnaturally quiet. I couldn't hear the usual hum of the refrigerator from the kitchen or the constant buzz of traffic noise drifting back from Main and Fannin. I could only hear the pounding of my pulse against my temple. Maybe it was because of my injury or maybe it was because of Mom's question, but that pulse inside my head seemed deafening. Even if I spoke, I wasn't sure I'd say the right thing because I wouldn't be able to hear myself speak. I remembered the long, embarrassed silence in the kitchen at church on that first Sunday morning when Brandon finished quizzing me over Dolly Parton and her tits. It was the same sensation all over again. A pause that passed in a few seconds somehow seemed to last an eternity.

I nodded my head and said softly, "Yes, I'm gay."

A surprising sense of peace washed over me. It was easier to say than I had imagined. I quickly glanced between my parents' faces, and I sensed nothing but the unconditional love

I had known for as long as I could remember.

Dad said, "Alex, we love you no matter what. You're our son, and nothing about you will ever change our love for you. Do you know that? Do you believe me?" I nodded, and a cascade of tears flowed uncontrollably. "You're the kindest, bravest, and most thoughtful boy we could ever hope for. You are everything we could ever want in a son."

Mom said, "We're here right beside you. We're here for you no matter what. We're on your side with nothing but love." She paused and seemed to choose her next words carefully. "Alex, do you think you have fallen in love with Brandon? Do you feel like you want to be more than just best friends with him?"

I didn't think I could speak through my tears, but an answer came from deep inside. "Yes, I think I have. He's my best friend, but I don't think about him the same way I think about Eric or Kevin or Abdul."

Dad asked, "Do you think he might feel the same way about you? Do you think he sees you as something more than his best friend? Is there any chance he's gay, too?"

That was where I felt lost at sea. As our friendship grew over the previous year or so, I noticed more and more how Brandon acted differently with me compared to the way I saw other friends act with each other. Not many guys threw their arms around their friend's shoulder as often as Brandon did with me. None of the guys at church sat so close to their friends in the pews. None of the guys at camp preferred to sit with their best friend on a swing or bench instead of playing sports. None of the guys at church seemed to take as much notice of Joel and Ben. I couldn't imagine any of my friends at school patting my abs or whistling if I took off my shirt in front of them. I couldn't imagine any of my friends at school filling a whole sketchbook with secret drawings of me or any other guy. He was different, no doubt, but was it the same kind of different as me?

I shrugged. "Maybe. Sometimes it seems he does like me the same way, but he's Brandon! He goes out with girls at camp and tells me I should, too. Sometimes he acts one way, and sometimes he acts another way. I don't know what he thinks or feels. Sometimes he's a total mystery to me. I don't know! I mean, I just don't know how he really feels about me."

Mom said, "Maybe he's confused, too. Maybe he doesn't know what he feels or whether he should feel the way he feels. Being a teenager is tough enough for everyone. If you have conflicting thoughts about whether you like boys or girls, it makes it even harder. And just think: there's nobody at his house he can talk to about this. He's all alone."

We went silent for a minute, the truth of Mom's statement weighing heavily on each of us. Dad sighed and said, "You look exhausted. You've been through so much in the last forty-eight hours. You've been so brave. Can we talk just a little more?"

I nodded.

"Your mom and I don't think there's anything wrong with being gay. You know that! Think of all the times we've had David and Nick up for dinner. We are just as comfortable around them as we are around all our neighbors. We let them babysit you a few times when your grandparents or Aunt Karen couldn't! You know how we feel about the mayor and her advocacy for the gay community. We are on your side, but we'd be neglecting our duty to keep you safe if we acted like everyone in Houston thinks like we do. They don't, and you learned that the hard way Friday night."

Mom chimed in. "Sweetie, you don't have to be ashamed of being gay. There's nothing wrong with you, but your dad is right. You have to be careful and aware. Nick and David are grown men, but they are very careful in public. They don't kiss and hold hands except in a few safe spaces. I wish you could just be you no matter where you are, but that's not the world we live in."

Dad said, "It's really important you find some way to keep

Brandon in check, whether he thinks of you as a friend or something more. We never intentionally eavesdrop on your conversations, but he can be so loud sometimes. We heard him teasing you to take your shirt off and admiring your abs when he came for his first sleepover. You two can't do that kind of stuff out in public anywhere.

"There have been a few mornings when you two lift weights after we run–" he hesitated, seemingly unsure of his words, "– when Brandon had his hands all over you... and he had this look on his face... like he could have kissed you in a heartbeat. It's something that can look both ways to someone passing by: either two boys goofing around or maybe something more. Whatever went on between you two at the football game attracted the wrong kind of attention from those two guys. We don't want that to happen again. You've got to be vigilant for the two of you."

I nodded. I knew they were right. I didn't doubt for a second that they fully affirmed my growing understanding of being gay, but I also knew they had a better sense than I did about the prejudice and danger that lurked around many corners in Houston. I knew they were trying to walk a fine line for my sake: they wanted me to know I was both normal and different.

Mom said, "You look worn out, sweetie. We'll have to talk more, but how about an early bedtime again? Are you ready?"

I let them see me to my room after I brushed my teeth. They rarely both tucked me in and kissed me goodnight. Perhaps they realized that night was the last time they would have the old bedtime routine with their impossibly innocent boy Alex. The boy who would wake up the next morning would be someone altogether new to them: their only son Alex who was starting to navigate his way toward maturity as a gay teenager and man.

· · ·

A little after 7:00 on Monday evening, Mom stuck her head in my room. Brandon was on the phone. My heart leapt a little, but I also felt some anxiety. I wasn't sure what to expect.

I ran down the hall and picked up the phone in the kitchen. "Hey, Brandon. I'm glad you called."

"Oh, my God, Alex. It's you! It's you! You're alive! Nobody would let me speak to you or come see you for days! I thought you were dead, and they were just waiting to break the news later. Are you okay? Are you in pain? Are you still dizzy? Are you still bandaged up? Does your back hurt where that asshole kicked you?" He paused, breathless. I sensed he was nervous. Did he think I might be mad at him?

"No, I'm okay, mostly. I'm still sore in my back, and I won't be writing or playing the violin for a while. But I'm gonna live and move on."

Brandon let out a loud sigh. "I swear, that dickhead could have broken your back or something. That's why I beat the shit out of him. Nobody messes with you! Got it? I mean nobody. I'll rip their heads off if I ever see those two guys again."

"I'm okay. What good will it do now? It's all over. I'm not made of glass. I'll recover. If you get sent to some jail for violent kids, how is that gonna help? And aren't you going to be in some kind of trouble for all this?"

I had been worried about what might happen to Brandon. Could those boys' parents press charges? Could Brandon get expelled from school? I had no idea what kind of consequences he might face for defending me.

"No, nobody's going to send me to juvie for defending you! They should be the ones thrown in jail. I wanna beat the shit out of those guys again and then send them to juvie! And then kick their asses some more when they get out!" He snickered.

"Okay! I get it."

"My dad did have to talk with my principal and one of the school counselors about it all. Then all four of us had this long meeting. Everyone understood why I did what I did. Nobody was upset that I defended you, but they all said I went too far. So, I have to do some school-based service, like cleaning up after lunch and picking up trash outside. I've got to do a total of 50 hours. I also have to go to this group session with my counselor at school." He sighed. "It's, like, a group for all the school misfits. I guess that means I'm a misfit, too, huh? I have to go and talk about ways I can be less angry. Maybe it'll help. Who knows…"

He paused. I wasn't sure what I wanted to say, if anything. I let the silence linger.

He went on, "I mean, do you think I'm an angry person? I only get angry when people are assholes. I wouldn't have started something with those guys, not for a million dollars, if they hadn't kicked you. Like, even if they had just called you a name, I wouldn't have started a fight. I just would've kept on going. I would never, ever start a fight. Do you believe me?"

"Yes. I do believe you. I think you are brave and strong, and I am glad you were there to protect me. I don't even want to think about what would have happened if you hadn't been there. I just worry about you. What if you get angry, even for good reasons, but end up in a situation where you're in over your head? What happens one day if you get mixed up in a fight with someone stronger than you who has a knife or a gun?"

He went silent again, but I wanted to lighten the mood. "There is a shortage of perfect chests in the world. It would be a pity to damage yours." I swear I could hear the frown on the other end of the line turn to a smile.

"Ha! Good one, Alex. But you forgot, dumbass, it's 'breasts,' not 'chests.'"

"I know, you even-dumber-ass. I was changing it on purpose to make it funny because you don't have breasts. Or have you not noticed?"

"Wow, that kick and fall didn't do much to soften you up! You are, like, knives out with your best ass-kicking friend." He chuckled. "Seriously, are you gonna be okay?"

"Yes, I promise. I'll be okay. I'll be at home tomorrow, and then we'll see about Wednesday. I don't want to miss too much school and get too far behind."

"Um, it's actually impossible for you to get behind! You're so far ahead, you'd have to miss, like, two years of school to get behind. You're in Algebra II, for crying out loud. I'm in plain ol' eighth grade math! You're literally two years ahead of me. And I bet your school's version of Algebra II is the college version. You are *not* going to fall behind in two days. Sheesh, man!" He snorted and chuckled.

"Yeah, well. I just don't want to miss a bunch and then have to stay late for several days when I go back."

"How about coming over this weekend? My parents said you could."

"I don't think I can this weekend. Dad said it's really important I take it slow and easy. Plus, I feel like going to bed at 7:30 every night. I am exhausted already. I don't think I'd be much fun. But I did already ask about next weekend; my parents said I could stay over at your house if your parents say yes. Ask them and tell me Thursday."

"Thursday? Dude, I'm calling you tomorrow night and every night this week! I gotta make sure you're okay."

"Well, don't get in trouble with your dad over it. I don't want him to cancel our next sleepover because of a few extra phone calls."

"No way, man. He thinks it's very mature of me to call you and check on you. He said so tonight. He said, 'I'm glad to see you thinking about someone else for a change, Brandon. It's a fine idea to check on your friend. Just don't tire him out. He may not want to listen to your non-stop gab.'"

"Ah, that's gonna be my new line: 'your non-stop gab'! I love it."

"Smartass!"

"Well, thanks for taking up your cross and suffering for

my sake!"

"Of course, any time. Any time. So, talk to you tomorrow?"

"It's a deal, non-stop gab and all!"

. . .

November passed in a blur. I quickly caught up at school. My wounds healed, though it was painful to hold a pen or pencil for several weeks. I missed a whole month of violin practice and orchestra. Brandon and I made up for the sleepover we missed on the night of the attack when I spent two nights at his house the weekend before Thanksgiving.

I dreamed about the attack several times in November. I woke up each time with a racing pulse and covered in sweat. I would hear that word, 'faggots,' over and over, and, in a kind of echoing response, I would hear the crack of bones as Brandon let loose on the hoodlum who kicked me. I woke up from those dreams with an erection every time, feeling equally confused and relieved.

I talked with Dad and Mom a few more times about my feelings toward Brandon. They listened patiently to my ramblings, never pressuring me to say more than I was ready to reveal. I got the sense they thought Brandon felt as strongly about me as I did about him, but I was still unsure. I started thinking about a way to sound him out, but I backed off quickly each time I came close to opening up to Brandon.

CHAPTER 9

Brandon spent the first weekend of Christmas break at our apartment. His family planned to leave for Nashville on Tuesday, December 20, and we didn't think we'd see one another until December 27. His weekend with my family was our chance to celebrate the holiday all together, even if a little early.

We sat close together on the couch in the living room on Saturday night, shoulder to shoulder, leg against leg. He sighed and said, "I can't believe what I just sat through for your sake! I can't believe it. I feel like you are milking my concern for you for all it's worth. I mean, that attack was almost two months ago." He poked me in the ribs. "The things I do for you, Alex N. Kennedy!"

"Oh, come on! I saw your toe tapping, and I heard you humming along. Even the scroogiest of hearts can't resist the Muppets and John Denver singing Christmas carols."

My parents found a battered VHS copy of *A Christmas Together* at Half Price Bookstore a few years previously, and I discovered it in my stocking on Christmas morning in 1984. Apparently, I had sat mesmerized when it first came on TV when I was four. I hadn't actually planned to show it to

Brandon, but he made the mistake of noticing it and laughing at it earlier in the evening. Then all I had to do was tee him up like a golf ball. He was his own worst enemy at times!

I said, "Get over it. This is payback for making me watch *Ernest Saves Christmas* last summer. I have a genetic disorder that makes me break out in a rash when I have to do Christmassy things way before December. Let's talk about the things I do for you!"

He looked at me in mock horror. "Now wait a second, Mr. I-Am-Too-Snooty-To-Actually-Admit-I-Laughed-At-That-Movie!"

"Go on! Go on! Tell me how wrong I am about Ernest! I dare you!"

"Listen, dumbass! You secretly like the movies I choose. You're just so stuck-up that you won't admit that *Ernest Saves Christmas* has a very good moral message. I mean, who thinks Christmas shouldn't be saved? Hmmm? I guess only you, Mr. I've-Got-A-Heart-Of-Stone-Call-Me-Ebenezer-Scrooge!   Only you!"

I rolled my eyes and sighed dramatically. "Ernest is not funny! It's like humor for three-year-olds! You're so immature!"

"Well, I just find it odd that Mr. I-Like-Choppin-and-Debusty can somehow also like something as babyish as the Muppets!" He snickered, knowing how it annoyed me that he continued to deliberately mispronounce the names of my favorite composers. "I mean, I think you and Joshua are actually destined to be best friends. I bet he's got two or three copies of this, just so he has a back-up if the first tape wears out. You ought to go over to his house this week and have a Muppets marathon. Want me to call him for you before I leave?"

"You better watch out! Karma's a bitch, you miserable, vomitous mass. I bet your Dayton cousins have some great hillbilly holiday albums cued up just for you. And some possum stew, too. You'll be paying for how badly you malign me in just a few days!"

He moaned, "Oh, God, Alex, don't remind me. I've got days upon days of sheer Dayton-cousin-hell waiting for me. I wish I could just stay here with you. Imagine me just hanging out here all week… nothing to do but annoy the hell outta you and chill with your impossibly cool parents."

"It would be the best Christmas present ever, Brandon. I wish you could stay."

He sighed and went quiet. After a moment, he said, "I've been meaning to ask you something. I mean, speaking of your cool parents, how in the world did you three ever start coming to Bissonet? Your parents are so *not* churchy. I don't get it. I don't think they believe three fourths… no, like, nine tenths of what they hear at church. And you guys only come on Sunday mornings now. I can tell their hearts aren't in it. I didn't think much about it at first. I was just so happy you showed up. But now, after all this time, it seems odd you three ever came to start with and that you've stuck around for so long."

"I thought you knew the story. Didn't my mom tell you one morning last summer? I thought I heard her talking to you about Douglas Wallis one time when you were over here."

"Well, yeah, she mentioned your dad knows him from work, but that's all she said."

"Well, Douglas works in the development office at the hospital, and he was putting together a committee to work on part of the annual campaign in 1987." Brandon looked confused. "You know, like, fundraising? Douglas helps the hospital raise money for research and patient support. Anyway, Dad got randomly chosen to sit on the committee, and he and Douglas worked together a lot. It was just before the end of school in sixth grade.

"Then Douglas and Sherry invited Mom and Dad out to dinner a couple of times over the summer. The first time, it was just the two couples. Then the next time it was Douglas and Sherry and about five or six other couples from your church. My parents didn't know about it until they got there and suddenly everybody was talking about the same church. Then Douglas and Sherry asked my parents if they wanted to come to church. My parents were pretty hesitant. I mean, they both grew up going to church, but they didn't really feel a need to go back as adults."

"I didn't know they grew up going to church. I thought Bissonet was their first church."

"No, Mom grew up Presbyterian, and Dad grew up Baptist. They had both left their churches by the time they got to college, and they just never started going anywhere again."

"I can see why your parents were targets for the Wallises. People in the church love to seek out you atheist families, act all friendly, and then go in for the hard sell." He snickered. "Repent and be baptized or prepare to roast forever! I mean, what a way to make friends, eh?"

"I know! My parents weren't interested, but they didn't want to be rude to the Wallises. Mom and Dad kept putting them off, but the Wallises were persistent. So, my parents agreed to come one Sunday just to be nice."

"And in you walked, Alexander Kennedy! I'm tellin' you, we were destined to be best friends." He rested his head on my shoulder.

"Well, actually, I've never told you this..."

"What? What?" He sat up straight in a flash and turned fully toward me. I shifted, too, so I didn't have to crane my neck to look him in the eyes. "You've got me worried! Please tell me you're gonna keep coming. If you stopped, there's no way Dad would let me be friends with you. I mean, it would be like you hadn't even been baptized! He's already a little pissed you three come less often than you used to."

I placed a reassuring hand on his knee. "No, no, no! We're staying put. Wild horses couldn't drag me away from you!"

He grinned. "That's what I like to hear."

"No, here's the funny, crazy, almost-impossible-to-believe part. My parents asked me if I wanted to go with them that first Sunday, and I said no. So, they made arrangements for me to spend the morning with Aunt Karen. She was gonna pick me up for an early brunch, and then we were gonna run some errands."

"I knew it! You really are a secret atheist in your heart! Why didn't you want to come to church?"

"I don't know. It just didn't seem interesting. I mean, I thought it was all myths and nonsense stories."

"You still think that! You are totally gonna roast for eternity."

"Well, I mean, come on! God created the world in six days, like six thousand years ago? Moses parted the Red Sea? Joshua made the sun stand still in the sky? Elijah went to heaven in a fiery chariot? Mary got bonked by the Holy Spirit in order to have Jesus without original sin?" He snickered. "And Jesus walked on the water and calmed a storm? Am I really supposed to believe all that actually happened? None of it makes any sense! If it was in some book other than the Bible, nobody at church would take it seriously!"

He shot me his most scandalized look. "You secret little heretic! You gotta keep your mouth shut, or my dad will go monkey-shit, shitting-balls crazy!"

"You've got such a way with words! You're a poet in the making!"

"Shove it, smartass!"

"I rest my case!" I chuckled and patted his shoulder. "Do you really think I'm gonna bring this up at the dinner table at your house?"

He laughed and put his hands on my knees. "Of course, not. But just don't ever let it leak out. Okay? Just like evolution. Keep your trap shut, my little stick-arm friend!"

"Got it." I winked and smiled at him. "Now, can I keep telling the story?"

"Yeah, sorry! Keep going."

"But Aunt Karen called us early that Sunday morning. She thought she had food poisoning. She'd been up all night."

"She should've listened to Marvin Zindler. He would've steered her straight." He chortled at his own joke. Zindler was a local TV personality on Channel 13. He had blindingly white hair and teeth, blue-tinted glasses, and a permanent tan that had a suspicious orange hue to it. He came on every Friday night, delighting Houstonians young and old with his over-the-top dirty restaurant report. Go anywhere in the world and say 'Slime in the ice machine!' If anyone looks your way and snickers, you can be sure they lived in Houston at some point in their life.

"And she was too sick to come get me. So, I had to go to your church with my parents... rather against my wishes, I have to add."

"You mean you weren't even really supposed to be there?"

"Nope! It's all because of some dodgy Chinese food that I even walked into the church kitchen that morning."

"You're shitting me! Come on!" He shook his head in disbelief. All the color drained from his face, and I swear a few small tears formed at the corner of his eyes. "You mean, we were that close to never meeting? You might not have come that morning... or ever?"

"I know! Just imagine."

"And you say you don't believe in miracles!"

"Then, soon after we started coming, my parents realized you and I were becoming such good friends. They figured your dad wouldn't let us be friends if we stopped coming. So, they just sucked it up and put on their best church faces a few times a month."

"You mean they don't believe, either? None of you really believe?"

"Well, I mean, we believe in God. It's just all that other stuff that seems hard to swallow."

"And they do it all just so we can be friends?"

"Yup! They love us that much."

"Holy shit! My friendship with you is, like, fiftieth on the list of priorities for my dad. I mean, we are below oil changes and getting the taxes done and booking the next dentist appointment. But we're top of the list for your daddy-o." He shook his head, and the tears finally fell.

He flopped on his back and rested his head in my lap. He looked up at me and smiled. "Find out where that restaurant is. We gotta make a pilgrimage there and offer them our thanks." He snickered. "I mean, thank God for dodgy Chinese food!"

. . .

ii.

Life hit warp speed in January. Homework took up more and more of my evenings. Brandon talked about increased homework, too, and I worried about his grades. I knew the slightest sign of trouble would bring down a ton of bricks on his head since Mr. Marshall knew Brandon's Achilles heel. Brandon and I seemed to skate on thin ice throughout those early months of 1988.

Fortunately, our luck held. Dad and Mom were impressed with my ability to keep up with my schoolwork. Brandon went to tutoring sessions after school several days a week and managed to keep his grades up, so Mr. Marshall was happy. The sword of Damocles held off for much longer than I expected.

Brandon continued to come on Saturday morning runs with Dad and me as long as the weather was dry. He usually stayed the rest of the morning and had lunch with us. Our parents still allowed us two Saturday night sleepovers each month. By some unspoken agreement, we always did our sleepovers at Brandon's house. He said we had more room and more privacy there. Plus, we had his weights and a TV to ourselves in his bedroom. He called it our little bachelor pad.

Mr. Marshall must have been in a particularly good mood in mid-February. He told Brandon I could stay over two nights on the last weekend in February. My parents agreed, saying it was a well-earned reward for all my hard work.

I went over on Friday night in time for pizza, salad, and ice cream. Brandon only took a small scoop of ice cream. He whispered to me, "I'm watching my figure, you know." Mrs. Marshall said she felt a cold coming on and went to bed early. Mr. Marshall had some reading to do in his study. Will left after dinner to go see some friends.

As we helped wash up the dishes, Brandon whispered to me again, "We're off the hook, A-man. No dorky family games tonight!"

When we got upstairs, Brandon pulled his shirt off and slipped into some shorts. He looked at me and smiled. "Okay, Mr. Two-Scoops-of-Cookies-n-Cream, you gotta work off all that food you ate."

I groaned. "I have it on good authority from Joel that eating ice cream or pizza or French fries occasionally is not a bad thing. You're not going to get fat. I'm not going to get fat. Let's just relax tonight. We can work out tomorrow. For once, let's just take it easy."

"Just relax? Just relax?" He walked over to me and lifted up the right sleeve of my shirt. "You have these thin sticks you call arms, and you have the gall to say to me, 'I just wanna relax.' No, sir!" He laughed and thumped my bicep. "You're killing me. I'm trying to help you out, and what thanks do I get?" He paused and squinted his eyes at me. "I get no thanks at all and tons of excuses instead."

I laughed and gave him a punch in his stomach.

He said, "Careful or you'll break a knuckle on these babies." He tightened his abs. I had been missing that sight for some weeks.

I slipped off my shirt, too, and put on some shorts. Brandon put me through my paces with a quick arm and chest work out. Then he made me do twenty chin-ups and so many crunches I lost count. To top it all off, he insisted I do a few hanging leg raises. He stood behind me as I struggled to lift my legs and not sway too much. He held my hips steady and cheered me on.

At one point, he kissed the small of my back and said, "See what I do for you, lazy ass. If it wasn't for me, you'd be a flabby little eighth grader who went on occasional runs with his dad. But with me, I'll have you trained into a little powerhouse before you know it."

Even after he let me take a break, I still felt the sensation of his lips on my back, not far from the place where that guy kicked me the previous October. In so many ways, I felt like I knew Brandon as well as I knew myself, but there were moments – like that brief kiss on my back – when everything about him seemed mysterious and impossibly beyond my grasp.

I was silent as I finished the last few leg raises. Brandon let go of my hips, walked around in front of me, and looked me up and down as I hung from my arms. "Not bad, overall! Not too bad. Joel will be proud of you. Now we just gotta work on those bean pole arms of yours!"

After a quick shower and brief run to the kitchen to get some snacks, we decided to watch *The Princess Bride* again. As usual, we laughed and quoted our way through all the best scenes. I think we could have watched it a million times without ever getting tired of it.

We sat together on Brandon's couch, shoulder to shoulder, as the credits rolled and Willy DeVille sang *Storybook Love*. Brandon let out a long sigh, turned fully toward me, and asked, "What is it about this movie that gets me every time? I mean, when we first watched it, I loved the action, the humor, the swordfights, the friendship between Westley, Fezzick, and

Inigo. Now, when I watch it, and I hear that music – you know that soft guitar music that plays the theme? – I always feel this kind of sadness in me. What is that?"

I paused for several seconds, wondering which of two paths I should take. Some unfamiliar voice inside me urged me to take a risk. I said, "I think it's just the power of a story about love. Westley and Buttercup love one another, and they have to overcome so many odds to be together. It's sad. It's romantic. It's real somehow, even though it's a fairytale."

Brandon looked up at the ceiling and said, "So that's it? You think it makes me feel that way because it's a story about love?"

There was a time when such a direct question from Brandon would have bewildered me. Back when we first met, I froze anytime he said anything that made me remotely uncomfortable. In many ways, I had grown more at ease with him as our friendship blossomed, and I understood myself better since the attack at Joel's game and all the conversations I had with my parents. Yet our sudden talk about love left me feeling tongue-tied and light-headed. I felt like Westley on the edge of the fire swamp. If I plunged in, would I make it out alive?

He looked back at me. I took a deep breath and said, "Sure, Brandon. Just listen to those lyrics. The whole song, the whole movie really, is about their love. It's all about love."

I softly quoted some of the lyrics I knew by heart:

> *"He said, 'Don't you know I love you oh, so much*
> *And lay my heart at the foot of your dress?'*
> *She said, 'Don't you know that storybook loves*
> *Always have a happy ending?'*
> *Then he swooped her up, just like in the books*
> *And on his stallion they rode away."*

Brandon held my gaze throughout and said, "Does love really always have a happy ending? Do you think people really end up happy in life like they do in books and movies?"

"I don't know. Maybe you have to take a chance on love. You have to say 'yes' to it, even if you don't know how it's going to end. Maybe you love someone, but you're not sure they love you the same way. You have to take a chance."

"Even if you have to go through fire swamps, and fight the R.O.U.S., and survive the life-sucking machine?"

"Yes, even if you have to storm the castle."

Brandon chuckled. "Maybe you need a chocolate-covered miracle pill from Max."

I held my breath for a few seconds. Could I say the words pressing against my lips from the inside? Could I say the words, once spoken, I could never pull back? I thought of Westley and the old hag who booed and hissed at Buttercup when Prince Humperdink announced their engagement. Love seemed so powerful, yet so fragile; so certain, yet so precarious.

To speak of love is a risk; to love is even riskier; to deny love is the greatest risk of all. I was in a risky spot no matter what I did, but I finally found the courage to speak.

"Well, I love you, and it does feel like a miracle."

He looked at me for several seconds, but I couldn't read his face. To be honest, I was glad for that. I had a hard enough time understanding what I was thinking and feeling. The thought of taking on Brandon's thoughts and feelings was too much for my pounding little heart. It felt so fragile in that moment. Whatever he said next could break it into a thousand little pieces or sending it soaring. I longed to know, but there was a kind of safety in our silence. As long as he remained silent, I could still hope.

"I know, Alex. I know you do." He glanced away for a good twenty seconds; his voice was even lower when he spoke again. "I love you, too. You're the best friend I could ever have. I don't know what I'd do without you."

We sat there in silence. It may have only been a few

seconds, but it seemed to stretch on for minutes and minutes. I dared not speak again. I had said what I wanted to say. I didn't want to break the spell or ruin our magic moment. I just wanted to sit there, Brandon leaning up against me, and revel in that moment I had feared for so long.

. . .

iii.

Brandon and Mrs. Marshall made a trip to Nashville during Spring Break. Mrs. Marshall's mother had been diagnosed with cancer in late January, and Mrs. Marshall's siblings in Tennessee had been taking turns looking after her. Mrs. Marshall wanted to give them a break for a few days, and she asked Brandon to go with her.

I teased him on the phone the Thursday before he left. "I know you'll be depressed without me next week, but you'll survive five or six days without me. You'll have a great time with your cousins from Dayton. Maybe they're gonna bring some friends. It could be like a ten-person hillbilly sleepover. You'd love that!"

He shot back, "Watch it, sorry-ass loser-man! I've already spoken to Joshua and told him you were free every day and wanted to hang out with him while I'm gone. He's got a whole week of cool things planned for you." He snickered. "He's got a snail collection, and I understand he needs help cleaning out their bowls." He snickered even more. "God, you're gonna love it. I think his sisters have some cats now, and they keep the litter boxes right by Joshua's bed. You can, like, squeeze between his little boy bed and the litter boxes. It'll be perfect."

"Actually, Mr. I'm-A-Hillbilly-At-Heart, I have two days planned with Joel during Spring Break. Once I knew you'd be outta the way, he and I made all kinds of plans behind your back."

He gasped and hissed, "I will beat your skinny little ass next time I see you, Alexander Nathan Kennedy. I will mop the bathroom floor with your hot-ass cute hair. What do you mean you've got two days planned with Joel? When did this all take place? When did you two sneak around and make all these plans without me?"

"Wouldn't you like to know, Mr. I-Love-My-Dayton-Cousins-More-Than-Life! Wouldn't you like to know!"

"Yeah, well, we'll see about this. I'm calling Joel as soon as I say goodbye to you, Mr. Benedict-Arnold-Is-My-Hero. I'll tell him you'd rather be with Joshua."

He was silent for a few seconds. His silences could still trouble me at times. He finally said, "Well, whatever you do, don't forget about me. And tell Joel I expect to have some days with him to make up for this. He owes me. And so do you, my little stick-arm friend."

. . .

I actually had no role in planning the two days with Joel. My parents arranged their work schedules so they could both be off on Wednesday, Thursday, and Friday of Spring Break. Without me knowing, they talked to Joel and asked if he had time to spend with me on Monday and Tuesday. I had no idea where that plan came from. Every time I thought I had those two figured out, they upended all my expectations. Life as their son was like a game of chess with some Russian champion. I thought I was two moves ahead at times, never realizing they had checkmate planned five moves ahead of me. I was a little pawn in their mystifying adult game.

Joel picked me up around 5:00 on Sunday evening. Our plans were pretty simple: hang out at his house Sunday evening, go for a run at Memorial Park on Monday morning, go see a movie early Monday afternoon, hang out at his house Monday evening, run errands on Tuesday, and finally drop me off at home around 3:00. I was both nervous and excited. Part of me knew we'd have a great time; another part of me wondered if Joel would get tired of me after the first day. Would I end up being a little pest who annoyed him? Even though Joel said Brandon and I were like the little brothers he never had, I'd never spent so much time with him alone. I was used to Brandon filling in the silent pauses and making everyone laugh with ease.

We grabbed some tacos from a small place off Holcombe as we drove to his house. I had never been to Joel's house before; he told me it was a few miles off Bellaire Boulevard. When we got there, his parents were waiting for us. Mrs. Thompson had prepared black beans, guacamole, and fresh salsa to go with our tacos. When I thought I couldn't take another bite, Mrs. Thompson surprised me with *sopapillas* she had kept warm in the oven.

Joel laughed when he saw me drooling over the *sopapillas*. He said, "So, first thing to know about staying here: we'll actually feed you! I know when you stay with Brandon, he measures out your food ahead of time and weighs every ounce. He's manic, but you gotta love him!"

Mr. Thompson laughed and said, "Absolutely! You can have anything you want. Feel free to forage in the kitchen. Go have a look in the pantry anytime you want. We've had four growing boys in this house for years and years. We're used to it. You can have whatever sounds good. Make yourself at home, Alex."

All four of us watched *Indiana Jones and the Temple of Doom* downstairs in the living room. Once it was over, Mr. and Mrs. Thompson went to their bedroom, and Joel and I headed upstairs. As we climbed the stairs, he said, "We've got extra bedrooms, the ones where my older brothers used to sleep. So, you can sleep in one of those. Or you can stay in my room." He paused when we got to the landing. "What's best for you? Where do you wanna go?

"I think I'll stay with you. Do you mind?"

He threw his arm around my shoulder. "No, of course not. It'll be way more fun that way. My other friends sleep in my room when they come over. It's not like we haven't seen each other half naked anyway!"

I thought to myself, 'Actually, Joel, I've seen you 100% naked several times! Don't tell me you've forgotten about the first Fall Retreat!'

Joel's room was smaller than I imagined, but it was obsessively neat and tidy. His car was always spotless inside, and I imagined his room would be the same way. Yes, I'd imagined his room a number of times.

He spread his arms wide and said, "Consider yourself at home!"

I whispered, "*Mi* room *es tu* room." He smiled and nodded.

I put my bag down at the foot of his bed. I excused myself and went down the hall to the bathroom. When I came back, Joel had changed into an old pair of running shorts. He was putting a tape into the small cassette player on top of his dresser. I stood for a second when I came into the room and admired his broad shoulders, chiseled back, trim waistline, and those legs that never seemed to end. He turned up the volume as Joan Baez sang out.

He must have sensed me standing there. "Hey, hey," he said. "How about some sister Joan to help us mellow out? Do you wanna get changed?"

I nodded and began to change into some shorts and a t-shirt. He whistled when I slipped my shirt off and said, "Your abs are coming along! You must be doing leg raises with Brandon."

"Yeah, I can't walk into his room with him making me do leg raises. He's just as one-track about me working out as he is about himself working out."

We leaned back on his bed and listened to the music for a while. Neither of us said anything. It was getting late, close to

10:00. Even though it was Spring Break, I was tired, and I kept yawning.

A wry smile crossed Joel's lips. "Sorry I'm boring you so much. I must be pretty dull compared to Brandon. I hear you two get up to all kinds of things at his house."

"No, you're not boring me! I'm just really tired. Last week was so hard at school. My teachers piled on the work. Then we ran errands all day yesterday, and I had trouble sleeping last night. It's just all catching up with me."

"Hey, no problem. I was kidding! If you're ready for bed, so am I. I had to work yesterday, and I got home late last night. Plus, we have two big days ahead of us. Let's go shower and brush our teeth. We can come back and talk till we fall asleep."

He hopped off the bed, stripped in front of me, and said, "I've already got towels and stuff ready for you in the bathroom. I'll shave at the sink while you shower. Okay? Just drop your clothes here, buddy."

I jumped up, stripped as well, and followed him down the hall. I had never stared so long at another guy's bare ass, not even Brandon's. I was mesmerized by the view from behind. Joel turned around about halfway down the hall and said, "God, you are the cutest thing on two feet. I do not understand why you don't have a... uh..."

He stopped himself, ruffled my hair, pulled me close to his side and said, "Well, I mean... Oh, never mind! Never mind." He blushed a deep red, something I had never seen before.

I was snuggled beneath the top sheet when Joel came back. He was naked and still slightly damp. Small beads of water sparkled like jewels across his rounded shoulders and down his taught torso. I thought about Brandon and imagined how miserable he was with his hillbilly cousins. As much as I missed him, being in Joel's naked presence was not a bad consolation prize.

Joel stood at the end of the bed for a few seconds, looking me straight in the eyes. "What are you thinking about, Alexo?"

He turned to the nearby dresser, pulled out a pair of briefs, and slipped them on.

"Mostly about Brandon. I miss him. I mean... I mean, it's great to be with you, too. I just miss him. It's like I'm missing an arm when he's not around."

Joel climbed into bed beside me, turned on his side to face me, and propped himself up on two pillows. I turned on my side to face him, admiring his freshly-shaved jawline up close.

He winked at me and said, "God, that's sweet! You two are something else. I think I said it before, but I am totally jealous of you two. I've never had a friendship like yours." He sighed and stared off over my shoulder. We both went silent for a good thirty seconds or so.

Joel finally cleared his throat and said, "So, I gotta talk to you about something. Do you mind if we talk about something that might be hard for you to talk about?"

I had a sense where he was headed, just like I did that night after the attack when my parents first asked me if I was gay. I didn't know what I could say to Joel. I couldn't imagine lying to him, but I wasn't sure I had the courage to tell the truth either. I knew I was on sure ground the night my parents asked me. I was much less certain about Joel's reaction – if he asked and if I answered honestly.

I nodded and mumbled, "Sure, I guess so."

"I've been thinking a lot about that night you got attacked at my game. I'm so sorry it happened to you there. If I hadn't invited you guys, that never would've happened. I've felt really bad about that." I tried to interrupt, but he held up a finger. "No, wait. I've got to say all this at once or I may chicken out. I feel really bad I wasn't around to protect you. You're the sweetest, nicest, smartest kid in Houston. The thing is, nice guys like you become targets for assholes like the guy who kicked you. I know Brandon beat the shit out of him, but he's lucky I wasn't there. I don't think anyone could have pulled me off him. I would do anything to protect you. And Brandon, too.

Even though he can be a dickhead at times, I'd crush anyone who messed with him. Do you believe me?"

"I do. Thanks for looking after me, but don't feel like you have to. I can outrun most guys who might want to hit me. If I can get a two-second head start, I'll be okay."

"Well, what makes you so amazing is also what makes jerks like that think they can beat you up. Does that make sense?"

I nodded.

"Will told me later what that guy shouted at you and Brandon. He told me the guy yelled the word 'faggots.' Is that true?"

I nodded again.

"Now, when I asked Brandon about it, he said the guy yelled 'faggot.' As in singular. Are you sure you really remember what he said?"

"Yes. He said 'faggots.' Plural. They were coming for both of us. I think they kicked me first because I'm smaller than Brandon. Then they were gonna go for him, but they didn't count on him being so fast and so strong. I mean I didn't see it all happen like that. But based on what everyone has told me about it, that's what makes most sense to me."

"That's what I was thinking, too. Now here's the next question. Do you think those guys saw you and Brandon earlier? I mean, I know what Brandon's like with you. He's got his arm around your shoulder all the time. He's got this puppy dog look in his eyes when he's talking to you. I've even noticed how he leans into you when you two are sitting side by side. I notice this all the time, but I don't think he knows he does it. Do you?"

"I guess I do and I don't, if that makes sense. He's just Brandon. That's what he's always been like. It's just who he is. If he was any different, he wouldn't be Brandon."

"I know! That's what he's like with you. All of us who know you two take it for granted, but these guys must have noticed, too. They saw you two come in. Maybe they were behind you walking in. Brandon probably had his arm around your shoulder – laughing and talking non-stop." True, he did. "He probably followed you to the seats and sat down as close to you as he possibly could." True, he did. "He probably laughed and smiled and entertained you like he always does. He probably shouted something ridiculous at the top of his voice." Yes, yes, yes; all true. I could see it all in my mind's eye the way it must have looked to those hateful guys.

Joel paused and sighed. "And I think those guys noticed. And they didn't like it because…"

Tears pooled in my eyes as I finished the sentence for him: "…because they thought we were faggots."

Joel held my gaze without saying a word. Perhaps for the first time since I'd known him, I was unaware of his over-whelming physical presence. The only part of him that existed were those two aquamarine eyes – bright yet deep; tender yet edged with protective steel.

My heart had been racing for much of the conversation. I felt it slow to a near halt. I had been holding my stomach in tightly, and I slowly released the tension. The massive boulder lodged on my chest rolled away, and I let a steady inhalation of air fill my lungs.

I knew I was on the cusp of another turning point in my life. I had only ever spoken of my desires to my parents. Un-expectedly, with the god of the youth group, I had the chance again. Could I say what I knew to be true about myself? Could I admit that I loved Brandon the way most guys love girls?

I hesitated and blinked. I looked over the top of Joel's shoulder for a few seconds. When my eyes came back to his, they hadn't moved. His gaze was squarely fixed on me. I didn't think he was even breathing. I wondered how could he be so still and calm knowing what my answer might be? Wouldn't he be disgusted? Wouldn't he throw me out of his room, out of his house, and out of his life forever?

If time was actually ticking forward, I had no sense of it. I felt like a spider dangling from an impossibly thin strand of silk. Then I heard the faint melody of *Storybook Love* well up deep inside my heart. To speak or remain silent?

Suddenly it dawned on me, an insight full of comfort and peace: unexplainably, reassuringly, and without a doubt, Joel already knew. He already knew my secret. He had known for a long time, and it had not mattered one bit. I sensed somehow, in the space between two heartbeats, that I was safe with Joel.

"I love him but not like friends usually love each other. I mean, I love him the way gay men love other men." I paused, my voice quivering. A few warm tears fell down my cheeks. "And I think he loves me that way, too. But I don't know for sure, and I am too afraid to ask him. I'm afraid I might push him away forever if he finds out I'm gay."

"Do your parents know?"

"Yes. We talked about it the weekend I got attacked and a few more times since then."

"Are they mad at you or okay with it?"

I smiled through my tears, little hiccups escaping as I said, "No, they're okay with it. They said they love me no matter what."

He smiled and ruffled my hair. "Well, you're lucky there. A lot of parents don't think that way, especially church parents. They can be the worst hypocrites in the world. Imagine if Brandon's parents found out. His dad would fucking kill him. I mean, he'd kick him out of the house and tell him to go to hell and then go to church and preach a sermon about loving your neighbor as yourself. That man's a mean-spirited hypocrite." The smile disappeared from his face as his jaws clenched tightly.

My tears came more heavily then. I knew Joel was right. I knew what it would cost Brandon if his dad ever found out about me. And if Brandon loved me the way I loved him – the way I dared to hope he did – it would come down like a ton of bricks on Brandon's head if his family ever found out. How in the world would we keep such a secret forever? How could we pretend for the rest of our lives?

I whispered, "Are you mad at me? Or mad at Brandon? Do you think we're faggots? Do you think I'm disgusting?"

He barely let me finish before saying, "God, no! No, no, no! Never in a million years. I know a lot of guys go around using that word and saying how they would kill a guy who tried to kiss them. They're just assholes. Most of them can't find the courage to kiss a girl, so they make up all this bullshit to appear tough. But that's not me." He cupped my chin in his hand and repeated, "That's not me. It won't ever be me. I've said all along that you and Brandon have a special kind of friendship. I'm so jealous of you two. You're so perfect together, whether it's friends or something else. I don't give a flying fuck. If two people are happy together, let them be together."

I once imagined an avalanche of thundering snow descending from an unseen mountain hovering above Houston if I ever spoke openly to Joel. Yet his steady presence remained – still breathing calmly, still smiling gently, still cupping my chin in his reassuringly strong hand. Whatever torrent of cursing and shouting I feared disappeared before it ever began. Everything I thought would vanish in an instant remained unshakably in place.

I wiped the tears from my eyes as best I could with the sheet. I realized what I was doing and apologized.

"Hey, little man, cry all you want. You are the bravest, wisest, kindest person I know. You can cry a river right here, and I wouldn't give a damn. I mean, I'd care about the fact that you're crying, but I don't give a damn about the sheets! We can wash them tomorrow if we need to." He leaned in close and patted my shoulder.

He said, "Do you realize it's after midnight? You must be

exhausted, especially after that. Mom says most of her clients go home and sleep for hours after they tell her a lot in a therapy session. Even she comes home tired, and all she does is listen and nod all day long. She says catharsis makes people tired. I bet I don't need to ask if you know what catharsis means, do I?"

I grinned. "It means release or letting go. Like, it was cathartic for me to tell you my secret."

"God, you're amazing! I hope it was cathartic for you to tell me. It took a whole mountain of courage, that's for sure. And speaking of courage, I was scared shitless, to be honest. I thought I would make you mad or hurt your feelings. Or maybe I was completely wrong, and you'd go ballistic. Little guys like you can do a lot of damage. You could get in a couple of well-aimed crotch kicks and be down the hall and out the front door before I could catch you." He snickered.

I grinned at him and said, "How do you think I keep Brandon on such a short leash? He knows not to mess with me."

"You are *so* wicked! I know all about the leash you have Brandon on. I've said all along I know who wears the pants in your friendship." He winked at me. "Am I right or am I right?"

We fell silent once our giggling trailed off. I was impossibly tired and immensely relieved. I yawned a few times and my eyelids drooped.

Joel spoke into the silence, startling me. "So, what are you gonna do? Are you gonna talk to Brandon or just leave things the way they are?"

"I don't know. I can't imagine doing either thing: speaking or staying silent. Well, that's not true. I tried to tell Brandon how I much love him a few weeks ago, but I don't think he got what I was saying." I narrated my conversation with Brandon when we talked about the special appeal of *The Princess Bride*.

Joel whistled. "Holy shit! Sounds like you were pretty brave and direct. And he didn't bat an eyelid?"

"No, he was quiet and thoughtful. I could tell he was trying to take it all in, but I don't think he really gets it. I mean, I don't think he gets me... that I love him the way I do. Maybe he thinks I love him like a best friend and almost-brother." I hesitated, and my voice wavered. "I'm so afraid I'll push him away or ruin the great friendship we have if I spell it out for him."

"I don't think you have to worry about that, Alexo. I really don't! Something tells me he either already understands and doesn't care or maybe he feels the same way but thinks you don't. Have you considered the fact that he may feel just like you? He might be afraid to say what he really feels because he doesn't want you to reject him." He paused for a few seconds. "Just think about tonight. Were you honestly afraid of my reaction? I mean, deep down in your heart, were you afraid?"

"I guess not... Um, or maybe I was and I wasn't. I think my head had a million reasons why you'd hate me and think I was disgusting, but my heart told me I was safe with you."

"Exactly! I think your heart knows the same thing about Brandon. I think your heart already knows or else you wouldn't have even said what you said to him a few weeks ago."

"Maybe. Maybe you're right."

"Trust me: I'm right!"

Another enormous yawn came over me. Joel turned off the small lamp on the bedside table. I let my head fall to the side, resting it against Joel's reassuringly solid shoulder.

"You really are the bravest guy I know. Sleep tight and dream of your best, most handsome friend." He chuckled. "I mean Brandon – not me, of course! And if you wet the bed, I'll throw your ass out the window in the morning!"

CHAPTER 10

A former congregant who moved away to a small town between Houston and Austin died early in the second week of June. The woman's family asked Mr. Marshall if he would preside over the funeral. He agreed and drove out to Brenham early Friday morning to prepare for the funeral on Saturday.

Mrs. Marshall would have normally gone with him, but she woke up with a high fever on Friday morning. One of her friends from church, Mrs. Lawton, came over around 8:00 and drove her to the doctor. Mrs. Lawton stayed the rest of the day, tending to Mrs. Marshall.

Will was in and out of the house several times during the day. He originally planned to spend the night at Joel's house but said he would cancel his plans and be back by 8:00 if Brandon and I stayed around downstairs in the early evening in case Mrs. Marshall needed anything before he got back.

Brandon and I occupied ourselves upstairs most of the day: softly talking and joking around, reading *Murder on the Orient Express* together, sketching, watching TV, and lifting weights.

Mrs. Lawton finally left around 4:00. We checked on the soundly sleeping Mrs. Marshall and went out to the pool.

Even for Houston, it was a sultry summer afternoon. The water beckoned as a welcome relief. We jumped in and swam a few laps, making an unspoken agreement to keep our voices low and our horseplay to a minimum since the Marshalls' bedroom window overlooked the deep end of the pool.

Within a few minutes, Brandon's resolve partially broke down. He remained quiet, but he couldn't resist an opportunity for horseplay. He began splashing me and trying to dunk me while making as little noise as possible. Ironically, he ended up making more noise than usual.

He grabbed me from the front, hands clasped tightly behind my back. Even though I knew it was futile, I struggled to free myself from his vice-like embrace. That sly ol' grin of his I sometimes saw in my sleep stretched from ear to ear. I took a deep anticipatory breath, preparing for him to take me with him and hold me under the water.

He didn't take me beneath the water as I suspected; instead, he pulled me closer to himself. I stopped struggling. We both went completely silent as we floated together in the middle of the pool.

I could hear the faint noise of rush-hour traffic drifting back from Kirby Drive. The wavy water's rhythmic lap against the pool's inner edge had a hypnotic effect on me, and I stared longingly into Brandon's alluring eyes. The warm, moist air between our faces crackled with imaginary electricity, ethereal yet undeniable.

I let myself go slightly limp in Brandon's embrace. His head inched closer to mine. We had been very close to one another on so many occasions and in so many ways, but something felt cosmically different in that moment. The density of the air around us seemed to intensify, as if it secretly willed to hold us together. Time ticked by slowly. Perhaps the sun slowed in its orbit; I couldn't say. In the space of a single breath, my perception of reality lengthened and expanded, then condensed and hurtled us forward.

Brandon pushed his lips up against mine. I opened my mouth in response, and our tongues found each other's. My eyes grew wide with surprise and delight. Brandon let out a deep sigh. I had dreamed about our first kiss so many times since we first met, but the reality of it swept away all those insubstantial imaginary longings.

Brandon used his left leg to prise my legs apart, and his dense thigh wedge up against my crotch. He pulled away from my mouth, still grinning, and I gasped at the wonder of what I felt.

He kept his right hand around my back, holding me close. I felt his left hand go down the front of my trunks and fumble its way to my penis. Our eyes held each other's fast. The world could have crumbled around our ears, Gorbachev could have dropped a thousand warheads on Houston, but nothing would have broken our mutual gaze. Months of repressed attraction and desire rocketed high, volcano-like, into the atmosphere of my being.

I brought my right hand up to Brandon's torso and caressed his contoured abs. Then I let it slip down further and felt my way inside his trunks. He was hard and throbbing. In that moment, I finally knew what I had often wondered and nervously doubted for far too long: Brandon wanted me as badly as I wanted him.

We drifted slowly toward the shallow end of the pool, our hands still exploring the other friend's trunks. We reached the point on the pool's sloped floor where we could both stand with the water lapping around our shoulders. He pulled his hand from my trunks and drew my head close to his. I took my hand out of his trunks and wrapped my arms around him mid-chest. We stood there for several seconds, toes struggling to keep purchase on the pool's rough floor, lost in each other's strong embrace. Lost for words. Lost in wonder.

He finally said, "God, Alex, I've loved you since that first morning you came to church. You stood there across from me with your knife and sticky hands, and something about you made me feel something inside me I didn't even know was there! You weren't like any other guy I knew, and I knew I wanted you. But I didn't understand it! I was so confused, and I've been confused all along. Have you? Have you been confused?"

"Yes! I felt the same way! I couldn't believe you were there, standing across from me that morning at church. I'd never met anyone like you. I already knew I liked boys and not girls, but I hadn't ever met a boy who made me feel all the things you made me feel. And it's just been like that every day since then. Every day I've loved you a bit more and wanted to know if you loved me, too. But I was so afraid. I was afraid you'd hate me if you really knew what I felt about you. I wouldn't let myself hope too much – that you might love me back."

He grasped me by my shoulders and said, "Me? Me hate you? You've never done the slightest thing to make me hate you. You couldn't ever make me hate you! But, God, I am the biggest dickhead in the world, and I've given you reason after reason to hate me. I've acted like such an idiot because I was so afraid of losing you. I was so afraid you'd find out what I was really like, and you'd never want to be around me again."

"I don't know how to say it any other way. That's never gonna happen. You're my best friend, and I love you. Nothing's gonna change that. Ever. You are stuck with me."

He said in a sing-song voice, "I'm so happy to be stuck with you... yes it's true, I'm so happy to be stuck with you."

I whispered, "Exactly." I leaned in and kissed him gently on his lips.

We waded over to the wide steps in the shallow end of the pool and got out. We went up to the deck, stripped off our trunks, dried off in front of one another, and put on some clean underwear and shorts. Brandon tiptoed inside the house and came back out with two thumbs raised. "Mom's still fast asleep. I don't think she's gonna move for a long time. And it's only 5:15. Will won't be here for hours. We've got the whole evening to ourselves."

"Sounds perfect."

"How's this for a plan? Let's go work out a bit, then we can eat, and then watch whatever lame-ass movie you brought, and then see what's next when we get there."

I grinned and chuckled. "Sounds like a plan."

This was the point where he once would have thrown his arm around my shoulder. Instead, he cupped my chin in his hands and kissed me on the lips again. He pressed his body up against mine as he did so, and I felt every hard muscle I had spent the previous twenty months longing to embrace without fear. I wrapped my arms around his chest and stroked his back with my hands. I rested my chin on his left shoulder, and he caressed my still-damp hair. He whispered in my ear, "Can we just stay like this forever?"

"Yes, please. It's all I want."

"As you wish, Alex. As you wish."

. . .

Later that night we climbed into Brandon's bed tired but indescribably happy. I was flat on my back, and he had turned on his left side to face me.

"Alex, can I feel your abs?"

"Of course!" I tightened them and held my breath. He reached over and ran his hand across my stomach.

"God, they're beautiful. You've come so far! I'd give them an A-." He snorted. "I mean, mine are an A+ to the tenth power, but yours are pretty fine, too."

I shot him the dirtiest look I could from my right eye.

He asked, "Can I hold your hand?" I smiled but didn't say anything. He took his hand off my stomach and grasped my right hand.

All the lights were off except the small lamp on the

nightstand next to him. The whole house was still and silent. Will decided to sleep in the guest bedroom downstairs so he could be nearer to his mom in case she needed anything in the night. Before we came upstairs, he threatened us with a week's separation if we made any noise and woke up Mrs. Marshall. We knew enough to take him seriously. One word from Will to Mr. Marshall, and we could kiss at least a week goodbye. Maybe more! The thought of any kind of separation weighed heavily on my own mind.

Brandon softly said, "So when did you first know?"

"I told you earlier! The morning I stood across from you in the church kitchen."

"No, I mean, when did you first know you liked guys and not girls?"

"Oh!" I paused and considered. "It was at the end of fourth grade. I was on the merry-go-round at recess with Kevin, Abdul, and some other guys. I don't think Eric was with us for some reason. We were all sitting around the edge with our legs pointing to the middle. One of the other guys named John dared us to say which girl we liked and wanted to kiss. No one had ever asked me that before. By some alignment of the stars, the guy next to me, Mark, started. Then it went to John, then Kevin. So, it was going around the long way to me. I'd be the last one to speak.

"And I just remember thinking the whole time that the only person I wanted to kiss was John. He was the coolest, most athletic guy in our grade. It hit me like a bolt of lightning: I wanted to kiss John. I could imagine my lips on his, but I could never in a million years imagine my lips on any of the girls. I mean, I thought some of the girls were pretty, like Sandy and Maria. But I didn't want to kiss them. I never, EVER thought about kissing a girl! Never once!"

Even in the dim light, I could see a twinkle come to Brandon's eyes. "Oh, so who is this dickhead, John? Do you still want to kiss him? Where is he? I'm gonna beat the shit out of him. Give me his address." He reached over and traced the curve of my upper lip with his index finger. "These lips are for me only."

I stifled the laughter that shook my body. "No, you moron! He's a total jerk! I thought he was hot in fourth grade. Well… he still is kind of hot, but he's an asshole! He's cocky, and he thinks he's about ten times smarter than he really is. His parents are mega-rich and donate money to every appeal from the school. Seriously, the school only keeps him around for his parents' money. We all think the teachers grade him on a curve just to keep him afloat."

Brandon winked at me. "That's what I like to hear. Just don't go letting your eye wander to his body. Or anybody else's."

"Don't worry! You could shoulder press him above your head. He may be hot and athletic, but I bet he's twenty or so pounds lighter than you. Plus a year younger. I like older guys, don't you know?"

He grinned and said, "Good! Just let me know if he ever makes a pass at you. He'll be dead meat!"

"So, what about you? When did you realize?"

"Right when you walked in. I don't know what happened inside me! You did something to me I had never known before. I mean, I had dated girls at camp and school and church, but that was all just for fun. I was just doing it because I was supposed to and because girls always seemed to like me and notice me. Joel and Will always told me who I should date and who I should avoid. I just did what they said! I didn't know any better!"

He chuckled, let out a wistful sigh, and said, "I remember the first time I kissed a girl at camp. Nothing really happened! We kissed, and I was, like, 'You mean that's it?' I thought it would be amazing, and it was just boring. And she was like a Hoover, you know? She just wanted to keep on kissing, but that one kiss was enough for me. I got my first serious scratch when I pulled away from her. She clawed and scratched. I was totally off-guard."

He shuddered at the memory and said, "Then you, Boy Wonder, walked into the church kitchen out of nowhere in your khaki pants and blue-and-green button down shirt, and I knew you were the one I wanted to kiss. I don't know why I felt that way or where it came from, but I knew right then. I wanted to kiss you, Alex, and only you."

He let go of my hand and reached to tilt my chin toward him. "And I knew that I could never have you, that you'd never want me, that we'd never, never, never kiss in a million years. So, I blabbed on and on about Dolly Parton and tits." He groaned. "I mean, fucking hell, I just wanted some lightning bolt to zap me in that moment. I was doing my best to be cool and make you like me, and then I saw your face. I saw your blush and the tears on the edge of your eyes. And I just wanted to die. But I kept going on and on about tits! Dolly's damn tits!"

I started to break in, but he placed his index finger gently over my lips. "No, let me go on. Then I realized you were this impossibly sweet, kind, thoughtful guy. You didn't know about tits. You didn't know about Dolly Parton. You didn't seem to know about any of the godawful shitty things my friends at school talk about all the time. You were, like, from another planet! And, God, you were so cute! So fucking cute! I mean... your hair and these lips of yours! Like you stepped out of a magazine! And I was a total asshole and embarrassed you in front of everyone. I felt like shit, Alex! I figured I'd lost you forever."

His words flowed out in healing waves. I had been afraid for so long, so afraid that I would lose Brandon forever if he knew what I felt about him. Ironically, he'd been so fearful of the same thing. He and I had overcome a thousand chances to mess things up and miss out on our friendship forever.

When he went quiet, I asked, "What made you kiss me tonight? Why tonight?"

"I just couldn't keep it in anymore! I felt like I was gonna explode. I knew I had to try even though I was afraid! I'd been thinking about it for so long. I felt like I would burst if I didn't give it a try."

Tears gathered on the bottom lids of his eyelids. He paused and his voice quivered slightly when he resumed. "I wanted to kiss you that night we talked about *The Princess Bride.* Remember? When you said sometimes we have to take a risk on loving someone? And you quoted those lyrics? Do you remember that? Something in me said you were saying all that about me. Like you were trying to send me some signal, but I couldn't let myself hope that was true. I was afraid that if I believed you, but it wasn't true, that I would break into a million pieces!"

I nodded. "Yes, I remember. I wanted you so badly that night, but that's all I could say. I was so afraid you would be disgusted with me if you knew what I was really thinking. I felt so brave about what I said. It was the most courageous thing I ever did." I chuckled slightly. "I look back now, and I know it's not. It was pretty lame compared to the courage it took you to kiss me today."

"God, I wasn't really brave! I was just desperate! I was gonna go crazy if I didn't try." He shook his head, tears still poised on his lower eyelids. "Isn't it crazy, Alex? We both thought the other one would hate us if we were really honest, but all along we were dying on the inside from not being honest."

"It is crazy! I wonder how much longer we would have gone on like that if you hadn't kissed me in the pool? Imagine if we had gone on for years."

Brandon laughed softly and said, "No, I couldn't have gone on for years. You make me so horny. I would have kissed you eventually. I couldn't have lasted much longer. You are too hot to resist."

A fiery blush spread across my cheeks. Even in the dim

light, Brandon noticed. "God, you're blushing, Alex. You're fucking blushing! I love everything about you, do you know? Especially your modest blushes."

There were so many thoughts in my head. I didn't know where to start. I felt an odd mixture of utter elation and desperate sleepiness. I wanted to talk all night, but I also wanted to sleep forever – afraid that, if I woke, I would never be so happy again.

"But, one thing, Brandon. How are we gonna keep all this quiet? Nobody can know. I mean, my parents know how I feel about you. But we can't give anyone else even the tiniest hint."

"They do? You told them?"

"I had to. I don't keep things from them. They asked me straight out a couple of nights after the attack at Joel's game. They knew what those guys shouted at us. I couldn't lie to them. They don't care that I'm gay. They love me and support me no matter what."

"Well, you know that's never gonna be the case with my parents. My dad will kill me. He will literally kill me. He has a gun! I've seen it! I can just see him chasing me down the street and shooting me dead as I tried to run away. He'd rather me be dead than gay! I do know that. He practically hates me as it is. This would just seal the deal."

I took Brandon's hand in mine. "He's an asshole for hating you. The only reason I'm glad he's alive is that you came from him. Other than that, he's a total dickhead and a waste of space. His sermons are just full of bullshit! I don't give a damn what he thinks about me, but we have to be careful and serious. We can't do anything to make anyone suspicious. We have to keep each other safe. There are plenty of guys out there who would beat the shit out of us. Your dad and Will are just the start!"

I wasn't quite ready to tell him about Joel. Unless he asked me directly, I'd leave that conversation for another day.

Brandon laughed a little and said, "God, you just dropped,

like, five or six cuss words in ten seconds. I guess my dad gets on your nerves."

"Yes, he does! As do all assholes. I'm tired of being nice to assholes, but, seriously, we have to keep things secret. I don't really want to get kicked again or beaten up or knifed!"

Brandon nodded earnestly. "I know! It's gotta be totally a secret! And I will keep you safe. No matter what! I'll fight off a dozen guys to keep you safe." He paused for a second and kissed my forehead. "Men can get put in prison for being gay here in Texas. Did you know that? We could go to jail if someone found out."

"No, that's not true. Nobody can go to jail just for being gay. It's only homosexual conduct that can get you arrested – if anyone sees it and reports you. My parents talked to me about the Sodomy laws a while back. That's what they're called. Aren't they horrible sounding words? Sodomy. Sodomites."

"Yeah, they're awful! And they're Bible words. Fucking Bible words! Can you imagine kids at church finding out?"

"I don't give a rat's ass what they think. Mom says they're all so repressed they'll be warped for life."

"I know! Why do you think so many guys get caught jacking off in the showers at camp? I swear, they all spit on their popsicles before they slide them in between their lips." He cackled. "You know I'm right!"

We fell into a comfortable silence for a minute or so. He rolled toward me and draped his arm over my torso. "I'm so tired! It's been the best night ever with you, but I feel like I could sleep for a decade."

"Me, too. But it's the best kind of exhaustion I've ever experienced." I kissed his forehead. "Let's just sleep as late as we can."

He gave me a lopsided, wry smile. "Oh, no you don't, mister! I've been waiting a long time to kiss you good night properly, and that little peck didn't count!" He kissed me fully on my lips for a good thirty seconds. We separated, slightly breathless.

I nestled in close to him. "And I've been waiting for months to sleep beside you without any fear, just like this. Just us; just like this."

He giggled, and a cute smile spread across his face. "Do you know what I thought about the first time we watched *The Princess Bride*? Hmm? I kept thinking that you'll look like Cary Elwes when you're his age. He is so damn hot in that movie, and I swear you'll turn out just like him when you're twenty-five. Except you've got better hair." He snickered and ran his hand through my hair.

"Well, as long as you don't turn out like Andre the Giant in ten years!"

He looked at me in horror and said, "I would not say such things if I were you! Say that again, and I'll challenge you to a game of 'to the pain'!"

I leaned up to kiss his cheek again. "Just kidding, Brandon! You're the hottest guy I know. I can't wait to see you in ten years. We'll be the hottest couple ever!"

"That's assuming I don't find someone hotter than you with some decent arms before then."

I was too tired to think of a come-back; I just rolled my eyes instead.

He reached over the other way to turn out the bedside lamp. When he settled again, he draped his arm around my head and squeezed my upper left arm.

"Good night, my little stick-arm friend. Rest well and dream of large women."

I giggled and said, "Thank God, I'm not Fezzick. No women for me. I just want you, Brandon. You and only you."

"Good! Let's just leave the ladies out of it!"

I turned on my side and pressed in close to Brandon. He kissed my forehead again and rested his chin on the crown of my head. I faded away in seconds.

. . .

Dad picked us up the next morning for our weekly run at Hermann Park. I caught him looking at us in a slightly bemused manner. Did he sense something had changed between Brandon and me? I couldn't be sure. At the same time, I was so filled with euphoria because of Brandon I hardly had time to scrutinize my dad's humored looks and knowing smiles.

Dad and Mom decided we three needed a night out. We went to one of our favorite places: Antonio's, a small Italian restaurant on Montrose, right between two gay bars. I remember a time in sixth grade when we had to wait on the sidewalk for fifteen minutes before a table became available. I was too young to put all the pieces together then, but I distinctly remember noticing that every couple that went into either bar was a same-sex pair.

All through seventh and eighth grade I had been wondering about those bars and a few others like them I had seen around our neighborhood. I eventually understood what they were all about, and a surge of excitement flowed through me as I imagined what it might be like to walk in there with Brandon when we were older.

After dinner, we stopped by our favorite ice cream stand on the way home and headed back for a quiet night reading together. We settled on the couch. Dad held Mom's old hardback copy of *A Room with a View* in his lap, marked where we left off the previous Tuesday. I could have sworn a lifetime passed since then. I was irretrievably different from the boy who sat there just a few nights before as we read about the initial blossoming of love between Lucy and George in Florence. I thought back to that first kiss between them and then to my own with Brandon. I struggled to keep a smile off my face as I hunkered down between my parents.

Dad didn't open the book as quickly as I expected. Mom shifted her body slightly my direction so she wouldn't have to crane her neck to see me. Neither of them said a word. Ah, I knew what was up! They wanted to talk. The patient, pregnant silence was their way of wordlessly signaling to me that they would wait for me to say what they already knew I was going to say. They played that game with me many times as a child! Their silences were more powerful and alluring than any words Mr. Marshall may have shouted. As the silence lengthened, I wondered if he ever considered my parents' tactic. Didn't he realize a child with a burning secret is much more likely to speak into a knowing, loving silence than the fearful, tenuous silence that followed his verbal outbursts?

I cleared my throat. I knew the hardest part of our conversation would be the first ten or so words. Not that I had counted them out, but the principle was sound: once the dam burst, there was no stopping the flow.

I reached for my glass of water on the low coffee table in front of the couch. I sipped. I sipped again. I could have sipped a camel's worth of water. I set my glass back down. My parents hadn't budged or sighed or shifted or cleared their throats. Loving but steely eyes looked back at mine.

The words gushed out of me: "Brandon kissed me in his pool yesterday. I kissed him back as hard as I could." I couldn't contain the smile any longer. "He told me he had loved me since the first day we met at church, and I told him the same."

Mom said, "Well, wow, sweetie! Wow! Just like that? All your questions and doubts disappeared in a second, huh?"

"Yes, everything changed in a second. Maybe less. In that fraction of a second when his lips met mine, I knew."

Dad said, "Alex, it's a beautiful thing to fall in love. I never really fell in love until I met your mom. I dated a few girls in high school, but your mom was my first real love. It was like nothing I had ever known, especially when I realized she loved me, too."

Mom took my hand and held it to her cheek. "Well, we knew something was going on inside your heart and mind.

Your dad said you and Brandon were smiling in some new way when he picked you up this morning. He sensed something was different and thought perhaps you two had found some way to speak of your love." She paused and chuckled. "Though we didn't imagine you had kissed already!"

Dad laughed and wiped his eyes. "Definitely not! I didn't even imagine the possibility of you boys kissing just yet!" He took my other hand and held it in his lap. "But if it's what you both want, then go ahead. Take a few steps and see how you feel as you go. A kiss can be a beautiful thing."

I wondered if I could tell them we had held each other's penises. Would they guess that? Would they think it odd? It seemed so intimate, and I wasn't sure I could tell them just yet.

Mom said gently, "It's important that you two go slowly. Even if you were attracted to a young girl, we would tell you to go slowly. You're not even fourteen yet. You're our precious, sweet, impossibly amazing boy, and your heart is experiencing things that are far beyond your years in some ways. Then when you add on the layer of you and Brandon both being boys..." She chuckled. "I mean, what else would you be, right? That was a weird way to say it. I just mean you are two boys, rather, you are two young teenagers, and what you've discovered with each other is different and rare. Let it grow and blossom, but let us help you through it in whatever way we can, okay?"

I nodded.

Dad continued, "Really, Alex, we mean it. If you were attracted to a girl who was a year older than you at this point in your life, we'd want to know what you were doing and how you were feeling. Part of what we love about you is your openness with us. We think you trust us."

"I do! I do trust you!"

"We know you do, but we also know there is a natural tendency to hold things back, especially about love, from your parents. My dad told me nothing about love or sex. I figured it out all on my own. Well, on my own and with the help of some randy boys at school. They talked smut all the time, and I soon knew more than I wanted to know. I think I was in fourth grade when I learned how babies were made." He laughed at the memory.

Mom said, "I had a little more guidance from your Grandma Allen, but I kept a lot back from her. We want you to trust us and talk to us and tell us as much as you can. There will come a day when you can keep your private life totally to yourself, but for now, as we allow you to spend time with Brandon and as he comes over here, we have a responsibility to know what's happening with you two. Does that make sense?"

I wasn't sure I grasped the full meaning of what she said. I had a sense there were deep waters all around me, and I was only floating on the surface.

Dad picked up her train of thought. The old, sturdy line that connected their brains held firm even in unexplored territory. "What we mean is we want you to take it slow with what you and Brandon do with your bodies together. You're both very young. We don't even know what you know yet about sex. It was a conversation we planned to have at some point when we thought you would one day come to like girls. When we realized that was perhaps not the way you were developing, we thought we'd wait. We were afraid that talking to you about physical touch and sex with girls might make you think we expected you to want that. Does that make sense?"

I nodded. For the first time since the conversation when I told them I was gay, I realized what a journey my parents had been on. They had to shelve 'the talk about girls' while they waited to see what was going to happen with me. I upset all their carefully laid plans. I guess they never imagined they would have to have 'the talk about other boys' with me!

Dad went on: "So, we just left things. We didn't think there was any rush. We didn't think you were going to get in any kind of awkward situation with a girl that we needed to prepare you for. And we couldn't imagine you had eyes for any boy but Brandon." I couldn't help but gasp. Dad patted my leg and smiled. "We figured things were in a holding pattern with him. So, it just seemed like we should leave it. We wanted to walk alongside you and not get too far ahead of you."

He smiled in that old familiar way that made me feel impossibly safe and loved. "And, remember, you're our first gay son! This is all new for us. We're kind of building the airplane as we fly it, so to speak. We're not totally clueless, but we are learning a lot as we go."

We sat in silence for a few seconds. I realized they were waiting for me. Somehow, they knew there was more to come!

I took a deep breath. "Brandon and I have touched each other. On our abs. And our arms. But we've done that for a long time. Just playing together." I gulped. "But when we were kissing, he put his hand down my swim trunks." I gulped again. "And I put my hand down his. We felt each other's penises."

A scarlet blush raced up my neck and face. I felt as if I was on fire! Damn my fair skin and blonde hair! Without missing a beat, Dad said, "It's okay, Alex. Keep breathing. You're okay; we're okay. Anything else?"

I shook my head. "Not really. We held hands as we fell asleep last night, and he kissed me a few times before he drifted off. But that's it."

Mom breathed a deep sigh of relief. Had she been worried about something else? "There's nothing wrong with any of that, Alex. But that's all that it needs to be for now."

Dad said, "We need to keep talking. This is as good a time as any. Are you ready to keep talking? Do you need a break?"

I shook my head. I was afraid to get up but also afraid to go on. I had a sense my parents were about to take me past the shallow waters of my limited imagination and experience.

Would I ever come up back to the surface?

Dad continued: "Men who have sex together don't do the exact things that heterosexual couples do together. Do you know what a man and a woman can do?"

"Yes, I know about a man putting his penis into a woman's vagina. I know that. Eric told me."

"Okay, so when men who love each other want to express the same kind of attraction at that level, they might have anal sex. You know what anal means, right?"

"Yeah, like your bottom." I realized in a flash where Dad was headed.

"Okay, so one man, who has an erection, could insert his penis in his partner's anus. That's one thing they might do. Are you okay with this information so far?"

I nodded meekly.

"And the other thing they may do is for one man to put his penis in his partner's mouth."

I went hard in a flash as I imagined Brandon kneeling before me, my enlarged penis in his mouth. It was surprisingly shocking and satisfying all at once.

Mom said gently, "Alex, we really want you to feel comfortable. Are you okay?"

"Yeah, I think so. I think I kind of knew about both those things. I mean, I heard someone at school talk about two men being butt-fuckers. What he meant didn't hit me for several days."

Mom murmured, "God, what do we pay those school fees for?"

Dad said, "Right. So, you know a little bit about both things. There's no reason for you and Brandon to do either of those things any time soon, certainly not before you feel like you might be ready. If it's not something you want to do, then don't do it."

Mom said, "And sweetie, this is important. Brandon is so much bigger than you are. I've seen you play and wrestle before, and I know he can overpower you easily. You mustn't ever let him do something to you if you don't want him to do it. Okay?"

I cried out, "Brandon would never, ever hurt me! I know he wouldn't! I swear. He's rough with other guys, but he's always gentle with me. Even when he overpowers me when we wrestle, there's a kindness in it. Last summer this jerk at camp challenged him to a wrestling match. Brandon didn't want to. He tried to get out of it, but the other guy insisted and called Brandon a pussy. Brandon slammed him into the ground so hard. I mean, there was a kind of roughness in Brandon that startled me. But he's never like that with me. Honestly. Never!"

"I know he's really gentle with you. But in the heat of the moment, when two people are strongly attracted to one another, all kinds of things can go wrong. And often, the physically weaker partner can get hurt badly. That's why we want to say these things now. We want you to know what's possible so you can protect yourself."

A deep sense of sadness washed over me. I truly believed I was impossibly safe with Brandon, but the thought that love sometimes went so wrong filled me with despair.

Dad let out a long sigh and kissed my cheek. "That's a lot for you to take in. We love you so much for telling us the truth. We're on your side, and the best way we can help you is to know what's happening and what you're feeling. Can we trust you to do that for us? Can we trust you to be honest? We don't want to hound you every time you spend time with Brandon. We are going to rely on you to let us know when you want to talk about things."

I nodded and smiled at them both.

Mom took my hand in hers. "Your dad and I have been talking with Nick and David quite a bit over the last several months. You know how much they love you. They said they would be happy to talk with the three of us and Brandon any time, if you think that would help. So, keep that in mind, okay? I think it would be good for you and Brandon. You don't have to do any of this on your own. Okay, sweetie?"

I nodded again.

"Right," Dad said, "let's see what Lucy and George are up to. I have a feeling you could teach them both a thing or two about a first kiss." He chuckled and opened the book.

CHAPTER 11

Mom had to speak at a work-related conference in the first week of July… in Hawaii! As a way to thank the Marshalls for all they did for me, Dad and Mom invited Brandon to come with us. The Marshalls agreed. They even let us pay for Brandon's airfare, though they sent him with spending money and told my parents not to spoil Brandon with extra purchases beyond what he could afford with his money.

Dad, Brandon, and I went to get some snacks once we found our gate at the airport. Brandon tried to pay for his own. Dad put his arm around Brandon and said, "I'll shove that wallet up your ass if you try to pay for anything else again. Got it?"

Brandon grinned with delight. "Yes, sir! Got it!" He slipped his wallet back in his pocket and winked at me.

A little later as the wait lengthened because of a short flight delay, Mom and I went off to the restrooms. When we came back to the seating area near the gate, Dad and Brandon were engaged in a serious-looking talk. Brandon, turned a quarter of the way in his seat, was leaning in close to Dad. Dad's left hand rested on Brandon's right forearm. I wondered if they might want another few minutes alone. A knowing look from

Mom telegraphed the same intuition had struck her, and we kept walking to a small newsstand further down the concourse.

Mom slipped her arm through mine and said, "Honey, your dad is going to try to walk this delicate walk with Brandon. He's not Brandon's dad. He can't really have a say in Brandon's life. He can't change a single damn thing about Brandon's father. I know Mrs. Marshall is very loving and tender with Brandon, but his father is a bit of a monster, to be honest. We'd have left that church long, long ago if it weren't for your friendship."

She sighed and turned to look at me while we paused next to a rack of magazines. "But your dad is going to do all that he can to be a father-like figure to Brandon every time we are together. He can't replace Brandon's dad, but he can compensate for some of what Brandon's missed all these years."

She leaned in close and kissed my cheek. "Will that be okay, sweetie? Do you understand that he won't have less love for you? In fact, loving Brandon is a way he can love you even more. Does that make sense?"

Soft tears fell from my eyes. I nodded. "Yeah, it makes sense. It's the best thing Dad could ever do for me. I want Brandon to know what a different kind of dad could be like. I want him to know the kind of love I get from you two. I think he needs it, especially from Dad. Plus, Brandon already loves you both so much. He thinks of you like a second set of parents."

"We love him, too, Alex. I'd like to knock him upside the head every once in a while, but that's because I do love him. He's got a heart as big as Texas. What else could we want in a friend for you and a kind of second-son for ourselves?"

We got to Honolulu late on Saturday afternoon. The island was magical, impossibly lush, and intoxicating! Brandon giggled with delight at every turn as we made our way in a taxi to the hotel. Mom's department gave her a generous travel allowance. My parents put in some of their own money, and we were able to get an ocean-facing suite at a beautiful hotel in Kahala. The suite had two bedrooms with private bathrooms and a large living space between the rooms. It seemed like heaven to Brandon and me. He kept looking at me and shaking his head, speechless and amazed. Perhaps he was thinking of all the 'vacations' he'd spent in Tennessee with his infamous Dayton cousins. Our Hawaiian vacation was the stuff of legends in his limited experience.

Mom's conference didn't begin until Monday morning. Dad and Mom hung around the hotel pool all day Sunday. I saw her working on some notes a few times and reading over papers and journal articles she brought with her. Dad lost himself in a paperback spy novel. Brandon and I spent the whole day at the beach just in front of the hotel. The day was a happy blur of white sand, blue water, swaying palms, and Brandon close by my side every second.

While Mom attended her conference Monday, Tuesday, and Wednesday, Dad, Brandon, and I toured the island just like we were a family who had taken similar vacations many times before. There were moments when it seemed as if he had always been a part of my life, as if those lonely childhood years somehow belonged to another boy named Alex.

Whenever Brandon and I separated, maybe to take a restroom break or take in a view from a different angle, Brandon would drift toward Dad. Dad would often pat the small of Brandon's back or ruffle his hair. It made me impossibly happy to see how much Dad loved Brandon and treated him like a second son.

Those three days were some of the best days of my life: we took a helicopter ride over a local volcano; we went on a hike to a waterfall; we had long waterside lunches; we toured a nearby pineapple farm; and we spent many hours at the beach. I hadn't seen Dad so relaxed and happy in a long time.

Brandon smiled every second of every hour. My own face

got tired just looking at his permanent grin, but I couldn't begrudge him his happiness. I'd never known anyone in my life who deserved a real family vacation as much as he did.

In the evenings at dinner, Brandon would regale Mom with tales from our adventures. He loved being center-stage, and the three of us turned the lime-light fully onto him as often as we could. He got Mom laughing so hard she had to leave the table to collect herself. We drew a few stares from nearby diners, but our little four-member universe remained impervious to all the sideways glances.

Brandon and I showed remarkable self-restraint and caution at every turn. There were times, as we toured around with Dad those blissful three days, when I'd catch Brandon looking at me with a startling intensity. I'd catch his eye and shake my head a bit in warning. He'd shake his head, too, as if coming out of a trance. He'd give me a wink and look away.

Other times he'd be standing very close to me, maybe with his hand on my shoulder. I'd wiggle my shoulder a bit, and he'd drop his hand in response. We had this kind of constant tug-of-war going on: his inclination was always to move closer, to touch me, and I had to be the one who pulled away slightly or stood apart just a little. All of it went against my true desires, but I was the one with a little more self-control and self-awareness. I had to do it for both our sakes.

On Wednesday, late in the afternoon, we were playing around in the ocean. Brandon was splashing me, dunking me, holding me close and tossing me around – all the normal things we usually did in his pool. Without thinking he dropped his hand to my crotch and felt his way into my trunks. I froze and looked around. He froze, too. We immediately plunged into the water so he could pull out his hand. While we were under the waves, he kissed me roughly on my lips. I looked around as we came up. Nobody was even looking our way, but I knew we had been lucky.

As we made our way back to the shore, he sighed and said,

"God, this is worse than I thought. I just wanna be close to you, Alex, and I have to be Mr. Hands-to-Myself here in paradise. It's like a kind of perverse torture. This friends-only act sucks!"

"Well, Mom once told me that pleasure denied is pleasure intensified. Just tell yourself when we can finally be alone, it'll be that much better."

He slipped his arm around my waist and said, "I don't care who sees me do this. Friends do this all time. I just gotta feel you near me for a while. If anybody says anything, I'll punch their teeth out. I've been very good all day, Alex. I deserve a little reward for showing so much self-control." I felt his hand slip just below the top of my trunks, but he stopped it from going any lower.

We wandered back to a secluded grove where we'd left our towels and beach supplies in the shade of some soaring palm trees. I sat down on my towel and dusted my feet off. Brandon leaned back and rested his head on my thigh. He looked up into my eyes and said, "It's so amazing to be here with you. You're the most beautiful guy on this beach... on this whole damn island, actually."

"I know. I *am* pretty hot!"

He snorted. "Come on, dumbass. You're supposed say 'no, not really' and then compliment me on my hotness."

"Oh, right! I didn't realize you said something nice about me just so I'd say something nice about you."

He stuck out his tongue at me.

I continued, "Well, after me, you're the hottest guy on the island. A distant second, but still in second."

He rolled his eyes. "That's not what I meant!" He went quiet for a few seconds before continuing. "You know, I've been watching some other couples the last few days. I mean some straight couples near our ages. I keep wondering if I'd ever want to be the guy in the couple. Know what I mean? Like, would I want to be with these girls we keep seeing? But

I don't even have the slightest interest in them. I mean, I don't want to kiss anyone but you. I don't want to play around with anyone but you. Just you. Even when you're a smartass, I just wanna be next to you."

"You do know you contradict yourself, right? One minute I'm a smartass; the next minute I'm a dumbass. You keep using that word. I do not think it means what you think it means." I winked at him. "It's funny you say that about seeing these couples because I've thought the same thing a few times. I've been jealous to see how easy it is for these straight couples, even Dad and Mom. They can be totally open no matter where they go or who's around, but I wouldn't trade places with a single one of them. I can't imagine walking down the beach hand-in-hand with a girl. Never in a million years. Only you."

"You mean, you're not gonna ask Sarah to go out with you if she's at camp again?"

"Oh, my God, Brandon! I did all that just to please you. I felt so bad for her. I cringed every time I had to hold her hand. I'm sure she realized it. She deserved a genuine boyfriend, not a fake like me. I don't know why I let you talk me into that. What were you thinking?"

"I don't know! I was a mess. I knew I was supposed to want to be with a girl. That's what everyone does at camp. I just went along with it. I was just trying to fit in and be like the other guys."

"And you dragged me into it! And then you blew up at me! I mean, I did what you wanted and then you screamed at me!"

"I was a dickhead! I realize it! I look back, and I don't even know what I was thinking. I was so confused. I think part of me secretly hoped you would refuse to go out with Sarah. Like it would have been a sign some part of me was looking for. But when you agreed to go out with her, I thought that was a sign you were into girls. I was miserable! I figured I didn't have a snowball's chance in hell with you."

"Is that what you said you couldn't tell me?"

"What do you mean?"

"Remember on the last day of camp when we were talking on the swing and you apologized again? I asked if there was something else on your mind when you hollered at me. And you said there was, but you couldn't tell me. Was all this on your mind?"

"Yeah, of course. I just didn't understand any of it. Every time I saw you with Sarah, I felt so lost and alone. I wanted to be the one holding your hand!"

"But you set us up!"

"I know! I know! It makes no sense." He shook his head. "Do you see now why I blew up? There I was with you and Joel, the two coolest and hottest guys in the fucking universe, but I couldn't say what I was really thinking. I couldn't admit that I wanted to hold your hand, not Cathy's. I wanted to kiss you, not Cathy. It's like part of me knew all that, but another part of me was lost and confused. And I just erupted because you were being so sweet about Sarah. I wanted you to be that sweet about me."

I reached down and stroked his hair. "Well, it's all over now. I mean, why re-live it and beat ourselves up about it? We're in this amazing paradise. Let's just enjoy this while we can."

He sat up in a flash, kissed me on my cheek, and wrapped his arm around my shoulders. "How did I get so lucky, Alex?"

"You're certainly punching above your weight!"

"What does that mean? I've got a mean-ass punch. You know it!"

"It means I'm on, like, level 10 on the hotness scale, and you're on level 7. Maybe 8 when those two pimples on your chin go away. You're outta your league with me, Brandon."

He dropped his arm from around my shoulder and turned to face me straight on, a mixture of exaggerated outrage and mischievous delight playing out across his shifting facial expressions.

"Oh, my God! You are so fucking full of yourself. Whatever happened to that impossibly sweet, shy, PBS-loving guy who walked into the church kitchen two years ago? I think I'm gonna call the FBI. Put out an APB. A boy named Alexander Nathan Kennedy is gone without a trace. We're gonna get his picture plastered on every milk carton in America. Your parents can do a teary-eyed interview with Barbara Walters."

"What do you mean what happened to me? *You*, Brandon! *You* happened to me! You totally corrupted me! You dragged me down to your dirty world of Dolly Parton's tits and Dick Clark's dick. All your swearing and cussing has totally polluted me! And you were the one who just said you were lucky. Your subconscious was talking there. You know I'm way outta your league. Just admit it and be glad I've stooped down to be your friend."

He tackled me with force, his irresistible, mega-watt smile spreading from ear to ear. He pinned me on my back, holding my arms firmly to the towel. "Well, if my arms looked like yours, I wouldn't be so smug. Smartass!"

"Keep on about my arms, and you'll be sleeping on the fold-out bed in the sitting room tonight. I am so done with your knees in my back all night long."

He hovered an inch or two above me. All I wanted to do was kiss him and slip my hands down his trunks. Then I wanted him to collapse fully on me, his legs stacked on my legs, his chest pressed firmly against mine.

"You little shit! I never corrupted you. I just brought out your secret side. I was like the match that lit some straw that was already waiting to burn. If it wasn't for me, you'd be sitting here on this beach by your sorry-ass-self with your nose stuck in a boring English novel waiting for Mr. Darcy to come swoop you up. I mean, who do you really want to be with: me or Mr. Nose-in-the-Air Darcy? Hmm?" He kissed the tip of my nose.

I kissed him back on the lips and said, "And you'd be sitting in your bedroom all alone, probably jacking off in front of Gary, fearing your dad would walk in any second and scream the house down all around you."

As soon as the words were out, I knew I had gone too far. In a fraction of a second, the light went out of Brandon's eyes, and his smile vanished like some phantom spooked by its own shadow. He heaved himself up and flopped on his back.

I rolled over to him and gently kissed his shoulder. "God, Brandon, I'm sorry. I didn't mean to go in for that low blow. I'm really sorry… really, really sorry, buddy."

"Oh, it's not that. Honestly! I deserve all the jabs you give me. It's just the mere mention of my dad. I haven't thought about him since the airport. I kept thinking he was gonna show up before we left and say he changed his mind and drag me out of the terminal, with my suitcase trailing behind me. Once we were in the air, I felt like the plane was flying because my own heart was flying. Like I was keeping us all in the sky. I literally haven't thought about him in days.

"But all of this is just a dream! It's all coming to an end! We have to go to camp soon and pretend we're just normal friends all week. I have listen to my dad's sermons at church and listen to his shouting at home. I mean, what's the point of a vacation like this if we have to go back to something so awful? At least you get to be with your parents all the time. But it's back to cock-sucking reality for me."

"You know we'd keep you with us forever if we could. It's just not so simple. We just gotta put up with your dad. I know you get the brunt of it. I'd take it all for you if I could." I reached over and tilted his chin toward me. "And this vacation is totally worth it. It's a like a piggy bank of memories. Next time your dad's outta control, just think about this right here, right now – you and me on the beach all alone. Think about this whole week. Pick your favorite memory and tip it out of the piggy bank whenever you need it."

I kissed him softly on his lips and said, "He can't take that away from you no matter how loud he gets."

Brandon let out a soft sigh and said, "We're back where we started."

"What do you mean?"

"Me wondering how I got so lucky!"

. . .

Once her conference was done, Mom and Dad relaxed at the beach all day Thursday. They parked themselves on lounge chairs under a shared umbrella, only moving with the shade and to take short dips in the ocean. Brandon and I went to look for souvenirs in the morning. We guarded our purchases carefully, lest we saw what we bought for one another. We had lunch on our own at a nearby hamburger stand; Brandon even splurged on a milkshake for dessert.

We spent the afternoon playing on the beach – tossing a Frisbee, flying a kite Dad bought us, building a sandcastle, burying each other in the sand, and running to get drinks for Mom and Dad. As we walked back to the hotel in the late afternoon, Brandon whispered, "Damn! My piggy bank is overflowing!"

We had dinner that evening, our second-to-last night, in the hotel restaurant. We got a table by itself on the far side of the dining room. Warm air and the soft sound of the surf drifted in through the wide-open sliding doors. We ate mostly in silence. Mom and Dad were oddly tired and relaxed all at once. The intense days of sun, surf, and non-stop revelry finally caught up with Brandon and me, too. The sun, which seemed to energize and inspire us for the previous five days, finally demanded her payment. We had worn ourselves out.

Later that evening, the four of us sat on the long sofa in our suite, looking out to the dark ocean and the last glimmer of the sunset. Dad and Mom sat at opposite ends. Brandon sat next to Dad, and I was next to Mom. Our legs were pressed close together, and he linked his foot behind my ankle, caressing the top of my foot with his toes.

Dad cleared his throat and said, "We want to talk to you two a little. Your mom and I..." He stopped and looked at Brandon. "Do you mind if I refer to us as 'Mom and Dad'? You're always so respectful to call us Mr. and Mrs. Kennedy, but you're like a son to us."

"No, I don't mind. I think of you like Mom and Dad, too. I just don't say it because I don't want to make you uncomfortable."

Mom said, "We know you have your own parents. They love you more than we possibly could because you are their own flesh, their own son. But we do love like a son. You can call us Dad and Mom anytime. If we had two sons, we would want them to be just like you and Alex. He's the best son we could ever ask for. We don't deserve him, and we don't feel like we deserve you either." She reached across me to take his hand. "You are so lovely in our eyes. Do you believe that? You are so lovely and so good."

Brandon nodded. I could feel him soften beside me, and a little of that hard shell he often projected weakened under my parents' tender words.

Dad went on. "We know about you and Alex... how much you care for one another. We know you have a very special friendship, and we know you feel an attraction to each other that is different from the way most boys your age feel about their friends."

He paused and turned toward Brandon a little more. "None of that changes a thing about you as far as we're concerned. We love you just the same. Or maybe even more, because we know it's not an easy thing for you to bear because of your family and the church. You've had to deal with so many things that other boys your age will never understand. We want you to know we love you and like you just the way you are. We both think you're wonderful in so many ways. It's important to us that you believe that about yourself. There's nothing wrong with you for loving Alex. Not a damn thing."

Brandon sobbed beside me. I had heard him cry before out of frustration, anger, and shame, but his tears that night were something different: tears of relief, release, and joy. He reached out to take my hand. Out of the corner of my eye I saw Dad slip his arm through Brandon's left arm. Mom got up and knelt in front of Brandon. She placed her hands on top of his legs. I leaned in closer, too, and rested my head against my friend's reassuring shoulder. We held him there between us, the love we three had shared for so long, wrapping itself around him as a kind of transforming cocoon.

We let Brandon sob and sob. Great drops of tears and snot fell from his face. Even in those painful contortions, he remained my impossibly beautiful best friend. In fact, he seemed even more beautiful, as if the inner Brandon, the part of him which was purest and most innocent, suffused his face and pierced his outer husk. I realized in that moment there was a kind of holiness to my friend, a sacred wholeness that had survived many fierce blows. It wasn't the self-righteous holiness I had come to know at church. It was, instead, an earthy holiness – an amalgamation of real flesh, real blood, real suffering, and the transforming possibility of unconditional love and absolute acceptance.

I had no sense of time apart from the gradual disappearance of light from the horizon and the faint glow of distant stars as they flickered to life in the dark dome above us. Slowly, Brandon's heaving lessened, his sobs subdued, and he settled into a deep hush beside me. His breathing slowed. The pulse in his vein-streaked arm, pressed in close to mine, beat placidly again. Dad and Mom eventually kissed us good night and walked arm-in-arm to their bedroom.

A little while later, Brandon held me in his strong arms as we lay on our sides facing each other in bed. I pressed close up to his chest, my head nestled safely between his arm and torso.

I had no thought in the world except for him. Exam results, freshman year class schedules, Mr. Marshall's immaterial lurking presence, the horrific attack of last October: none of it mattered. I was full of gratitude. I knew how impossible it was that Brandon and I could have made it to such a point in our lives. With every odd stacked against us, we had found our way to each other.

I whispered, "You okay?"

"I am. I'm more than okay. I've never felt like this before. Please don't tell me I'm dreaming. I couldn't stand to wake up in the morning and realize this had all been a dream."

"No, you're not dreaming. It's like a dream, but we're fully awake. It's all true."

"Yeah, but for how long, buddy?"

"I don't know, but I'm happy enough right now. This is all I want right now."

. . .

Brandon and I assumed our last full day in Hawaii would be like the one before: a lazy day of sand, sun, and sea. My parents had other plans. They filled us in as we sat on the hotel patio enjoying a leisurely breakfast.

Dad set down his coffee cup and smiled. "So, boys, we've been saving the best for last. I know you were planning on a day at the beach. I'm sorry to ruin your plans, but your mom and I have something educational planned. You've wasted so much time here doing nothing. It's time to engage your brains just a little."

Brandon eyed me suspiciously. He looked disappointed. I, however, knew my parents better. They never delivered bad news so casually. I looked over at Mom. She held her coffee cup in front of her mouth for an impossibly long time. I could see the edges of a smirk peeking out on both sides of the rim, and her eyes sparkled with that mischievous radiance I knew so well. I thought I'd play along and see where things went.

I sighed and rolled my eyes. "Come on, Dad. We deserve one more fun day. I spend my whole life doing educational things."

Brandon chimed in. "Yeah, Mr. Kennedy… I mean *Papa-Numero-Dos*. Alex is the hardest working student I know. And all your educational stuff is lost on me. He knows I am a total dumbass." He froze. "Oh, God, I mean, he knows I'm not anywhere as smart as he is!"

Brandon actually blushed! God, this was gonna be fun.

I put on my best pleading act. "Come on, Dad. I'll read extra books when we go back. I'll make Brandon read Dickens with me all next week. And *War and Peace* the next week… and the week after… and the week after that. Just let us have one final fun day."

Brandon gulped loudly. He looked startled, his eyes imploring me to break down my parents' defenses.

My parents were sly ol' foxes. A knowing look passed between all three of us. They knew I knew they had no such 'educational plans' in mind. They knew I knew something of a totally different caliber was on tap for the day. I bet they even knew I had a pretty good clue about what they had in store.

Mom sat down her coffee cup, a semi-scowl fixed firmly in place. "We indulge you all the time. We have given you two every chance to be carefree all week. We don't think it's too much to ask you to spend a few hours in some museums today."

Brandon gasped. I shot him my best 'quiet-you-big-loaf-or-you'll-make-it-worse' look. He gulped again and looked down.

Dad cut in, "We're really not having a discussion. We gave you free reign all week. Today is ours to do what we want to do. You two are coming with us. That's an end to it. If you want to be happy today, you can. If you want to be miserable, you can. You and Brandon decide which way you'd rather spend your last day here."

We finished breakfast in silence. Brandon mostly stared out to sea. I think he was more disappointed in the way my parents broke the news than in the actual thought of going to some museums. He had come to be very comfortable with their easy-going manner. He seemed confused and hurt by their sudden abruptness and inflexibility. I almost wished we could call off the charade. There were times when he seemed so fragile; even a second's worth of upset was more than I could bear to see him endure.

Mom tapped my toe under the table just before we stood up to leave. I looked across to her. She gave me a wink and nodded at Brandon. She pressed her finger to lips and pretended to zip them shut.

Mom leaned over to Brandon and gently kissed his cheek. "We'll have a wonderful day, sweetie. We're not mad at you. We're only firm with Alex like this when we think he's being a bit selfish and immature. The two of you have weeks and weeks ahead of you to spend together. Let your old parents have their own kind of fun today."

Brandon smiled. He looked between my parents, then back at me, and said, "I know what you mean. For Alex, it's 'all about me' twenty-four-seven. His little world revolves around him." He winked at me. "It's about time you put him in his place."

He leaned toward Mom and kissed her cheek. "I'm happy with whatever makes you two happy today. This has been the best vacation ever. I'd go to fifty museums today to show my thanks."

Dad cleared his throat and said, "Well, we have a new favorite son. No doubt about that!"

Brandon beamed. He looked at me and winked again. It felt so good to let my friend have his moment. I'd be in the doghouse with my parents for a year as a trade-off for making him smile. He brought out every good-natured, generous cell in my body.

As we stood up from the table, I made a small dolphin-like noise under my breath. Brandon didn't even notice but Dad did. He winked at me and linked his arm through mine. He whispered, "He won't know what hit him!"

When we got back to the suite, Mom pulled me aside while Dad steered Brandon out to the balcony on some pretense. She whispered, "Tell him to change into shorts and a polo shirt for the museum. Pick out a pair of swim trunks and a couple of t-shirts, clean undies, and whatever else you think he might need. Be discreet. If you can, set the things outside the door when he's not looking, and I'll put them in my big beach bag."

Twenty minutes later, the four of us made our way out of the hotel lobby and hailed a taxi. Dad went around to the driver's side and whispered something. As we other three piled in, Dad shouted loudly, outrageously so, "Honolulu Museum of Art, please."

A few minutes into the drive, Brandon realized we were heading away from the city. He whispered to me, "I think the ol' taxi driver is lost. I remember seeing the museum that day coming back from the pineapple farm. It's right in the city, not out here."

I shrugged and pretended ignorance.

A little later, we pulled up to a small kiosk near a jetty where a large catamaran bobbed idly in the water. Brandon looked at me askance. "What's going on here?"

I shrugged again but couldn't hide a smile.

Mom and Dad chuckled as we tumbled out of the taxi. I grabbed Brandon's arm and pointed to a sign above the kiosk. He read it aloud in a soft voice: "Ocean's Dream Snorkeling Adventures: See Dolphins and More".

Brandon began hopping from foot to foot. "Wait, wait, wait! There is no museum tour, is there? You've been bull-shitting me all morning?"

I burst out laughing and slapped him on the back.

"You knew all along? You little rat fink! You total turd butt of a rat fink!"

His head whiplashed to Dad and Mom. "And you two! You had me going. You so had me going! I was so ready to brave the museums just for you, just to show up my little stick-arm friend here, and it was all a show! It was all a show!"

Dad said, "Well, you made it too easy for us. We were gonna trick you both, but he knows us too well. We let him play along!"

Brandon hooted with glee! "I can't believe it! This is my life's dream! I get to swim with dolphins with my best friend!"

He grabbed me in a huge bear hug and spun me around about twenty times. We staggered apart, dizzy with excitement and joy.

"Well," Mom said, "we're not going to actually swim with dolphins. It's not a very good thing for the dolphins. We read up about it before we came. You can find guides who will take you swimming with dolphins, but many scientists who specialize in dolphin well-being say it's not good for the dolphins the way these companies do it. It can be quite traumatic for the dolphins."

Brandon's face melted. "You mean, it's bad for the dolphins if we go swimming with them? I had no idea. Why do those bastards do it?"

Dad said, "Well, those bastards are just out for money. We decided to follow the advice we got from the tourist agency. This boat will take us snorkeling in an area where we are likely to see dolphins. It's the best way to keep the dolphins safe and happy."

"That's all I want. I want them to be safe and happy. I never knew it was harmful to swim with them. They always look so happy when I've seen other people do it on TV."

Dad put his arm around Brandon's waist. "Well, this is a way to make both of you happy: you get to see dolphins fairly close up and they get to stay at a safe distance where they won't feel stressed or in danger. They may come close, but it will be their choice. The boat won't go chasing them down." He looked at his watch. "Now, you two have about five minutes to go in that bathroom and change. We'll go pick up the tickets and wait for you down by that dock. See where the rope is? Meet us right there." He clapped his hands. "Hurry! Hop to it!"

Mom tossed me the bag with our clothes, and we ran over to the bathroom, Brandon hooting and hollering the whole time.

Just as we came out, he stopped dead in his tracks.

I asked, "What's wrong?"

He said bleakly, "I just saw that sign with the prices. I don't have that much money! Not even close. I've got, like, $25 left."

"Oh, come on, you big moronic loaf of bread. As if they're gonna let you pay for your ticket! This is their gift to you. To us. Get it?"

"But my dad will have a cow if he ever finds out. It's one thing when they buy me ice cream, but a $110 ticket is something different."

"Well, he won't ever find out. My lips are sealed. My parents' lips are sealed. Your lips are sealed. Nobody will ever know!"

He snickered and said, "Well, I'll see about unsealing your lips tonight." He grabbed me by the hand and pulled me behind him as we raced down to the dock.

. . .

Later that evening, Brandon and I sat beside each other on the small balcony outside our bedroom. Two balconies to the left, Mom and Dad sat on theirs. They only glanced over at us one time. They seemed lost in their own world, content to leave us in ours.

Brandon's left arm was draped around my shoulder. I

leaned my head up against the side of his chest.

"How about that deal now?"

I gave him a puzzled glance.

He clarified, "That deal to unseal your lips, dumbass."

I giggled and said, "Well, I suppose you can. I'll let you try this one time."

We tilted our heads close together and lingered in a long kiss.

Brandon finally pulled away. He turned onto his back and rested his head in my lap. I laid my right hand on his chest and ran my left hand through his hair.

"So how was today? Was it what you imagined?"

He beamed up at me. "It was magic. Pure magic. I always had this dream of swimming with dolphins. That was when I didn't know it was harmful to them. I didn't mind giving up that dream. Snorkeling today was the next best thing in every way. I can't believe all the fish we saw. It was the coolest moment of my life when that pod of dolphins came swimming by! Even though they held off a bit, it was amazing to be so close, to know we shared the same water. And then they hung around! It's like they knew we were admiring them, and they were putting on their best display. Strutting their stuff just for me!"

"Well, it's good to know you could die tonight a happy guy."

He squinted at me through narrowed eyes. "I would not be a happy man if I died tonight. I mean, my supreme joy in life is tormenting you. If I had to give that up in exchange for eternal bliss, I'd tell God to take a hike for a few more decades."

"I guess we're stuck together, then!"

"Absolutely! Stuck like super glue."

We both went silent for a moment or two.

"Serious question for you, Brandon."

"Shoot!"

"How do you know about Mr. Darcy?"

Brandon winked at me. "Well, contrary to what you think, I do know how to read. I got along in school just fine before I ever knew you. I may not be a mini-Einstein, but I can hold my own."

"Says he who shudders every time he walks by my bookshelf with Dickens."

"Well, Dickens is one thing! I asked your mom one time to tell me the name of one of your favorite novels. She said you were rather partial to *Pride and Prejudice*. So, my mom and I read it together back in May – kind of like the way you read books with your parents."

"Why'd you do that?"

"Well, I wanted to be able to talk with you about it one day and not seem like a total moron. I wanted you to casually mention it, and then I'd be all ready to respond with some sophisticated thoughts about the themes and motifs of nineteenth century English novels." He snickered. "Not that I know what any of that means, but my mom prepared me with a few ideas."

"Oh, yes! I was just about to ask you how the themes in *Pride and Prejudice* intersect with modern feminist hermeneutics and shifting ideas around gender roles and identity. I mean, I'm all ears. Please enlighten me!"

"Smartass! You and your fucking big words." He leaned up and kissed me.

"I can't believe you read a book just to impress me."

"Well, don't let it go to your head, Fitzwilliam. I mean, I totally get why you like Mr. Darcy: handsome, aloof, brooding, and mega condescending. He's, like, your role model for life. It's like he's both you and what you think you want in your dream man. It's actually a little odd... like you love yourself way too much, Alex."

"Well, Jesus said we should love our neighbor like we love ourselves. I figure the more I love myself the more I can love you. And vice versa."

"I can do a little vice versa for you, my little stick-arm friend! Actually, I can give you whole truckload of vice versa!"

We lingered on the bench long into the night, blissfully happy and so in love it was silly.

. . .

Life back in Houston fell into a comfortable rhythm again. We lingered around the pool through impossibly lazy afternoons. We chuckled and bickered during daily workouts by ourselves and with Joel every Friday. Camp sped by in a flash, and we avoided every girl like she had the plague. We only had eyes for one another, and if anyone else noticed or cared, their prurient curiosity never affected us.

Joel drifted in and out of our orbit. Will and he were busy with college preparations, and they had less time to taxi us around. We didn't really mind. Every time we went out in public, whether alone, with Joel, or with the youth group, we had to put on our friends-only act. This became less and less appealing in those weeks after our Hawaiian vacation, and we eventually came to prefer our own company to the exclusion of everyone else.

Brandon and I celebrated our birthdays together with a cozy weekend at my family's apartment in mid-August. Dad and Mom took us out to Antonio's on Friday night. We went for a long run with Dad on Saturday morning while Mom was at her yoga class. We all got back to the apartment at the same time, and Mom insisted on teaching us some yoga poses before anyone showered. Brandon was a sight to behold, shirtless in our living room, falling over every few seconds with a thud, laughing non-stop. Mom gave up after five minutes, all three of her favorite men collapsed in a pile around her.

We exchanged presents Saturday evening after Mom's best quesadillas, black beans, and guacamole. I gave Brandon a tie-dyed tank-top with the words 'Hawaiian Dreams' printed across the chest. I also gave him a coffee-table book about dolphins, full of vibrant photos taken around the bay where we had snorkeled. He looked through the book reverently, touching the photos and sighing with nostalgia.

"Wow! Just wow! This might be the best present I ever got. Whenever I come home stressed from school this year, I'm pulling out this book and that Bach CD you gave me for Christmas. It'll help me remember all my favorite people, my favorite place of all time, and just how much you've changed me."

I opened his present to me. It was a simple necklace made of small pieces of polished coral strung together. In the center of the necklace a flat piece of coral-tinted glass bore an engraving: *Aloha.*

Tears filled my eyes. Brandon looked at me and said, "I chose that because the word *Aloha* means hello and goodbye. So, it's like a way of saying we don't really have to say goodbye once school starts. Saying goodbye is not really goodbye. It's just *aloha*. It means hello already for the next time."

I teased him too often for being dim and slow-witted, yet he possessed a depth of feeling and sensitivity beyond my own. Maybe I had learned the periodic table faster in eighth grade than he would learn it later in tenth grade. Maybe I understood Einstein's famous equation in a way he would never even have to. But there were deeper things – matters of the heart – which he grasped more intuitively than I did.

I mumbled a soft 'thank you' and let him put the necklace on me. He kissed my neck when he closed the clasp. Dad and Mom looked on without a flicker of discomfort or censure. In fact, I'm sure I saw a few tears slip from Dad's eyes.

. . .

ii.

"So, you little enigma, how's your summer been? Something's up, right?"

Joel stretched out in front of me on his bed. I was sitting cross-legged, my knees touching the left side of his torso. It was two Tuesdays before school started again. I usually stayed at home on Tuesday nights in the summer, but Joel was leaving for UT at the end of that week. He invited Brandon and me over for tacos, a movie, and a final sleepover. Mr. Marshall changed his mind at the last minute, so I went to Joel's on my own.

I couldn't subdue a massive grin. "It's been pretty wonderful. The best ever."

"Oh, yeah? I have a feeling there's a lot more you could say about that. I've noticed a change in you and Brandon these last few weeks in our workout sessions. There's something different between you two. I could tell it with my eyes closed."

I grinned even wider. "Brandon kissed me in his pool back in June. We finally figured out each of us likes the other one as much as we like the other one, if that makes any sense."

Joel hooted and hollered. He jumped off the bed, danced around in a small circle, waving one hand in the air, the other one perched on an imaginary saddle, as if he was riding a horse.

"God, the horses are out of the barn! You two kissed? Like, on the lips? Full on kiss?"

"Yes, and more than that."

Joel stopped mid-buck and stared at me open-mouthed for a few seconds. "Tell me you didn't go all the way! Tell me you didn't! You just turned fourteen!"

"No, no, no. We haven't done anything more than kiss and hold hands. You know… that kind of stuff."

"Wow! So, what's it like?"

"It's like dreaming with my eyes open."

"You sly little devils. How in the world did it happen? He just kissed you flat out? You didn't talk about it? You didn't send any kind of signals?" He snorted. "Well, I mean other than that 'I want you so bad I can hardly stand it' look you've been giving him for two straight years?"

"Did I really look like that?"

"Um, yes! Totally! But it was two-way. And Brandon's look was ten times more serious. There have been a few times when I thought he was about to lean in and kiss you right on the lips. Even at church!" He sat down on the bed, legs crossed, knees right up against mine.

"No, we didn't say anything about it before it happened. It just happened! We were swimming, and he grabbed me like he normally does when he's about to dunk me, but he didn't dunk me. He just pulled me closer and kissed me right on my lips. It took a second for me to realize what was happening. I mean, at first, I thought he was trying to head-butt me or he was just playing. But I knew in two seconds what it all meant."

"Oh, my God! I've been over here on the sidelines, like, watching you two circle one another forever and ever. I just wanted to shove you together, but I knew you had to get there in your own time."

"So, did you really know Brandon was gay all along? Even before I came along?"

"No, I don't think I did, but it all made sense after we talked when you came over that first time. I mean, there are all kinds of friendships between guys. Some guys are close and talk a lot and even touch each other as friends, but there was just something different about him. It's not like I know tons of gay guys, but I do know one or two at my school. They mostly seem like all the other guys, but there's something different about them."

He paused and smiled at me. "I don't mean that what's different about them is bad. It's just different. You gay guys have to keep it such a secret. Maybe that's part of why you seem different. Like there's a part of you, one of the most important parts about you, that you have to keep quiet about. Maybe it makes you different, not because you're gay, but because you have to spend so much energy pretending not to be."

He shook his head. "I don't know. My mom's the psychologist; not me. Maybe I don't know what I'm talking about."

"You think I need to see a psychologist?"

"No! I mean, my mom understands some of the reasons people act the way they act. She says everybody has secrets. Everybody has a part of them they keep hidden from other people. She says we all have a persona, like a mask, that we wear so we can keep our hidden parts hidden. We just show on the outside the parts of us we think everybody will like and understand. It's like everyone you know is putting on an act of some kind. You're the last person I know who needs to see a psychologist. I mean, you're a little weird, okay? But you're so wise and calm even with your weirdness."

"Thanks, I think."

He stared into my eyes for a good minute. I had a sense he wanted to say more, so I stayed silent.

Joel opened his mouth, hesitated, and shut it again. He cleared his throat and finally said, "You know, I think I like both guys and girls."

He stopped and looked down for a second.

I laid my hands on his knees, trying to telegraph to him that he was totally safe with me – as safe as I was with him when I told him my big secret.

He looked up with tears in his eyes. "God, I wasn't gonna cry. I wasn't even gonna say anything to you. I'm supposed to be like an older brother to you. I shouldn't tell you things that are hard to understand about me, but I have to tell someone. I think you're the only one I can tell. You're the only one I wanna tell! I think you'll understand."

"Go on, Joel. You can tell me whatever you want to say. You know it won't make any difference to me. That's what you've taught me: to love without conditions."

"Did I really teach you that? God, if I did, it was all by accident. I don't know how I could do that since I don't really love myself. Can you love someone else if you don't love yourself?"

I didn't know what to say or how to answer.

Tears welled up in Joel's beautiful eyes. "So, yeah, that's my secret. I like guys and girls. I mean, I can be totally turned on by a hot guy just like a hot girl. I've kissed lots of girls and even two guys. It was fun with guys just like it was fun with the girls. But I think that's what's different about us. You've kissed girls and Brandon, but the girls never made you feel anything like what you feel with Brandon, right?"

"Yeah, that's it. I kissed one girl at school, that girl at camp last summer, and Brandon. Kissing the girls was like one bar of mediocre music; kissing Brandon was like a symphony."

Joel smiled through his tears. "God, you're a hopeless romantic at heart, aren't you? I'd love for someone to think kissing me was like a symphony. Nobody's ever gonna say that about me."

"Of course, they will! You just have to wait until you find the right person. If I was your age, I'd kiss you a thousand times over! I've thought you were so hot from that first morning I met you."

Joel's electric smile lit up his face. "Would you really, Alexo? Would you really kiss me if we were the same age?"

"In a heartbeat! Brandon would, too! I know he would!"

"Well, I don't give a rat's ass about our age difference! I'd kiss you right now if it wasn't for you and Brandon being together. I mean, that would feel like a betrayal of a kind, wouldn't it?"

"For sure. Plus, I might just be too much for you. I might be too hot to handle."

He laughed and lunged at me, pinning me beneath him on the bed. The heat and pressure of his body made me go hard. I loved Brandon and only wanted him, but in some other version of reality I could have done anything Joel wanted to in that moment. It didn't take much imagination to see myself all over Joel, kissing and touching whatever I could.

He rolled off me and stretched out beside me.

"I can't believe I told you all of this! I've told myself for years that I was just confused, that I really liked girls the most, and that whatever it was I felt about other guys was gonna pass or change. But seeing you and Brandon together has made me wonder about that. You two made me wonder if I really like guys the most deep down. I can't figure it out. It's been so confusing, and there's nobody I can talk to. I've had to keep it all locked up inside."

"What about your mom? Do you think you could talk to her? I mean, she helps all kinds of people with their secrets."

"Trust me, I've thought about it. I mean, in one way I think she would be okay, as a psychologist. She works with people no matter what they believe about God or even if they don't believe in God at all. She has to set her religious beliefs aside when she works with someone in her office. But it's different when it's me, you know? It's not like she can set aside what she believes about God when she's dealing with me. I think she'd want me to change. Or she might make me talk to Michael." He shuddered. "Or even Brandon's dad. God, that would be torture."

"You could talk to my parents. They'd listen. They'd understand, and they don't care about all the God stuff. I mean, they care about God, but they don't really fit in at church. They don't believe the same things most people do. They don't care if people are gay or straight or Muslim or Hindu. Not that being gay is like being Hindu. I just mean they don't get angry about that stuff, people being different."

He nodded. "I know. I've noticed that. Everyone at church

notices. My parents have even talked about it! They think your parents are liberals. Mom even whispered to me one time, 'I think they voted for Mondale in eighty-four.'" He snickered. "I mean, that's like the worst thing you can say about someone at our church: that they're a Democrat. I always assumed your family stayed at church because of you and Brandon. I can't imagine Mr. Marshall letting you two be friends if your family left the church."

"It's true! That's the only reason they've stayed these last two years. But seriously, you can talk to them any time. They really like you. Mom said you were the most sensitive jock she ever met!"

"Did she say that? Wow! That's sweet. Your parents are amazing. You're so lucky."

We both went quiet for a few seconds. Joel yawned and said, "Remember that first time when you told me you liked Brandon? You were so tired when it was over. Now it's my turn to be exhausted after finally sharing something so secret. I feel like I could sleep a million years."

"You should. And you'll feel better in the morning. I know I did that next morning after I talked to you."

"Good, I'm glad that helped you. You've helped me tonight. It's funny to think about a guy going off to college sharing something so personal with a guy just about to start high school! But you're basically ten years older than you are – the heart, mind, and soul of an adult in a little body." He snickered. "And God, what a cute little body you have!"

"You sound like Brandon now. He always says I have a cute little body."

"Because it's true. He's so lucky to have you. He's hunky, for sure, but you're so goddamn dreamy! I don't think I'll ever find anyone like you. I don't know if I should try. I could spend my whole life looking for my own version of Alex Kennedy, and I'd finally discover God broke the mold after he made you."

My heart swelled to three times its normal size! I loved Joel more than anyone in the world after Brandon and my parents. Yet a heavy sense of sadness settled on me as we went to brush our teeth and use the bathroom one more time. I realized how lonely Joel must be. He had kept his secret for so long. I knew the kind of toll that takes on a young guy.

By some lucky alignment of the stars, Brandon and I found each other when we were so young. We found some way to build a friendship despite our differences. And against all the odds, we found the courage to express our love for one another. On top of that, we had my parents by our side to listen to us, to cheer us on, and to love and support us. Joel didn't have any of that. He was alone in so many ways.

As we settled back into bed in Joel's darkened room, I turned on my side. I kissed Joel lightly on the cheek, the way I might kiss Dad or Mom. "Someone is gonna be really lucky to find you one day. It might be a girl. It might be a guy. But whoever it is will feel like they've won the lottery. And you'll feel the same way. That's when you'll know you found the right one."

Joel nodded silently, took my hand in his, and held it on top of his chest. I drifted off in seconds.

CHAPTER 12

FRESHMAN YEAR:
FALL AND NEW YEAR'S EVE 1989

My worst fears about high school came home to roost within the first few weeks of September. The amount of work and the pace of each class fairly took my breath away. Latin alone seemed to eat up an hour or more each evening, and I struggled to find an even footing.

Brandon and I made do with the little contact our parents allowed us: phone calls every Thursday evening around 7:30, somewhat regular runs with Dad on Saturday mornings, sleepovers as often as we could, and church on Sundays. Just before Christmas, we counted up our sleepovers. We had only managed seven sleepovers since school started, and three of those were during Thanksgiving break! Nothing was the same. We both felt the lack of one another. We both missed our closeness, and we both wanted it back.

Brandon, Will, and his parents left for a short trip to Nashville three days before Christmas. They usually made the long drive spread out over the course of two days. For the first time ever, they flew there and back.

Brandon came home late in the afternoon on Tuesday, December 26. We both had to return to school a week later on

Wednesday, January 3. Luckily, our parents gave us free reign that week. Brandon stayed over with us for three nights starting on Tuesday. He didn't even unpack. He just brought his suitcase with him straight from the airport and crashed in my room. Then I spent three nights at his house. I hadn't been so happy since the end of August.

Joel and Will took us with them to the Odeon on West Gray on New Year's Eve. We saw *National Lampoon's Christmas Vacation*. It wasn't my first choice; I had my eye on *Driving Miss Daisy*. I knew, however, the other three had been looking forward to Chevy Chase's festive antics for weeks; they would have simply out-voted me and barreled-over any resistance I offered!

We got back to Brandon's house a little after 11:00. Mr. and Mrs. Marshall had already gone to bed. Will was going to stay the night with some old high school friends he hadn't seen since graduation. Brandon and I had the whole upstairs to ourselves.

As we climbed the stairs, he said, "I say we skip Dick Clark this year. He brings back too many unhappy memories. Okay with you?"

"Fine with me!"

"Good," he said. "There's only one dick I'm interested in tonight." I giggled, and Brandon pulled me close to him as we walked down the hallway to his room.

In those very last hours of 1989, our desire for one another shone more brightly than that ridiculous descending ball in New York. We spoke very little. We didn't need any words. We only needed to know we were close together again and inseparable for the night. The new year would roll our way, and the rigors of school would crest and crash over us again in a few days. We knew we had to make the most of every second we had together.

After a few minutes of tender kissing and caressing, Brandon jumped up from the bed to turn off the overhead lights. When he got back in bed, we turned on our sides and gazed at each other in the dim light of the single bedside lamp.

Brandon asked, "Where is this all going?"

"What do you mean?"

"I mean us. Our friendship. Our secret. Our love. All of this. Where's it going?"

I knew what he meant, but I didn't feel up to such a conversation. I had no idea where we were going. I couldn't imagine any kind of a future where we could continue as we were. At the same time, I didn't want to imagine a future where we didn't.

I sighed and said, "Well, we have tonight and tomorrow morning. Maybe that's enough for right now. My parents and I were talking about this on Christmas Eve. They don't know where it's going any more than I do. If they can't figure it out, what hope do we have?"

He looked over my shoulder and said, "Well, I have an idea that could buy us some time and maybe confuse people."

I caught a hint of hesitation in his voice. I propped myself up on the headboard. "Oh, yeah? What?"

He stayed on his side but craned his neck to look me in the eyes. "Now, don't go ballistic, Humperdink! I, uh, was... I was thinking I should probably get a girlfriend."

I couldn't believe my ears! "Oh, come on, Brandon! What the hell would be the point of that? It's just like adding one more secret on top of all the others. It makes what we feel about each other and what we do together seem shameful."

His eyes widened. He sat up in a flash, turning his body fully to me. "You think we're shameful? Really? I'm shameful to you? Our love is shameful to you?"

"No, no, no! I mean how we feel about one another is something that other people think is shameful. Or, you know, some people think it's shameful. And we..."

He interrupted me. "Correction. Just about everybody we know would be totally disgusted with us. Other than your parents, I can't think of one person I know who would think you and are just fine together. They would call us perverts and faggots and sinners and Sodomites and queers and who knows what else. What we mean to each other is not normal to anyone else, Alex. Nobody's ever gonna think it's okay."

"I told you Joel knows all about us and doesn't mind at all. He's so happy for us!"

"Well, that's three people – your parents and Joel – versus millions and millions who think we're perverts!"

"You know that's not true. Think about Nick and David. Everybody in our building knows all about them, and nobody treats them any differently. Think about those two bars by Antonio's. Every time we go eat there, we see gay and lesbian couples lined up outside. And there's a lot more bars and clubs like them all over Montrose and Midtown. It might be shameful in your family and to everyone at church, but there's actually a place out there in the adult world where nobody cares. They hold rallies for gay rights at the Unitarian church. That's on the corner of Southmore – like three blocks from my apartment! A lot of people right here in Houston don't give a damn who other people love. Why is it anybody else's business?"

"Well, in case you hadn't noticed, we're a fucking long way from being adults. You're still fourteen, dumbass. We have a whole decade before we could even begin to live like adults. How in the world would we get through college? We don't even know we'll be at the same college. You'll go to Harvard, and I'll have to go to HCC and work at McDonald's. How in the world do we even get through that? You'll fall in love with some brilliant Harvard student, and I'll never see you again."

"Who said I'm going to Harvard? And why are we talking about this now? I don't wanna fall in love with someone else. I don't wanna talk about this right now. It's New Year's Eve. Let's celebrate the amazing year we just had. The year we first kissed! The year we went to Hawaii! The year I told my parents about us and found out they don't give a damn. It's been an amazing year! Let's worry about 1996, or whatever future year, when it gets here."

"God, Alex, you're always the sensible one. You're the one who thinks ahead and plans out every scenario from here to fucking kingdom come! And now, when something really important is on the line, you're Mr. Ostrich! Head in the sand! Or up your ass, or something. Like we'll just walk down the fucking yellow brick road into Oz without a care in the world. Like we'll kiss on the big screen like Westley and Buttercup and the whole world will cheer for us!"

"Brandon, stop cussing at me."

"I'm not cussing at you. I'm cussing in your general direction." He waved his hand above my head. "I'm cussing into this space up here. Six inches above your head. Big difference, you skinny-ass know-it-all."

We glared at each other for a few seconds but broke into laughter in quick succession. I reached over and put my hand on his mouth.

"Shhhh! Your dad would kill us if we woke him up."

He kissed the palm of my hand and held it to his chest. We scooted close to one another, legs crossed, knees touching. He grinned with delight.

I said, "Let's not talk about college right now. It's more than three years away. Can we just forget you started this argument? Can we just start again?" I winked at him.

He rested his palms on the inside of my thighs. "Nah, I don't want to start again. I like it when we argue. It makes me want you even more. You're so damn hot when you get angry with me. It's like I know you want to reach out and clobber me, but at the same time you wanna reach out and kiss me. All your love and anger mixes together." He whispered. "You make me so hard. Please get angry with me any time you want."

He inched his hands up my thighs and slipped them into

my shorts. His index fingers gently touched my penis. "Oh, I see I have the same effect on you."

I rolled my eyes. "We gotta get back on topic. My problem about you getting a girlfriend is that it seems really unfair to the girl. I've seen girls eyeing you all the time. It's not fair to take advantage of some girl who really likes you. Remember those two girls on the Catamaran in Hawaii? They couldn't take their eyes off you. I mean, they were practically drooling. It would be cruel to take advantage of any girl like that."

"You turned a few heads on the beach, too. That face and your hair and your abs can melt any heart of stone. It's just a shame about your bean-pole-arms. How can we workout so much and you only put on a few grams of muscle in a year?"

He pulled his hands from my shorts and caressed my upper arms.

"Come on! It isn't the right way to treat a girl."

"Wait! Here's my plan! Just listen. Don't get mad. Well, do get mad because you are so damn cute when you get all self-righteous!"

"Get on with your plan! I'll listen, but I won't approve. Never, ever!"

"Well, that just defeats the whole point of a conversation, my little stick-arm friend."

"Just get on with it."

"Okay, okay. Sheesh! I know a girl at school who is hot but super mean. She goes through guys one right after another, and she is always the one who dumps them. She's like a predator, you know? Always on the look-out for the next victim."

"And you think it's a wonderful idea to welcome this girl into your life? Into OUR life? You think she'll just roll over and play nice because you're the biggest stud of your high school."

He chuckled, "Well, I'm not the biggest stud. I mean, there are a few other guys who..."

"Answer my questions! You think you won't get hurt in

the process? What if you're the one she finally learns to like? Then you'll be stuck with her! What if she wants to spend tons of time together? What if she wants to kiss you every time she sees you? What if she wants to touch you the way I touch you? What if she wants to have sex with you? God, have you not thought two seconds about this? It's a mega-bad idea! I can't think of one reason why it would work, and I can imagine ten thousand ways it could go really bad really fast."

He went silent, the kind of silent that was his own personal mixture of confusion and hurt. I knew I had pushed back against his idea too vigorously. I said words I would've paid a million dollars to take back. I'm sure I sounded just like his dad – the very last thing I ever wanted to do.

I scooted up closer to him. I took his chin in my hand and said, "I know why you want to do this. I really do, and it makes me love you even more. You're trying to protect us, to protect what we have. It makes me feel so good to know you want to do that. It's just that this plan could go wrong and make things even worse. What if you hold back when kissing her or she pressures you for something more than a kiss? What if she insists on screwing you? What are you gonna do? I can just hear this super mean girl saying to her friends that her boyfriend must be a fag because he won't grope her and sleep with her. Then it's even worse."

"I know, I know! You're right. It's a horrible idea. It's just want to do something that could kind of take attention away from us. I don't want people snickering at us behind our backs or spreading rumors. I swear some of those counselors at camp looked at us funny a few times... like they sensed some-thing was up. I don't want that for you or me."

"Well, there's not much we can do about that. We can't control what people think or say. To hell with what they suspect! We just have to be super careful and keep things low-key between us when other people are around. I don't know what else there is to do."

"Oh, wait! I, uh, just had another idea. I could date a super sweet girl who would never in a million years try to kiss me or want to have sex. I can think of ten girls at church who would be perfect. We could just say sweet things to each other, talk on the phone once a week, and that would be it."

I sighed and shook my head. "But then you're being really mean to a sweet girl. You'll break her heart. Think about all the times we felt like our hearts were breaking before we kissed the first time. Imagine putting some sweet, innocent girl through that on purpose. That's cruel!"

"I know, I know. You're right about that, too. You're just about always right."

"I want that in writing from you next time we get up!"

"Fuck off, Alex." He snickered. "Your head is already as big as a battleship. I'm not going to add to it by actually admitting on paper you're smarter than I am."

"Well, whenever we take the SAT later in high school, we'll have written proof then."

"Wow! You did not just say that." He reached over and began to tickle my waistline.

I squirmed in vain and said, "Please stop! I don't wanna wake up your parents."

He ceased and patted my abs.

I said, "You know I'm just teasing you. I don't give a damn what score you get on any test. You already proved you were impossibly smart when you fell in love with me and became my best friend."

"True, but I don't think my brain had much to do with that. Some other organ was in charge there." He snickered and shot me a sly look.

We lapsed into silence for a minute or two.

"Can I ask you a question?"

I nodded.

"You know when we were talking about other people thinking what we do is shameful or dirty or perverted? I don't remember the exact words, but you know what I mean, right?"

I nodded again.

"Well, what do you think, Alex? Is there actually something wrong with us deep down? Are we wrong for how we feel?"

"Honestly, I never really thought about it until I started coming to church. When I first realized I wanted to kiss other boys I didn't think it was wrong or bad. I knew none of my friends talked that way. So maybe on some level I sensed it wasn't common, but I don't think I thought it was wrong. I didn't feel ashamed when I thought about those boys. I didn't feel dirty for wanting to kiss John or other boys."

"Boys? Boys? I thought you said John was the only boy you wanted to kiss. Now you're going plural on me! Who are these other little fuckers? I have a right to know who you're looking at behind my back!"

"Chill out! I just mean I thought about kissing several boys in fifth and sixth grade. Trust me, none of them hold a candle to you." I paused and kissed his cheek. "But when I saw you bare your arm while scraping off that glob of jelly on that first Sunday, something totally different happened to me. I started getting hard every time I saw you and Joel or thought about you. That's when I started wondering if there was something wrong with me for feeling that way. Remember when Michael gave that lesson at my first devotional at your house? That was such a shock. I realized there was a huge gulf between what my parents thought and what church people thought, but I never really believed Michael was right."

Brandon let out a deep breath and said, "I remember a time when Michael and his wife came over for dinner. It was just after he came here to start being the youth minister. I was in third grade. I don't remember anything about the conversation except the word gay kept coming up. I can hear that word over and over again, even all these years later. Michael and my dad were just saying how it was dirty and against God's will. I know that's what they'd say about me now. And you. They'd say we're going to hell."

He paused and stared over my shoulder for a minute. "So, yeah, I knew it was dirty and a sin according to everyone at church, but once you came along I didn't care."

His eyes turned to mine again, and I said, "Dad bought this book about the whole issue, about what the Bible says about homosexuality. He said it's important to realize from the beginning that the Bible doesn't talk about homosexuality. It just talks about same-sex behaviors. People back then assumed everyone was straight, so it seemed wrong to them whenever people of the same gender did sexual things together. They didn't have any idea that some people are born gay. Does that make sense?"

He had an intense expression on his face. I took it as a sign to plow ahead.

"Anyway, this book was written by some Bible scholars who know Hebrew and Greek and understand the context of various passages. He wants me to read it. I just haven't had time yet. But he's walked me through each of the chapters, so I have a pretty good idea of the issues. Do you know about the six passages?"

"Not really. What do you mean?"

"Well, there are six main passages in the Bible about homosexuality – a few in the Old Testament and a few in the New Testament. Do you want me to tell you about each one? I don't think I remember all the details, but I kinda remember the basic points."

"How about one now and then we can do more later? I get enough crazy Bible lessons from my dad every night after dinner. Maybe you could get the book and we could read it together. Or with your parents, maybe. Would they want to?"

"Yeah, sounds good! They would love to read it with us. I'll tell 'em as soon as I get home. They'll be so excited!" I winked.

"Okay, so you know about the story in Genesis about Lot and his guests, right?"

"Um, rings a bell…"

"Well, Lot was Abraham's nephew. He was in a place called Sodom–"

"Which probably sounded normal before it got turned into a dirty word."

"Yeah, really! Anyway, two visitors show up in Sodom, and Lot invites them to stay with him and his family for the night instead of sleeping in the town square."

"Who were these visitors? You mean they were gay?"

"Um, it's a little confusing because the Bible says they are messengers from God. And we normally think about angels as being messengers from God, but it's pretty clear in the story that these are real men because they have a big meal with Lot that evening. Just when they're about to go to sleep, all the men from the town show up, bang on Lot's door, and basically say they want to gang-rape the two visitors in Lot's house."

A horrified look crossed Brandon's face. "Like, they say, 'Hey, Lot. What's up? We'd like to rape your guests. Send them out, please, if it's not too much trouble.' Really?"

"Yes, pretty much. And Lot says – get this – he won't send his guests out to get raped. However, he's got a couple of virgin daughters, and he's happy to send them out instead."

"Good God! Talk about throwing your kids under the bus! What the hell's wrong with the Bible?"

"I know! It's another great example of biblical fatherhood for you. It's as bad as Abraham thinking God told him to sacrifice Isaac."

"Well, that whole family sounds fucked up. I mean, Abraham and Lot are, like, the worst fathers ever. They make my dad look like the Easter Bunny, Santa Claus, and Mr. Rogers all rolled into one." He snickered.

"I know! So here are the main things to think about." I ticked them off on my fingers. "One, there's a good chance that all or most of the men from the town who show up at Lot's house are actually married men. Back then, people got married really young, and basically everybody got married. So, they are straight men who are married, and they want to gang-rape Lot's guests in order to humiliate them. The problem in Sodom is straight, married men who want to gang-rape other men. And two, like you said, Lot's a shitty dad! I mean, if you think the whole point of this passage is to say it's wrong for gay men to have sex together, then the corollary is to say that this passage also teaches that gang-raping young virgins is no big deal."

"What do you mean 'corollary'?"

"I just mean that it follows... like, one argument follows the other. If what's actually being condemned in this passage is man-on-man gang rape, then it follows that the passage is actually honky-dory with man-on-young-virgin gang rape. But you know today, we'd say rape is just wrong all around – man-on-man, man-on-woman, woman-on-woman, man-on-virgin, man-on-boy, woman-on-boy..."

Brandon smirked and said, "Man-on-donkey..."

"Exactly! All of it is disgusting and wrong." I was about to get to my third point, but Brandon cut me off.

"Oh, wait, I get it! I get it! Here's the point, right? What you and I feel about each other and do together is not about rape! I mean, it's so obvious. If one of us tried to rape the other one –" he shuddered and grimaced, "or some other guy, it would be wrong – not because we're both guys but because rape is wrong. Forcing yourself on someone is the real issue no matter who's involved."

"Exactly! Dad said this passage is not about you and me. It's not about two best friends who just happened to have fallen for each other. It's not about gay couples like Nick and David who've been living together for, like, a decade."

"It all makes so much sense now! It's actually a story about perverted, disgusting *straight* men! How come nobody at church talks about this? Why does everyone think it's a story about gay men?"

"Good question." I poked him in the ribs. "Why don't you ask your dad and let me know what he says? I bet he'd love to have this conversation with you. I can imagine him being totally open to a conversation about gang-rape in the Bible."

He gave me a withering scowl. "Smartass."

I leaned in and kissed him on his lips. "Dad says people at church are just so stuck in their ways and so sure they're right and so afraid to change their minds. Plus, people see what they want to see. You can basically make the Bible say anything you want. So, people start with what they want to believe – like gay people are disgusting and going straight to hell – and then they go looking through the Bible until they find a verse that seems to back them up."

He went quiet for a few seconds. I could see the mental wheels turning. I didn't want to pile on too much, but something else Dad said seemed important to share with Brandon.

"You know, the other thing you have to keep in mind is that not everybody believes the Bible is inspired the way your dad does. I mean, everybody at our church thinks the Bible came straight from God, like it's exactly what God would write if God had a hand and a pen and a piece of paper handy. But Dad says lots of other Christians think about it differently. There's obviously a lot of stuff in the Bible that is considered wrong today – like support for slavery, men having multiple wives, all those passages about God commanding the slaughter of women and children, and, of course, Lot thinking it's a good idea to toss his virgin daughters outside to a bunch of angry rapists. The Bible was written by people, not God. You can take it seriously but not think that every part of it is true and universally applicable today."

"Universally applicable? Use normal words!"

"Just because something's in the Bible doesn't mean we have to do that thing now. We don't have to believe and follow every single line in the Bible. Dad says we have to use our brains and follow our conscience."

"I never knew any of that. You mean God doesn't think we're perverts? God's not gonna send us to hell?"

"No. God loves us and made us the way we are. Why would God make us this way and then tell us we are bad?"

"Holy shit! I never even thought about it that way."

"I know! Holy shit, indeed. We can talk about any of this with my parents any time you want to. You don't have to be embarrassed or ashamed. They love you so much. They only want to help us."

"I know. That sounds good. I can't talk to my parents about any of this, but I think I could talk to your parents about anything. Have you held anything back from them? I mean, anything about us?"

"Not really. I try to be open with them. I know I'm safe with them no matter what, so it's easier to be honest.

"I can't even imagine feeling safe with my parents. I don't even know what that would feel like. I just know what fear feels like." He sighed a little and cleared his throat. "Okay... something else I have to ask you. You said you get hard when you see Joel or think about him. Do you really?"

"Yeah, absolutely. He's so gorgeous. I can't stop myself. I know you do, too, Brandon. So, don't deny it!"

"What? How do you know that?"

"I looked at your crotch one Friday two summers ago when we were working out with Joel. I noticed you were hard just like me. We were both sitting there staring at him while he rested between sets. He was catching his breath, covered in sweat, and he just looked like some Greek god come to life."

"Oh, my God! I had no idea you noticed me then, but I think it's sweet. What did you think? I mean, what did you think when you saw I was hard?"

"Well, I was a little confused. I couldn't imagine why you were hard while looking at Joel. I thought maybe other boys got hard around really big guys, even if they only like girls." I felt flustered and began to stammer a bit. "I don't know. I mean... It was all so confusing. I was hoping Joel didn't see me. I was hoping you didn't see me. I was trying not to look at your crotch. I was trying not to look at Joel too much or in the wrong way. I was a mess! I was afraid of pushing you two away. I was so afraid you'd notice and make a huge deal about it and walk out of my life."

He reached over and ran his hand through my hair. "God, you poor guy. I don't remember being hard then, but I bet I was. I got hard the first time Joel came over to swim years ago. He had the most amazing abs I had ever seen. They were way better than Will's! I couldn't take my eyes off him. I was so scared Will would notice. There was even a time in the pool when Joel's hand brushed against my trunks while we were wrestling, and I swear I don't know how he didn't feel the bulge."

We both giggled and shook our heads. I said, "We've spent so much of our lives being afraid of who is going to find out about us and who's gonna hate us when they do. I get exhausted thinking about it."

"Well, we need to keep on being afraid in one sense. Nobody can ever find out. I mean, I'm not ashamed, but I don't understand how we can let anybody but your parents know."

"We have to be careful. You're the one I'm worried about. You gotta keep your hands off me when we're out in public."

"I'll try. I'll try." He paused and glared at me through narrowed eyes. "Hey, Mr. I-Can't-Stop-Panting-After-Joel, do you think Joel's better looking than me?"

"Honestly, no! He's gorgeous for sure. He's older than you and bigger than you, but there's something about you that nobody else has. You're like a magnet for me."

"Do you know he weighs about 190 pounds? I mean, that's like really good for his age and height. Do you know how much I weigh?"

"Oh, God, here we go!"

"Come on, guess!"

"I don't know! Maybe 160 pounds."

"Oh, you're so close. 163! Or at least last time I checked!"

"What about you? Do you even know?"

"Actually, I do know because the nurse weighed me the other week when I went to the doctor for that check-up. I was 128."

He leaned in and kissed me. "I knew it! I was thinking 130 or so! You're 128 pounds of pure attraction. That's why your abs are so pretty! Not an ounce of flab on you! Now we just gotta work on those arms. I'll be damned if your arms defy me much longer!"

He reached over and switched off the lamp. I turned on my side, facing away from him. He slipped his arm over me and draped it down my chest. He kissed my shoulder and whispered, "Sweet dreams, my skinny-ass best friend. Sweet dreams."

CHAPTER 13

Disaster struck in early February. I was neck-deep in Latin verbs, wondering again for the fortieth time why I agreed to study a dead, morose language. I had my eye on the clock, anxious for Brandon's usual Thursday evening phone call. I was missing him so much. We only managed one sleepover after school started up again. My parents and I had stayed home from church the previous two Sundays so we could all catch up on rest and chores around the apartment, so I hadn't seen him in person in nearly three weeks. My call with Brandon the previous week was cut short because he was studying for an Algebra test. His dad had him on a tight leash that night; we barely said hello before Mr. Marshall picked up another receiver at their house and ended our call without warning.

I wanted to talk to Brandon for hours. Ironically, I had a feeling I would likely feel worse, not better, after talking to him. Hearing his voice would only remind me that I missed him and that it would probably be weeks before we could have any kind of fun time together.

A little after 6:30, Mom stuck her head in my room. "Sweetie, Brandon is on the phone."

She placed her hand on my shoulder when I got to the door. "He sounds upset, and you are very stressed. You've raised your voice with your dad and me twice tonight. You need to watch your words and how you react if he's got bad news." She kissed me lightly on the cheek.

Mom walked back to her bedroom. Dad was in his study preparing for a presentation the next day. All three of us were stressed and tired. I realized I'd been a jerk to them. I knew it deep down before Mom said anything. As I walked to the kitchen, I told myself I would apologize later. I took a deep breath and put on my brightest voice as I picked up the phone.

"Hey, hey! Why are you calling early? Did you finish already?"

"Alex, I'm so sorry. I am so, so sorry."

"What? What's going on?"

Brandon's voice quivered as he began. "I failed my last two Algebra tests, and I hid the notes from my parents. I was supposed to bring home a note for Mom or Dad to sign to say they knew I failed the tests." He gulped. "I forged Dad's signature on the first one. I threw away the second one. But I forgot that if you fail two tests, Mr. McWhirter also calls your parents in addition to sending the second note home. He just called to speak to Dad about an hour ago. Dad didn't know about either note. He went ballistic, and I'm grounded for at least six weeks."

I erupted before I could think or stop myself. "God, how could you be so stupid? What the hell were you thinking? How did you think you were going to get away with something like that? And why didn't you let me know you were struggling? I would have helped you! I'd do anything for you, but I can't help you out of this crazy mess you've made now. I mean, what the hell, Brandon?"

A tense silence fell between us. I wanted to kick and scream at him, but I wanted to kick and scream at myself even more. Mom had just warned me to keep my cool. It took five seconds for me to lose it. I felt like the biggest jerk in the world. In the space of one evening, I had hurt the feelings of the three people I loved most in the world.

"I'm sorry! I'm sorry I just said that. Please forgive me."

"It's okay, Alex. I'm pretty mad at myself. I deserve to be screamed at. I don't know what I was thinking. I thought I could pull myself together. I thought if I just went over the problems in the book again and again it would all make sense. But it doesn't! Mr. McWhirter hardly helps us. He just does a few problems on the board and tells us to use those to help us figure out the problems in the book. Then his tests are nothing like any of those problems. I just sit there and stare at his tests. I managed to get a C last semester, but I feel lost right now."

"Can you ask him for help?"

"I have! Over and over again. He does a tutoring session after school two days a week, but it's just more of the same. I leave just as confused. He talks about 'a+b equals this and that,' and all I can think of is you. Alex plus Brandon equals us... equals love." He paused and sighed again. "And then I made it all worse by forging that signature and tossing the second note. I just panicked! I can't explain it. I don't know... I don't know."

"Hey, hey, hey. It's okay. At least you've come clean now with your parents."

"Oh, God, Dad hit the ceiling. He's been shouting for the last thirty minutes or so. I'm grounded from you for the next six weeks. He's banned me from watching any TV. He's taken the weights out of my room. He said I wasted too much time with you and dreaming of gaining muscle. He said I was wasting my life away on things that didn't matter. He even said my sketches were a waste of time if I can't pass Algebra. He threatened to take away my sketchbooks and pencils. Mom talked him back from that." He sighed. "I can hear him downstairs yelling at her right now. All she does is try to keep the peace, and she gets yelled at."

"I'm so sorry. I've seen him hit the ceiling before, and I was scared. Are you okay?"

"You know, he doesn't scare me. Honestly! But I can't stand that yelling and screaming and the things he says about me. It's not like he's going to beat me or hit me." I had wondered before if Mr. Marshall ever hit Brandon. "I mean, seriously, if he hit me, I'd hit him back. He knows it. I'd knock his fucking head off if he ever touched me or Mom, but he knows I won't scream back at him. I just won't do it. And he knows that's the power he has over me. He knows he can hurt me with his words. And he does. He knows he can ground me from you and that's his other source of power. He knows just what to do to me to hurt me most." His words were muffled by increasingly loud sobs and gulps for air. "What kind of father does that? I mean, what did I do to him to make him hate me so much?"

"I don't think he hates you." I caught sight of Mom out of the corner of my eye. She was standing near the sofa in the living room, looking my way. I motioned her over with a tilt of my head. She came closer as I continued, and Brandon's sobs got louder. "Listen to me, Brandon. Even if he does hate you, it's not because you deserve it. You don't. None of the shouting is your fault. No son ever deserves to hear the kind of things your dad says to you. You deserve to hear the kind of things my dad says to me and to you. Your dad is an asshole, and you shouldn't even care what he says."

Mom's eyes widened; a sly smile followed.

I asked him, "Are you alone upstairs?"

"Yes."

"Can I put Dad on to talk to you?"

Just as I asked the question, Mom turned and hurried away, seeing where my train of thought was going.

"Sure, Alex. I'd like that."

"Hold on. Just a second..."

Dad and Mom came into the kitchen. I think Mom had

given him a synopsis of what she gleaned from the part of the conversation she heard. He took the receiver from me.

"Hey, Brandon, it's *Papa-Numero-Dos*. What's up?"

I could only hear bits of the conversation. Brandon's voice was loud but muffled again by sobs and moans. God, how I wanted him to be in our apartment: safe, loved, and far away from his dickhead bully of a dad.

Dad broke in after a good minute of letting Brandon go on. "Hey, Brandon. Catch your breath. Breathe. That's it. Take a deep breath. Come on. Slow breaths. Deep breaths." I could hear a slight tremor in Dad's voice. Mom stood close by me, one hand at the small of my back and the other on my shoulder. "Good, that's good. Now listen. Whatever this feels like now, you've got to remember it will pass. I know you feel like shit right now, but it will pass. I love you like you're my second son. If I had a million boys to choose from, I'd pick you first for a second son. You are very dear to me, and to Elizabeth. We really love you. Okay? Do you trust us?"

Dad paused and glanced my way, giving me a big wink.

He went on: "I know we can't fix this for you, but I don't want you going to sleep later without these words in your mind. The three of us love you more than you could possibly know. If we could snap our fingers and change your dad, we would. We'd do anything to make things better for you, but we can only do so much. And you can only do so much. But you have to know what that is. You have to know what you can do and then do it with all your heart. We're here cheering you at every step. We're here for you no matter what, even if it's going to be a few weeks before we see you again."

Mom grabbed the receiver. "Honey, it's *Momma-Numero-Dos*. I love you, sweetie. Just remember everything James told you. Don't go to sleep tonight thinking of your dad's words. Go to sleep thinking of our words. Just our words. Are you gonna be okay?" He must have reassured her. "Well, good then. I love you, Brandon. I'll pass you back to Alex. Sleep well, sweetie. Call us any time you want to! Any time!"

Brandon's calm voice came across the line. "Hey, man. Your parents are stars. God, Alex, you are so lucky. I just wish I could come over there to stay and live with you three. I don't think I can keep living like this over here." His voice broke again. "I can't do it. I cannot do it. Not three-and-a-half more years of this bullshit."

"If we could make it happen, you could come live with us. I mean, it would solve so many of our problems and…"

There was a click on the phone. Mr. Marshall's voice broke in. "Brandon, are you still on the phone with Alex?"

"Yes, sir."

"Well, I was trying to be patient and give you time to say goodbye to him for the next six weeks. You're time's up. Hang up, Brandon. Hang up now."

Brandon only managed to whisper, "Aloha." Then his breathing vanished from my ear. My heart skipped a beat or two. It felt like six years, not six weeks, of separation stretched out in front of us. We didn't even really get to say goodbye.

Mr. Marshall said, "Alex, you've been a good friend and example to Brandon. I wish he was half as smart as you and maybe half as honest, too. I know you make stellar grades, and your parents tell me you never lie to them or keep secrets from them. I wish Brandon would learn from you."

Rage coursed through my veins. I knew my voice was way too loud, but I couldn't help myself. "Brandon is the best friend I've ever had. I may get better grades than he does, but he's taught me more about being a friend and really caring about someone else than anybody I've ever known. I wish you saw that side of him. I wish you saw him the way I see him and the way my parents see him. We love him like he's part of our family."

"You are a kind, thoughtful boy. I only let Brandon be friends with you because I think you're a good influence on him. Since he's become your friend, his grades have improved and he gets in far less trouble at school than he once did. But you should remember your place. I am his father. I know him infinitely better than you do. Don't you dare presume to tell me what I do and do not know about my son. Do you hear me, Alex Kennedy? Don't you dare. He is your friend, but I am his father. You mean nothing in the big scheme of his life."

I wanted to reach down the phone line and rip out Mr. Marshall's larynx. I never wanted to hear his menacing, sanctimonious voice again. Just as I opened my mouth to let loose a torrent of cursing, I felt Mom's hand on my shoulder. I looked up and saw her mouth the words, 'Just say goodbye.'

I froze and held my tongue in the nick of time. If I had said what I really wanted to say, Mr. Marshall might have ended my friendship with Brandon for the rest of high school. After a brief pause, I managed to say, "I'm sorry if I upset you, Mr. Marshall. I've got to get back to my Latin homework."

His end of the line went dead without a single parting word. What a colossal prick!

Mom said, "It's no use making him mad at you, sweetie. You need to be careful with him. If he turns on you, you can kiss seeing Brandon goodbye until he's old enough to go to college." She took my chin in her hand. "Seriously! Do not antagonize that man! Ever! Let us do that. He likes us way more than we like him, so we have some leverage with him. And Suzanne is as sweet as they come. She can get Robert talked down from his moral high horse. So, trust your dad and me. Let us deal with the adults."

Dad came up from behind me. "Yeah, leave him to us. We'll get something sorted out." He grasped my shoulder and turned me toward him. "I love you so much, Alex. If I ever, ever, ever start to sound like that man, you have my permission to cuss me out and punch me in the gut." I started to snicker. "Seriously, if I ever sound like that, sock me right between the eyes."

"Well, dear," Mom said, "if you ever sound like that, Alex

will have to tear me off of you before he can get a clear shot. I'll rip you limb from limb."

I snorted. "Whoa! Kung-fu yoga mom is on the loose! Watch out, Dad!"

Dad pulled the two of us close to him. We all stood in a tight embrace. I felt exhausted. The thought of finishing my Latin aorist verbs and a doing quick chemistry review thoroughly depressed me.

Mom must have been reading my thoughts. "What about an early bed-time? I can get you up a little early tomorrow to finish anything you don't complete tonight. Do you have much left to do?"

"No, maybe thirty minutes of Latin. I was gonna review for the chemistry quiz, too. But, honestly, I could take the quiz blindfolded and get an A. I spend too much time reviewing what I really know. I'm always scared there'll be something I'll miss or forget."

Dad said, "Well, there speaks a man who knows something about himself." He chuckled. They always gave me a hard time for studying too much. "I think you should go brush your teeth, turn the lights down, listen to some music, settle your heart, and drift off to sleep. You've just been through the wringer. You gotta hold yourself together for Brandon's sake. And ours."

He kissed me on the forehead. "We can hold up Brandon with you, but we can't hold you both up." He winked at me and patted my bottom. "Now, off to bed. Close your books. Forget about Latin, and get some sleep, my little star."

I started to walk off, but he pulled me close for one more long, tender hug. He whispered in my ear, "I love you more than you'll ever know, Alex."

"I love you, too. You're the best dad I could ever ask for."

Mom walked me to my room. "You can only do so much for Brandon right now. It's important you don't let his problems completely weigh you down. This storm will pass, and things will be easier in a few weeks. I know six weeks seems like a long time, but you'll get through it. I know you will. Keep telling yourself that keeping the peace with Mr. Marshall now will mean lots of time with Brandon this summer. Keep the long-view in focus, okay?"

I kissed her on the cheek and hugged her tightly. "Thanks. I love you. And thanks for what you and Dad said to Brandon. You can get to him in a way I can't."

"He's a sweet boy; troubled, but sweet. He just needs some love and attention. I can do those things without breaking a sweat!"

A few minutes later, I curled up in bed. The soft, sweet sounds of the oboe in the largo movement of Dvorak's *From the New World* symphony soothed my troubled heart. I thought of Brandon lying in his bed just a few miles west of me. I imagined him on his side, alone on the quiet second floor, alone in his spacious room, alone in his bed, alone in his sadness and confusion. I yearned for him in that moment in a new and unexpected way. I wanted to be near his body – not to touch it or admire it. I simply wanted to pull him close and let him know he would never, ever be alone; to say to him that whatever his dad said about him was just background noise compared to what I could say about him.

. . .

ii.

The following Thursday, my parents and I had a silent dinner. Each of us had been through a grueling four days. Before we sat down to eat, Dad put on one of his favorite Debussy recordings. The music calmed our frazzled nerves. We took our plates to the sink when I finished my last bite and returned to the table to have some yogurt and fruit

Dad turned off the CD player and said, "Listen, buddy,

we're going out tomorrow night. It's last minute. Aunt Karen is going to come over and stay with you for the evening."

"But I don't need a babysitter. I could spend the evening alone just fine."

Mom said, "You haven't seen her since Christmas! She isn't coming to babysit you. She's coming to see you. She misses you!"

"I'm sorry. I didn't think of it that way. It'll be great to see her. Is she eating here?"

"She said she would order pizza for you two. I got some more ice cream at the store today. She'll bring those cookies you love. So, you can have a Friday night treat. How does that sound?"

I nodded and smiled. Aunt Karen was good company. It would be fun to see her.

She came over to the apartment about 5:30. She had the code to the elevator and a key to the front door. I heard the door open and shut, and she came bustling in while I added the finishing line to a Latin translation.

She called out from the hallway. "Alex, sweetie, I'm here. Where are you?"

I came out of my room and ran to her outstretched arms. She kissed me on my cheek then held me at arm's length. "Goodness, Alex. I think you've grown two or three inches since Christmas. You must be hitting a little growth spurt. You're taller than me now!" She leaned in to kiss my nose. "And you're cuter than ever. God, your eyes and your hair! They make me jealous! I spend hours on my hair, and it just defies me at every turn. I bet you do nothing to yours, and you get this!" I blushed, and she laughed with glee.

We chatted for a few minutes. I told her about the mountain of work I always felt buried under.

She asked, "Do you need some time to study? I brought a book just in case you didn't have time for a movie!"

"No, the weekend workload is manageable; I can finish the

rest tomorrow."

"Good! Because we are gonna have some pizza. Your mom said there's fresh ice cream. I brought some cookies, too. And a video." She looked in her shoulder bag and pulled out a tin of homemade cookies. Then she grimaced.

"Oh, I left the video under the front seat. I went to Blockbuster yesterday to get a good selection before the crowds swept in tonight. You know what Blockbuster is like on a cold Friday night. If you get there after 5:00, all that's left are absurdist French movies from the fifties and old Carol Burnett shows!

"I put it under the front passenger seat when I left the store so I wouldn't take it into my house and forget to bring it over here. Run and get it for me, sweetie. Here are the keys. I'm parked where I normally do. Right by the corner, where that big oak tree is. You know where I mean?" I nodded. She had a regular spot right off Fannin.

I ran back to my room to put on shoes and a jacket. It was a cold night for Houston. There was a gusty north wind. I shivered as the first blast of cool air hit me on the sidewalk. Other than the wind, it was quiet all around. Fannin was busy all day but grew calmer in the evenings as the last office workers left downtown for points south. A lone plane came in low on its descent to Hobby Airport. The sidewalk was deserted.

Just as I reached Aunt Karen's car and bent over to unlock the driver's door, I heard the rush of footsteps behind me. Some hidden part of me sent up an instinctual, primal surge of terror. I thought I had put the attack at Joel's game far behind me, but in that flash of a second, when I heard those rushing footsteps, the entire scene burned brightly in my mind. Before I could turn or scream, strong arms wrapped around me. I was petrified with fear and panic. I couldn't make any sense of what was happening to me.

A breathy voice spoke in my left ear: "What are you doing

out here at night all alone, my little stick-arm friend?" I recognized Brandon's muffled laugh before I connected that unexpected voice with my best friend.

He held me tight and spun me around a dozen times until we were both dizzy. He stumbled and let go of me. I turned to face him in a jumbled mixture of relief, surprise, diminishing panic, and surging anger. The anger seemed to be first out of the starting gate as I spoke.

"What the hell are you doing here, Brandon? And, my God, you almost gave me a heart attack. I thought someone was attacking me. God, you scared me to death! I mean, what are you doing? What were you thinking?"

He roared with laughter, doubled-over. "I got you, Alex! I so got you. This is payback from that morning in Hawaii when you had me thinking we were really going to the museum. I've been waiting for the perfect moment. It's just a shame it's taken me, like, eight months or so! But I finally got you!"

I socked him as hard as I could on the shoulder. "Yeah, but you really scared me. It was like Joel's football game all over again when I heard loud footsteps running up from behind me. I just panicked! I was seriously afraid. I thought I was about to get beat up or something. I was really afraid." My voice trembled more than I meant for it to, and my heartbeat raced like a jet engine.

Brandon's self-satisfied grin dropped from his face. He stood up straight and held out his arms. Neither of us even bothered to look around. He pulled me in close to him and said, "Oh, God, Alex. Sorry! I didn't even think about that! I just wanted to surprise you! I just wanted to make you laugh and wonder what the hell I was doing hiding behind a tree outside your apartment!" He kissed me gently on my lips.

My fists loosened, and my heartbeat began to slow.

"I'm okay now. I'm just so surprised! And what are you doing here? How long have you been waiting there? What if I never came out? Did you run away from home? Please say you didn't run away."

"No, no, no. I'm not that dense. I'll tell you the whole story inside. Come on. We've only got about three hours. We gotta make hay while the sun shines!"

We started to make our way back to the front doors, when I remembered the video. Then I wondered: was there really a video? What was going on? Why was he here? Who else knew? What in the world was happening? I still hadn't put all the pieces together.

I ran over to Aunt Karen's car, unlocked the driver's door, and reached across to feel for the video under the passenger seat. Bingo! It was *The Princess Bride*. I hurriedly locked the door and ran back to Brandon. He grinned when I showed him the movie.

"Awww, your aunt is the best! I wonder how she knows we love that movie so much."

Aunt Karen was all smiles as we stumbled into the apartment, arms around each other and laughing non-stop. She hugged Brandon and launched into the full story after I peppered her with a dozen or more questions. Brandon interrupted from time to time, overflowing with excitement.

Aunt Karen started. "Your mom called me Wednesday and told me they had a plan to help Brandon. They wanted to take the Marshalls out to eat so they could present their plan to them, and they enlisted me to get Brandon over here and stay the evening to keep you two out of trouble!"

Brandon jumped in. "Yeah, apparently, your sweet momma knows somebody at Rice who coordinates a program where some of the students studying math for their degree volunteer to help high school students who suck at math! Like me! They take pity on us poor losers and try to help us out."

Aunt Karen said, "You don't suck at math. You just need a different kind of teaching. If a student doesn't learn something, it's not the student's fault normally; it's usually the teacher's fault."

She winked at me and said, "Anyway, they're going to present this plan to his parents at dinner tonight. It's all free, and your mom can arrange all the details. So, they're hoping his parents will say yes."

"Yeah, it sounds awesome. I think Dad will go for it. I know Mom will. I'm hoping he'll say yes. Lord knows, I need all the help I can get or I'm just gonna keep on failing Algebra. I can't do that, or we'll never see each other again!"

I swear he almost leaned in for a kiss, but he stopped himself just in time.

He went on. "And your parents said I could come over for pizza and a movie with you and your Aunt Karen. I think Mom had to talk Dad into agreeing to let me come over. But he did agree in the end. I mean, what else were they going to do with me? They rely on your parents to have me over when they want to go out with their friends! Dad didn't think that through when he grounded me for six weeks." He gave me a sly grin and a thumbs-up. "So, I figure the ice is already starting to melt, and maybe if I can start passing my tests, he'll even end the six weeks of punishment early. I mean, I have to have some glimmer of hope, or this semester will never end."

"I can't believe all this stuff has been going on, and I didn't have a clue. Mom and Dad didn't say a thing."

"I know! I didn't know you didn't know until Aunt Karen came. She arrived right as your parents came to pick up my parents. She told me I was coming with her, and that we were coming to babysit you! So that's when I told her I had to get you back for your dirty trick in Hawaii. Then she and I came up with the plan about the 'forgotten tape in the car.'" Full air quotes from Brandon. "She told me to hide in the back seat at first, but I was afraid you'd see me. So I went to hide behind the tree near where she parked. Then I waited. And, God, it took you long enough to come down. What did you do? Go style your hair and change clothes three times before coming down? I was freezing my balls off."

He blushed and looked sheepishly at Aunt Karen. "Sorry!"

She patted him on the cheek. "Don't worry. I've heard the word before. Trust me!"

Brandon threw his arm around my shoulder, and I slipped my hand behind his back and around to his stomach. I could feel the edge of his abs through his long-sleeve t-shirt. I had been missing those abs.

"So, we have a few hours to hang out with cool Aunt Karen and actually see one another for more than ten minutes or so at church. God, I've missed you!"

"I've missed you, too!"

Aunt Karen looked at us and smiled. "You two are impossibly cute. I don't think I've ever seen two such close friends. Now, what kind of pizza are we going to order?"

After a short argument, we decided on supreme with no onions. Brandon hated onions; I loved them. In exchange for my valiant act of sacrifice, he promised to make it up to me later. He giggled and kissed my neck when Aunt Karen turned away to order the pizza on the kitchen phone. I wondered for the first time if she knew I was gay. And if she did, did she know about me and Brandon?

As we finished our ice cream about an hour later, Aunt Karen asked me, "So what is this movie all about? I asked your mom what movie I should get, and she said you two loved *The Princess Bride*. I don't think I've ever even heard of it. I don't remember seeing it advertised at all."

Brandon said, "It's our favorite movie of all time. It's got action, drama, humor, dastardly plots, revenge, poison, spells, monstrous rats, swordfights and some of the funniest lines in any movie ever."

I added, "And it's got love. It's all about love."

"Yeah, that's the best part. It's all about love."

Aunt Karen beamed at us. "Well, how could I turn that down? It sounds perfect. A movie about love and two hot boys to hang out with. All my girlfriends will be so jealous when I tell them what I did tonight!"

We settled on the couch after Brandon got the VCR started. Aunt Karen sat on the left end, I sat in the middle, and Brandon sat to my right. We didn't stay upright long. Aunt Karen let me rest my head on a pillow in her lap. She played with my hair throughout the movie, chuckling at Brandon and me, as much as at the movie itself.

Brandon and I had regular parts when we watched *The Princess Bride*: I always quoted the lines for Westley, Inigo, and Humperdink; he quoted Buttercup, Fezzick, and the Man with Six Fingers; everything else was a mish-mash of overlapping giggles and interruptions. Oh, and I was always the old crone who shouted at Buttercup at the announcement of her engagement to Humperdink. We had our act down to perfection. Aunt Karen snorted the whole way through.

Brandon rested his head on a pillow wedged against my waist, his legs perched up on the far end of the couch. I wanted him even closer to me, but I was happy to be as close as we were. Being together was living on borrowed time. I treasured every second with him, and, at the same time, dreaded the cold, dark two miles that would separate us by night's end.

When the movie finished, Aunt Karen hurried off to the bathroom. Brandon and I both sat up and scooted together. He turned toward me and kissed me hard on my lips. I slipped my hand up the bottom of his t-shirt and let my fingers caress my favorite abs in the world. After a minute or so, we gently pulled apart.

"God, Alex! I've been wanting to do that for weeks and weeks! Now aren't you glad we didn't get onions on the pizza?" He chuckled. "And you know what? The last three hours were the hardest of the whole last month or so. To have you so close and not be able to kiss you or touch you... it's like the worst torture ever."

"I know. It's easier when you're two miles away than when you're two inches away." I leaned my head up against his shoulder. He kissed the top of my head.

I said, "It's all gonna work out. This tutoring will make a huge difference. I know my parents well enough to know they're gonna do some sweet talking tonight. Your dad thinks they have done a perfect job raising me..."

"Which they have done, my perfect *amigo*!"

"...and I think they're gonna make some gentle suggestions, you know? Like, they'll say, 'What works with Alex when he won't do his work is this and this.'"

"But you always do your schoolwork. Nobody else on the planet does their work like you." He chuckled and kissed my ear.

"But I mean, they're gonna make it sound like they have to stay on top of me. See? They're gonna make it seem like they have some secret to parenting, and your dad might listen to them. They'll suggest that Mr. Marshall dangle some kind of carrot in front of you in order to make you work harder – instead of shouting."

He grinned from ear to ear. "And you think you're the carrot that will motivate me, do you?"

"Yup! I bet that's their plan."

"God, your parents are the best." He pulled me even closer and kissed my neck. I let my hand rest on his crotch. Then we heard the muffled sound of the toilet flushing in the guest bathroom.

He leaned in. "One more kiss, you sorry-ass loser-man! Who knows when the next one will be."

We straightened up a few seconds later when the lock released on the bathroom doorknob. I let my hand linger on his crotch for another second or two. He pressed his hand on top of my crotch and said, "Well, talk about carrots! You got something stiff down there, for sure!"

. . .

Some of our predictions came true; some did not. Brandon's test grades soared in the following weeks as the tutoring sessions took effect. He kept me informed when we saw each other at church. He said his tutor was a thousand times better than Mr. McWhirter. Algebra was finally making sense. I felt so happy for my friend.

At the same time, Mr. Marshall did not budge in the weeks leading up to Spring Break. Brandon and I shared neither phone calls nor sleepovers. Brandon figured that if it had only been a matter of failing those tests, his dad would have relented sooner than six weeks. Mr. Marshall remained angry about Brandon's forgery and lies. Brandon said Mr. Marshall still brought up the lying and forgery at dinner several times a week.

Brandon and his mom planned to go to Nashville at Spring Break as usual. He called me the Thursday before they left. I was so excited to hear from him.

"Guess what, A-man." He never paused to let me guess anything. He just plowed ahead. "I got an 88 on my Algebra test." He whooped and hollered. I had to hold the receiver a few inches away! "We took our test early this week since Mr. McWhirter thought a lot of people might be gone tomorrow. He gave them back today! 88 baby! How about that?"

"Oh, my God! I can't believe it! I mean, I can believe it. You're smart enough. You just needed somebody who would explain it to you well. That's amazing. I'm so proud of you. Give me a second."

I held the phone away from me and shouted from the kitchen, "Brandon got an 88 on his Algebra test."

My parents came out of their room, both grinning wildly. They circled around me. I held the phone up in the air. Their voices overlapped: "Well done, Brandon. We are so proud." "We knew you could do it." "We love you!" "Get back over here soon. We miss you." "Please! Come take Alex off our hands. We haven't been out for dinner alone in weeks!" "We love you, sweetie!"

I put the receiver back to my face. "Did you hear that?"

"Yeah, they're the best. Tell them I love them and miss them. All my dad said was, 'Well, I'm pleased to see you've decided to take things seriously. Let this be a lesson to you.' But get this! Mom was standing right there, and she said, 'Well, I think you deserve a reward. How about a sleepover with Alex this weekend? You can do it here or there.' I could tell she hadn't checked with Dad, but he didn't say a thing. She just winked and gave me a kiss."

"Wow! That's amazing. Yes, yes, a thousand times yes! Let's do it! Your place or mine?"

"Oh, mine! Come. Over. Here. Please."

"Deal. We've got a lot of time to make up for!"

He snickered. "Oh, yeah, baby. I'm gonna put you through the toughest work out ever. I bet you've gone soft all over in the last two months."

"Well, not everything's gone soft! Not everything..."

"Alex N. Kennedy! I swear you are the raunchiest teenager alive."

CHAPTER 14

We plowed our way through the rest of the semester, snatching whatever time we could be together on the weekends. Brandon's dad let us resume our periodic sleepovers, and Brandon joined Dad and me again for our long runs on Saturday mornings.

Brandon worked harder and harder in Algebra. With the help of his tutor and a few tidbits from me, he ended up with a 73 for a final average. That, along with all As and Bs in his other classes, seemed to be the salve that finally smoothed Mr. Marshall's outraged parental psyche.

As June approached, we realized our third summer together would be a little different from the previous two. Brandon's tutor offered to work with him one morning a week for most of the summer. Brandon's parents jumped at the offer. Brandon was upset at first, but then his mom made a suggestion which involved me. He told me about it as we talked on the phone on the last Thursday of the school year.

"So, Mom thinks you should come with me to the tutoring sessions on Tuesday mornings. I'll have homework to do between each session. If you're there with me, you can be like a secondary tutor when I'm doing homework. How about it? I know you did Algebra II, like, five years ago, but I figure you still know it all by heart."

I was hesitant at first, easily imagining the bickering that might transpire if I tried to help Brandon with tutoring homework on a regular basis. Despite our easy-going friendship, we both hard sharp edges. He was inclined to blow up when faced with a challenge, and I had next to no patience for explaining to others what was obvious to me.

"Do you really need me to come? I thought Jason explained it all to you so well. I don't want it to be confusing if he says one thing and I say something different."

"He has helped, but sometimes he goes a little fast. I get lost but try not to show it. He usually circles back when he sees my mouth hanging open and a tiny trail of drool starts going down my chin." He chuckled to himself.

"Oh, yes! I know that look of yours. It's pretty much permanent, in case you hadn't noticed."

"Smartass!"

"Listen up! I won't tolerate any nonsense from you, Humperdink. If I'm gonna help you, you gotta realize it will be on my terms. I'm serious! If you get outta line, it's wedgie time for you!"

Brandon cackled with delight. "Actually, sorry-ass loser-man, your wedgies are like microscopic wedgies. I can't even feel them, and you're back there pulling my undies with all your might. I mean, I can eat a sandwich while you give me a wedgie. I can take a nap while you give me a wedgie. I could knit a sweater while you give me a wedgie. Wedgie, my ass!"

I did my best Inigo Montoya impersonation. "I do not think you would accept my help, since I am only waiting around to kill you."

He replied as Westley, with a tinge of an English accent. "That does put a damper on our relationship." We could go on like that for hours, maybe a lifetime.

On the whole, we did all right. I lost my patience with him

a good dozen or so times in June alone, but I only erupted twice. He loved it when I got angry with him, so we managed to avoid any major melt-downs while factoring polynomials and graphing quadratic functions.

Brandon's parents also enrolled him in driver's education. He went every Friday afternoon from 1:00 to 4:00. He was in countdown mode all summer and talked endlessly about the things we'd do together once he could drive us anywhere.

I teased him and said I would make plans with Joel every Friday while he was in drivers' ed. class.

"Hey, hey, you little smart-ass. I'll rip your arms off if you ever go around spending extra time with Joel like you did that time at Spring Break. No more sneaking around behind my back."

"Your broad, chiseled back?"

"Got that right! If I tried to sneak around behind your back, it would take two seconds, you little bean-pole-for-a-back loser. You'd get lost behind my back. It's that wide!"

"Okay, okay, Mr. I'm-More-In-Love-With-My-Body-Than-Is-Even-Normal. Stop making yourself hard thinking about yourself."

He gasped. "You dirty little shit! I can't believe you just said that. Everyone thinks you are so wise and calm and mature and perfect, but you've got the dirtiest mind I know. Like a kitchen sink, as my grandma likes to say. And you drink like a fish!"

"What? I do not! I take, like, three sips of champagne or wine from time to time!"

"No, I mean that's what she says. Come on! Stay with me, Alex." He snickered and snorted. He loved it when I didn't follow his shifts in conversations. "Those are her two famous lines: 'So-and-so has a mind as dirty as the kitchen sink' and 'You know, so-and-so drinks like a fish.' Those are the two worst things in her book. A dirty mind and drinking too much alcohol."

"And yet she loves you! Love really does conquer all!"

"Oh, funny. You're a laugh a minute. Let me see if I can stop laughing." He paused dramatically and sighed. "Um, yep. It took exactly one fourth of a second to stop laughing after that attempt you made to be funny, dumbass."

My parents made plans for a family vacation to Washington, D.C. and New York at the beginning of July. We invited Brandon to come with us, and his parents agreed again. Tragedy struck just a few days before we were due to leave, though none of us were terribly surprised. Mrs. Marshall's mother passed away after her long battle with cancer. Brandon and his family flew to Nashville for her funeral the very morning we flew to Washington for the start of our vacation.

Brandon came back from Nashville with an awful stomach bug. He was too sick to go to camp. I was actually quite relieved. Neither of us wanted to go in the first place, but Mr. Marshall was insistent. When I found out Brandon wasn't going, I asked my parents if I could stay home. They agreed, and I ended up spending a few lazy days with Mom while Brandon recuperated. It was better by a mile than going to camp without Brandon.

. . .

Brandon and I spent our usual nights together the rest of the summer and, through some strange luck, added on Saturday nights without any pushback from our parents. My parents seemed happy enough to have me home Sunday, Monday, and Tuesday nights, and Brandon's parents seemed to accept that I was suddenly there every Saturday night.

The only exception to those nights at Brandon's house was August 11, the Saturday before my birthday. My parents wanted all four of us to go out to eat, and they invited Brandon to stay at our apartment that night. We went to Antonio's again. Aunt Karen met us there as a surprise and went back home with us for dessert.

Aunt Karen left after we had our cake and ice cream, and the four of us sat together on the balcony overlooking the north end of Hermann Park. Mom made decaf coffee for me and Brandon. She and Dad had the real deal. Even though it was a hot August evening, the coffee tasted good and made me feel grown-up as I inched closer to turning fifteen.

Our chairs were in a semi-circle: Dad on the far left, Mom next to him, Brandon next to her, and me next to him.

We fell into a companionable silence after Dad told us a story about his fifteenth birthday. Mom spoke first. "We want to talk to you two before school starts up again. Alex is going to have a very busy year ahead. If last year felt hard, this year is going to make it seem like kindergarten." She winked at me. "But he can do it. He can manage."

Brandon said, "I know. He's a little Einstein. There's nothing he can't learn. He'll do great this year. Now, me, on the other hand. I've got Algebra II to survive and Chemistry. It's gonna be rough. My tutor is good at Chemistry, too. So he's promised to help with that if I need it... which I will." He paused for a second and took Mom's hand in his. "Oh, and thank you again, *Momma-Numero-Dos*, for setting all that up. Jason's been a life saver. And a friendship saver, too." He looked at me and smiled.

Mom pulled his hand to her lips and kissed it. "Well, sweetie, that's part of what we want to talk to you both about. The next few years of high school are going to be hard for both of you. We want you two to spend time together. We think you two are such sweet friends – and more than that, of course. We know you kiss and hold hands! We see you, and there's no problem with it." She turned a little more toward Brandon. "Honestly, Brandon, I know you don't hear that from anyone else, so it's important you hear it from us. We couldn't be happier that you two are friends and that you love each other the way you do.

"At the same time, you two are still very young. These high school years are full of emotions and stress, and so many other things are going on. It's really important that you two trust us to help you through it all. Does that make sense?"

He nodded. She looked at me. I nodded, too, though I sensed there was more to come.

Dad said, "So this is the issue, boys. We want you to keep having about two sleepovers per month. We know your parents are okay with this, Brandon. We've spoken to them. And once you're able to drive legally, it will make our lives easy. We won't be shuffling you back and forth so much. But here is a really important thing for you to get right now: we will put limits on the places you go together once you're driving. We don't want there to be any surprises. A lot of teens think their car is their ticket to go anywhere, anytime, but we are going to put limits. So, you might as well get that processed in your brains right now. Do you understand?"

We both nodded.

Dad went on. "We'd be saying this to you if you were just friends, but we also have to say this because of your relationship. To be honest, your mom and I have talked about our fears for you. We are lucky to live in this part of Houston where you two can actually see gay couples out and about. Someone at work told me the zip code that centers on Montrose and Westheimer is the gayest neighborhood anywhere between New York and San Francisco. That's only a mile or so up the road, but there's still a lot of hate and misunderstanding out there. Do you remember that crazy man who ran for mayor back in 1985?" Brandon shrugged his shoulders and furrowed his brow. "Well, he said the surest way to stop the spread of AIDS was to shoot the queers. Those were his exact words."

Brandon said, "But Whitmire beat him by a wide margin. I remember because my dad was so angry."

"She did beat him handily, but there are people all over this city who share those beliefs. They may not be the majority, but there are plenty of them." His voice quivered as he continued. "There are people out there who'd just as soon shoot you two as look at you if they knew you were gay. You have to be unbelievably careful when you are out and about. I know you already are in many respects. I remember how cautious you were in Hawaii. You have to maintain the friends-only act. Looking like friends is the best camouflage for how you really feel about each other... to keep you safe. Not many people would suspect you're both gay as long as you keep your hands off each other. And no kissing in public, *ever*. Got it?"

We glanced at each other and both nodded. Dad was right. Brandon and I had been fantastically lucky on so many occasions. It could all go horribly wrong in two seconds if we let our guard down around the wrong people. The episodic nightmares I still had about the attack at Joel's football game were necessary, if grim, reminders of what was at stake.

Dad went on. "The other part of keeping you safe is the duty we owe your parents, Brandon. Elizabeth and I talk about it frequently. We feel a little conflicted about the secrets we keep from your parents. If you were involved in drugs or stealing, we'd feel a duty to tell your parents at some point. We think this is different. We can't really explain it. We just know what the stakes are; perhaps we understand them better than you two can, though I know you understand a great deal.

"We've agreed it's your business to tell your parents when you're ready. We've also agreed that we have to do everything in our power to keep you safe because we do owe that to your parents. None of this is easy for any of us, and perhaps we'll look back one day and think of a thousand things we could have done differently. But for now, as we said to Alex when he first told us about his feelings for you, we're building the plane as we fly. We just don't want to run it into the ground and take you two down with it."

Mom cleared her throat. "And we want to talk to you about your relationship. It's really important you're both honest with us. Alex tells us a lot about your relationship. We never force him to say things, but it's important you both trust us. Part of trusting us is being honest with us.

"We know you two kiss and show each other a lot of affection when you're around us. We know you touch one another and kiss when we're not around. We notice that you often shower together." Brandon shifted a bit in his chair. Mom had never been so direct with him before. "It's really important that you tell us when you start to think about something more. There's nothing shameful about your bodies. There's no shameful part on your body. What you feel for one another isn't shameful, and what you want to do with each other isn't shameful. Do you believe me, Brandon?"

He gazed at her silently. I tried to read his facial expressions as a clue to his thoughts and emotions. I could tell he was anxious on some level, and perhaps embarrassed, but I knew he knew he was impossibly safe with my parents.

He finally said, "I think so. I mean, a part of me thinks how I feel about Alex is wrong. I know my parents think it's wrong. I can't imagine ever talking to them about this. They would never say what you're saying. They would say I'm disgusting and perverted. Well, that's what Dad would say. Mom would be crying too much to say anything."

"Well, sweetie, it's really important you listen to what I say: there is nothing shameful about your body, your love for Alex, and what you two do together. You have to be sure about it because plenty of people – at church, at your school, in your family – do think it's wrong and shameful. You're going to have to learn to drown out all those voices and just hear our voices until you one day find more people who do understand."

A few tears slid down Brandon's cheeks. I reached over and squeezed his hand. He laced his fingers between mine, his palm resting on top of my hand.

Dad continued. "We've told Alex that we would say the same thing if he was with a girl instead. We'd want to know what he was doing with her, and we'd want to know what he was thinking about doing with her. Not to put a stop to it necessarily, but so we can talk about it. Because whatever you feel like you have to hide from us will feel shameful to you. When you hide things, especially about your body and your sexual desires, you usually hide them because you think they're shameful. Nobody wants the kind of love that feels shameful. What you feel is very natural, but it can become quite unhealthy if you bottle it up or pretend you don't feel the way you feel."

He turned to Brandon and said, "Is there anything you feel a little ashamed about?"

We all sat in silence for a moment or two. I could tell Brandon was working up the courage to say something. He finally did. "Well, I sometimes feel like I shouldn't want to touch Alex's penis. It feels good and wrong all at the same time... if that makes any sense."

Dad said softly, "That's what we mean. Tell us what you're up to so you don't feel ashamed. You don't have to keep it secret. Your penises are just a part of your body. You do something quite special with them, but you can also do special things with your hands – like sketching and playing the violin. You shouldn't feel ashamed of holding hands, should you?" Brandon shook his head. "So why feel ashamed of touching your friend's penis?"

Brandon nodded a little and gave a faint smile.

A burden lifted from my shoulders. I had felt ashamed at times about my deep attraction to Brandon's penis, but I saw Dad's logic. Why was one body part so shameful? What was the difference between a hand and a penis, other than the things you do with them? A penis could never shoot a gun, wield a knife, or knock someone's teeth out, but a hand could do all that. Hands can do real harm, and nobody gives hands a second thought. But I had heard so many messages at church that made me think my penis, maybe the gentlest part of my body, was something I ought to ashamed of. My thinking was a bit muddled at times, but Dad was right: talking openly made it clearer and helped me feel better instantly.

I looked at Dad and said, "I do like holding his penis, and he likes holding mine. But we haven't done any of the other things you told me about."

Brandon chuckled nervously. Mom looked at him and said, "Do you know what he's talking about, Brandon? Do you know the other things men might do with another man's penis?"

He nodded, eyes slightly cast down.

"Well, that's good, and it's important you say the words and not be ashamed. Some day you two may be ready for oral or anal sex or some kind of masturbation together, but you need to be really comfortable before you get there. I mean, I know you are comfortable with each other. You love being together, and it's obvious you enjoy touching and kissing. But until you feel really comfortable with more, you need to enjoy what you have right now."

Dad said, "If you two aren't comfortable talking about sex with us and with each other, if you can't even say certain words without embarrassment, then just wait a bit. We'll keep talking with you. You keep talking with us. Then when the time is right, you'll know it, and you won't go around feeling ashamed."

I nodded. Brandon squeezed my hand and shot me his best mega-watt grin. I wondered what he was thinking.

Mom said, "We know you can't talk to your parents about this, so that's why we want to keep talking to you two like this. Like James said, we have a duty to keep you safe: physically and emotionally. You're too young to figure this out by yourselves without getting hurt and hurting each other."

"Hey, *Momma-Numero-Dos*, I need all the help I can get, and you're right: I could never talk about this with my parents. But I hope you know I would never, ever hurt Alex. In fact, my main mission in life is to keep him safe from all assholes."

She chuckled and said, "I know that! You've proven that. What I meant to say is that you could both easily get emotionally hurt if you were trying to figure this out alone. That's why we want to have these kinds of talks with you."

"I know. I feel so lucky to have you for second parents. I think Alex and I would be messed up if we were trying to keep this a secret from you two also. Well, he'd be messed up, but I'd be okay mostly." He gave me a wink.

Dad said, "Oh, of course, of course. We know you'd be perfectly fine, Brandon!"

Brandon looked alarmed and said, "Oh, God, no! Not really! You can't think that! You three are the only people who keep me sane and normal. I'd be lost without you. I mean, so, so, so lost."

Mom blew him a kiss. "Well, believe it or not, our little threesome would be kind of lost without you, sweetie. You are one of us now for as long as you want to stay around."

Mom and Dad stood up at the same time and leaned into one another for a hug. Brandon and I took our cue from them. We stood in tandem, and I leaned in close to kiss him. He dipped me dramatically and lingered on my lips. Dad and Mom laughed; then Dad dipped Mom, too. The four of us stood there for a long time: two happy couples locked in strong, safe embraces. I couldn't imagine another family on the planet where that would have been possible. We were one-in-a-billion, and I was the luckiest soon-to-be-fifteen-year-old alive.

. . .

ii.

Brandon's parents threw a surprise sixteenth birthday party for him the following Saturday evening. They enlisted my help a few weeks earlier, mainly for advice on who to invite from Brandon's school and from church. Mrs. Marshall admitted to me, "We really don't know who his other friends are. He's always surrounded by a group of boys when I pick him up from school, but I know nothing about them. The only boy in the youth group he ever mentions is Joshua. So, I thought you could help me make a small list. Maybe five or six from school and the same number from church. Be sure to include Joshua." I suppressed a giggle at the last suggestion.

I struggled to come up with names of his school friends. I ended up having to be a little devious and wrangle names out of Brandon by stealth. He didn't seem to think I was up to anything, and he was truly surprised when I brought him through the front door of his house on that Saturday evening. My family had taken him to lunch and a movie to give the Marshalls all afternoon to prepare.

Later, as the guests were trailing out, I reflected back over the evening. In some ways, Brandon was the life of the party, especially with his school friends. Each of his friends from school seemed a little wild to me. They were the kind of public school guys I easily stereotyped in my mind: average grades, good at sports, insolent with their teachers, grumpy with their parents, and disdainful of any kids who didn't seem cool enough to fit in their group. I didn't think they were the most popular kids in his grade, but they didn't seem to be misfits or kids on the fringe either. Why he liked them was a mystery to me.

All the church kids hung out together on one side of the living room. All the school kids hung out on the other side. I mingled in between the kitchen and the living room. Every few minutes Brandon would come up to me, exhausted from bouncing back and forth between the groups. He did have a certain social flare that lit up the room. He was funny and charming. Both groups of friends seemed quiet and awkward until he came back to their side, and it was interesting to see how he tried to adjust himself to the differing expectations of each group.

The school kids definitely acted like he was the coolest one of them. He stood a good head taller than any of them. He was bulkier than any of them by at least fifteen or twenty pounds. They stood around looking up at him and hanging on every word. At the same time, he didn't seem comfortable with them. He seemed to know his role in that group, and he played it well. But his heart wasn't in it. I could tell as I watched him sway nervously from foot to foot and fidget with his collar. Every time he came back to me, I sensed a frenetic weariness in him, as if he were a high-wire artist struggling to maintain his balance, wary of plunging off the impossibly thin cords of twisted metal.

He didn't seem any more comfortable with the church friends. Maybe he was even less comfortable with them. They knew him better in some ways, and I think they saw through the persona he often projected at church. He was the preacher's kid, and everybody at church expected him to walk on water and turn water into wine. His older brothers played the role perfectly. Brandon gave it a shot at times, but he never pulled off a convincing performance. All the church kids knew Brandon could curse like a sailor; next to drinking, doing drugs, and having sex before marriage, cursing was about the worst thing our church friends could imagine. They knew he snickered when people said odd things in prayers. They knew he lost his temper quickly in sports. The boys knew he would bulldoze over them if he got a bit competitive in a game of football or baseball. He was wild and unpredictable in their eyes, and all of them were slightly afraid of him.

Perhaps for the first time since we had become friends, I

saw him clearly through the eyes of the people who populated his life before I came along. Yet, maybe that's not exactly correct. Those people didn't see him clearly. They only saw him for who they wanted him to be and as he wanted them to see him. In a moment of clarity, I realized Brandon must have spent years pretending to be someone other than who he was. And, in another startling realization, I realized he kept up his two personas with those divergent groups of friends even after he and I became such fast friends. The Brandon I knew was the Brandon he wanted to be. His frantic back-and-forth between sets of friends with misguided expectations showed me the extent of the gift he found in our friendship and in my family. We had seen him for who he was, and we had loved him even more for it.

The very last guest didn't leave until nearly 9:45. Brandon heaved a sigh of relief as he shut the door. We helped his parents clean up, though Mrs. Marshall and I did most of it while Brandon and all the party guests played 'Win, Lose, or Draw.' That game was the one part of the evening that everyone seemed to enjoy.

Brandon and I climbed into his bed a little after 10:30. Brandon turned on his right side and took my hand in his. He seemed sad and distant in some inexplicable way.

"You okay? You seem a million miles away. You'll be legal to drive in a few days. I thought you'd be grinning from ear to ear."

He sighed a bit and said, "Yeah, I'm okay, I guess. It's just that this party kind of showed me how I don't have any friends but you." He paused and looked over my shoulder for a few seconds. "I mean, I wouldn't want it any other way... I mean being best friends with you. But it makes me wonder what my life would have been like had we never met. You would be just fine without me. All my school friends think you're impossibly cool. They all thought you were, like, two or three years older than me – just really short for an eighteen-year-old guy." He snickered. "You would make friends wherever you go. I just don't think I could."

I started to say something, but he gently put his hand on my shoulder as a silent request to let him finish.

"It's like, I only want to be a certain way... the way I am with you. But nobody else wants me to be that way. I can't tease my friends at school the way I tease you. I can't talk about love and classical music and Agatha Christie and sketching and Mr. Darcy with them! And I can't talk about working out or tell dirty jokes or say what I really think about God with my church friends. It's like I don't belong in either world. Somehow I fit in your world but nobody else's."

I reached out and stroked his chin; then I let my finger trace its way down the center of his bare chest. "Sure, I get it. It makes sense. And you shouldn't say things are easier for me. Do you think I would fit in with your school friends? Maybe they think I'm cool and mature. Maybe they like my hair." I winked at him and got a small smile in return. "But we have nothing in common. Do you think *they* want to hear about Dickens and Elgar and Chopin? Do you think *they* want me to quote the lyrics of *Storybook Love*? Come on, Brandon! I'd be just as lost with them as you feel. I'd have to pretend, too. Maybe my friends at school don't mind me talking about Emily Dickinson, Thomas Tallis, and Horton Foote, but they would never let me hold their hand or touch their chest or kiss them anywhere!"

"Which one of them do you want to kiss and touch?"

"None of them, you moron. That's not the point." He looked away, and I softened my tone. "I just mean there's nobody like you in my life, and there's nobody like me in your life. It's that simple. We were lucky enough to meet each other and become best friends. Then lucky enough to discover that we loved one another in a way we never thought possible. Why spend all this time wondering about how different it would be if we hadn't met? Not tonight of all nights! I mean, you're almost sixteen! A driver's license is on the way, and you're getting a gently used car from an anonymous generous person at church. How cool is that? How many kids get a free car out of the blue?"

"Well, it is a bit of an old clunker, but you're right. It's better than nothing. Better than... what was that phrase in that book you read to me? 'Better than shank's pony'?"

"Yes, exactly!"

Brandon smiled and pulled me closer to him. "Well, it is a pretty special birthday. You're here. Never in my wildest dreams could I have dreamed you up and imagined you'd be right beside me in bed."

"I know I'm pretty dreamy! You don't have to keep telling me!"

I winked. He winked back.

He asked, "Can I touch you?"

I giggled.

He slipped his hand down my shorts.

"I'm so glad your parents talked to us about this, Alex. I think there was a time I wondered if it was dirty. Well, I know I thought that, but your dad was right. It felt wrong because we kept it a secret. Once we talked about it and they said there was nothing shameful about it, it was like a curtain rose up. All this light came flooding in. What I thought was a dark room we had to keep hidden became so bright. Like our love became brighter, too."

He let go of my penis and withdrew his hand from my shorts. He smiled and said, "See, that's all it is, isn't it? Just a touch, and I can let go. Like a kiss, and we can stop. Like a hug, and we can separate. Nothing wrong about any of it."

I traced my finger back and forth across his chest. The small dip between his pecs which so attracted me that first Sunday in 1987 had finally become a canyon. "You're getting so big, Brandon! It's funny how I see you all the time, but then I also kind of forget how much you've changed in the last year or so. Does that make any sense?"

"I think so. Sometimes I even forget how much I'm growing. The other day, I looked at a few of those pictures your mom gave me from last summer in Hawaii. I've definitely added a lot of muscle this year. Joel said it will just accelerate over the next few years if I stay serious about working out and eating well. He said he put on a lot of muscle after he turned sixteen."

"Sounds like a plan!" I reached over and ran my hand over his peaked bicep and around to his bulky tricep. He flexed his for me.

"What do you think, A-man? How's the ol' arm looking?"

"Very good from this angle." I leaned in and kissed the hard ridge of muscle on the outer head of his tricep.

"Oh, yeah, what about this angle?"

He reared up in front of me on his knees. He gave me his best double-bicep pose. I whistled with satisfaction.

"As you would say: 'Wow! Just wow!'"

"And check this out." He put his palms behind his head, elbows akimbo, and tightened his abs. I was mesmerized, and I wondered how an almost-sixteen-year-old could be so beautiful. Mom liked to remind me that beauty is only skin deep, and I knew what she meant. I would have loved Brandon just the same if he was shorter and skinnier like me, but the beauty of his body was like a dollop of whipped cream on the best ice cream sundae ever. It wasn't the most important part of the sundae, but it was hard to imagine enjoying the experience the same way without it.

I sat up and leaned in close to his abdomen. I tried to kiss each ridge of Brandon's six pack. He started laughing so much he couldn't hold his pose any longer. I only got up to kiss number three.

He looked at me with a crooked grin. "You horny little guy! Where'd you get that idea?"

"From Joel. He told me one of his girlfriends kissed his abs one time. I've been thinking about kissing his and yours ever since. Mainly yours these days."

"Did you say mainly? Mainly, Mr. Kennedy? As in, in addition to kissing my abs, you think about kissing his abs? Or someone else's? God, you are so sex-obsessed!"

"Oh, shut up. I just mean when he first told me about that girlfriend, I wondered what it would be like if I did that to him or to you. I mean, if he was here now and said, 'Hey, Alexo, have a kiss if you want,' I wouldn't say no."

"Hor-or-ny! That's what you are! If only the whole world knew!"

"Oh, and you wouldn't kiss mine or his?"

He gulped. "Well, now that you mention it…" He grinned and reached for my shirt. "Take this off, or I'll rip it off you. Come on, come on! Being friends is about sharing and taking turns. Or did you not learn that in kindergarten? Were you too busy learning Shakespeare and Algebra I?" He snorted at his own joke. I giggled, too.

I raised myself up on my knees in front of him and pulled my shirt over my head. I tightened my abs.

Brandon snorted and said, "Wow! Just wow! How can you have such skinny arms and have these rocky abs? It's like you're a freak of nature."

I couldn't control my giggling. "I can either hold my abs tight or you can tease me. What's it gonna be?"

"Okay, okay, okay. My lips are sealed." He snickered. "Well, not totally sealed. I mean, that would be lame and defeat the point." We both chuckled. "Okay, stop laughing! Get serious. Pretend I'm Joshua, and I just invited you to a week-long sleepover!"

He gently slapped my abs with the back of his hand. "Come on, come on. I've not got all night."

I tightened my abs again. He leaned in close. I felt the soft warmth of his lips caress me six times. He looked up and grinned. "God, you're something else, Alex!"

I put my hands on each side of his head just above his ears and pulled his head up against my torso. He patted my crotch and grinned. I was so hard. Brandon slipped my shorts and underwear down and brought his lips close to my throbbing penis.

He looked up at me. "Can I?"

I wondered for a second: 'Can he? Should he? Did I want him to?'

I nodded. "Yes, but just a kiss."

"Okay. Just a kiss."

A pulse of warm energy passed through my entire body as Brandon's lips gently touched my penis, and I marveled at the softness of his lips as they lingered in a few places. He let out a contented sigh or two, and then, ever so gently, he let his tongue linger an extra few seconds on the tip of my penis. The whole encounter left me breathless, and, like our first kiss, the reality of the moment made me feel alive in a new and startling way.

Brandon looked up at me and smiled. "How was that, smartass?"

"Impossibly wonderful! I could die now and be happy with the life I lived!"

"Well, like I said, even if you were too busy memorizing the periodic table in kindergarten, I learned you have to take turns if you want to be a good friend. Do you want a turn?"

I nodded. "Oh, baby, yes!"

Brandon slipped his shorts and underwear off. He rose up on his knees, just as I had done. I brushed my lips against his hard penis and gently licked the tip. He let out a soft moan. I had an urge to slip his penis in my mouth, but I remembered my parents' advice. Not now... later... there would be time later.

"I've been dreaming about this for months. I love you so much. This is the best birthday present ever!"

"I love you, too, Brandon. Every inch of you, inside and

out."

I wrapped my arms around his waist, and we tumbled onto the bed together. We held each other tight in a long embrace. I kissed his chest and neck and made my way to his lips. He pulled me in even closer and used his free hand to hold my head firmly against his cheek. A thousand marching bands could have paraded through his bedroom; his Dayton cousins could have stood around the bed and hooted in derision and disgust; we wouldn't have noticed a thing!

Brandon led me to a room in my soul I had never entered before, but I knew it by heart as soon as my eyes first fell upon it.

CHAPTER 15

FALL 1990

By the time, October rolled around, Brandon and I felt comfortable with the demands of our sophomore year. Maybe some academic hurricane was quietly gaining strength offshore, but I was coping well and keeping my head above water. Brandon said he was doing well, too, though I took that with a grain of salt. He sometimes didn't know when he was drowning at school. At least that was my observation from a distance. Nevertheless, he managed all As and Bs on his first report card. Our parents let us have a rare two-night sleepover in mid-October as a reward for our successes of the first six weeks.

Brandon arrived at our apartment a little before 6:00 on Friday evening. He still wasn't allowed to drive completely by himself. So, he drove himself and Mr. Marshall over; then Mr. Marshall drove Brandon's hand-me down Corolla back to their house.

I could tell something was wrong the moment Brandon entered the lobby of the building. His eyes were red, and I could see a faint line of mucus along the bottom of his nose. A small wave of fear and uncertainty welled up deep inside me.

I slipped my arm through his as we walked toward the

elevator. "What's up, man? You look upset."

He shook his head. "I can't say it here. If I do, I won't be able to get in the elevator. Let's just get upstairs, and I'll tell you three together at the same time."

We rode up the elevator in silence. My parents hurried to greet Brandon as we made our way in. They, too, instantly sensed his troubled state. They looked to me, and I shook my head slightly, telegraphing my own bewilderment.

Mom hugged Brandon and asked, "Do you want a drink? Coke? Or some juice or water?"

He shook his head. Tears welled up in his eyes. I put my arm around him and guided him to the couch in the living room. We sat down together. Mom sat next to me, and Dad sat next to Brandon. He sobbed for several seconds. Mom handed him some tissues, and he wiped his nose and eyes.

His voice quivered as he began. "There's no good or easy way to say this. I don't know how to say it." He gulped. "We're moving to Nashville." He leaned against me and sobbed even harder.

As my own eyes flooded with tears, an image flashed across my mind: that trick where someone whips a tablecloth off a table so fast and skillfully that all the china, crystal, and cutlery stays in place. Except in my case, in my life, all I could hear was a crescendo of shattering glass, silverware, and china as my life splintered into a million tiny shards.

I gasped, "No, Brandon, you can't move! Not now! Not ever! Why?"

Mom slipped her arm through mine and took my hand in hers. I felt her pulse racing fast against my thin wrist.

"Dad got a new job with a church in some suburb of Nashville. We're moving there during Christmas Break. They just told me today when I got home. Dad's announcing it on Sunday to the church." He sobbed more heavily and said, "It's all over. Everything is ruined."

Dad leaned into Brandon on the other side and patted his thigh. "We're here for you, Brandon. You just cry or scream or do whatever you need to do. If you need to punch something, we'll get Alex to stand up right here."

Brandon's sobbing only increased. Like we did that night in Hawaii, we surrounded my friend with our presence and love and let him cry as much as he needed.

After a few minutes, the tears ceased flowing so freely and his breathing calmed a bit. He placed his hand on my thigh and rubbed it up and down.

"You gotta believe me. I had no idea this was coming. I had no idea. I would have told you, I swear. Don't be mad at me."

"I'm not mad… just incredibly sad. We only have about two months."

"I know. I used to think we had forever to be friends! Like, we would muddle through high school and then figure out how we were gonna do college." He smiled for the first time all evening. "I never told you, but I had a plan. I was gonna wait to see where you got into college, then I was gonna apply to some junior college in the same place or near it. I thought I might get a degree in art so I could become an art teacher someday. I thought we could get an apartment together or something. I don't know. We were gonna figure it out. I just knew there was a way to make it happen." A slight tremor stole into his voice again. "I don't know now. It all seems so confusing. How do we go for over two years in separate towns? Separate states even?"

Mom said, "Sweetie, let's just take a second and not get too far down the road, okay? Let's just get through this right here, right now. We never dreamed this would happen. But I guess now that I think about it, it makes a lot of sense. I always knew your parents wanted to go back to Tennessee to be near all your extended family. I guess we just thought they'd let you finish high school first."

"I know, I know! That's what I thought. I never thought

they'd live here forever since all their family is back in Nashville or near to it. I mean, except for my three older brothers, all the family is back there. I just thought they'd let me finish high school here, but Dad said the opportunity was too good to pass up."

I felt numb and raw; empty and utterly lost at sea. I was a small sailboat on a storm-tossed sea, and the familiar, beckoning light I usually used to steer a steady course vanished without a trace. I simply couldn't imagine my life without Brandon.

We all sat in silence again for several minutes. There wasn't much to say. An unseen fault line running beneath the soft soil of my life shifted in an instant and everything safe and familiar crumbled around me. Words didn't seem to matter. Nothing I said could change the inevitable: Brandon would move in sixty or so days.

Brandon filled us in on more details over dinner. "My parents plan to make a couple of trips out there to look for a house. They're gonna ask you closer to the time if I can stay the weekend here when they make those trips. The plan is to have the movers come the Monday after school finishes. Mom's sisters are coming to help with the packing while Mom finishes up her teaching. Then we'll actually move out there around December 20. So... two months from now. It'll all be over then. I'll be gone. Gone for good."

I cut in, "No, not gone for good. Just gone for a bit. We'll figure out ways to see each other. I mean, now that we are so old, you could come spend the whole summer here." I looked at Mom and Dad. "I mean, right? He's always welcome."

Dad nodded. "Of course! You can come here any time and stay as long as your parents will let you. We'll even pay for your plane ticket, and we'll arrange for Alex to fly to see you. Maybe a week after Christmas and at Spring Break, if your school there has the same Spring Break. We'll make it work. Then we'll see what happens in a few more years.

"Boys, we do our best to never speak down to you or to act like you are immature or naïve, but don't lose all your perspective on this. It may seem like this is the darkest day of your life. It may seem that there are only dark days ahead, but you'll get through this. We'll help you get through this. Life can be pretty shitty sometimes, yet those shitty times often help us grow and mature and become wiser and more resilient in the end." Brandon and I shot each other sly looks. Dad hardly ever cursed!

Mom said, "Your dad and I spent two years apart after college when he went to Stanford and I went to Columbia. I know we were older, and things were different for us. But we made it through, and we were more in love because of our long separation – not less!"

Brandon teared up again. "I knew you two would help me see this in a better light. Mom tried to say some kind things, but Dad kept cutting her off. He kept saying I was being immature and unreasonable. He said he and his brothers moved four times when he was a kid. He said he never made a scene like I was making. He said, 'It's time you start acting like the young man your body is already becoming! You look like you're eighteen, but you act like you are eight. It's time you toughen up, son.' He's a total dickhead."

We all fell silent again. I thought about how hard the years ahead would be for Brandon. My parents had become the heralds of a different kind of message, the opposite of the message Brandon heard from his Dad over and over again. Who would be his new cheer section? Who would listen to him and offer him a different perspective from his father's insistent criticism?

Mom's thoughts were moving in the same vein. "We'll have to keep up our phone calls. We want to hear everything that's going on in your life once you get there. You're our second son, and that won't change. We can love you and cheer you on across state lines, you know? We'll make it work, sweetie. Somehow, we'll make it work."

Later that evening, we pulled out our well-worn VHS copy of *The Princess Bride*. Mom and Dad joined us. In between bites of ice cream and cookies, Brandon and I quoted our way through the whole film. For a few moments here and there I actually forgot about the bad news. As soon as the final credits appeared and *Storybook Love* began playing, however, the grim weight of reality descended like a crushing blow. I staggered beneath its assault.

Brandon and I crawled into bed a little after 10:00. We were both drained from a grueling week of school, and Brandon's tragic news left us even more deflated. We turned on our sides, inches apart, legs entwined.

He said, "I wonder how we get through the next two months? I can't imagine even trying to focus on school. I mean, the thought of going to school on Monday depresses me beyond belief. I just want to spend every second with you and your parents."

"I know. I've got three big exams next week. I feel ready for them, but my heart's not in it. My heart is here with you." I reached over and patted the left side of his chest. "Right here."

"Mine, too, but I guess we should have known it was all too good to be true. It was a one in a million chance you walked into the church kitchen that morning. And another one in a million chance we became friends and somehow found a way to show our love to each other. I suppose we used up all our good luck in the last three or so years. It was too good to keep on being so good."

"We gotta think about it in terms of the big picture. Like Dad said, it feels like the end of everything, like it'll be shitty forever, but it's really not. It's the end of this chapter, but we can write new chapters. We can make it work. It's just a detour."

He chuckled. "My wise friend, Alex! You always know just

what to say." He slipped his hand down to my crotch and patted it. "You're right. It's just a little break in the story. There are more chapters ahead."

He snickered as he slipped his hand inside my shorts. "But, man, am I going to miss holding onto you like this. Your stick-arms, not so much; but this, yes! Nothing in Tennessee can be as good as this."

. . .

ii.

The rest of October and all of November flew by in a blur. For all the criticism I heaped on Mr. Marshall, he was incredibly generous in those final fleeting weeks. Brandon and I spent every weekend together, alternating between his house and our apartment. In addition, I spent the first four nights of Thanksgiving Break at Brandon's, and he stayed with us until the next Saturday. He even came to our family's Thanksgiving celebration at Dad's parents' house so he could say goodbye to my grandparents and Aunt Karen. It was a teary celebration that day. My whole family loved Brandon, and they loved our friendship. They all felt with us for our loss, and everyone threatened him with great harm if he never came back to visit.

Right after Joel came home for the holidays, the three of us went to Ninfa's for enchiladas on the Friday evening before the last week of school prior to Christmas break. Then we headed to the Galleria for ice skating and a movie. The evening was bittersweet and nostalgic for all three of us. Joel had been a constant figure throughout my friendship with Brandon. I often wondered if Brandon and I would have developed the friendship we did without Joel's presence. He seemed to draw something out of us that helped us find the courage and clarity we needed as we forged our friendship in those first few tentative months.

Back when we went to Hawaii, I told Brandon that I had told Joel about us. He was amazed when I reassured him over and over again that Joel didn't care – not only that he didn't care, but he actually rooted for us all along and wanted nothing more than to see us happy together. Joel eventually gave me permission to tell Brandon about his own journey toward self-understanding. Of course, Joel was all but gone from our lives by then, but he was a kind of anchoring presence – unseen for many months at a time but never far from our thoughts.

We laughed ourselves silly at Ninfa's and the ice rink. Brandon was in fine form all evening. He entertained the entire rink, alternating between break-neck speed, daring maneuvers, and purposeful clumsiness, usually taking me down with him each time he hit the ice. He drew several rounds of applause from the amused onlookers who ringed the rink. I often worried he might turn morose and withdrawn as moving day approached, but he found some inner reservoir of resilience I never knew he possessed. I took it as a hopeful sign. He had a long, lonely road ahead of him. He needed to draw on a well of interior strength and confidence if he had any chance of surviving, let alone thriving, in Nashville.

We got to Joel's house a little after 11:00 and crashed in the Thompsons' living room, settling down on a makeshift pallet of unzipped sleeping bags and blankets strewn across the floor. The two of them wore each other out in a friendly wrestling match as I looked on with delight. Brandon dragged me in near the end. Joel and I quickly turned the tables on him. Joel held him tightly to the floor, and I tickled Brandon's torso until he begged for mercy.

Joel turned off all the lights except his family's Christmas tree. It was sweetly fitting that the once-a-year ambiance only a Christmas tree provides shed a soft glow over our last night together as a threesome.

Brandon's voice held a playful tone as he said, "So, Joel... Alex tells me you have a boyfriend at UT. Why've you been holding out on telling me about him? Come on, spill the beans! We want details – every juicy detail!"

"I dated two different girls my freshman year. They were both really nice, but it just didn't feel right. I mean, we kissed and played around a bit. It was fun, but I never wanted anything more. It didn't seem right to let either of them think we had something more.

"Then I met Justin at the gym at the beginning of this year when I started going off campus for my workouts. I didn't know he was gay at first. I noticed him the first time I went there. He's impossible not to notice. He's so handsome. Then I started seeing him there every time, and we chatted off and on. Then he asked me out! It all happened so fast. He finished his bachelor's degree two years ago, and now he's working on a doctorate in US history. He wants to teach college some- where when he's done. It's so different from being with either of those girls from last year. Maybe I know now. I mean, maybe I know what I'm really looking for – whether it's Justin or another guy somewhere down the road.

"I was confused for so many years because I can be attracted to both guys and girls, but somehow I know deep down I really wanna be with another guy. It just seems clear now. I talked about this with a counselor at UT, and she said some people are somewhere between gay and straight. Like, not everybody fits into either category. I guess that's me on some level." He chuckled, but I also sensed a weightier tone in his voice.

Brandon chimed in, "God, I want to meet him. Do you have any pictures of him?"

"Only a few, and I don't have them with me. They're back in my dorm room. He's about my height but about twenty pounds lighter. He just works out to stay fit, not get big." He paused and looked down for a second. "And he's got an afro. I mean, he's black. I mean, I know you don't care, but I think you might be surprised if you saw us together and didn't know that beforehand."

He paused again and sighed, "So, yeah, not only am I gay or whatever, but I've fallen for an African-American guy who's a Marxist! I don't imagine my parents will even know what to think. They'll literally be speechless."

I said, "You know we don't care about that. I mean, Kevin, my best friend at school, is black. And Abdul's a Muslim. Brandon and I are both gay. Most of the boring people we know are straight, white, Christian men. Why fit into that group? You know we'll never get all worked up about the differences between people. I say love who you want to love!"

Brandon chuckled and said, "See, this is what I'm worried about. Alex is gonna go chasing after other guys when I'm gone. He's all about free love! I'm already bracing myself for that 'Dear John' letter I'll get in about two months."

"You dork-butt! It's not like there's a line of gay guys waiting outside my apartment just waiting for you to move. Chill out!"

Brandon shot back. "Listen, Humperdink! I've got three words for you: drop your sword!"

Joel cut into our bickering. "Hey, I thought we were talking about me! Anyway, Justin's coming here right after Christmas to spend a few days. So at least one of you will get to meet him and tell me what you think."

I grinned at Brandon. "See, you warthog faced buffoon. That's what you get for moving away. I'll get to meet hot Justin while you're hanging out with your Dayton cousins. I'll get Joel to arrange a sleepover for us. We'll think of you for, um... like a few seconds."

"Smartass! I'm gonna whip your skinny butt in about five seconds."

"Right! I'd like to see you get past Joel! He'll snap you in half before you even get close to me."

As if on cue, Joel rolled over on Brandon, pinning him to the floor.

Brandon glared at me. "Well, later then. When you least expect it next weekend, my little stick-arm friend. I'll come down on you like a ton of bricks."

Joel laughed, rolled off Brandon, and turned to me. "Now, that's the only thing about Justin. I really like him in a lot of ways, but we don't have the kind of bond you two have. He's quiet and shy in many ways. I like that about him, but I also wish he was a little more fun at times. He never teases me. When I tease him, I get the sense he takes it personally. You two have way too much fun together. I could listen to you bicker all night."

Brandon said, "We can arrange that for you! It'll be a sacrifice, but we can make it for you!"

"Actually, it will get very boring for you. Brandon uses the same comebacks he did back when we were in seventh grade! It's like an old tape. Just the same lines over and over. You've heard it all before!"

Brandon propped himself up on his elbow and playfully glared at me across Joel's chest. "Oh, yeah, sorry-ass loser-man? Oh yeah? Well, go ahead! Since you know me so well, tell me all about my limited number of comebacks."

"Gladly!" I winked at Joel and raised my index finger in the air. "Brandon's first go-to insult: 'smartass.' This usually follows a pithy, funny, often ironic, and completely brilliant comment I've made which causes Brandon to realize how giant my intellect is compared to his puny, chimp-like brain."

There was a delightful twinkle in Brandon's eyes. He and I both knew these kinds of exchanges were among the things we'd miss the most in the months ahead of us.

Joel snickered and said, "Score one point to Alex."

I stuck up my next finger. "Brandon's second go-to insult: 'dumbass.' This usually follows a withering attack I launched against some argument or idea that Brandon has spent days cultivating. When it takes my superior brain about five seconds to see seventeen thousand colossal holes in whatever he just said, he is reduced to one pitiful word: 'dumbass.'"

Joel hooted with glee. "Oh, my God! This is, like, the best take-down I've ever witnessed in person!" He munched from an imaginary bag of popcorn. "I mean, go ahead. Don't mind me. I love this front row seat. I believe we are at 30-love, Alex."

Brandon rolled his eyes. "Oh, yes! Please continue, my most arrogant and obnoxious blonde haired friend." His exasperation was only skin-deep; I knew my good-humored mocking turned him on!

Third finger. "Brandon's third go-to insult: 'my little stick-arm friend.' This is an all-around comeback. It's easy for Brandon to remember because there are only five words. He usually fires this one at me when he himself realizes the futility of his argument before I get the chance to refute it thoroughly. In that sense, it is a sign of some intelligence, but it's really a desperate, last-ditch effort to save some face."

Joel burst out laughing and said, "Alexander Kennedy! You're on fire! Whatever happened to that sweet kid I teased at the first fall retreat? I mean, I thought you were an innocent wall-flower back then. Who knew you were some giant cactus with five-foot thorns?"

Brandon spluttered a second or two before saying, "Exactly, exactly... I mean, well... I know! He had us all fooled for so long. I thought he was the sweetest guy on the planet – no, in the whole fucking universe. And then Alexander 'Call-Me-Scissors-Tongue' Kennedy came along, and the cute, impossibly sweet ol' Alex has never come back! And you have no idea how horny he is when I'm just in my boxers. He's unbelievable."

Fourth finger. "Brandon's fourth, final and ultimately predictable go-to insult..." He actually said it with me! "...'sorry-ass loser-man.' This is Brandon's all-around, all-purpose comeback, though it often follows a comment that someone else made that completely bolsters my thoughts and comments while simultaneously tearing Brandon's ideas into tiny, infinitesimal pieces."

Joel cackled with delight and gave me a round of applause. I stood up quickly and bowed. Brandon lunged at me before I was prepared. He giggled and snickered as he took me down. We fell onto some pillows with a thud. He pressed his chest down against mine and brought his thigh up to my crotch. He kissed me roughly on my lips. I looked over at Joel; his eyes were wide with surprise and perhaps a tinge of jealousy.

Brandon spoke through gritted teeth: "Oh, yeah... oh, yeah! Well, just you remember this, you impossibly gorgeous smartass: I've got something on my body that you're gonna be missing so bad in about ten days." I heard Joel stifle an enormous laugh. "And if you get too big for your britches, you better believe I will keep the object of your desire stored well away from you and your groping little fingers the next time I see you. You'll be paying for this for a long time, sorry-ass loser-man."

Joel couldn't hold it in any longer. He rolled over toward us in a fit of laughter. "You two are impossible!"

I kissed Brandon back and said, "Well, just don't rub yourself raw before I do see you again. I know how you'll be remembering me in the long weeks ahead."

A sly grin cropped up on Brandon's face. "There you go! Straight from the horse's mouth: Alex N. Kennedy really is the horniest guy alive! That whole shy, innocent act was just to reel us in."

Joel winked at me and said, "Well, Brandon, I think you fell for it hook, line, and sinker. You fell for it bad!"

Brandon chuckled and said, "I know! Alex took Jesus literally when he said we should be fishers of men. He set his eyes on me that first Sunday and lured me in like some master angler. Just without the camo hat, buck teeth, and bad Southern accent."

"I worked a long time to get you in the right place! I'm a helluva patient guy."

Brandon leaned in close and kissed my cheek. He whispered softly, "Patient, gorgeous, funny, and my amazing best friend."

Joel snickered. "Seriously, you two have something special. Whatever you do, don't let this thing between you flicker out."

A short silence fell between us. Brandon spoke up first. "Well, Joel, whoever falls in love with you is going to be so lucky. You've got it all: hot body, great looks, kind heart, and sense of humor. You really care about people, especially people who are weak or hurting. You'll make some guy really happy someday. Maybe Justin; maybe somebody else. We're both cheering for you. I mean, if it hadn't been for you, I might have pushed Alex away forever. You were the one who helped me see that I was hurting him by being so sarcastic and critical. You helped me see that I had to change."

I added quickly, "You've been the best kind of friend we could have asked for. Sometimes Brandon and I say it was a million-to-one chance we met, a million-to-one chance we fell in love, a million-to-one chance we found the courage to kiss that first time..."

Brandon cut in. "Um, who found that courage, smartass? Who exactly? We would have been dealing with dentures on our first kiss if I waited around for you. So, *who* found the courage, O Wise One?"

"You did! You know I always give you credit for that first kiss. It may have never happened if you left it up to me. I totally admit that!"

"Damn straight. You owe it all to me!"

I winked at Joel and went on: "Anyway, as I was saying... then it's another one in a million chance that you were at the same church, already friends with Will, and somehow became our friend even with the big difference in our ages. I mean, it's like everything that needed to go right aligned perfectly, and you were right at the heart of it all."

"I'll never forget when I stood over you that morning at the first retreat. I was naked and dripping wet, and you had no idea where to look. I could tell you wanted to stare your eyes out, but you were so shy and unsure."

"You're right about that. I stared at you every chance I got when I thought you wouldn't notice."

Brandon snorted again. "See! You were horny right from the start while pretending to be Mr. I'm-Already-Perfect-So-I-Don't-Need-To-Get-Baptized! I saw through you right from the start!"

Joel said, "You were so cute back then, and now you're just too hot for your own good. I have a feeling you'll be batting away the girls more and more in the years to come." He turned to Brandon. "You better hope he doesn't forget about you. Because he could date whoever he wanted in a heartbeat."

"I know... I know... I'm the lucky one in all this. He could have any guy or girl who wanted him, but nobody on the planet would put up with me but Alex." He sighed. "I'm the luckiest guy alive."

I snickered. "I want that in writing! Add it to the list of Brandon's best lines."

Joel stood up from where he was lying between us. "Far be it from me to keep you two apart tonight." He stepped over me and settled down on my left side. I scooted toward Brandon, nestling up against his shoulder. He sighed contentedly and draped his arm across my chest.

He whispered, "Well, we've got tonight, tomorrow at your apartment, and then next Friday at my house. Then it's all over for who knows how long."

"Tonight's been perfect. The next two will be perfect, too. We'll be heading forward on the fumes of these perfect days for a long time to come. We gotta make every second count."

"Every second, indeed, my little stick-arm friend."

. . .

iii.

Seven days later, the long-dreaded last weekend arrived. Just after Mom dropped me off for our final night together, Brandon and I walked around the ground floor of his house in a daze. It was a warren of boxes headed to Nashville and piles of items destined for Goodwill or the church benevolence closet. The house's state of disarray matched my mood too perfectly. I felt a diffuse yet powerful internal sense of vertigo, as if I might tip over any second and never stand upright again.

We stood for a moment in the foyer, right on the spot where we sat that Sunday night at the youth group devotional back in October 1987. I sat down and motioned for Brandon to join me. He collapsed beside me, leaning up against my shoulder. Our thoughts, as usual, flowed in tandem.

"Do you remember how I just talked and talked that night we sat here for the first time? I think I talked you to death. I couldn't tell if you liked it or if you found me annoying. You were such a mystery to me those first few months. I wanted you to like me so much. Nobody had ever made me feel that way before. I didn't know what to do but talk!" He chuckled. "God, I was annoying, wasn't I?"

"Not really. I was just confused. I couldn't get enough of you, but I also couldn't take you in. Does that make any sense? I wanted you to keep going, but I also wanted you to stop! But I was afraid if you stopped you might never speak to me again, so I just listened and listened." I sighed at the sweet memory. "I especially remember when you showed me the mosquito bites on your arms. I couldn't take my eyes off your arms. I just wanted you to leave your sleeves up and let me keep looking, but I was so afraid you'd notice how much I wanted to keep looking. I can't believe that was three years ago. I look back, and that seems like a different me. A different you. Back when we weren't 'us.'"

He put his arm around my shoulder and drew me closer. His parents and his small army of aunts had gone out to eat. We were totally alone. He kissed me on my right cheek and said, "I wanted you to keep looking! I wanted you to notice me and like me! It's so crazy, isn't it? We both wanted the other one to like us, but we were so afraid of making one wrong move and ruining things forever."

I turned fully to him and kissed him back on his lips. I slipped my hand up his shirt and felt his abs. I couldn't imagine going months and months without being near Brandon, without kissing and touching him! My future stretched out before me in a bleak, unvarying string of boring school days and lonely, quiet weekends. In other words, it was back to life 'BB': Before Brandon.

He grinned and said, "We gotta make this a night to last us for a long time, *mi amigo*. I wish there was some way to bottle it up and take it with me... take you with me."

Later on, after a quick drive to get tacos and queso, we watched *The Princess Bride* one more time. They had already sold Brandon's old TV, and the family TV from the den was all wrapped-up in advance of the movers. All that was left was the small TV/VCR combo in the empty guest bedroom. We took it upstairs with us.

Brandon's room was completely prepared for the movers: the walls were bare; all his sketches were stashed away somewhere; his various posters were rolled up tightly in a cardboard tube; the weights were in boxes; the contents of the closet and dresser were packed away in boxes lining the hallway; even his drawing table had been disassembled and packed away. All that remained were the big pieces of furniture and a couple of suitcases with the clothes Brandon needed for the following four or five days.

A wave of intense nostalgia washed over me. I wish I had

thought to take a few pictures of Brandon's room before he began packing up and taking everything down. Going forward, our safe refuge of so much happiness and intimacy would exist only in my sweetest memories.

We set the TV/VCR combo on a stack of boxes at the foot of his bed. All his sheets were packed away. He had unzipped his sleeping bag and spread it out on his bed. A spare sheet from downstairs and a thin blanket lay folded at the foot of the bed. I brought two of my own pillows from home since he told me all his extra pillows were in some unknown box downstairs.

We nestled as close as we could to one another, heads propped up on pillows against the headboard, hands clasped, his right leg draped over my left leg. By some unspoken agreement, we didn't quote any of our favorite lines. We let our beloved make-believe friends do all the talking for us on our final night. The end credits appeared too quickly, and we sang *Storybook Love* together one last time. It was a night of too many last times.

Thirty minutes later, after a final shower together, we climbed into bed, but our bodies resisted sleep in that darkened, ready-to-move room. I couldn't have cried if I wanted to, but I felt a depth of sadness I didn't think was possible for someone my age. I knew a guy at school who lost his mom to cancer our freshman year. I wagered I felt like he did the day he left school early to see her one last time in hospice. I never knew I could hurt so much.

Brandon said, "You know, I don't feel the despair I did back in October. I didn't tell you this, but Mom made arrangements for me to see Joel's mom three times over the last month or so. She's been so helpful. She lets me talk about all this and say whatever I want. It feels just like it does when I talk with your parents. But in a way, it's even easier with Mrs. Thompson because she's not the one I am going to miss. Does that make sense?"

I nodded.

He went on, "I can't believe we leave here for good on Sunday morning. I wish you could stay tomorrow night, too! But Dad said no. So, it's now. Our last night is now. I never, ever thought we'd say that: that this is our last night together for who knows how long."

"I know. I feel the same way. I feel sad and empty, but I don't feel quite as hopeless as I did back when you first told us. Back then it seemed like life would never be the same again. I guess it won't, in some ways. But in other ways, I know it's gonna go on, and we'll find ways to stay in touch and see each other." I sighed deeply. "I just wish it didn't have to be like this."

He leaned his head up against my shoulder. I turned my head and kissed his brow. He took my hand in his and squeezed it tightly. We didn't say anything else for several minutes. What was left to say we hadn't already said over the previous few weeks? We had been saying goodbye over and over again, remembering happy times spent together, and making plans for some kind of rendezvous again in the near future.

I turned on my side and looked fully into his face. He turned, too. His chest seemed to have exploded since he turned sixteen. I traced my finger over the two mounds of hard flesh as they rose up sharply from his breastbone. He reached across and stroked my arm.

"Hey, hey, Alex! You're finally putting on some arm muscle. It's so noticeable. Your body finally got the signal from all the lifting I taught you to do." He grinned. "Miracles do fucking come true!"

I flexed my bicep for him, and he hooted as loud as he could.

I instinctively put my index finger against his lips, not wanting to disturb Mr. Marshall.

Brandon kissed the tip of my finger and said, "What does

it matter now if I wake Dad up? What's he gonna do? Ground me from you next weekend? Let's just scream the whole house down! It'll serve him right for separating us like this!"

I snickered and nodded.

He squeezed my bicep again and said, "Keep using those weights your dad bought us. I've already given him the list of what he needs to buy you next. So, I expect to see results by Spring Break or summer." He glared at me. "No excuses, you sorry-ass loser-man. You'll have tons of time on your hands; so hit the weights, buddy. Hit 'em and hit 'em hard!" He barked and growled like a dog.

"For you, Brandon, I'd hit 'em all day, every day."

"That's what I like to hear. And no straying eyes, my friend."

"Well, that's one more upside to being gay. Other than Joel, you're the only gay friend I know. It's not like I could find a ton of replacements for you, even if I wanted to."

"Yeah, you better not."

"And you better not. Those little boys at your new school in Tennessee are gonna take one look at you and decide they'd like to be gay! If anyone could turn a straight boy gay, it's you. Well, you and Joel." I sighed. "God, I'm gonna miss you so much."

"And I'm gonna miss your impossibly handsome face! I don't say it enough, but you get more beautiful every week, I think. All those poor girls at your school must be so confused! They must wonder why this teen model, I mean the hottest model ever, won't give 'em a second look."

"Yeah, Kevin says that all the time. He says a dozen or more girls have asked him to ask me to go out with them this year, and he's gotta deliver the sad news over and over again."

"Do you think he knows about us? I mean, I think of all your friends at school, you might tell him."

"I've never told him. I don't think he knows. He's never said anything, but he wouldn't care if he did know. He's not like most guys."

"Maybe he's gay."

"No, I don't think so. I mean, all he talks about are the girls. Girls, girls, girls, all the time."

"Well, he can have them. I just want you!"

"Ditto! Ditto all the way to Tennessee and back."

. . .

We woke early the next morning to Mrs. Marshall's insistent knocking on the bedroom door. Dad was coming at 7:00 to get me out of the way so the Marshalls could get on with their final day of packing. Mrs. Marshall, her sisters, and Brandon were leaving early on Sunday morning. Mr. Marshall was staying behind to supervise the movers on Monday. Then he would leave Houston on his own early Tuesday morning.

Brandon and I sat up quickly. It had turned cold in the room overnight. We both threw on the warmest clothes we had to hand. We went downstairs for a quick bite of cold cereal in disposal bowls. We climbed the stairs wearily a little after 6:30 to spend a final few minutes together before Dad arrived.

"This is it. Our last time in your room. I remember the first time I walked in here. I thought it was the coolest room I had ever seen. I just wanted to move in and live here with you forever."

"Trust me. I had the same idea. I wanted you to stay forever. Now it's all coming to an end."

"Well, this part of our time together is coming to an end. There's more to come."

"Yeah, the best is yet to come."

He kissed me and went to his closet. He came out holding two presents. "These are for you, Alex. It's like Christmas and farewell rolled into one. Or two, I guess. Two presents to say more than I could ever say in words."

He handed them to me. We down sat on the floor near his

bed, and I opened the first box. It was one of Brandon's sketchbooks, the one I had discovered that day he was at the dentist two summers before. I couldn't believe my eyes.

He looked a little hesitant. "I don't know if it's a dumb present. I mean, I am giving you a bunch of pictures of yourself! As if you need to know what you look like. But I thought maybe this was a way I could show you what I see in you. Like, this is the you I see through my eyes. It seems a good way to say goodbye."

I teared up as I flipped through the pages. I saw the familiar sketches from two summers ago, plus a whole host of new ones. He was right: the drawings were a way for me to see how he saw me. I thought back to all those uncertain, hesitant months before our first kiss and smiled to myself. I'd seen the proof of what Brandon really felt about me when I first saw the sketchbook, but I allowed fear and doubt to get the better of me time and time again all the way up to our first kiss!

"I love it! It's the most meaningful thing anyone has ever given me. I'll see you seeing me every time I look through this. It'll be like you're right next to me looking at me." I chuckled as I flipped some more pages. "Wow! You certainly caught my hotness in every drawing. I love it!"

He tickled my torso. "I should have thought about that. Now your way-too-big head is gonna get even bigger."

I opened the next box. It was a new copy of his favorite weightlifting book. He grinned at me. "I expect to see this looking well-thumbed the first time I come back. If it's dusty and sitting on a shelf in your room, there will be hell to pay." He leered at me and punched one fist into the other palm.

"Got it! I will definitely use it. Now that you and Joel are both gone, I've got to rely on all the extra help I can. I'll put it to good use." I flipped through a few pages to one of our favorite photos, a man with some of the best-looking abs on the planet. I whistled. "If nothing else, I can look here when I miss you." I gave him a sly look and leaned in close to bump his shoulder with mine.

I pulled two presents out of my large overnight bag. "Now it's your turn!"

He opened the first one. It was labeled: "To: Brandon, From: Your second and forever family." He traced his finger over the label and looked up at me. "This is from your parents?" I nodded. He opened it up and took out the small scrapbook inside.

Mom had spent the previous few weeks sorting through old negatives and getting reprints of some her favorite pictures of Brandon and me. She arranged them artfully on each page, with small comments in her neat handwriting noting the date, place, and something funny about each photo. There were pictures of us lifting weights in the park after a Saturday run with Dad; pictures from some of our dinners together at Antonio's; pictures from Hawaii; pictures from camp she must have tracked down from someone at church; pictures of me and Brandon, and sometimes all four of us, all around Houston – at the Zoo and Japanese Gardens, in front of the Alley Theater and Jones Hall, hiking along trails in Memorial Park, falling over each other while skating at the Galleria, canoeing on Buffalo Bayou, at the entrance to Astro World, and on and on.

It was a pictorial timeline of our amazing friendship – condensed, preserved, and ready to be remembered at the mere turn of a page. The final snapshot on the last page was the best: the two of us together on the balcony at our apartment on my previous birthday, lips kissing lips, my arms slipped around his waist, his strong arms resting on my shoulders.

He looked up with tears in his eyes. "This really is THE best present ever. I only have a few photos of us; just the ones Mom took from time to time. I never thought to ask your mom for any of these. I should have! I just didn't think." He looked back down at the final picture. "And this one! Oh, my God, Alex. I didn't know she took that photo. I must have been thinking about something else at that moment." He snickered. "But I'm so glad she did. I swear, I think I'll look at this every day."

"I'm glad you like it. She did a scrapbook just like it for me! We've got identical scrapbooks. So, when you flip through it some day in Nashville, you'll know I might be looking at the same page. But you'll have to be careful with that last one. Do you notice she didn't glue it down? It's just got tape on the back. So, you can take it out if you need to. Just don't lose it, man!"

"God, no, never! Never ever."

I handed him a second box. "Here's the next present! It's from me. Go on! Time is running out."

He unwrapped the second box and gasped as he looked inside. It was a first edition copy of *The Princess Bride* by William Goldman. He held it up tenderly and leafed through a few pages.

"It's a first edition copy from 1973. It's quite rare, and it's pretty valuable now that the movie is so popular. Dad got it from an auction house in New York. It just came in the mail about a week ago! Dad said don't ever put it in a garage sale or loan it to a friend or set a Coke on it. Treat it like a big pile of money!"

"Of course! I'll treasure it. It's my second most-prized possession after this scrapbook. Nobody touches this or I mess with their face." He held it close to his chest. "I'll keep it safe forever." Tears filled his eyes again. "Wow. This makes my book for you look so lame. That was only, like, $20 at the Book Stop. This must have been a lot more. Did you buy it yourself?"

"Yes and no. I saved up as much of my allowance as I could since November and gave that to Dad. And now I basically owe them two years of allowance to pay off the balance." I snickered. "I've gone in debt for the first time in life just for you."

He leaned in and kissed me. "Alex, you're a star. The best friend I could ever have."

We heard the doorbell ring.

"Oh, God. That's my dad. Help me get all this in my bag. Run and check to see if I left anything in the bathroom." Brandon ran down the hall and brought back my jeans from the previous night. I started to shove them in my bag. He grabbed them back from me.

"Wait! Leave those with me."

"What? Why?"

"Leave them with me. I'll 'find' them later and insist we bring them to you Sunday morning on our way outta town. We'll get one last, last goodbye tomorrow."

"You're a genius! Yes... here... take them! I'll just zip up my bag now and not look for anything else. Maybe you'll find more of my things! Just tell your parents I was distracted and distraught!"

I slung the bag over my shoulder and we headed to the door. Just as Brandon reached for the handle, I put out my hand.

"One last kiss. This is the last one for a long time."

He drew in close. We heard his mom shout up from the foyer. We ignored her and kissed again, trying to somehow preserve our final few seconds so they would last us through the long drought ahead. Mrs. Marshall shouted again. Brandon pulled away, opened the door, and hollered back, "We're on the way." He looked at me. "One more, Alex! Please!" We leaned in close again.

All four of our parents were waiting for us in the foyer. I didn't expect Mom to come, but I was glad she did. She and Dad had already said their final goodbyes the previous weekend when Brandon stayed over the night after our sleepover at Joel's. I guess she wanted one more chance to say goodbye, too. There were hugs all around, long sighs, and soft sobs as the six of us said goodbye and exchanged final endearments.

My parents stood with Brandon in a mutual embrace for a long time as the Marshalls and I looked on. Soft whispers passed between the three of them. Dad looped his arm through Brandon's, and they walked out the front door into a fine, cold mist. Mom turned to shake hands with Mr. Marshall, and they followed Dad and Brandon onto the front sidewalk. I started to follow when Mrs. Marshall stopped me with a hand on my shoulder.

She pulled me in tightly. Her pretty face was streaked with tears and her voice trembled in my ear as she said, "I never wanted us to leave so soon, Alex. I'm so sorry for you and Brandon. I promise you can come see him any time you want, and I promise he can come back here to see you next summer and maybe even the week after Christmas." She held me a little bit away from her and looked directly in my eyes.

She said even more softly, "I gave up a lot of ground when I agreed to this move, but I got a lot of concessions for you two. You won't have any trouble with his dad from now on. I'm the one who gets to say when you come to see us and when Brandon can come see you." She winked through her tears. "I promise."

I nodded and smiled. "Thank you. I'm gonna miss him so much."

She pulled me closely to her again. "I know you will. I just hope he can make it without you. We all love you so much, and I love you especially for being my baby's best friend. I couldn't have ever dreamed up such a friend for him." We walked to the door arm-in-arm and stepped out into the morning's chilly embrace.

Dad and Mom climbed in the front seats. The Marshalls stood on the porch, arm-in-arm, slightly shivering in the colder-than-usual December morning.

Brandon walked beside me to the car, his arm around my shoulder. He took the bag from my hand and tossed it in the back seat behind Dad. We walked to the opposite side and stood by the rear door. I wrapped my arms around him tightly, and he rested his chin on the crown of my head. I breathed in his familiar scent and hoped the sensation of holding him so close would linger for months. There were a thousand things I could have said, but all those words seemed like sawdust on my tongue. None of them felt substantial or real.

"I never imagined I'd have a friend like you, Brandon. I'm the luckiest damn guy on the planet."

"That you are, my little stick-arm friend. That you are." He chuckled and lowered his voice. "I love you, Alex. More than I can say. I love you, and I'm gonna miss you like hell."

I ducked in the car before I started crying any more. Brandon tussled the top of my head. He leaned in and said to all three of us, "I miss you already. I love you, and I'll see you sooner than you might imagine." He winked at me through teary eyes. I tried to wink back, but my eyes were too full to obey my will.

I nodded, and he shut the door. He placed his hand on the window as Dad started the car. I mouthed the words 'I love you' to him. He beamed at me, gave me a thumbs-up, and placed his hand on his heart.

We backed down the driveway, turned out into the foggy street, and headed west to the early morning bustle and glaring lights on Kirby Drive.

. . .

Brandon's ruse worked. He and his mom dropped by a little after 6:00 on Sunday morning to deliver my jeans and my pillows. It was a quick stop, and we only got a brief hug and a final last goodbye. But it was worth it.

Dad and Mom looked at me slyly as the small procession of cars disappeared down Fannin Street. Mom said, "How about back to bed, a late breakfast, and a day doing nothing?"

I nodded and asked, "What about church?"

Dad grinned. "I think we've earned plenty of stars in our crowns... maybe we'll take a little break."

"Sounds great, Dad. Sounds perfect!"

CHAPTER 16

SPRING & SUMMER 1991

Brandon and I spoke on the phone every Thursday. He seemed to settle into his new life in Nashville quicker than I imagined he might. His parents found a house they liked just three days after Christmas, and they moved in around the middle of January. Brandon was already plowing ahead at his new school by then. He told me one Thursday in late January that it was a breeze compared to his old school in Houston.

"It's fucking crazy! I'm getting As in all my classes! I have about half the amount of homework here. It's, like, the easiest school in the world. Mom said they just have different standards here in Tennessee. All I know is, I actually feel like one of the smart kids at school for once in my life! Someone actually asked for my help in Algebra II the other day! Me! They asked *me* for help! Tell your mom to pass that message to Jason. He'll flip out!"

"Who asked you for help? A friend?"

"Just some guy. Not really a friend. Why? Are you jealous?" He snickered.

"No, of course not! I want you to make friends out there."

"Well, his name's Billy Bob or Tom Bob or Wayne Bob. I forget. About half the guys out here go by two names, and the second name is always Bob." He snickered again. "And then there's the girls. They go by three names. Anna Michelle Bob. Susie May Bob. Christy Rachel Bob. Sarah Coon-dog Bob."

We both laughed so hard we couldn't speak for a good two minutes.

Our Spring Breaks didn't fall on the same weeks, much to our disappointment. The long drought apart stretched on through April and May. As soon as school ended for us both, my parents let me fly out to Nashville for the three weeks. Brandon and I had an amazing time together. In some ways, nothing had changed between us. It felt just like the good ol' days in Houston, only in different surroundings. Maybe the only substantive change I noticed was a new level-headedness and maturity in Brandon. In some way I couldn't have predicted, the upheaval of his family's move and the new start in Nashville helped Brandon grow up a little more.

I remarked on this to my parents one night at dinner soon after I got back to Houston in late June.

Mom replied, "Well, I didn't say so at the time, but I had a sense that Brandon might do some growing up as a result of the move. I thought it would require him to be a little more responsible and do some maturing without you around all the time. Does that make any sense? You two are so close and so sweet together, but you were pretty mature to start with. Even in seventh grade, you were a wise little sage in a boy's body. But Brandon was all over the place. He kind of got stuck there while you kept maturing because he could rely on you to be the level-headed, emotionally stable one. He was growing muscles everywhere all those years, but he remained a little boy on the inside in some ways."

I nodded. "Yeah, I see what you mean. I was kind of worried it might be different when we saw each other, even though he's been the same ol' Brandon on the phone for five months! I was worried for nothing. It's like all the best parts of him got better, and the parts of him that needed to mature a bit got the chance. He's been seeing a counselor since March. He told me just after I got there. He sees her every two weeks. He told her he's gay. She supports him completely. So, he doesn't have to keep that a total secret from everyone there. I think that's helped him, too... to know there's at least one person out there who understands and supports him being gay."

"That's lovely, sweetie; really lovely." She leaned in and kissed my cheek.

. . .

ii.

Brandon flew to Houston a week later on July 3. We stayed up late talking and playing around, as if we had been apart for ten months, not just ten days. My parents let us sleep late the next morning, and we stumbled out of my bedroom around noon.

Mom and Dad made small talk while we all ate lunch together. I could tell they had something on their minds. Their faces were strained, and Mom's eyes were moist and red. We moved to the living room after we cleared the table. Mom and Dad sat on the floor with their backs against one of the couches, and Mom motioned for Brandon and me to sit right in front of them. Mom reached over and caressed my cheek. My stomach dropped. I had no idea what they were about to say, but every cell in my body was in fight-or-fight mode. The whole catalog of fears that rested somewhat fitfully in the deep recesses of my heart played out like a movie in my mind: Did something happen to Aunt Karen? Or one of my grandparents? Did one of my parents have cancer? Did Brandon's parents somehow discover his secret, our secret? Were *we* going to move? Did they think Brandon and I needed to end our friendship? A vivid image of each possibility projected itself in garish colors on a screen somewhere behind my eyes.

Dad started the conversation. "Boys, something horrible happened last night. It was all over the news this morning and in the paper. We want you to hear it from us first."

Brandon tensed up and leaned into me.

"A young man – a young gay man – named Paul Broussard was murdered outside a night club in Montrose last night. A group of thugs attacked him, beat him, and stabbed him. Right up the road... just a few blocks away while you two were sleeping safely here."

I teared up and linked my arm through Brandon's. Memories of the attack at Joel's football game came racing back, and the deepest sadness I had ever known descended on me, a fog that felt more like lead than water vapor. It took so little effort to imagine either of us – or both of us – lying on the ground, curled up like a fetus, praying for the end to come quickly as a steady stream of curse words and violent blows rained down like hailstones. It was too much to bear.

"Oh, shit," Brandon muttered. "Those goddamn mother fuckers! Those goddamn cock-sucking mother fuckers!" His voice broke, and through soft sobs he said, "That poor guy..."

Dad said, "He was only 27. He was a graduate of A&M, and a group of assholes beat him to death because he was gay."

Tears cascaded down Mom's cheeks. "It's so important you two realize what can happen to gay men right here in Houston. We take so much for granted because of our neighbors and the fact that a lot of people in this part of town are open-minded, but not everyone is. They think these guys who attacked Paul drove in from The Woodlands. They seem to have come to Montrose specifically to attack gay men. They came just to..." Her voice broke, and she reached out to draw me close.

She whispered in my ear, "It can't happen to you. It can't happen to either of you."

Dad placed his hands on Brandon's knees and said, "We don't want to overly scare either of you. I mean, the odds of something happening to you are so low. There are plenty of gay men at bars and clubs every night of the year in Houston, and there have been for years and years. This attack is random and out of the ordinary, but it hits too close to home for all of us. Too damn close to home."

He lost control of his voice for a second and wiped tears from his eyes. He gathered himself back together and went on. "And it's a reminder to you two. You have to double-down on your commitment to be safe. You have to keep your distance from each other and look like you're simply good friends. I know you get tired of it and just want to be carefree like other couples..." He trailed off.

I finished for him. "But we can't. It's never gonna be easy and carefree for us. We'll never get to be like other couples, and the price is too high if we forget that around the wrong people."

Brandon pulled me in close. He kissed my forehead and said, "I swear to you, Alex, I'll do everything I can to keep you safe. I don't think I could go on if something like that ever happened to you."

I nodded, too overcome by my own sobs to say anything in reply. The four of us sat there for several more minutes, each couple leaning in close, lost in a world of our own thoughts, yet keenly aware of the very worst imaginings playing out in everyone else's minds.

Dad let Brandon and me read *The Chronicle* after we all talked some more, and the four of us watched the evening news together. The news coverage extended into the subsequent days. We followed it closely, horrified as more details came out. The initial police response was underwhelming and demoralizing. Yet we also found a small glimmer of hope as Houston's gay community and its many allies rallied for justice and kept the spotlight on Paul's brutal murder.

As the shock of Paul's death slowly faded, Brandon and I slipped into our old, effortless companionship, and it felt like just another summer in Houston with Brandon by my side from sun-up to sun-down. My parents and I decided to forgo a vacation so Brandon could stay longer. They both took a week off work, and the four of us alternated between lazy days around the apartment and several jam-packed days at some of our favorite spots in Houston.

Brandon and I were always conscious of our proximity to one another and kept our distance whenever we left the apartment. It was a way we could honor that brave young man. If Paul's death made us more conscious of our own safety, perhaps he had not died in vain. It seemed to be one of the few rays of hope I could find in the midst of such evil.

For years to come, Paul's death was a very personal version of the space shuttle *Challenger* disaster for Brandon and me. It became one of my life's major emotional touchstones: just as I would forever remember the shocking moment when the *Challenger* burst into a ball of flames and the two booster rockets carried on without it, the tragic murder of Paul Broussard left a lasting mark on me, a psychic wound that seared my impressionable young heart.

We trudged off to camp in the middle of July. Neither of us really wanted go, but we consoled ourselves that the alternative would have been worse. Brandon was originally scheduled to go to camp with the youth group at his new church at Mr. Marshall's insistence, but Mrs. Marshall intervened on our behalf. Mr. Marshall relented in the end and said he was just happy that Brandon was going to church camp of some kind.

I felt odd going to camp since we left Bissonet after the Marshalls moved, but Michael assured me it was no problem. "You're always welcome to come along for anything! We still miss you. You're the easiest kid in the youth group. Or, I mean, you were until you left us! And it'll be great to have Brandon back at camp. It'll be like old times again. You just have to keep him calm on the football field!"

. . .

iii.

We didn't see one another again until just after Christmas. Brandon flew to Houston on December 26 and stayed with us until New Year's Day morning.

Brandon and I lay on our sides facing one another in my bed just after 1992 rolled into existence. The previous six days had been incredibly wonderful. Brandon was his old self in many ways, but, in other respects, I kept discovering something new about him in every conversation. It was like meeting my best friend for the first time over and over again. I initially found the changes unsettling and jarring. Then I began to see them for what they were: additional confirmation that Brandon was maturing and finding his own authentic way to be himself.

He started a conversation about college without any prompting from me. "So, I've been thinking about college. I definitely want to do an art degree. My art teacher says I could probably get into any art college I wanted to. She said the sky's the limit with my talent. I could go anywhere, even with my mediocre grades – as long as I don't fail any core classes. But that's not a worry anymore. It feels really good to know I can go to college almost anywhere I might want. Dad says college is mandatory, so he's happy with me for once. He used to think I'd never go to college, like, back when I was a freshman. Now he's just relieved. He said he wasn't picky where I went as long as I could get a good scholarship. My guidance counselor at school is helping me with all this. She's amazing. Where are you thinking about going?"

"I'm still aiming for Harvard, Columbia, or Yale. The

whole point of St. Martin's is to get into one of the best colleges. I've got the highest grades in the whole school, and I did really well on the Pre-SAT. My counselor says I should aim high. Harvard is my dream. Boston would be fun, but I really loved New York City when we went the other summer. It would be an amazing place to go to college. So that makes Columbia really appealing."

"Well, I'll get in somewhere close to wherever you go." He snorted. "I mean, you'd be lost without me in the Big Apple or anywhere up there. I'll be there to make sure you don't miss your momma too much... or your little boy bed."

"I haven't had a little boy bed in years. You know it!" I punched him on the shoulder. "Seriously, that would be awesome if we could be in the same city, but I don't want you to make your college decision based on where I go. You should choose what's best for you. Even if we're both in the Northeast, we could probably see each other every few weeks."

"But that's just it, dumbass! I want to go where you go so we can be together every day. You're what's best for me! Imagine sharing a dorm room or an apartment! New York would awesome! If you went to Columbia, I bet I could get into some other college in the area. There are tons in New York City." He paused and considered. "I'll see if my counselor and art teacher can help me start looking at which colleges offer art degrees near Yale and Harvard, too. And let me know if you apply to other places. I can check out options wherever you apply. That would be a start, right? Wouldn't it be amazing to be in New York together? All those gay guys there! And gay bars! We could actually have friends who were like us. We wouldn't have to hide anymore."

"That sounds pretty amazing."

"No more hiding and keeping secrets. I keep thinking I'll tell my mom before I go to college, but I'll ask her to keep it quiet from Dad. If I don't get much of a scholarship, he might have to pay part of my tuition. If he knows I'm gay, it would be all over. I'd be stuck in Nashville until I could pay my own way to college or art school." He snickered. "I have this dream of letting him pay for some of my college, like my living expenses and stuff, and then telling him I'm gay the minute after graduation!"

"You know you can talk to my parents. They can help with some of your college costs if your dad won't."

"No, I couldn't ask them for that kind of help. They've been the best parents in the world to me in so many ways, but I couldn't ask for money!"

"Well, first, who do you think keeps paying for your plane tickets here, you muscley moron? And second, you wouldn't have to ask! I know they want to help. They've already spoken to me about it. If I get a full scholarship somewhere, they can use my college savings fund for you. They've been saving for years but secretly hoping I'll not really need the money for college or grad school. They'll kill me if they have to spend that money on me!"

"God, no, Alex! I mean, no way. That's your money! If you don't need it for college, save it for a car or a trip."

"But I won't need it! We've got enough for those other things even without the college savings. That's the whole point. They'd rather spend it on you than on anything else in the world."

"Really?"

"Really! Don't argue! You may be rising to the top of your class in that hickville high school you go to, but don't forget I have a superior intelligence in every way. Resistance is futile. What's mine is yours. Got it?"

"Oh, I know what you have that I want. That's for sure!" He winked at me and licked his lips.

I drew in closer toward him and stroked his bare abs. My, how I had missed his abs! He grinned and tightened them for me.

"I guess you've missed these, babies, eh?"

"You could say that. You could say that for sure."

"Well, I have missed this face of yours. Honestly, you're more gorgeous than ever. There's not a guy at my school who looks as good as you. A few of them are pretty hot in the body department, but they've only got average faces." He leaned in for a kiss. "There's nobody like you, as far as I am concerned. And your arms! Your arms!" He had been talking about my arms constantly for six days. "It's like they were just waiting for me to leave and BOOM! They started to grow! You've got some damn fine arms now."

I said in a playfully aggravated tone, "Well, as I told you EVERY week on the phone, I've been working out hard. I find I really enjoy it now, especially since you aren't here to tease my poor muscles all the time. I mean, my arms were psychologically scarred from being shamed constantly by you. They just needed some encouragement... and not being constantly overshadowed by your arms."

"Well, I don't care about their hurt feelings. I just wanna see them grow and get hard. Go on! Give me a flex!" I complied. "Wow! That's been worth the wait, my friend." He squeezed my bicep and drew his finger along my finally-blossoming tricep.

We both turned on our backs. He draped his arm across my arm and rested his palm on my stomach. He sighed and said, "So, it's back to reality tomorrow. Back to hickville and everybody's-married-to-their-second-cousin Nashville. God, it's a weird place. I never appreciated Houston so much until I left. Don't even think about finding a good taco in the whole goddamn state. You can get bar-b-que anything – bar-b-que possum, squirrel, and dog, I kid you not – but there's not an edible taco or enchilada within hundreds of miles. And don't get me started on their salsa. It's like ketchup with a few onions thrown in." He shuddered. "I mean, seriously. It's like, here, have some oniony ketchup with your tortilla chips before we serve you the nastiest taco imaginable."

I bent my head down and kissed his dense forearm. Maybe the tacos were horrible, but the Tennessee water, or something out there, was like Miracle-Gro on his body.

He said, "Remember when we kissed each other's penises last summer when you came to Nashville?"

"I remember!"

"Why you been holding out on me this visit? Have you gone off me? Are you ashamed of my dick, Alex? Hmmm? If your arms get their feelings hurt so easily, imagine my poor little John Henry down there. Imagine how he feels knowing you've turned your back on him!"

I turned toward Brandon and placed my right hand over his mouth. He grinned. I rolled on top of him and pressed my groin hard up against his. His heart thudded against my chest. He sat up quickly, tossing me aside. He let me pull down his shorts and underwear, and I let him remove mine.

"Well, if your little John Henry feels bad, I know how to make him feel better!"

Brandon gasped and chuckled. "Like I always said, you are a horny little bastard! You're no saint, no matter what everybody else says!"

CHAPTER 17

Brandon and I kept up our weekly Thursday evening phone calls and started calling each other on Sundays by the time February rolled around. I never got tired of hearing from him. I'd often put him on speakerphone in Dad's office, and he'd entertain all three of us with anecdotes from school, his new church, and life around Nashville. He had a good ear for accents, and he perfected the Nashville twang to our delighted amusement.

Once again, our Spring Breaks fell on different weeks. His was a week after mine, but Dad and Mom let me miss two days of school as a special treat! Without Brandon's knowledge, I flew out to Nashville early on the Friday morning of my Spring Break. Mrs. Marshall picked me up from the airport. We had lunch together and reminisced about some of our former times in Houston. Then we went to pick up Brandon from school. I hid down low in the floorboard behind the front passenger seat with an old blanket draped across me.

Brandon got in the car without noticing me. He was talking fifty-miles-a-minute about how much he needed Spring Break and how he planned to do absolutely nothing for nine days. I reared up stealthily behind his seat and slipped my hands over his eyes, saying, "And you: friendless, brainless, helpless, hopeless! Do you want me to send you back to where you were? Unemployed in *Greenland*!" He flipped out and shrieked so much Mrs. Marshall had to pull over.

He told me later that night, "That was one hell of a surprise! I mean, I've never ever been so surprised in my life. Well, except for that time in Hawaii. THAT was a surprise! I knew from the beginning of our friendship you were a little man of mystery. You've always got something up your sleeve! Feel free to sweep me off my feet any time you want. I mean, I'm just waiting on your big master plan to get me the hell back to Houston. I am so done with goddamn hickville."

I flew back to Houston just after lunch on Tuesday and dragged myself wearily to school on Wednesday, pretending that I was recovering from a 48-hour cold.

. . .

That summer after our junior year went much like the previous summer. I spent most of June with Brandon in Nashville, and Brandon came to Houston in early July. Since we never had a proper vacation the summer before, we made up for it with a ten-day trip to the Florida Keys. Brandon came with us. We didn't give much thought to anything but the blindingly white sand, the impossibly blue water, the warm gentle breezes, and the safe, easy company the four of us lovingly shared.

Once again, Mr. Marshall had insisted that Brandon attend summer church camp in Tennessee. Once again, Mrs. Marshall intervened on our behalf, and I made arrangements for us to go to Camp Brazos Hills with the youth group from the Bissonet Church of Christ.

We spent the week between the Keys and camp doing as little as possible. A couple of times, I caught myself thinking back to the first summer we spent together in 1987. Brandon had every second of every day planned a month or more in advance. There was a kind of frantic intensity to his plans. Perhaps he thought that would be our first and last summer together. Perhaps we both sensed that first summer together was destined to be the last 'best summer' of our young lives, and we endeavored to fill every second of it with endless fun.

Inexplicably, there we were, five summers later, content with long morning runs in the park, cool showers before lunch, lounging about all afternoon – reading our way through the Christie canon, listening to classical music, sketching, and playfully wrestling – all capped off by long conversations, sometimes serious, sometimes funny, over dinner with the two people in the world who loved us more than we loved each other.

And the nights! They were so simple and so sweet. We left aside most of our playful banter and teasing. Just to lay side-by-side, arm against arm, legs impossibly tangled, silent, breathing gently in tandem, without a care or concern: those were the tender moments that prepared us for the fiery ordeal which descended with sudden ferocity only a few days later.

. . .

ii.

We met our new counselor shortly after we arrived at camp. He greeted us at the door to our cabin. His name was Stephen. He had just finished his freshman year at Harding University in Arkansas, and it was his first time being a counselor at Camp Brazos Hills. They normally didn't assign first-time counselors to the older guys, but it seemed nearly all of the counselors were new that summer. Whether by chance or design, poor Stephen got stuck with us veteran campers in cabin nine. Some of the senior guys sensed Stephen's fear and circled around him like sharks, waiting for a chance to assert their bravado in some macho battle of wills against our wet-behind-the-ears counselor.

Over the course of the first two days, Stephen watched Brandon and me like a hawk. I had never seen a counselor pay so much attention to us before. We normally seemed to fly under the radar of the staff's watchful eyes since they were so busy trying to keep the guy-girl couples at reasonable distances. Even though I felt generally safe at camp, the recent anniversary of Paul Broussard's murder had me on edge. I wondered what emotions played across the eyes of his killers as they watched him leave that night club with his friends. Were they anything like the animosity I thought I saw a few times when I caught Stephen staring me down?

Late on Tuesday afternoon, Brandon and I sat together on one of our favorite swings. We had a fine view over the west side of the camp. We could see the rooftops of some of the girls' cabins off to the left, and farther off in the distance the rolling hills of central Texas stretched out for miles under the unrelenting summer sun.

I said in a low voice, "I've been watching Stephen watching us. He doesn't like us. I don't know what we did, but he doesn't like us. I think we've been extraordinarily careful. More than last summer for sure."

"I know. He's tried four times to get me to sit somewhere else at lunch or dinner. He keeps asking me why I don't hang out with those guys from Marble Falls. Apparently, that whole youth group makes up the high school football team. I guess he thinks all the big guys should hang out together." He sighed. "He's a dickhead! What's his problem?"

"I don't know, but we need to watch out. Have you noticed he doesn't really hang out with the other counselors? I mean, he's with them a lot, but he never seems to join in. He kind of hangs back just on the edge."

"Yeah, well, if he says anything to me, I'll knock his goddamn head off. If he lays a finger on you, I'll kick his ass all the way back to Arkansas. I'm a foot taller than him, and your arms are bigger than his! He's just a little asshole. He probably imagines my body and jacks off in the bathroom when nobody's around. He can go fuck himself."

"Okay, okay, okay! Enough cursing!"

He leaned into me slightly. "Sorry! You know I can't stand bullies. Especially bullies like him. There's an anger behind all his talk about God and being a good Christian. He's just a fucking fake." He stopped and put his hand over his mouth. "Sorry!"

I chuckled. "It's okay, but I think I should start a swear jar with you! Every time you swear, you have to pay me a dollar!"

"Hell, no, Alex!" He grinned and pressed his leg up against mine. "Well, if we do that, then I get to start a hard jar."

"A what? What's that?"

He chuckled and said, "Well, we are at church camp. You should be holy and pure this week. So every time you go hard thinking about me, you have to pay me one dollar. I may be a math dunce, but I know who'd be richer at the end of the week." He snorted. "I mean, contrary to what you think, I can control myself. But you?" He snorted even more. "You are outta control when you start thinking about me. Out-ta control, my friend!"

I glanced around. We were totally alone as far as I could see. I turned to him slightly. He rested his arm on my leg, the underside facing up. I used my finger to trace the ropey veins that streaked beneath his flesh from his wrist to the crook of his elbow. When I got to the bottom of his bicep, he flexed. I marveled at the beauty of that rock-hard flesh. God, he was right. It took so little to arouse me!

"So, that's a dollar, kind sir. One dollar to me!" He snickered and leaned into my shoulder even more.

We heard some branches snap off to left and immediately scooted apart. A small gaggle of junior high girls came out from between some trees and low brush. There's no way they could have seen or heard anything between Brandon and me. In fact, they looked more scared of us than the other way around. They all averted their eyes and clomped away, giggling and whispering with heads held close. It was a timely reminder! In one way, we felt lazy and carefree, but the danger was equally palpable. Complacency was both our enemy and our constant companion.

Wednesday was a blazing hot day. All the high school guys planned their usual 'Hotter Than Hell Soccer Game', as it had come to be known in camp lore over the previous few years. Brandon and I never played. Each year, Corey, the camp director, allowed the two of us extra swim time during the soccer game in return for extra kitchen duty, just as we had done with Joel all those years ago. We made our deal with Corey again, happy to have the pool to ourselves for two hours in exchange for helping with cleanup duties after lunch.

We saw Stephen head off for the soccer field. He and some of the other counselors were splitting themselves between the two teams. Everyone looked deadly serious. The game had taken on a life of its own. The losers held grudges all year long, and both sides bargained fiercely for the allegiance of the new guys who might be hidden soccer stars.

Brandon and I breathed a sigh of relief as the gate to the pool enclosure latched behind us. It was the first time all week we had been alone together for more than ten minutes. We draped our towels on the deck chairs at the far end of the pool. Memories of our big fight on that spot were fresher than I had expected. Brandon's thoughts kept pace with mine.

He looked at me sheepishly. "God, I was such an asshole that summer. Why did you ever put up with me back then?"

"Well, I've always had a soft spot for hopeless causes, and you were chief among them!"

He snickered. "Well, I felt same way about your arms. God, what little sticks you had back then. But look at those biceps now! And those fucking triceps of yours!" He reached out and drew me near to him. Our lips brushed against one another's.

I pulled back and said, "Careful. We gotta be careful."

He nodded and sighed. He turned away quickly and took a running jump into the pool. I followed close behind him, jumping on his back once I found my bearings in the water. He spun me around and around. We both cackled with delight. It felt so good to hold his body next to mine, even in a playful, innocuous-looking way. I let my hands drift from his shoulders down to the mid-point of his chest. He brought his arms down over mine, lacing his hands behind my back, pinning me closely to him.

We bobbed in the water like that for several minutes. I kissed his neck, and he bent his head down to kiss the top of my hand where it rested on his chest.

An ebb and flow emerged between us: we'd wrestle playfully yet intently for a few happy moments; then we'd separate to float or swim apart. Together, apart; together, apart; together, apart. Finally, with our hearts and minds in tandem, we gave up and gave into our desire. We held each other tightly, chest against chest, legs intertwined, lips finding lips in a passionate kiss.

My ears registered two seconds too late the familiar sound of the gate's metal latch as it dropped into place after closing on its spring-hinge. I saw one second too late a faint movement out of the corner of my water-blurred left eye. And half a second too late I recognized a frisson of fear pass through my body like a high-voltage shock. Brandon, oblivious to it all, held me even more tightly, lost in the revelry of days' worth of repressed contact and intimacy.

A strident, angry voice shattered the silent, shimmering heat that hovered just above the water's surface. "Get out of the pool, you dirty faggots! Get the hell out of the pool now!"

Stephen stood by the side of the pool, legs and arms streaked with dirt from the soccer field, his face contorted by rage and disgust, arms trembling, fists balled tightly.

Brandon turned in a flash, and realizing who was speaking, roared back. "Get the fuck out of here, you rat-faced bastard! I bet you get off on watching us together! Go the hell away!"

Stephen shouted back, "God, you're in so much fucking trouble! You are totally screwed! You are so done, you dirty, nasty perverts!"

Before I could stop him, Brandon was charging to the side of the pool. He screamed, "I'm gonna kick your scrawny ass so hard it comes out your nose, you dickhead."

I cried out, "No, Brandon, stop! Stop!" He didn't even turn back or slow down. He was inches from a ladder on the side of the pool, ready to pull himself up and out of the water. I knew Brandon could do real harm to Stephen.

Stephen must have sensed it, too. He stepped back and looked a little uncertain as Brandon grasped the ladder's rails. In that brief second, I saw Corey a few feet behind him, standing in the darkened shade beneath the entry to the shower rooms.

Corey stepped forward and shouted, "Stop! Both of you! Stop!"

He grabbed Stephen by the shoulders and turned him around, pulling him away from the pool. He screamed at Stephen, "You've shown me what you wanted to show me! Now get the hell outta here! Go! Go straight back to the field. No stopping. And don't you dare say a word to anyone, or I'll fire you so fast you'll be sleeping on the highway tonight. Go! Now! I'll deal with this."

He gave Stephen a hard shove toward the gate. Stephen stumbled and shouted back at us, "You will rot in hell. Both of you, you dirty faggots!"

Brandon was out of the pool by then, but Corey stood between him and Stephen. He put his hands up against Brandon's chest. "Stop, Brandon! Stop! Don't make this worse. Just stop. Leave it. Leave it." Corey was somewhere in his mid-twenties. Brandon matched him eye-to-eye in height, but Corey was a bit pudgy around the middle. He looked rather weak next to my best friend, with his wide chest, peaked biceps, and white-knuckled fists ready to let loose a dozen fierce blows. Brandon could have knocked him out flat, but he didn't. He simply dropped his fists. He glanced back at me, bewildered, like a wild, wounded animal caught in an unexpected trap.

I cried out, "It's okay, Brandon. It's gonna be okay."

I made a move to leave the pool.

"No, Alex, stay there for a second," Corey said. "Just stay there. Please just stay in the pool." I obeyed his instructions but moved up closer to the shallow end where I could easily stand.

Brandon turned back to face Corey. His shoulders were gently shaking. I knew that posture so well. My strong, beautiful friend was seconds away from full-body sobbing.

Corey put his hand on Brandon's left shoulder. He whispered something I couldn't hear. Brandon looked around dazed. He didn't meet my eyes. He wandered to the back of the enclosure and toweled himself dry. I watched him the whole time. He glanced at me for a brief second. He slipped his shirt on and walked around the far side of the pool.

Corey said a little more loudly, "Go on up to the office. It's cool in there. Pull yourself together. Don't talk to anyone on the way. If anyone asks you, tell them I'm meeting you in less than five minutes. And stop crying!"

Brandon shuffled to the gate. He turned around and met my gaze just as he stepped out of the pool enclosure. He looked like he did all those years ago on New Year's Eve after the Dick Clark incident as his dad browbeat him with Bible verses. I cursed myself because I let my own desire get the better of me. I was the one who should have resisted. I should have been strong enough for both of us. I could have saved us from all the shit that was about the hit the fan if I had been on my guard. I held back my own tears as I thought about Paul Broussard and my one-in-a-billion best friend. I had let them both down, and the shame of it burned like a furnace in my heart.

Corey looked down at me. "Get outta the water, Alex. Dry off and come with me."

As I climbed out of the pool, I said, "Corey, that was all my fault. Brandon just feels sorry for me, and he lets me kiss him from time to time. He just gave in to me to make me feel better. It's not his fault. Please, Corey! You have to believe me! Do what you want to me, but leave Brandon out of it. Please!"

Corey shook his head. "I've watched you two for the last few summers since I first became director. You two have always been way too close. All the counselors noticed, but nobody thought you were *this* close. There's no way it's a one-way street. Now that I look back, I've seen him looking at you so many times. This is about both of you, Alex. There's something really wrong with both of you. You're both dirty and sick."

I stood inches away from Corey, dripping with water, trembling with fear and sadness, my stomach clenched in a tight ball of anxiety and uncertainty. Even in that state of confusion and shock, my only thought was for Brandon. I had to protect him at all costs.

"Listen, Corey. Punish me! Do whatever you want to with me! I can call my parents right now, and they'll be here by tonight to get us. We can go. In fact, I want to go! I don't want to be here, but none of this is about Brandon. He's not dirty." I looked Corey right in the eyes. "And I'm not dirty either. There's nothing wrong with either of us."

Corey shook his head in dismay. "God, you're perverted *and* deluded! You are so messed up. Go get your clothes and follow me."

My parents raised me to be respectful of all authority figures. However, as I made my way through high school, they began to help me develop a more nuanced appreciation of when to submit and when to think for myself. I was beginning to discern more clearly when I had a duty to obey an adult and when I had a duty to be true to my own conscience. I didn't have an ounce of respect for Corey or any of the adult leaders at camp, and I didn't feel any need to jump at his commands.

I walked to the back of the enclosure, dried off, and put my shirt on. I turned back towards Corey, determination and confidence building in me with each step. I looked him in the eyes as I drew near and said, "Go to hell, Corey! Go to hell!"

He reached out to grab me, but I was already moving too fast. I threw open the gate, and sprinted down the dirt trail to the camp office, which was inside the old farm house that had stood on that land since the time it was a working cattle ranch. I ran up the steps of the back porch, threw open the screen door, and called out for Brandon.

"I'm up here, Alex!"

It took my eyes several seconds to adjust to the darkened corridor in front of me. I ran up the long hallway to the front of the old farm house. Brandon was sitting by a window in the former dining room near the battered desk where we all registered when we arrived.

He jumped up and hugged me. "Oh, God, Alex! What are we gonna do? Do you think they can call the cops on us?"

"I don't know, but Corey's gonna be here in seconds." I took Brandon's chin in my hand. "Come on, Brandon! No crying, babe. Okay? And let me do all the talking. Trust me, Brandon! Trust me! Okay?"

He nodded.

I said fiercely, "Tell me, Brandon. Say it. Tell me you trust me."

"I trust you. You know I do."

I heard the rear screen door fly open. Corey shouted down the hallway. "Where the hell are you, Alex?"

I winked at Brandon and whispered. "This will all be over

by tonight. Trust me."

Corey stumbled into the room and shouted, "Get away from one another! Alex, over here! Now!"

I let go of Brandon but didn't leave his side. "I want to call my parents. You have no right to keep me from calling them. I'd call them myself, but I don't know the long-distance code from this office. Let me speak to them. They know all about us and don't give a shit."

Corey glared at me and said, "Just shut up, Alex. And enough with the cuss words. You are not in charge here. I am. You've broken every camp rule in the last ten minutes, and you've broken every law God has, too. You're not in any place to tell me what you want or what you're gonna do."

I stood resolutely by Brandon's side. "What are you gonna do, Corey? There's nothing you can do to us. Just call my parents, and we'll leave as soon as they come. We'll be gone forever. We don't even need to pack. You can throw all our stuff away or even burn it. I don't give a shit. Just let me call my parents."

"You better drop that language right now! I'm sick of your foul mouth and your dirty mind."

Brandon tensed up beside me. I took his hand in mine and squeezed it firmly.

Corey shouted at me, "Let go of his hand you dirty pervert! Let go!"

I refused to let go. Corey glared at me. He took a step towards me, and Brandon let go of my hand. He stepped up to Corey and stared him down. Neither of them spoke, but Corey finally took a small step back.

"Alright. Let's call your parents, but I'm calling Brandon's first. Let's see what they think of their faggot sons."

Corey turned around and looked through a filing cabinet, searching for our parents' numbers. I looked up at Brandon and winked. He leaned down and silently kissed me.

Corey turned back around and sat down at the desk. He

picked up the phone. His first call took me by surprise.

"Hey, Jack. Come over here to the office, will ya? And bring as many of the crew as you can. I need your help with some faggot campers."

Jack was the camp caretaker. He lived in a small double-wide trailer about two-hundred yards from the office. Jack's two sons, Eddie and Shawn, were both home from Abilene Christian University for the summer. In addition to Jack, there were two men from the local town who worked as handymen and groundskeepers during the summer. I assumed this was the crew Corey was summoning

Corey stood up and left the room. He came back in with a baseball bat. He stood across the room from us. "Brandon, if you threaten anyone or say a word, I swear to God, I will come at you with this bat. And when I finish with you, I'll start on Alex. You may be big and fast, but I guarantee you: you can't get past this bat or the ten fists coming into this room. Now, both of you, sit the hell down on that couch, and don't say a word."

The front door opened. Sure enough: Jack, his sons, and the two handymen came in. Not a one of them was under six-feet tall. Brandon might be able to inflict some harm on one or two of them, especially the older handymen, but we were outnumbered and overpowered.

Corey spoke up. "Jack, you and your boys, take Brandon back with you to your house and lock him in a bedroom. If he gives you the slightest trouble, give it right back. You'll have no trouble from me if you do, and nobody will believe his word over yours."

They moved toward us where we sat on a small, tattered couch. I said to Brandon, "Go on, go with them. I'll be okay. Mom and Dad will be here tonight."

Corey sighed and said, "Get him outta here! Now!"

Eddie and Shawn grabbed Brandon's arms and pulled him with them. He didn't resist. Corey handed his bat to Jack. "Use this if you need to. He talks to no one and says nothing. Got it?"

"Yes, sir. Got it. I'll put him in the small back bedroom."

They took Brandon from the room. He tried to turn around as he left, but Jack shoved the bat up against his spine and muttered, "Keep walking. Keep walking, you faggot."

Corey nodded in my direction. "Take him to the back room on the left. Lock the door and bring me the key."

The two handymen moved toward me.

"You can't do this to us, Corey. We're not your prisoners. Just call my parents and they'll come get us. Just leave us alone."

"Shut up, Alex. I'm so tired of your yapping. You're the smuggest kid I've ever met."

Eric and Adam grabbed me roughly and pulled me off the couch. The taller one, Eric, wrenched my left arm behind my back. They dragged me between them down the hallway. Eric gave me a harsh shove through the door. I stumbled and shouted back to him, "God, you're gonna hurt me. Stop it, assholes!"

He slammed the door without a word. The lock clicked. I slumped down on the floor and wondered how long it would take my parents to get to camp. Maybe six or seven hours from the time Corey called them until they pulled up the dirt lane leading to the camp parking lot? Hopefully not more than that.

There was no clock in the small storage room, but I soon heard the bell ring for the end of free time at 4:30. Thirty minutes later, the supper bell rang. I didn't feel hungry, and I had no regrets about missing camp dinner. The thought of hot dogs and fish fingers made my already tight stomach turn over again and again.

Corey came in a few minutes later carrying a tray from the dining hall.

"I brought your dinner. Do you need to go to the bathroom?"

"No. And I'm not hungry."

"Suit yourself. I'll just leave it here in case you change your mind."

"I'm fine. Leave me alone."

"I've called your parents. They're on the way to get you. They'll be here by 10:00 or so depending on the traffic getting out of Houston. I'll come get you around 7:00 when the evening activities begin, and we'll go get your belongings."

I didn't reply. He set the tray on the floor, shut the door and locked it. I heard his steps retreat down the hallway.

The light in the room slowly began to fade as the sun dipped below the trees on the west side of the old farm house. My thoughts were all over the place. I was worried about Brandon. I was so mad at myself for losing control and giving into my desire. I should have been stronger. Brandon always thought it was his duty to keep me safe from assholes, but I had been convinced for years that it was my duty to protect us both from the consequences of our own desire. I had failed Brandon so horribly. I knew what was at stake for him, and I feared what was going to happen when he had to face his father. Brandon and I thought the world came crashing down around us when he moved to Nashville, but I had a feeling that would seem like child's play compared to Mr. Marshall's immanent fury.

I thought about Grandma Allen's steadfast belief in the positive power of luck. It seemed a bit naïve and ill-advised as I considered my immediate circumstances. For the first time since I met Brandon, I truly believed that our luck had turned against us. We always talked about the long odds we overcame to be friends and how fortune seemed to greet us at every turn. The odds were tired of their losing streak. I feared the deep well of cosmic goodwill Brandon and I tapped into had finally run dry.

I figured it was nearing 7:00 when the door opened again. Corey stood in the doorway. He had another baseball bat in his hand. He looked down at the tray of food. "Sure you don't want this? Cold food is better than no food." He sighed. "God, what a mess this is, Alex. Come with me. Let's go get your stuff."

We headed out the back door and across the large field at the center of camp. I heard raucous noise coming from one of the large covered pavilions where the campers gathered for evening activities. It seemed hard to believe it had only been twenty-four hours since Brandon and I happily joined in with the three-legged races and dizzy-bat relays.

Corey remained silent the whole way, which was fine by me. I wasn't in the mood for any sanctimonious bullshit. I thought the bat was a bit over the top. What did he expect me to do? Jump him?

He stood outside the cabin as I went inside to gather my belongings. I noticed at once that Brandon's belongings were already gone. A deep sadness washed over me as I thought of him collecting his belongings under the hateful, accusing eyes of Jack and his sons. I thought, too, of the other guys in our cabin. They'd return around 10:00 after the campfire and see two bare bunks and perhaps not have any clue what had happened.

Or would they? Would rumors about me and Brandon race like wildfire around this narrow-minded, insular group of teenage fundamentalists? Had some of the campers noticed we had been missing for hours? What had the other counselors told them? What kind of mean-spirited gossip about us might Stephen circulate? Part of me – most of me – didn't give a shit, but a more primal and vulnerable part of me felt exposed and naked. It angered me to think that the special love Brandon and I shared might be the subject of teenage snickers and lewd innuendoes.

Corey and I returned to the farm house in the descending dusk. He held open the door to the small back room. I set my belongings on the floor in the hallway. He shut the door behind me without a word. I collapsed on the floor and nibbled at the soggy fish fingers and impossibly congealed macaroni-and-cheese. I drank the lukewarm milk and realized I had to pee. I looked around for some kind of container. I found an old empty coffee can at the back of a small closet and peed in it. I set the can back in the closet and shut the door. Someone else could deal with that after I was gone. I thought about flipping on the lights, but I relished the gloomy calm after the garish, blinding sunlight of the afternoon's poolside scene.

I missed Brandon with a physical ache. I had never before wanted him near me so desperately. What was he thinking? Was he sad? Confused? Calm? Crying? Was he hungry? Was he injured in some way? Had he put up a fight? Would they have really beaten him with a bat? Could those Christian men be that cruel? I knew what they thought about us – they'd call us faggots, queers, and Sodomites – but, surely, they would draw the line at physical abuse! Surely!

The farmhouse-cum-office was eerily quiet. All the commotion of slamming doors, hushed conversations, and mumbled phone calls were long over. Judging by the utter lack of light in the room, I thought it might close to 9:00. I assumed the campers would be finishing their evening canteen break and heading toward the fire circle for the devotional and campfire. A smile spread across my face as I realized I'd never have to sit through another ridiculous camp devotional or sweat to death as a roaring campfire roasted our already sun-kissed faces in the 95° heat of a Texas summer evening. I suppose it was a testimony to the triumph of the human spirit that I could find a silver lining in the middle of such a predicament.

I heard a faint tap at the window. I didn't move at first. I thought it might have been some animal or bird. Then I heard a pattern of knocks – three rapid-fire knocks followed by another three. I jumped up. I knew it was Brandon.

I drew back the curtains. Brandon's face smiled up at me,

lit from the left by an outdoor light on the corner of the old farm house. I raised the window.

"Oh, my God, Alex! I am so glad to see you. You're a sight for sore eyes." As he drew closer to me, I noticed a large gash across his right cheek.

"Shit, what happened to you?"

"Those fuckers actually punched me. Well, that kid named Shawn did. I hit him back and bloodied his nose. I think I broke it! His dad shoved us apart and stood with that damn bat two inches from me. He would have swung if I moved. I thought of you, and I didn't move an inch."

"Oh, God! Your poor face." I leaned toward him across the windowsill and kissed his cheek right below the broken skin. "Does it hurt?"

"Not too much. They did give me some ice for the swelling."

"But what...? What are you... I mean, what are you doing here? How did you get out?"

He smirked. "Those dumb fuckers! They locked the door, but, hello, there's a huge window in that room. I just opened it, popped the screen out, climbed out, put the screen back, and closed the window." He snickered. "I was playing possum the last two times they checked on me after I got my stuff from the cabin. Then I heard them start a movie. You know that loud music before an HBO movie? I heard that come on. I waited a few minutes. Then prison break, baby! I came to see you!"

I leaned toward him again and kissed his lips. "But what if they notice you're gone?"

Brandon flashed me his brightest grin. "Come on. No time for all that. I overheard Corey tell Jack that your parents are coming at 10:00. It's already 9:30 or so. The campers and counselors are all distracted. The fucking hillbilly sons back at Jack's are jacking off to some porn movie." He snorted. "Just leave your stuff. There's not a thing we need. We'll run down the dirt road to the highway and wait for your parents there. Then we're gone. I know for a fact your parents signed all the right forms so that they have permission to pick me up. Nobody can stop me leaving with them." He smiled and leaned in to kiss me. He held out his hands. "Come on! Nobody's around. But we gotta go now before the campfire breaks up or Jack's inbred sons come looking for me!"

I took his hands. He helped me out the screenless window. We ran between scattered oak trees up to a small parking lot near the mailbox and a white wooden sign with the words 'Brazos Hills Church of Christ Youth Camp – You belong here!' painted in red letters. Brandon gave the sign a middle-finger salute as we passed by. I followed suit and offered it a double-barreled farewell of my own. He snickered when he saw me and said, "Kiss our asses, you narrow-minded bigots!"

We sprinted down the dirt road toward the main entrance. I looked back once or twice. Nobody followed us. No hue and cry rose up from the Jack's house or the old farm house. Maybe, just maybe, we'd see the headlights from my parents' car sooner than I dared to hope.

We slowed down a bit as we neared the end of the long camp road. Brandon chuckled and said, "Man, where's Fezzick when you need him?"

I looked at him askance. "What do you mean? Do you need a piggy-back?"

"No, dumbass! Like at the end of the movie when he shows up with four white stallions! We could use two white stallions right now. We'd just ride off into the proverbial sunset until we saw your parents!"

We reached the end of the road and turned left. We slowed our pace. The small country road was deserted. We couldn't hear any sounds from camp. Other than the flash of a few lightning bugs and the nighttime chorus of invisible chirping insects, it was utterly dark and quiet.

We stayed well to the side of the road, close to a small

barbed-wire fence that marked off the camp's property. I turned to Brandon and said, "I'm so sorry about all of that. I shouldn't have let us get to that point. I let you down. I'm so sorry."

The shock, anger, fear, and anxiety of the last six or so hours crystallized in me at that very second, and great heaving sobs erupted from my body. I crumpled into Brandon's arms. Perhaps for the first time in our long friendship, I was the one who fell apart and needed most to be held.

Brandon's strong arms wrapped around me. He pulled me close. I felt safe in those dense, familiar arms. He peppered my head with tender kisses, and great streams of my own warm tears tumbled down his thin t-shirt. I squeezed him even harder.

He whispered softly, "It's not your fault, Alex. None of this is your fault. It's not my fault either. There's no blame between us. Only love. Only love." His voice quivered. "I was so afraid they were gonna hurt you. I was so afraid I would find you bloodied and bruised. I kept thinking about poor Paul and what might happen to you. That's my worst fear – that someone beats the shit out of you because you love me." He paused and took a deep breath. "None of this is our fault. It's their fault, those assholes back there. They have the problem. Not me." He took my chin in his hand and tilted my face up to his. "Not you. Never you in a million years."

We stood on that dark, silent country road and kissed one another as deeply and lovingly as we ever had. Relief flooded over me. Perhaps the very worst part of our secret's revelation was over. Perhaps what we had feared for so long was behind us. Finally, the world beyond my parents knew about us; or at least a small part of the world knew. Word would travel fast in our old church circle. There would be Brandon's parents to deal with, but I hoped the very worst was behind us. How could it ever get worse than being threatened with baseball bats and locked in rooms at camp?

We heard the steadily growing rumble of a car heading our way. We pulled apart but remained hand-in-hand. A pair of headlights finally crested the small hill in front of us.

Brandon let go of my hand and said, "Stay a little behind me. Run back to camp if I say run."

The car accelerated slightly as it coasted downhill. I caught sight of Mom's profile under the interior roof light she was using to follow a map.

Brandon must have seen her, too. He cried out, "It's them! It's them!"

He ran out into the road. Dad braked quickly. Mom looked up, slightly dazed. Brandon ran to the passenger side as Dad put the car into park. They both flew out of the car. Mom grabbed Brandon's neck and mine at the same time and pulled us tightly to her. She was crying. Brandon was crying. I was crying. I felt Dad come up behind me and wrap his arms around my shoulders. He was crying, too.

Mom said, "Oh, you poor boys. You poor, brave, beautiful boys." She started to kiss Brandon's cheek and saw the ugly gash. She gasped. "Oh, God, Brandon, please tell me an adult didn't do this. Please tell me they didn't."

"No. It was the caretaker's son. I'm okay. I broke his nose in return. Asshole."

They let loose a flood of questions.

"What are you doing out here?"

"How did you get here?"

"Are you hurt, Alex?"

"Where are your things? Where are your bags?"

"Does someone know you're out here?"

"Where is the actual camp?"

I finally cut them off. "We'll explain it all! I promise. Just take us home. Please just take us home."

We all tumbled into the car. Brandon and I launched into a confused, overlapping account of the awful afternoon and evening before Dad even started the car.

Dad shut us down with a loud whistle. "Hold it, boys! Just a second. Do you know where your things are?"

I nodded.

"Then we're going to get them."

He started the car. My stomach sank. I had no desire to go back.

"Please," I begged. "Let's just go home. I don't need any of that stuff. I don't want to see any of those people ever again."

He was stonily silent. Even in the darkened car, I could see his white knuckles and the taught tendons in his hands as he gripped the steering wheel.

I looked at Brandon and shrugged my shoulders. He winked back.

Dad asked me, "How do we get there?"

"Turn up there. Where that street lamp is. That's the driveway."

We rocketed down the dirt road, a swirling cloud of dust rising behind us. We pulled into one of the rutted parking spaces near the white welcome sign. I sighed at the irony of that message. Not everyone was truly welcome. Only certain kinds of kids were welcome.

Dad turned around to me and Brandon. "You two stay here. Do not get out. Do not speak to anyone who comes to the car. Your mom and I will handle this. Just tell us where to go."

I said, "My stuff is in that building straight ahead. It's down the hallway near the back. Just go straight in and straight down the hall."

Mom hopped out of the car. Lights were on in the front room of the old farm house. Katie Millwood, the assistant camp director, came to the screen door when Mom knocked. Katie opened the door, and Mom disappeared inside.

"And mine's in that trailer over there." Brandon pointed to Jack's house. "They may not know I've gone. We put my stuff in their living room, right by the front door."

Dad got out and walked over to Jack's front door. In a flash of fear, I wondered if Jack had a gun. Or guns. A fair number of people in rural Texas had as many guns as toes and fingers... sometimes more.

Brandon whispered, "If I think for one second something bad is going down with your dad, I am so outta this car. I feel like whipping some ass."

We kept our eyes peeled on Dad's silhouette up against the soft light streaming from Jack's front door.

Within seconds, Mom came out the front door of the office and down the porch steps. Katie said something to Mom, but she didn't turn back or respond. I reached up to the front dashboard to pop open the car's trunk. Mom lifted the trunk's lid, set my stuff inside, and came back around to her seat. Her face looked strained and angry.

Just then, we heard the door shut over at Jack's. Dad carried Brandon's belongings in his hands. He walked over to us smiling. He put Brandon's stuff in the trunk and got back in the car.

"See? Easy as you please!"

He winked at Mom. She leaned over and kissed him on the cheek.

I wanted to ask a million questions, but I decided to let sleeping dogs lie. I had no doubt in my mind that my parents gave Jack and Katie a piece of their minds. It didn't take much imagination to conjure those exchanges!

Dad threw the car into reverse. We headed back down the driveway and out to the small county road that would lead us to the junction with the main highway. We turned right at the crossroads and sped toward Austin and away from Camp Brazos Hills forever.

We drove on in a mutually-agreed upon silence. Brandon scooted to the middle of the seat and leaned heavily against me. He kissed my cheek lightly, and I rested my head on his shoulder. I struggled to keep my eyes open. Somehow, miraculously and unexplainably, we had survived our first public exposure better than I expected. As we drove toward the lights of Austin, I prayed that was our first and last such ordeal.

When the sign for Bee Cave came into view, Mom turned slightly and said, "Your dad and I have a thousand questions for you two. Maybe you have a thousand questions for us. We are tired and hungry. I imagine you are, too. Let's save all the questions and explanations for tomorrow, okay? We stopped on the way and booked a room at a hotel on the other side of Austin. We'll stop up here at the first place we see that's open and get a bite. Maybe a McDonald's or Sonic or whatever we see. Then we'll drive on to the hotel. We all need a shower and a soft bed. Okay?"

I said, "Sounds good. Thanks for coming to our rescue."

Dad caught my eye in the rearview mirror and gave me a big wink.

I did have one burning question that couldn't wait. "Can I ask one thing? Do Brandon's parents know?"

Mom sighed and said, "Yes, baby, they do. The camp tried to call them first, but they couldn't get anyone at home. They called us next. Some man named Corey called about 3:00. He told me what happened. If he expected me to rage and vent, he was gravely in error. I told him we knew all about you two, and we had no problem with it at all. 'In fact,' I said, 'we encourage them in their love and maintain an open dialog with them regarding the way they express their physical affection for one another.'" She snorted with laughter. "He went silent for several seconds. I said we'd be on our way to collect you both as soon as Dad could get away from work."

She turned around and reached for Brandon's hand. He extended it out to her.

"I have your mom's office number, so I called there first. She was just about to leave. I told her what happened. She loves you so much, Brandon. She wasn't really surprised by all this. She said she thinks she knew on some level, even though she didn't want to believe it. She said she can't support you, but she won't stand in your way. So, that's something. She said she would tell your dad when he came home. We've scheduled a call with them tomorrow evening at 7:00."

She sighed and looked at Dad.

"I think more than anything, she's mad at us for keeping your secret for so long. I can't say I blame her on one level. She feels it was a deep betrayal, and I understand that. Perhaps we were wrong, but I don't think so." She let go of Brandon's hand and turned fully back to the front.

Brandon's voice quivered slightly as he said, "Well, at least it's all out now. I mean, I was sure I would die if they ever found out, and now they know. I'm still alive; still here; still with y'all. Maybe I could just stay with you and never go back."

. . .

We made it back home a little before noon on Thursday. Even though we had a good eight hours of sleep at the hotel, all four of us looked shell-shocked. Mom and Dad had dark circles under their eyes. Brandon's eyes were puffy, and he teared up from time to time. He never burst into a full-throated sob like he once would have, but I could tell he was in a fragile state. I knew he feared the looming conversation with his parents.

Dad went into work for about three hours after a quick sandwich and a short nap. Mom let Brandon and me sleep from right after lunch until nearly 5:00. Dad came home just as we woke up. We all headed out for dinner at our favorite pizza place up on Kirby. We were a subdued bunch. Nobody seemed in the mood for talking. Brandon picked at his pizza. Sadness affected our appetites inversely: I ate more; he ate less. He was intensely quiet, and none of my smiles, winks, or kisses pierced his pensive mood.

My parents went into Dad's study a little before 7:00. Brandon and I drifted out to the balcony. We sat next to each other on the wooden bench, looking out over the Museum of

Natural Science and the Hermann Park reflecting pool beyond it. It was a sultry, windless evening. Muted traffic noise from Main Street drifted our way. I could also hear a group of young men playing soccer on one of the big green spaces near Miller Outdoor Theater. I thought about Stephen, fresh from the soccer game, glaring and shouting at us, his face twisted in anger and disgust. I asked myself, 'Was that really just a day ago?'

I felt like I had aged ten years since that scene at the pool. I had a feeling I would never be the same. Everything had changed. I hoped the changes would all be for the better, but I dared not hope too much. If Emily Dickinson was right, hope sang all the more sweetly in the fiercest gale. I wanted it to be so. I didn't know if I could handle another blow of any kind.

Of course, my favorite poet from Amherst also said that each beloved moment – and I had experienced so many with Brandon – required a kind of payment in return:

Sharp pittances of years —
Bitter contested farthings —
And Coffers heaped with Tears!

Perhaps my bill was past due and some cosmic accountant demanded payment in arrears. Could it be that my best times with Brandon lay behind me, and I had nothing but barren, lonely years ahead of me?

I turned to Brandon and said, "No matter what happens, the three of us are here for you. No matter what! I think you should come live here with us. That would solve everything."

"It's not that simple. You know that, but thanks for saying it. It's the only thing that gives me any hope right now: your love and your constant friendship."

We sat in silence as dusk deepened around us. When the three citronella candles we lit finally burned out, we went inside. I offered Brandon some ice cream, but he declined. I had some anyway as we sat in silence at the dining room table. Muffled voices drifted out of the study. They had been talking almost forty minutes.

Mom came out of the study and beckoned Brandon with her finger. He rose and went toward her. She whispered something to him I couldn't hear. She kissed him on his uninjured cheek, and he stepped into the study.

Mom came to sit by me. I offered to get her some ice cream. She, too, declined. She whispered, "His dad is irate, but his mom is calm and in control. I think she's going to win out in the end."

"What do you mean? Win out how?"

"Let's just wait and see what Brandon says. It's all up to him."

She stood up, went to the living room, and started the CD player. Glenn Gould's interpretations of Bach's *Goldberg Variations* rang out. I felt calmer than I had since we left for camp the previous Sunday. I put my dish and spoon in the sink and joined Mom in the living room where she stood by the CD player. She wrapped her arm around my shoulder, and we sat down together on the couch.

About twenty minutes later, Brandon came out. His eyes were red, but there was a spring in his step and a slight smile on his lips. He looked at Mom and whispered, "I said yes! I said yes!"

She leaped up and hugged Brandon fiercely. He kissed Mom on her forehead and spun her around and around. She giggled with delight.

What had he said yes about?

I jumped up and said, "Someone tell me what's going on! Please!"

Brandon set Mom down gently. She wobbled a bit. He turned to me and wrapped his arms around my waist. "You've got a new roommate, dumbass. That's what's going on!" He picked me up and spun me, too. "My parents are gonna let me live here. I'm gonna live here, Alex! With you!"

I couldn't believe my ears! Why would his parents let him move in with us? Was that even legal? Can kids just move to a new family? It seemed impossible! He wasn't an orphan! He already had a family. How could he become part of ours? Nothing made any sense!

I was speechless and dizzy. Brandon collapsed to the floor and pulled me down with him. He shook with great convulsions of laughter. His eyes filled with happy tears. He was utterly transformed.

He lay on his back, and I sat cross-legged right next to him. "What? How can you come live here? I mean, are we adopting you? How can that be? How can you just leave your family?"

"It's not often I know more than you do. I kind of like this!" He reached out to poke me in the ribs. "No, you're not adopting me! That would be weird! It's even better. I turn eighteen in, like, three weeks. I can do what I want then, and this is what I want. Your parents are what I want. You're what I want. I want this for as long as I can have it."

I fell over on top of him and kissed his irresistible neck and made my way up to his lips. My brain was processing information so quickly I was dazed. I had been expecting the worse and bracing myself for unmitigated bad news, but things had turned on a dime! Somehow, miraculously, Brandon and I had cleared another seemingly insurmountable hurdle. Emily's bird sang out sweetly, almost deafeningly, in my joy-infused heart.

The full story came out later as the four of us had some celebratory ice cream.

Brandon started, "Dad said I had to come back and go to some shitty school for delinquents. He knows some man in Nashville who runs this program that tries to get gay kids to become straight. He said I could never see or talk to you again, but Mom just said no. She said no, no, and hell no." He shook his head. "I can't believe it. She finally stood up to him for my sake! Well, I mean, I can believe it. She has put up with so much shit from him for so long. She was always the calm one, the voice of reason. He was always blowing up and screaming, and she had to go around picking up the pieces. I don't think I ever really realized until tonight just what a hard life my mom has had. She deserves better than him. I wish she could get away, too."

He went silent for a few seconds before continuing. "Anyway, she said I didn't have to come back. She said I could make my own decision when I turn eighteen. And if I already knew what the decision was, then I might as well make it now.

"She told Dad she would divorce him in two seconds if he forced me to come back and go to that fucked-up school and go to some crazy-ass psychologist who wants to make me straight. As if that was even possible or I even wanted that!" He snorted. "Dad knew she meant it. He'd be fired from his church so fast his head would spin, even if Mom was the one who wanted the divorce. He'd never get another job as a preacher. He'd be toast!"

A smug smile spread across Brandon's face.

"So, Mom said it was up to me. Your parents were already in agreement. We figured you wouldn't care!" He reached over and patted my cheek. "Right? Right? So, it was up to me. I could go back to Nash-loser-ville or I could stay here." He stood up and spun around in fast circles. "And I'm staying here, Alex! I'm staying here!"

Later that night, Brandon and I lay beside one another in my bed. The previous two days of our lives had been a roller coaster on every level. I couldn't remember the last time I felt so worn out and overwhelmed. At the same time, a sense of peace and euphoria settled in my heart. It seemed an odd juxtaposition: I felt so happy I wanted to dance, shout, and cry; at the same time, a delicate blanket of peace covered me with a silent, serene comfort.

"I can't believe it. I can't believe you're gonna live here with us."

"I know it keeps hitting me over and over again. I've dreamed about living with your family since the first time I visited here. I've always thought this was the life I was meant to have and that other life I had with my family was not really me."

"And now it's coming true. We'll get to spend our senior year together! You'll be in the next room, not three states away! We can hang out all the time and still have sleepovers on the weekend." I giggled. "You can come to my room. I can come to the guest room... I mean, your room. It'll be incredible. I just can't believe it."

I turned and placed my head on his shoulder. He slipped his arm under my neck and drew me a little closer.

"No more secrets. No more pretending to be something we're not. No more keeping all this from my parents." He sighed. "I'll miss Mom for sure, but I was going to be leaving for college next year anyway. And if I had started kindergarten on time, I'd be heading off to college next month. Isn't that funny? I'm still gonna leave home when I'm 18, just like all my brothers. So I'm not really leaving home early."

"It's a miracle! I feel like we won the lottery!"

He turned and kissed my forehead. I snuggled up close to him, my nose pressed right up against his shoulder. I kissed it gently. He slipped his hand down to my crotch.

He said, "God, just imagine. If we were still at camp, we'd be in separate beds, listening to Stephen drone on and on in the cabin devo. That guy Seth from Austin would be farting like a chimpanzee. Joshua would be picking his nose as inconspicuously as possible. We'd be swatting mosquitoes and trying to figure out what was worse: staying on top of the sleeping bag and getting eaten alive or burying ourselves in our sleeping bag to escape the mosquitoes but sweating to death instead! But now we're here! For a whole year! Until we figure out where to go to college." He sighed and reached inside my shorts. "And if we were still at camp, I'd only be able to dream about doing this for another three days."

I looked up and said, "Well, dream no more, my hunky roommate. Dream no more..."

Mom flew to Nashville with Brandon the following Monday. They stayed at a hotel near the airport. Early the next morning, they drove a rental car to Brandon's house. Mr. Marshall had already left for work, making it clear he had no desire to see Brandon. Mrs. Marshall met them at the door in a flood of tears. She was torn asunder: she loved Brandon so deeply but could not say she supported or approved of his sexuality. At the same time, she promised him she would always make a place for him in her heart and in her life. She said she would never cut off ties with Brandon, no matter what anybody else in the family decided. Mom told Mrs. Marshall she could come visit us in Houston any time she wanted.

The three of them spent the day packing up Brandon's clothes, personal items, and a few mementoes from his room. Mom and Brandon were gone by the time Mr. Marshall came home from the church office. They spent another night at the hotel and began the long drive back to Houston in the rental car on Wednesday morning.

CHAPTER 18

My parents arranged for Brandon to enroll at my school for his senior year. He was slightly embarrassed to find out he would be taking classes filled with freshmen and sophomores. Most of the senior-level classes Brandon would have taken at any local public school came along much earlier in students' plan-of-study at my school. After the first week, however, he was completely at ease. He fit in more easily than I thought, and my friends treated him like they'd known him for years. Every time he came out of class, a small flock of ninth or tenth graders huddled close by him, looking up in wonder at the six-foot, 180-pound god who descended from Mount Olympus and deigned to mingle with such lowly, gangly mortals.

We did our best to project a low-key relationship at school. We knew we were safer if we kept up the friends-only act. I'm sure a few observant students may have wondered about us from time to time. If anyone ever put two and two together, they kept it to themselves as far as I could tell.

I had already told my small circle of best school friends about Brandon and me our junior year, and none of them even batted an eyelid. Kevin said he had suspected for a long time that Brandon and I were more than friends. Eric was all smiles and high-fives. Abdul even said, "I'm sure the Prophet will slay for me saying so, but I'd be gay for Brandon's sake any day he wanted me to be! I can't believe Brandon's real. You are definitely blessed!"

The fall semester passed in a blur as Brandon settled into his new life with us. At least once a day, sometimes more, I'd catch him grinning and he'd say, "I just can't believe I'm here. I think about last year, and I think about now... and I just can't believe it."

By early February, I had four tantalizing acceptance letters in hand: Harvard, Columbia, Yale, and Rice. My parents told me I'd be a fool to turn down the offer from Harvard, and I knew they were right. Yet I felt unsure; I didn't know what Brandon would say. Would he want me to say yes to Rice and stay close to home? Close to him?

I asked him about it one Saturday night after we finished a movie. He grabbed my shoulders and turned me to him. "I will literally beat your skinny ass into the ground and stomp on it when I'm done if you say no to Harvard! Why are you even asking me, dumbass? You know I want the stars for you! Go to Harvard! Go to the fucking school of your dreams! I'll break up with you if you don't!!"

"But what about you? I feel bad about leaving you here. What are you gonna do?"

"Hey, we'll sort that out soon. I like your parents' plan! If they'll let me stay here and take some classes at U of H, I'll be totally happy. It'll give me time to figure out what I really want to do, and I can work out how I'm gonna get into a college or art school near you by next year! I know I can't waffle around forever, but I need some more time to make a firm decision. I don't know if I want to teach or go into some design work or maybe do art history. It makes sense for me to stay and for you to go. It's just a year! You know this! You know I'm right!" He took my chin in his hand and kissed me gently.

"I know it makes sense, but I could stay here and go to

Rice. It's not exactly a school for dummies! It's the best college in the south by a long shot. It's called the 'Harvard of the South' for a reason!"

"But you've busted your ass for six years to get into the *real* Harvard. Don't throw it away! Not for me! Not for anyone. Plus, I'm so fucking proud of you! I mean, I can tell people that my boyfriend goes to Harvard! How cool is that?"

"Don't go around saying that!"

"What? That you go to Harvard?"

"No, that I'm your boyfriend. Even if I'm not here, you gotta be careful. Please swear to me you'll be careful when I'm gone."

"Of course, I will. I mean, I won't really say that. Not in public at least. I know we have to be careful. I'm just tired of it. I used to think we'd get past the stage of being secret once my parents knew, but it just seems like it's never gonna end. We'll spend our whole lives looking over our shoulders and wondering who's gonna flip out. It's exhausting just to think about."

"Maybe it won't be forever. Maybe our love will outlast all the hate."

"You've been watching Oprah behind my back again, haven't you?"

I giggled and gave him a big wet kiss.

I said yes to Harvard in the end; I swear, Brandon was happier about it than I was.

· · ·

ii.

My parents planned a joint graduation party for us on the second Saturday in June. Mrs. Marshall flew in from Nashville the Wednesday before. Brandon sobbed with relief and delight when she walked through the door from the jet-way into the terminal. I knew he missed her more than he admitted. My parents and I had done so much for him, but I was old enough to know we never could take his mother's place in his affections.

Mrs. Marshall and Brandon spent Thursday together, revisiting some of their favorite Houston haunts and catching up with each other's lives. Mom, Mrs. Marshall, Brandon, and I spent most of Friday shopping and running errands in preparation for the party. Then, on Saturday morning, they turned us out of the apartment so they could focus on final preparations.

We went for a long run in Hermann Park and then headed to the gym for a brief workout. When Brandon moved in with us, my parents added him to their gym membership. He dragged me to the gym all through our senior year whenever we had a free afternoon or Saturday morning. I liked to moan about it just to get under his skin, but I secretly loved every second at the gym with Brandon.

We took showers at the gym, changed into fresh clothes, and went to have lunch at our favorite Greek deli in Rice Village. While we were eating, Brandon relayed part of a conversation he had with his mom on Thursday.

"So, get this! You know Mom and Joshua's mom are good friends. I think you know they moved to Abilene the summer after we moved to Nashville." I nodded. "Well, Joshua got to Abilene and fell head-over-heels in love with the oldest daughter in the family next door. Her name is Laura. They've been a couple ever since. They're both going to Abilene Christian in the fall. Apparently, they've already been talking about marriage. I mean, they're not getting married soon, but they're planning on it at some point. Joshua told his mom to tell Mom to tell us both hello when he heard she was coming here. So, there you go! Joshua's done alright for himself. All our teasing didn't do any lasting damage."

I shook my head in shame. "But we were too mean to him!

Well, I guess we were never super mean to his face. We never teased him in person like we did when it was just us two, but I've always felt bad about it. He knew on some level we didn't like him. He was clueless about some things, but I'm certain we hurt his feelings. He looked rather crushed a couple of times after we brushed him off at church or camp."

"Well, he made it hard on himself. Remember that year at camp when he brought all his Legos with him? He had a whole suitcase full of Legos! What guy in high school carts his whole Lego collection with him to camp and then talks non-stop about his favorite sets? He used to collect ash from the campfire and pretend it was moon dust so his Lego spaceships could land in it!"

I snorted at the memory. "I know! He was hard work. I just wish we had been nicer. It's not like it would have hurt us. We could have included him on some things we did together."

Brandon choked on his drink and said, "Over my dead body, Alexander Kennedy! Like I wanted him crowding in on our limited time! You forget how little we saw of one another at times. We used to go weeks and months without sleepovers. I would have killed you if you'd ever invited him to join us."

"Well, like you said, he's turned out okay. I just hope he doesn't think too badly of us."

"Do you think he knows we're gay and that we're a couple? Mom's never really told me who knows and who doesn't."

"If he does know about us, it was sweet of him to send a hello through your mom. He didn't have to do that." I paused for a second. "Tell your mom to give his mom my phone number and say that he should call us this summer." I winked. "Let's make an effort with him if he is willing. A phone call or two now can make up a little for us being jerks back then."

Brandon reached across the table, unconcerned about any onlookers, and took my hand. "God, I don't deserve you, Alex. You're the kindest guy I've ever known."

"You *are* pretty lucky! If I hadn't been so nice back in

junior high, I would have told you to take a hike after that first retreat we went on. Joshua never treated me like that!"

I pulled my hand back slightly, even though nobody was paying us any attention. We were both in sandals, and I felt him slip his bare left foot over my right foot. It was a losing battle at times!

"I would have deserved it! Like totally deserved it. You've put up with so much shit from me."

"Yes, well, I'll let you make it up to me later. Deal?"

He snickered and leaned in close across the table. "Kind but horny: that's what you are, Alex N. Kennedy. Kind but horny."

. . .

The party started at 2:00. My best friends from school all came: Kevin, Abdul, Eric, Michael, and Juan. All of our building neighbors dropped in. Nick and David showed up in stunningly coordinated outfits, flowers in hand for Brandon and me! Some of my parents' colleagues and their families arrived with cards, balloons, and small gifts. Mom invited a couple of fellow graduates from the Unitarian Church where we had been attending, and Mrs. Marshall somehow made contact with two of Brandon's friends from his old high school. He was ill-at-ease around them. They clearly didn't know a thing about our relationship, and I caught their looks of surprise when Brandon and I gently kissed as other guests mingled upon arrival. The two guys left about ten minutes into the party without a word of goodbye. One minute they were there, and the next minute I heard the groaning of the elevator as it carried them out of Brandon's life for the last time.

In the midst of all this, Joel literally burst out of the coat closet in the foyer about ten minutes into the party. Brandon and I couldn't believe our eyes. We hadn't seen him since Christmas break.

He pulled us in close for a huge hug. "How could I not come to your graduation party? Your mom called me a few weeks ago, and I drove over just to be here. I've been in that damn closet for about twenty minutes! The things I do for you two!!" He snickered. "Listen, I'll be around all next week. So, let's spend a few days together. How about Galveston, maybe Astro World, and a workout or two?" We nodded with glee and promised to call him Sunday to come up with a plan for the latter part of the week.

A few minutes later, Joel's boyfriend Justin arrived. Joel howled with delight when he saw our faces. "How could I not bring Justin along? He's been dying to meet you, Brandon, and he'll be around all week, too. We'll all hang out as much as we can."

The doorbell rang again. Mom went to answer it. A man I had never seen before stepped into the apartment and looked around hesitantly. A spark of recognition fired in my brain, and I realized I *had* seen the man before – in a picture in Brandon's old bedroom. It was his oldest brother, Jacob.

I looked across the room to Brandon. He was deep in conversation with Kevin and Abdul, entertaining them with some anecdote from when he and I first became friends. I looked next to where Mrs. Marshall stood talking with Dad. A wide smile lit up her face when she caught sight of Jacob. Dad gave me a wink and a nod.

Just then, one of those odd moments that eventually happens at every party came to pass: every conversation in the room, except Brandon's, simultaneously paused. Brandon noticed me looking at him and quickly lowered his voice. I motioned my head toward the foyer where Mom stood by Jacob. Brandon did a double-take and let out a small gasp of surprise.

Conversation in the apartment picked up suddenly. Brandon excused himself from Kevin and Abdul and made his way across the living room toward Jacob. My eyes were glued to the scene. I didn't exactly expect the worse, but I was uncertain and slightly worried.

Brandon and Jacob held each other in a tight hug. I couldn't see Brandon's face, but soft tears streaked down Jacob's cheeks. My own eyes teared up slightly. I excused myself from the small group of neighbors I was speaking to and made my way over to the foyer. Mrs. Marshall arrived from the other side at the same moment. My parents came and stood by me, wrapping their arms around my shoulders and gently holding me back for a few seconds. Mrs. Marshall joined her sons in their shared embrace.

They eventually separated a bit. Brandon held out his hand toward me. I walked over, and he linked his right arm through my left arm.

"Jacob, this is Alex, the best, best, bestest friend on the planet. He's amazing, a friend in a billion. And Alex, this is Jacob, my long-lost best brother ever."

I reached out and shook Jacob's hand. He was remarkably handsome, and I saw again the strong resemblance between Brandon and Jacob I first noticed in that photograph so long ago. Jacob let out a small chuckle, almost exactly like Brandon's.

"So, you're the famous Alex. I've heard so much about you. I can't believe it's taken us so long to meet."

"You heard about me from Brandon?"

"No, from my mom. She's the only one in the family I have contact with. She keeps me up to date on Brandon, and you two seem inseparable. I've heard tons of stories about the things you two get up to."

"Yeah," I said, "we're pretty much inseparable. He's the best period... just the best everything. It's really nice to meet you after all these years. Welcome to our home."

Mom stepped up behind me and offered Jacob a drink. Brandon followed them into the kitchen.

Dad came up beside me, put his arm around my shoulder,

and pulled me in close. He spoke softly into my ear. "Before you start asking a ton of questions, I'll just answer some for you. Yes, we're the ones who invited Jacob. Yes, Mrs. Marshall knew he was coming. We got his phone number from her. No, Brandon didn't know he was coming. And, finally, he's gonna hang around after the party and talk as much as you and Brandon want. His wife is at home with their two girls, so Jacob's free to stay as long as he wants."

I gasped. "Two daughters! You mean Brandon is an uncle twice over?" I shook my head in disbelief. "I don't think he knows. In fact, I'm sure he doesn't."

"I think Suzanne is the only one who knows. The girls are twins. They're about a year old. It's a long story. You'll get all the details later. But in the meantime, let's not neglect our other guests." He smiled and patted my ass. "Come on. Back to the party! Keep milling around. Just another hour or so to go."

I milled as instructed, but I must have seemed like a catatonic moron to our guests. I kept asking people to repeat themselves. I couldn't focus on anything since my thoughts were a million miles away. Well, not really that far. It's more like my thoughts were just across the room with Brandon and Jacob as they stood close together in a little world of their own amidst the clamor of the party for another hour.

Once all the guests had left, Brandon, Jacob, and I sat alone in the living room. Brandon and I sat side-by-side on one of the couches. Jacob pulled an armchair close to face us and sat with his knees right up against Brandon's knees. My parents and Mrs. Marshall were cleaning up after the party and left the three of us to get on with our conversation.

Jacob started. "So, Alex, I have to start by saying that I know about you and Brandon, and I don't give a damn. Well, I mean I *do* give a damn because it makes me happy you're both happy together, but I don't judge you or think there's something wrong with you. I've had my own brutal conflicts with my dad and people in the church. I would never put either of you through that. In fact, I like you more knowing you're gay. Why be like everyone else, right?"

"What do you mean? What kinds of conflict have you had with Mr. Marshall? Can you tell me?"

"Sure. I can tell you. Brandon knows some of this because I told him earlier, and I know he wants you to know." He sighed and looked at Brandon with great tenderness. "I was the golden boy growing up. Dad thought I was the best kid ever. Everyone at church thought I was the perfect Christian. I ate it all up. I didn't know any better. I thought Dad was right about everything, and I naively assumed everything I heard at church was true in every sense of the word.

"Then I went off to MIT on a scholarship. I left right after Brandon's fourth birthday. And, like a lot of teens who go off to college, I discovered what a small, insular world I had come from. Even though I was doing a degree in programming, I took elective classes in physics, philosophy, and even comparative religion. Well, that was at Boston College the summer term after my freshman year.

"Anyway, my whole world turned upside down because of all the things I was learning. Then I met Prisha at the end of my first summer in Boston. She was a student at Harvard. Her family lived in New York, but her parents' families both immigrated from India just after the partition. I fell head-over-heels for her. I mean, I was mega in love with her.

"As you can imagine, Dad went ballistic when I told him about her. We had already clashed a few times about religion, metaphysics, and epistemology when I called home my freshman year. I left him tongue-tied and angry every time. Then I brought Prisha home for Christmas my sophomore year, and it was horrible. He insulted Prisha. He said that Hinduism was a dirty, doggerel religion that, I quote, 'gloried in cow pats and human squalor.' It was horrendous. We stayed two nights and left. I don't think Brandon remembers any of that. Do you, buddy?"

"Not really. I mean, I have this vague memory of Mom and Dad fighting by the Christmas tree one year, but I don't connect it with you. I don't really have many memories of you at all. I really only have one memory of you – from that New Year's Eve dinner we all had. You said it was the year before because that was your last New Year's at home."

"Yeah, New Year's Eve 1978 was my last one at home. Then my last Christmas was 1979, the year Dad insulted Prisha and her one billion fellow believers. I never came back after that. Prisha and I got married in the summer of '81. Nobody from our family came. I never heard from Mom until three years later when I sent her my phone number in a letter and asked her to call. That was in May 1984, not long after my birthday. Prisha said it was time to try to make contact with Mom."

Brandon said, "And I thought I was the one who messed up our family. I mean, I thought you three were perfect and that I came along and messed it all up. But it was messed up long before I started going wild."

Jacob leaned in closer. "Listen, Brandon. You aren't responsible for anything that's happened in our family or in our parents' marriage. It's all down to them, and 99% of that is all down to Dad. He's a messed-up motherfucker, even with all his religion and affected holiness. You and I know what's he's really like. Nothing he does at church or says from the damn pulpit makes up for any of the shit he's done to us."

He paused and looked at me. "Sorry for cursing. I don't mean to offend you."

"It's okay. If there's anyone I know who deserves a few curse words tossed his way, it's your dad."

Jacob smiled and put his hand on Brandon's knee. "I don't want you to hate him. That'll only drag you down. We're both free of him. He's in the past. He can't hurt us now. The only power he has over you is the power you give him in your own heart, mind, and memory. You just have to let it all go."

A few tears fell from Brandon's eyes, and he rested his head on my shoulder. I grasped his hand and held it in my lap. Jacob moved from his chair and sat down next to Brandon. He took Brandon's free hand in his own.

"Leaving you behind is the one big regret I have over all these years. You were the sweetest kid on the planet! You used to let me hold you and read you stories. I used to give you baths when you were a toddler. I gave you endless piggyback rides. You wore me out, but I loved it. I loved every second we had together. You were glued to my side from the time you could walk until I left for college. You used to stand outside my room and bawl when I was doing my homework and couldn't play with you. I'd finally give in, and then I'd have to stay up late to finish my homework once you were in bed. But I secretly loved it. I tried to love you the best way I could because I realized that Dad never really had time for you.

"It's like, with each son that came along, he had less and less time for us because he was so busy trying to be the perfect preacher. Mom said you were inconsolable for weeks when I finally went off to MIT. And you cried your little heart out when I went back at the end of the Christmas holidays that year."

Brandon smiled through his tears, and my own eyes finally filled to overflowing.

Jacob continued, "But I didn't know how to be your brother after that last Christmas at home. Dad told me I was never welcome to come back until I repented in front of the whole church for my disbelief and broke up with Prisha. I knew neither of those things was ever gonna happen, so I just had to wash my hands of the whole family. I didn't really want to break contact with you and Mom, but I didn't know what else to do.

"You have to believe me: I grieved for you and cried over you for years, knowing what you'd have to face growing up with that man. If I'd ever had the slightest idea you were gay,

I would have come and kidnapped you once we moved back to Houston. I never intended to live so close to Dad again, but the job offer was too good to pass up. And Prisha secretly prayed for years that our family would somehow reunite again. I guess her prayers finally worked for you and me. I'm just so sorry for all you had to go through. I'm so sorry I waited so long. Do you forgive me for waiting so long?"

Brandon nodded. "Of course. How could I not?"

"And look at you now! Who would have thought that cute little three-year-old who wouldn't leave me alone would turn into a teenage Adonis? I used to hold you in my arms and sing you to sleep when Mom was busy getting Matthew and Will ready for bed." He chuckled and shook his head. "But look at your damn arms now! I mean, holy hell, Brandon! I'm as straight as they come, but you are totally turning me on. I mean, can I say that as your brother? You're hot as hell!"

Jacob grinned at me. "And wow! Look at you! Mom told me you were a cute kid, but she didn't say you were handsome enough to be a model. I get why you two instantly felt drawn to one another. If I were your age and gay, I'd be drooling all over myself and panting after you, Alex. Brandon is so lucky!"

It was odd to hear such language coming from a man in Brandon's family. They had been an implacable block set firmly against us both for so long. It was surreal to have Jacob in our apartment and to hear his playful, hedonistic banter.

Brandon turned to kiss me. His lips brushed against mine briefly, but he leaned back just a bit to look at Jacob before we kissed more fully.

A bright smile crossed Jacob's handsome face. "By all means, Brandon. By all means. Don't let me stop you. This party was for you two after all. Who am I to stand in the way of young love?"

We kissed more fully, and Brandon put his arm around my shoulder. He turned to Jacob with a puzzled look. "I think I'm still confused on some of the timeline. It's all so much to take in. Just tell me again when you got married, when you contacted Mom, when you moved here. I'm just trying to think how old I was at each point. Nobody ever said anything about you. It's like you were never really there! I just don't understand it."

"Well, we got married in July 1981. You would have been six, almost seven. We both graduated in May 1982. I went to work right away at a small technology firm in Boston. Prisha carried on in the law school at Harvard. She finished in '84 and did some work with a civil rights firm in the city. Then I got an out-of-the-blue job offer from Compaq in November '86. We moved here in February 1987. You would have been twelve by then. Prisha started working for a small firm which also focused on civil rights. Mom and I were already back in touch by then. She came up to see us one Saturday not long after we moved here. I think she had to lie to Dad and sneak away. She brought me some pictures of you. I was so happy to see you, if only in photo form. She came to see us a few more times in the spring and came every other week that summer."

He choked up a little. "I honestly wanted to reach out to you then, but Mom said Dad was on your case all the time. I guess you were giving them some grief that year. She said it would make things worse if I tried to see you or even call you. Dad's overriding fear was that you'd turn out like me. He was afraid I'd lure you over to the dark side."

Brandon said, "That was right about when Alex here came waltzing into my life. We met in September 1987 when he first came to church. You wouldn't believe what an asshole I was to him. I mean, on his very first Sunday I embarrassed him so badly. He ran from the church kitchen in a flood of tears. If the earth would have swallowed me up right then, I would have gone gladly to her deepest, darkest pit. But somehow, Alex forgave me, and we kept making these small steps to building a friendship. Every setback was my fault, but we made it in the end." He sighed and patted my leg. "We'll tell you the whole story sometime."

I shook my head and said, "Don't let him tell you the story that way! I did my fair share of stupid things! I said some really harsh things to him a few times, and I was the one who wanted the earth to swallow me up each time. I heard myself doing the exact thing your dad did to him, and I hated myself for it."

Brandon turned to look in my eyes. "I never knew you thought that. You thought you sounded like Dad when you were angry with me? You mean like that time I got grounded from you for six weeks and you raised your voice at me? You thought you sounded like Dad?" He chuckled and squeezed my hand. "Lemme just tell you: no, no, and hell no. You never sounded like Dad. Even when you were at your angriest, I knew you loved me in some unshakeable way. I could take whatever you dished out to me. Plus, you're so damn hot when you get mad and flustered. Your ears go all red, and your eyes narrow. You're impossibly sweet even when you're angry."

Jacob smiled and looked back and forth between us. "God, Mom was right. We were talking on the phone not long before they moved to Nashville, and she said you two were the sweetest friends she had ever seen. She said she didn't get it, but she was so happy you two found a way to be friends." He looked at me with misty eyes again. "She said she dreaded to think what may have happened to him had you not come along."

We all lapsed into silence for a few seconds. Just then, all three parents, as if on cue, came through the living room from the kitchen to tell us goodnight. There were hugs, kisses, and whispered endearments all around.

Mrs. Marshall, Jacob, and Brandon stayed locked in a tight hug that must have lasted three or four minutes. Mrs. Marshall's body shook with great sobs. When they pulled apart, I heard her whisper: "Maybe something good has come out of my marriage. I couldn't be prouder of you two, and nothing in the world would make me happier than to know you two are reunited for good. You both deserved so much more than I could give you. I am so, so terribly sorry."

Jacob, Brandon, and I sat up for another couple of hours, exchanging stories and trying to learn a little more about each other. At times, I forgot that he had only been in the apartment for a few hours. He seemed to have been around since the beginning of my friendship with Brandon. He belonged with us in a way I hadn't anticipated.

After regaling us with anecdotes about his first year of fatherhood, he said, "You must come over soon. We want you to meet the twins. You're probably the only Marshall uncle they'll ever know. I mean, maybe Matthew and I will find a way to reconnect. But who knows? I want you to come over often! We've got a lot of lost time to make up for!"

"Sure! I'd love it! Can Alex come, too? We kinda go together, like chips and salsa. You get one, you get the other." He snickered.

"Absolutely. In fact, you'd be in trouble if you came without him. I'd like to be a kind of older brother to both of you... that is, if you'll let me, Alex. Maybe one Marshall is all you need in your life."

"No, I'd love that. I'd be honored to have you be like an older brother."

"Honored, eh?" Jacob winked at Brandon. "You did tell me he's a charmer. Now I know what you mean."

I said, "And Mom and Dad want you and Prisha and the girls to come over here for dinner. You can bring all your baby stuff and just invade for the evening. They really want you to come."

Jacob grinned and said, "I'll hold you to it. And we'll catch up each time you come back from college – Thanksgiving, Christmas, Spring Break. Maybe the three of us can go on a vacation together next summer. I can pay. It'll be my treat and a small way for me to make up for all the lost time with you."

Brandon grinned and teared up again. "Cool! I'd love it. Before Alex and I plan anything for next summer, we'll make our plans with you so you can arrange it with your work and with Prisha. We'll go whenever is best for you. And I'll be around all school year while Mr. My-Brain-Is-Too-Enormous-To-Be-Normal here is at Harvard! I'll be coming to see you all the time!"

They high-fived and threw their arms around each other's shoulders.

. . .

Thirty or so minutes after Jacob left, Brandon and I snuggled up close to one another in my bed. He yawned and kissed the top of my head.

"God, what a night. I never, ever imagined I would see Jacob. And even if I could have imagined seeing him, I couldn't have ever imagined him being so... so... cool and unbelievable. I mean, Will thinks I'm going to hell, according to what Mom says. But Jacob's like, 'You're gay? No big deal. It makes me love you even more.' I mean, who would have thought a son of my father would ever be okay with me being gay?"

"Well, you're a son of your father, and you think it's perfectly amazing to be gay, right?"

He chuckled. "Score a point to you. That's an excellent point. You're all logical even at the most emotional of times. I love you, Alex."

"I love you, too, and I'm so happy he loves you just the way you are. You deserve to have a brother like that. I'm so jealous. Even though he says he wants to be like an older brother to me, you'll always have a different kind of connection with him. I'll never quite know what that's like. You're so lucky."

He pulled me closer to him. "Oh, come here, you little hottie. That may be true on one level, but he'll never have what we have – this incredible love. I don't care how much he loves his wife, no couple on the planet has as much fun as we do. He's my amazing and wonderful older brother, but he's no Alex Kennedy."

I leaned my head toward him and kissed his cheek. He smiled and took my hand in his.

I asked, "So, what do you feel deep down? What does your heart tell you about meeting your long-lost brother?"

"I feel like someone opened a really dark room in my heart that I never knew about. I mean, I never knew that Jacob loved me so much. I never knew he missed me. I never knew he thought about me. I guess Mom kept it all from me to spare my feelings. Maybe she was trying to protect me from Dad. Maybe she thought if she told me all about Jacob that I'd want to see him. Dad would never have allowed that, and it would have been one more source of conflict for us."

He sighed and shook his head. "I don't know why she kept it all from me, but it's almost like some part of me knew. Maybe my heart remembered how much I loved him and followed him around when I was a toddler. Then that part of my heart kind of died when he went away. But now that we've reconnected, that part of me is alive again. A little part of my heart that had shriveled up is beating again."

"That's so sweet. You deserve it after all you've been through. You deserve to have someone in your family who loves you just the way you are." I paused. "You know, I think your mom is coming around. She's not quite there yet, but I think she's getting close."

He teared up. "God, Alex, I keep crying every five seconds tonight. I think I've cried more in the last six hours than the last six months. I think you're right about my mom: she is slowly getting used to it all. But even if she never can quite totally approve of us, it's okay. I know she loves me the best way she can. It's enough for now."

We both went silent for a few minutes. I wondered if he

had nodded off as his breathing slowed, but he stirred slightly when I shifted my weight a bit.

"Hey, Alex."

"Yeah?"

"Are you okay?"

"Yes, of course. Perfect. Here with you is always perfect."

He ran his hands through my hair.

"Well, I think I'm ready."

"Yeah, I'm pretty sleepy, too. It's been a long day. I think it's your turn to get the lamp."

He snickered. "No, you chump. I mean, I'm ready for you. Ready to have you in me."

I sat up and looked him in the eyes. "You mean my penis in you?"

He nodded. "Is that okay? I mean, are you ready? I know it's a big step for us, but I feel ready. I can't stop thinking about you. You know that, don't you? Even when I was talking to Jacob tonight, I knew where you were at every moment. My heart skipped a beat every time you crossed my line of sight."

"Same for me. I can't take my eyes off you if you're anywhere in my field of vision. You're my own real, live Adonis in impossibly sexy briefs!"

He snickered. "God! I think about all the people who think you are so perfect. Nobody on the planet could imagine your horny little mind, but you don't fool me. You don't fool me!"

I grinned and said, "So, my love, how do we do this?"

He sat up beside me. "Well, I think I slip off these sexy briefs, as you call them. I'll kneel down, open wide, and let you in." He snickered. "That is, if you can manage to get hard. I mean, I know it takes a lot of work to get your little pecker past caterpillar stage."

I socked him as hard as I could on the shoulder. He leaned in and kissed me roughly on the lips. He patted my crotch and smirked. "Oh, I see. Your little caterpillar has a mind of its own. I'd say you're ready!"

He rolled off the bed, slipped off his briefs, and got down on his knees. I scurried off the bed and slipped off my briefs. I stood in front of him, and he ran his hands up and down my legs. I kissed the crown of his head and placed my hands on his shoulders.

"One serious question first! Are you gonna swallow?"

Nick and David had talked to us a few times about oral sex so we'd be prepared once we decided we were ready. We kind of knew what to expect, but I was a little nervous. I figured we'd probably fumble about a little as we gave it a shot.

He smiled and said, "Oh, God, I didn't think of that. Um... I don't think so. Let's just take it slow this time."

"Well, we need a glass or something."

"Lemme run to the kitchen."

"Like that? Not a stitch on you?"

"I'll be five seconds. Back in a flash!"

He stuck his head out the door, looked both ways, and darted down the hallway. He was true to his word and came through the door glass in hand, still hard, and looking impossibly chiseled from head to toe.

"God, you're beautiful, Brandon."

"Thank you, kind sir. I aim to please."

He knelt down on the floor in front of me again. He looked up at me and giggled. "Wowzers, Alex! Your chest actually seems big from this angle. Every inch of you is perfect. I wouldn't change a thing about you."

He leaned in and kissed my penis. I placed my hands on his head and drew him closer to me. He let his cheek rest against my right thigh, and I could feel the breath from his nostrils brush across my penis.

He hesitated and looked up again. "Are you totally sure? We can stop. I want you to be totally comfortable. If you're even 1% unsure, we can stop. Okay?"

I nodded and grinned. "I'm never more comfortable than when I'm with you. I feel impossibly safe with you. I'm 100% sure."

He kissed my navel and the flat plane of flesh below it. He whispered, "I love you, Alex. I love you inside and out... so much."

He opened his mouth. I leaned forward a bit and let my penis slide between his lips. He let out a small moan. I had imagined our first attempt at oral sex for so long, but nothing in my wild imaginings prepared me for the bliss I felt as Brandon's mouth enclosed my penis.

I didn't really have any sense of time. I just wanted him to go on and on forever. Yet, more quickly than I wanted, I felt myself ready to ejaculate. Why did it come so soon?

I mumbled, "Get ready! Don't choke!"

Brandon's eyes widened in surprise. He reached beside him and brought the glass to his mouth. He spat into the glass and smiled at me. He set the glass behind him on my desk.

I asked, "Are you okay?"

"Yeah, for sure. That was just so unexpected. I mean, I knew it was coming at some point. I just wasn't quite ready."

He stood up in front of me. He wrapped his arms around me and held me closely to him.

He whispered, "How was it? Everything you dreamed of?"

"Yes, yes, yes! A thousand times yes!"

We collapsed on the bed and held each other in silence for a few seconds.

"Alex?"

"Yeah?"

"I feel like I need to go rinse my mouth!"

I giggled. "Yeah, I was wondering about that! Go on! You won't hurt my feelings."

He rolled out of bed, grabbed the glass from the desk, and headed toward the door.

I whispered, "Brandon! Briefs!"

He looked at me sheepishly, set the glass on the floor, grabbed his briefs, and slid them on.

I reached for some tissues while he was gone and wiped

myself off a little bit.

He was back in a minute. He jumped into bed and snuggled up beside me.

"Sorry, I had to wash all your little potential Alexes down the drain. It felt kinda cruel."

"That's okay. I have a feeling we'll be doing that a few more times in the days and weeks ahead. We gotta make every moment count before I head off to Boston!"

"Oh, yeah baby. Speaking of... do you want your turn? I mean, your turn in me?"

"Would you be upset if I wanted to wait?"

"No! As long as it's not because you're upset with me."

"Of course not! You've not done anything wrong at all. Just the opposite. I just want to wait. Let's do it tomorrow. Okay?"

"Like in thirty minutes when it's officially Sunday?" He snickered. "I know you, you horny little bastard."

"No, I mean tomorrow night. Let's just enjoy the um... um... afterglow of that experience. How's that?"

"Enjoy our afterglow? I like the sound of that. Honestly, just being by your side and holding you close is so perfect. Anything else is being greedy. So, yes, I can wait until tomorrow. It'll give me something to look forward to all day."

. . .

We all woke late the following morning and made a free-ranging brunch out of leftovers from the party. A little after noon, we took an old blanket and a small cooler with cold drinks and headed out to the park. Our parents said they needed to talk to us about something. I prided myself on being able to better read my parents ahead of time as I matured through high school, but they were very enigmatic as the five of us made our way to a large stand of oak trees alongside the reflecting pool just north of the zoo. What was coming my way? Good news? Bad news? I had no idea

We settled on the blanket in a circle – Brandon, Mrs. Marshall, me, Mom, and Dad.

Mrs. Marshall took the lead.

"Boys, I have some news to tell you. There's a meandering way to get there and a direct way. You're both old enough for the direct way now." She took Brandon's hand in hers. "Your father and I are getting divorced. It will all be final in a few weeks. It's been a long time coming. I've thought about it for years, but I kept telling myself that things would get better. I kept believing I could get the old Robert back. I thought that saving our marriage was my job, but I finally realized the extent to which I was kidding myself. Marriage is a two-way street, and your father put up so many roadblocks on his side. It's simply impassible and impossible now. We are past the point of no return." She paused and caught her breath. "So, there. It's out. Now you know."

Brandon leaned into his mother's shoulder and gently kissed her cheek. "I'm so happy for you. I mean, I'm not happy you're having to go through this, but I am happy you'll finally be free of him. Jacob said I was finally free of Dad, that he's in my past forever if I want to leave him there. I thought about you when he said that. I wanted that for you. More than anything else, I wanted that for you."

Tears filled her eyes. "You're the sweetest boy I could have ever hoped for. You and Jacob are two of the biggest reasons I made this decision. When your dad ordered me to cut all ties with you and Jacob, it was a moment of clarity. He was asking me to do something no real mother would ever do. What kind of man demands the loyalty and obedience of his wife at the expense of her love for her own sons? It was too much. It was the last straw."

"What are you gonna do?"

"Well, sweetie, I'm moving back here... back where I can be near two of my sons, my daughter-in-law, my two grand-daughters, my two best friends in the world, and my baby's sweetheart. I've got a new job all lined up. I'll be back in my old department at HCC, not the same exact position, but I know I'll love it. And I'm meeting with a realtor tomorrow to look at some condos around Midtown. I want you to go with me. You've got to help me pick one with a bedroom you'll like!"

"You mean you want me to live with you when you come back?"

"Of course, sweetie. It's your choice, obviously, but I want you with me for as long as I can have you. Maybe we can make up for some lost time."

Brandon looked at my parents. "Is that okay with you two? Do you mind if move in with Mom?"

Dad said, "Of course, we're okay! We're over the moon for you! We want you to be back with your mom. It's where you belong for now. We'll miss you, but we'll see you all the time. We'll have you and your mom over often, and you're welcome to invade every time Alex comes home."

Brandon looked at me and winked. "That's assuming he doesn't find some totally hot brainiac at Harvard."

"As if I'm even gonna be looking around!"

Mrs. Marshall said, "Jacob and Prisha are going to do some house hunting in West U. They want to live closer in and be nearer to me. Matthew is talking about coming back here with his girlfriend. He wants to start law school at U of H in January. So, I'll have three-fourths of my sons within a few miles of me. It feels like it would go a long way to help all of us do some healing after the last thirty years."

Brandon leaned back and laid his head in his mother's lap. She reached down and ruffled his hair. "Honey, there a million things I want to say to you. There are details to talk about – finalizing things with your dad, moving here, getting settled here, helping you get sorted for next year. And there are more things about our family – our past – that we have to talk about. There'll be time for all that. But right now, right here, in front of Alex and his parents, I want to say: I love you so much just the way you are. You being gay doesn't change my love for you. In fact, it makes me love you even more. It makes me want to know you better and understand you more fully, so I can be the very best mom I can be. I am so sorry I couldn't say that for so long. I'm so sorry for what I did that made things harder for you. I'd go back and change it all if I could. I know I can't, but I hope you'll forgive me. And I hope we can make a new start. I'm here for you. Always. No matter what."

Brandon turned his head toward his mother's torso and wept. Great convulsions shook his body; between a few gasps for air he finally said, "I do forgive you. It's all in the past. It's all behind us now."

. . .

iii.

Brandon came for a sleepover on my last night in Houston before leaving for Harvard. We spent a good deal of the evening reminiscing about our long friendship. We quoted our way through *The Princess Bride* a final time and snuggled close in my bed in anticipation of our upcoming separation.

"Do you know what this reminds me of?"

"Our last night together before you moved to Nashville?"

"Exactly! Except I think we are a little wiser and more mature. I know you think I held myself together back then, but I didn't! I may have been cool and calm that Sunday morning when we dropped off your jeans and pillows, but I was sobbing by the time we got on 59. I cried all the way to Texarkana... and for the next three months."

"I was pretty weepy for a few weeks, too. I'll probably cry tomorrow when we have to say goodbye, but I don't think it'll feel the same. It felt like the end of everything when you moved to Nashville. It feels different this time around. Deep down, I know there's a real future for us."

"As long as you don't fall in love at Harvard and leave me for some nerdy intellectual. I had a dream the other night you met some Nietzsche-wannabe philosophy major. He wore a beret and smoked tiny little French cigarettes. He went around quoting Keats, Elliot, and Dickinson. His dad was a hedge-fund manager, and they were fabulously wealthy. He swept you off your feet, and you never spoke to me again. You didn't even break up. You just disappeared to the Hamptons and cut me out of your life."

"Oh, God, Brandon! Don't dream like that! It's not gonna happen. I promise! And there's no way you dreamed all those details about him! You don't even know who Nietzsche is."

"You are so damn conceited, you sorry-ass loser-man. I did actually learn a few things at your school last year. I mean, I heard Nietzsche's name in that snooze-fest of a philosophy class I had to take."

He glared at me in mock-disdain.

I said, "Well, that guy sounds totally un-hot. You know I hate cigarette smoke. That's a major turn-off."

"I know, dumbass! I just like to goad you every chance I get. Annoying you on the phone is about a tenth of the fun as annoying you in person. I gotta squeeze in every chance I can before tomorrow." As he said this, he reached inside my briefs and gave my penis a squeeze.

He went on: "And it helps to know you and Kevin are gonna be roomies. I told him to keep his eyes on you. He'll be watching you like a hawk. Your dad and I bought him a long-distance phone card so he can call us anytime he thinks your eyes are straying. I told him to be especially watchful for the philosophy majors. I know you have a soft-spot for smooth-talking, emaciated philosophers." He snickered and snorted.

"I can't imagine meeting anyone I'd want to be with more than you."

"Ditto, Alex. It's been an amazing six years! How about another sixty?"

Brandon fell asleep before I did, and I thought back to my first Sunday at Bissonet Avenue Church of Christ. I never could have imagined where that initial encounter with Brandon would lead. If you had given me a million possibilities to choose from, the real outcome would have been one of the half dozen I thought least likely to ever come true. It just goes to show that Grandma Allen was right. Life is a lot like a lottery: we can't ever predict when the most unexpected and unimaginable chance might land squarely in our laps. All we can do is remain open and hopeful.

I thought, too, about Westley when he said to Buttercup: "Life is pain, Highness. Anyone who tries to tell you differently is selling something." Too often, Westley was right. Life is full of kicks to the back and angry imprecations shouted poolside. I had lived long enough to know that much was true. But Westley was only partly right, just as he was only mostly dead when his friends took him to Miracle Max. Just as Westley and Buttercup discovered the power of true love at the end of their perilous, seemingly ill-fated journey through the Kingdom of Florin, Brandon and I discovered that pain was only part of life's tapestry. Hope and love were always present, even in the darkest moments.

I didn't have a crystal ball, and I couldn't predict what the future would hold for us as young gay men. I knew what kind of world we lived in – a world where young gay men like Paul Broussard got murdered outside a night club just a few miles from my apartment. Yet I also knew that world was slowly changing. Perhaps Brandon and I might be part of a generation of gay men who could eventually live in less fear and secrecy. We might never have Westley and Buttercup's fairy tale ending displayed on a screen for all the world to see, but we could lay claim to our own version of a storybook love. I hoped it would be enough to see us through the uncertain years to come.

As sleep slowly washed over me, I visualized the thread of

hope that ran through the long story of my friendship with Brandon. At every turn, I had held on tightly to hope, often in the face of overwhelming odds and contrary evidence. Time and time again, hope had a way of bearing me aloft. Hope was the melody I'd whistle to myself on the winding road ahead of me.

And if things ever got too intense so that even hope's sweet tune failed to lift my most pessimistic mood, I could always call to mind an equally potent source of inspiration, a phrase that I sometimes heard in my happiest dreams: "As you wish, my little stick-arm friend, as you wish..."

AFTERWORD

If you want to change the world, throw a better
party than the ones destroying it.
– Rick Ingrasci

I liken the world of 'coming-out, coming-of-age' literature to an expansive banquet table where all are welcome. We live in a time when formerly untold and marginalized stories attract a wider audience and a deeper appreciation. Ample room exists for a multitude of narratives as we open our hearts and search within for our own authentic voice. No single story can represent the rich diversity of the LGBTQ+ community. We queer readers and writers owe it to one another to value the stories that are different from ours *precisely* because they are different. If we want to change the world, we have to throw a better party than the folks who insist there is only <u>one</u> story to tell. We who have been on the outside looking in for so long should be the first to make room for every honest 'coming-out, coming-of-age' story. In our rush to tear down the idol of heteronormativity, let's not raise another one in its place that demands an equally unappealing dogmatic uniformity. Let's honor the particularity of every queer story, even when we do not see our own story mirrored back to us in its totality. So, pull up a chair and share your unique voice! #ownvoices

Alex's story is only loosely autobiographical. Like him, I developed a love for Agatha Christie and classical music at a young age. I fell in love with *The Princess Bride* when I saw it in seventh grade at a cinema in Houston, and I remember dreaming about Westley for months on end after that first viewing. Like Alex, I encountered the Christian religion for the first time at a fundamentalist Church of Christ when I was twelve. The rest of Alex's journey is pure fiction. It was a delightful and life-affirming experience to write for him a story so different from my own as an adolescent.

You, dear reader, were on my mind every time I sat down in front of my computer. You didn't know it, but the blinking cursor I stared at became a doorway: a magical portal through which my heart could reach out to yours. Though I do not know you personally, I sense a connection between us since you walked alongside Alex and Brandon for six amazing years of their lives. Perhaps you love a good coming-of-age story and don't care about the gender identity or sexual orientation of the characters. Perhaps you are queer. Perhaps you wonder if you are queer. Perhaps you wonder if your child or sibling or friend is queer. Perhaps you are straight but want to better understand the queer experience. Perhaps you have been deeply wounded by unhealthy religious communities and toxic notions of God. No matter what compelled you to read Alex's story, I hope you found a life-giving passage or two. I hope you read something that caused you to think about yourself and your world a little differently. Above all else, I hope your own heart opened up a little more, enabling you to love yourself and other people more freely than you may have done in the past.

All of the political events in *The You I See* are historical! Kathryn Whitmire was elected as mayor of Houston, Texas in 1981. She was the first female Democrat to hold that office. She was a vocal advocate for the gay community in Houston throughout her ten years in office. Many in Houston's fundamentalist/evangelical Christian community organized their considerable force against her and the city councilors who sympathized with her efforts. This quasi-Christian political movement advocated for a so-called 'Straight Slate' political platform in the municipal elections of 1985. [I leave it to you to imagine what the 'Straight Slate' was all about!] Fortunately, none of the 'Straight Slate' candidates won city-wide office that year. Additionally, Mayor Whitmire handily defeated former mayor Louie Welch, who was caught on tape suggesting the way to stop AIDS in Houston was to "shoot the queers." Annise Parker came along twenty years after Whitmire's final term, becoming the first openly lesbian mayor of a major U.S. city in 2010.

The murder of Paul Broussard in the very early hours of July 4, 1991 was a turning point for an already-changing Houston. The details of Paul's brutal murder, the ineptitude of the EMS crew that responded to the attack, and the hesitant, tepid initial response of the Houston Police Department shook the city to its core. Houston Public Media produced a short documentary called *A Murder in Montrose: The Paul Broussard Legacy* in 2016. You can find a wealth of related information and watch the documentary film online.

https://www.houstonpublicmedia.org/projects/a-murder-in-montrose/

Religion is an important theme in Alex's story because religion is a powerful force in the lives of billions of people around the world. Religion continues to inform ideas about sexual morality in ways that are both helpful and harmful. As a former fundamentalist Christian, I can only speak about my own journey. I no longer believe that the Christian scriptures are a repository of divinely inspired stories and truth statements which function in an authoritative manner for my life. Just as I reject the authority of biblical texts that govern the acquisition and use of sex slaves (Numbers 31:17-18;

Deuteronomy 20:10-15), I reject the authority of texts that seem to condemn same-sex behaviors.

I hope Alex and Brandon's conversation about Sodom (Chapter 12) serves as a starting place for any readers who still look to the Christian Bible as a source of authoritative information about God and how they should live. Dozens of resources can aid interested seekers on a journey to a more sophisticated understanding. A few of the best are: *God and the Gay Christian: The Biblical Case in Support of Same-Sex Relationships* by Matthew Vines; *Unclobber: Rethinking Our Misuse of the Bible on Homosexuality* by Colby Martin; *Changing Our Minds: Definitive 3rd Edition of the Landmark Call for Inclusion of LGBTQ Christians* by David Gushee.

The Human Rights Campaign offers helpful information for Christians and members of other religions in the 'Religion and Faith' section of its website:

https://www.hrc.org/resources/religion-faith/

The resources section of their website also addresses topics such as: 'Coming Out', 'LGBTQ+ Youth', 'Parenting', and 'Sexual Health'. Check it out!

You know your story best. It's utterly unique yet ultimately universal... and you get to tell it the best way you can!

ACKNOWLEDGMENTS

I am so thankful for the small cadre of friends who read various iterations of *The You I See* and offered helpful – and often pointed! – feedback. I couldn't have done it without you. Thank you: Michael, Carter, and Tom!

I am also deeply grateful for the kind, prompt, and professional expertise of the entire team at Atmosphere Press. From the very first phone call through dozens and dozens of emails and more phone calls, you all have been a pleasure to work with! Thank you: Trista, Kyle, Alex, Ronaldo, Erin, Sarah, Cammie, Hayla, Claire, and Christina.

Finally, I owe a special debt of gratitude to all the teachers who helped develop my love for reading and writing, especially those teachers who pushed me to write often and write well: Mrs. Armitage, Mrs. VanLuezen, Mrs. Hooks, and Mr. Flemming.

ABOUT ATMOSPHERE PRESS

Atmosphere Press is an independent, full-service publisher for excellent books in all genres and for all audiences. Learn more about what we do at atmospherepress.com.

We encourage you to check out some of Atmosphere's latest releases, which are available at Amazon.com and via order from your local bookstore:

Possibilities with Parkinson's: A Fresh Look, by Dr. C

Just Be Honest, by Cindy Yates

Detour: Lose Your Way, Find Your Path, by S. Mariah Rose

Sacred Fool, by Nathan Dean Talamantez

My Place in the Spiral, by Rebecca Beardsall

My Eight Dads, by Mark Kirby

Dinner's Ready! Recipes for Working Moms, by Rebecca Cailor

Without Her: Memoir of a Family, by Patsy Creedy

ABOUT THE AUTHOR

Danny Freeman is a native Texan: born in Dallas and raised in Houston. He is a former elementary school teacher and intervention program coordinator for a large Texas school district. Danny now lives for a living and resides outside the Lone Star State in a happy spot somewhere between his head and his heart. He is busy writing his second novel. If there is an afterlife, he hopes he'll get assigned to a small cottage between his two favorite couples in the world: Westley and Buttercup, and Alex and Brandon. *The You I See* is his first novel.

CPSIA information can be obtained
at www.ICGtesting.com
Printed in the USA
LVHW100808041122
732159LV00006B/484

9 781639 883110